THE REWRITE MAN

Both as a film-maker and as a novelist, Bryan
Forbes has always been drawn to aspects of love.
Following his controversial last novel,
FAMILIAR STRANGERS, he now returns
to his professional origins and, with THE
REWRITE MAN, he has written what could well
come to be regarded as a landmark in the fiction
of the film industry. He has created a deeply
poignant love story of stunning authenticity,
peopled with brilliantly drawn characters – a
novel which goes beyond the usual second-hand
evidence. It is a subtle, brutally frank and
erotically absorbing story of obsession, written
by an insider who has been described as
'staggeringly gifted' in many fields.

THE REWRITE MAN is a major work by a
master entertainer.

THE REWRITE MAN

'A marvellously readable, funny and poignant story . . . Bryan Forbes has created some splendidly living characters, sparkling dialogue and a truly touching novel of obsession and jealousy'

Sunday Express

'His novel of love and lust and betrayal is absolutely convincing'

Sunday Standard

'A winner . . . a fascinating backroom tale of the movie industry'

Girl About Town

'Bryan Forbes has written a very good book indeed, based on all his experience of the film business . . . it's a long time since I felt such enthusiasm about my bedside reading'

Mail on Sunday

'An intriguing love story of deep meaning with strong characters'

Newcastle Journal

Bryan Forbes is vastly experienced in every field of motion picture production as author, actor, screenwriter, director and producer. From small-part actor he has risen to become one of the most highly talented and respected film directors in the world.

Born in 1926, Forbes served in British Intelligence during the war. In 1959 he formed a production company with Sir Richard Attenborough. He went to Hollywood in 1963 to write and direct KING RAT, and from 1969 to 1971 he was Head of Production for EMI Film Productions at Elstree Studios.

His published fiction includes a collection of short stories, TRUTH LIES SLEEPING (1951), THE DISTANT LAUGHTER (1972), and FAMILIAR STRANGERS (1979) – a highly acclaimed novel of betrayal, deceit and divided loyalties in the world of British espionage, in which he anticipated the scandal of 'the Fourth Man'.

He is married to Nanette Newman and they have two daughters.

The Rewrite Man

Bryan Forbes

CORONET BOOKS
Hodder and Stoughton

Copyright © 1983 by Bryan Forbes Ltd

First published in Great Britain 1983
by Michael Joseph Ltd

Coronet edition 1984

British Library C.I.P.
Forbes, Bryan
   The rewrite man.
   I. Title
   823'.914[F]   PR6056.O63

   ISBN 0 340 35485 2

Printed and bound in Great Britain for
Hodder and Stoughton Paperbacks, a
division of Hodder and Stoughton Ltd,
Mill Road, Dunton Green, Sevenoaks,
Kent (Editorial Office: 47 Bedford
Square, London, WC1 3DP) by
Richard Clay (The Chaucer Press) Ltd,
Bungay, Suffolk. Photoset by
Rowland Phototypesetting Ltd,
Bury St Edmunds, Suffolk.

This book is for
The Doubting Thomases
Wherever they are

'No man is rich enough to buy back his past'
Oscar Wilde

'Whatever you condemn, you have done yourself'
Georg Groddeck

'If . . . one considers the important part which the sexual impulse in all its degrees and nuances plays not only on the stage and in novels, but also in the real world, where, next to the love of life, it shows itself the strongest and most powerful of motives, constantly lays claim to half the powers and thoughts of the younger portion of mankind, is the ultimate goal of almost all human effort, exerts an adverse influence on the most important events, interrupts the most serious occupations every hour, sometimes embarrasses for a while even the greatest minds, does not hesitate to intrude with its rash interfering with the negotiations of statesmen and the investigations of men of learning, knows how to slip its love letters and locks of hair even into ministerial portfolios and philosophical manuscripts, and no less devises daily the most entangled and the worst actions, destroys the most valuable relationships, breaks the firmest bonds, demands the sacrifice sometimes of life or health, sometimes the wealth, rank and happiness, nay, robs those who are otherwise honest of all conscience, makes those who have hitherto been faithful, traitors; accordingly, on the whole, appears as a malevolent demon that strives to pervert, confuse and overthrow everything; – then one will be forced to cry, Wherefore all this noise? Wherefore the straining and storming, the anxiety and want? It is merely a question of every Hans finding his Grethe. Why should such a trifle play so important a part, and constantly introduce disturbance and confusion into the well regulated life of man? . . . The ultimate end of all love affairs, whether they are played in sock or cothurnus, is really more important than all other ends of human life, and is therefore quite worthy of the profound seriousness with which every one pursues it.'

Schopenhauer
The World as Will and Idea

The initial mistake was his. All the rest were mine. It could well be that I have always played host to the virus of self-destruction and that Martin merely activated it from afar – just as ultra-violet is said to revive the dormant *herpes simplex*. Certainly I would think of it afterwards as being Martin's fault, though in truth there was nobody to blame but myself. My worst failing is to expect too much of people – continuous friendship, permanent emotion and, where women are concerned, passionate fidelity. Love makes us irrational and ridiculous.

Not that it began as a love story. It began with Martin phoning me, unexpectedly. There was an urgent message when I returned home that night six years ago. In those days 'home' was a converted barn on the water's edge in Darien, Connecticut. I had rented it from a friend who had gone to Europe to recover from a particularly traumatic divorce. Unfortunately the conversion closely resembled his lifestyle and was lacking in creature comforts. It remained a barn in winter and in summer a vast sweat box. But like second-hand clothing it served its basic purpose without adding much dignity and it suited my mood that year. I wanted my life to be misshapen, I wanted discomfort, a degree of ugliness. The garden, which I never cultivated, I came to regard as an extension of myself, a constant reminder that, like the flower beds, the contours of my life had become blurred, tangled with spent relationships.

At such times one derives certain masochistic pleasures from the chaos of borrowed surroundings – confusion without responsibility. I had brought few possessions of my

13

own, just the tools of my trade: an electric typewriter well past its prime, some reams of paper and a generous supply of correcting fluid. For the rest I had sufficient for my reduced needs; all I lacked that summer was inspiration.

My absent friend's library, like most of his furniture, betrayed a catholic lack of taste, but again that fitted my mood and during the long, humid nights when old anxieties peaked, I would sit outside and read one of his supply of trashy novels. There is something uniquely compelling about manufactured best-sellers – their sheer awfulness renews one's belief in all that is worst in human nature. As a cure for insomnia I also found them cheaper and faster than Dalmane.

Even at midnight the heat and humidity in that wooden box sapped all intelligence. So when I returned home that night – opening the front door to enter a charnel house – I stood, stupefied and dripping with instant sweat, listening to Martin's recorded message, and for all it conveyed at first it might well have been a voice from another planet. Although what he had to say was short and to the point, I had to replay it three times before the sense penetrated. He ended with a long string of numbers, repeated twice with his precise British enunciation, which I would need in order to obey his summons.

It wasn't only the heat that slowed me down: I was genuinely surprised to hear from him, surprised he even remembered me, since it had been one of those summers when I assumed that most people thought I was dead. I tried to remember how many years it had been since last we worked together, and whether I had enjoyed the experience. Not too many people enjoyed Martin. They endured him – as I did, because as a freelance screenwriter I couldn't afford to strike off anybody from my dwindling Christmas card list, especially a director like Martin, who although not God's gift to the cinema was one of those curious hybrids who went from film to film while being constantly reviled by the critics. He had a positive Midas touch for mediocrity.

Because of this, I hesitated before returning his call – almost certainly it meant a job. Martin didn't make social calls to screen-writers who lived three thousand miles

14

away. The country code he had given me was for France, the area code for Nice and the surrounding districts. He had fled there during one of those mass migrations that armchair socialists make from the old country whenever a Labour government comes to power. Martin was a dedicated believer in the brotherhood of man as long as the brothers did not foul up his many and various tax avoidance schemes. It was said of him that he would rather go to bed with his accountant than his wife.

I could never quite put my finger on it, but there was something vaguely bogus about his whole life style. Not that I've ever understood the British. In appearance Martin gave the impression that he had bought a do-it-yourself Rex Harrison kit, but had never quite worked out the instructions. I tend to cast people according to their nearest movie counterparts. To my ear his accent was would-be Professor Higgins, but then most Englishmen of his ilk sound the same. He had taken all the familiar trappings with him when he upped and deserted mother England and now acted out the grand seigneur on a sizeable estate in Mougins – the sort of ultra-perfect, but unreal setting that is invariably featured in *Architectural Digest* – but made no concessions to the French. Being Martin, it was roast beef and Yorkshire pudding for Sunday lunch and Bath Oliver biscuits sent out from Fortnum and Mason to have with his imported Cheddar cheese. I wouldn't have put it past him to have tried to organise a local cricket team.

I started to calculate the difference in hours between Connecticut and Mougins, then recalled that few film executives have ever been concerned with the intricacies of international time zones: they exist for the masses but not for studio heads or directors. In Hollywood, in the beginning was not the word but the telephone.

After replaying the tape to check the long sequence of numbers, I dialled carefully. Martin picked up immediately after the first ring. Before I could say anything by way of introduction, he gave me an example of the charm that had endeared him to film crews on three continents.

'And about fucking time too! Have you any idea how long I've been sitting here waiting for you to return my call?'

'I'm sorry, Martin, but I only just this minute got in.'

'Don't your staff pick up your messages and contact you? You should always keep in touch with base.'

As a breed the Martins of my world take it for granted that their rarefied way of life is common to all. My 'staff' consisted of a non-English-speaking Puerto Rican handyman who came in once a month to chlorinate the pool.

'Yes,' I said. 'You're absolutely right. I'll make sure they do in future.'

'I suppose you were out looking for pussy as usual. No wonder nobody knows where the hell to get hold of you. Still, I guess I'm just jealous of your energy. What d'you take for it, intravenous ginseng?'

I was immediately conscious of the fact that his speech bore little resemblance to the voice on my answering machine. The familiar accent was still there, but slurred, the delivery had been changed by something – pain, drink, drugs? – the choice, God knows, is there for us all.

'Anyway, sod that, that's your problem, at least you finally dragged yourself to the old blower . . .' That was another thing I remembered about him; he often lapsed into that arcane dialogue which was once the hallmark of all those British war films. 'Keep in touch with base', 'Get on the blower' – it was like listening to the late-night movie with your eyes closed.

'. . . and listen, chum, old pal, the thing is, I didn't mean to bark at you just now, but the thing is, as you well know, you're my fucking life-raft in this mess, and if I don't talk to you who am I going to talk to? Must have one chum I can trust . . . You got somebody with you?'

'No.'

'Who was that talking just then?'

'Talking? Nobody.'

'I could have sworn I heard another voice. You wouldn't hold out on me, would you?'

'I promise you, I'm on my own. You often get a sort of echo on these phones.'

'Or else you get bugged.'

'I'm not worth bugging. You've made too many spy movies.'

'I know *you're* not worth bugging. If they wired you

16

they'd only wire your bed. I haven't been to bed all night. And that means I'm going to feel like death warmed up.'

Then he must have dropped the receiver. I heard a crash, the sound of breaking glass. A dog started barking. Martin shouted at the creature to shut up and when he came back on the line his voice was fainter still and I had to strain to hear him through a burst of static.

'The thing is . . . if I can only stop beginning every sentence with the same bloody three words . . . there have been developments.'

'What sort of developments?'

'Well, give me a chance, and I'll tell you. But before I get to that, I have to ask you a question, and I want a straight answer, none of your usual . . . usual, humour-the-old-sod-stuff . . . We've both been to the edge of the world and looked over, right?'

'Right.'

'On occasions, right?'

'Right.'

'In our gilded youth, when the sap was rising?'

'Right.'

'We have had our little moments of truth with the opposite sex. But . . . and I want to choose my words very carefully . . . But, the fact is that up until now, we've always been able to climb out from under and lived to fight another day . . . And yet you're such a cagey bastard, you don't give out much, that's why I want to ask you this. Have you ever been taken to the brink of clinical madness by an obsessive passion?'

It goes without saying that I have spent a fair proportion of my working life thinking up unusual opening lines for my fictional characters, but nothing in my previous experience of Martin had prepared me for such a question.

'Passion?' I said, playing for time.

'That's the word I used. What d'you usually call it? Do I have to draw a picture for you? Passion, from the Latin to suffer. A crucifixion, chum.'

By this point his entire dialogue was beyond my comprehension. I had no idea what it was all leading up to, except I doubted whether it had anything to do with my being

17

offered a job and what really irked me was I was paying for the call.

'No, I guess not, not in the way you mean.'

'Too true. And you know why? Because you never take a real risk. Your idea of taking a risk is to use somebody else's toothbrush. That's your style, but I'm talking about going the distance, right to the lemming edge of the cliff and then, whoosh! – taking the long drop. And I've taken it, I'm on my way down into the abyss.'

What you've taken, I thought, comes in little white packets.

'I mean, we're not discussing one of your little escapades, because you're such a faker, and maybe in the past I've done my share of faking, but this time no way, chum. No way. You remember *Love is a Debt?*'

'Yes, of course.' I didn't. As a general rule I made it a point of honour never to pay to see any of Martin's movies. If dragged I might attend a preview or a DGA screening. *Love is a Debt* had been one of his major commercial successes and had actually attracted a few good notices into the bargain. I knew that he considered it a landmark in his career, on a level with *Casablanca*, conveniently forgetting that he and his writer had lifted much of their plot from that classic.

'Well, this has all that intensity, and at the moment it's heading for the same tragic end.'

'Sorry to hear that.'

'I knew you would be. That's why I had to talk to you.'

'It's what friends are for.'

'She's something else, chum. Sheer bloody perfection. I mean, I've had my share of beauty, been around it all my life, directed it, photographed it, played grand opera with it, woken up to find it on my pillow and I thought I'd seen it all until this one came along, and it's destroying me, chum, destroying me. I've got a bad case, and that's not good at our age. If we can't love them and leave them we're in deep trouble.'

'Well, enjoy it while it lasts.'

'Don't say that. That's not what I want to hear. Anyway, how can I? You know my situation with the dear wife . . . What was that?'

'What?'

'I definitely heard something then. Like somebody picking up on an extension. Listen!'

I listened. All I heard was a sound not too far removed from the imagined roar of the sea one believed in as a child, holding a shell to one's ear.

'Maybe I'm just getting paranoiac.'

'Understandable,' I said.

'Jesus, it's good to have somebody to confide in. I was saying something, wasn't I? What the hell was I telling you? Oh, yes . . . well; I suppose I've reached the stage where I could chuck it all in, leave this place, give the bitch the lot, let the lawyers have a field day, and just take off with my sweet darling, have a little fun in my remaining years, and don't think I haven't given that a lot of thought. I could do just that, chum, believe me, the way I feel about her. The age difference would be a problem later on, but at least I would have had that moment . . . It is a madness, but I could come to terms with everything else except *him*.'

'Him?'

'Yeah, and I'm not going to mention the name over the phone, but you know who I'm talking about. And the reason I was so desperate to talk to you is that I'm convinced he tried to kill us last night.'

Once again I could think of no immediate response. He was giving me a crossword puzzle to solve without any of the clues. Across and Down. I suppose what really fazed me most, though, was the fact that he was talking to me as though to a close friend. Now at that time I had no idea where I stood in Martin's estimation. Whatever I thought of his work, he was where he was – near the top of the pile – and I was half-way down the slopes. My previous contacts with him had been purely professional. I had done rewrites on three pot-boiler scripts: he and I had always got on reasonably well but I hardly included myself amongst his intimate circle. Few relationships in the film industry have any durability now that the old studio system with its contract writers and executive dining rooms has disappeared. You work closely for a few weeks or months and then it's off to a personal Siberia again until the phone rings. In any one of the crises that punctuated every film

Martin directed it was, I am convinced, a matter of pure chance whether my name found its way to the head of his panic list. If it did, if I received the statutory midnight call for help, and if I was available and my agent's asking price was within budget, I got offered the job. If not, he moved to the next name on his pad and I would be forgotten again until his occupational insecurities forced him to thrash around for a malleable rewrite man. Certainly I had never thought of him as an insurance policy where I was concerned. He demanded total loyalty from his regular acolytes, but seldom returned it. 'They're lucky to be working,' I had often heard him say, 'and luckier still to be working for me. And if they don't like my style, they know where they can go.' Not that his arrogance was anything out of the ordinary in the places where I earn my living: the film industry is a kindergarten for assassins – every kid in the mail room is a potential hit man.

'Kill you?' I finally answered. 'Why would anybody try to do that?' I took his statement as a typical piece of bullshit. Maybe some electrician wished he could drop a lamp on him, or a small-part actor wanted to put strychnine in his Nescafé – those I could believe, but anything else was hard to take. There is murder in many people's hearts on a film set, but the death rate among directors never approaches the national average. Dear old Otto is living proof that wishful thinking alone seldom produces a corpse.

'I'm sure it was him,' Martin said. 'You know me, I don't scare easily, but this thing has really shaken me – on top of all my other worries, because I still have to finish the film. Anyway, I'll give you the latest. I went over everybody's head down here, ignored all the local jokers, because as we both know they're into the graft up to their fucking eyebrows. Don't forget the French invented the art of evasion. And what really bugs me is that I only came to their bloody country to revive the local film industry . . . I mean, who's doing who the favours? You agree?'

I murmured some vague assent, but he was in full spate by now. I thought, barking, he's barking mad, stoned out of his skull with something.

'Course, the real truth is they don't like us, never have liked the British, never forgiven us for fighting on the

20

fucking beaches and winning the war for them . . . You still there?'

'Hanging onto your every word,' I said.

'It took time and effort but I finally got to the top man on the police totem pole. So, I pulled rank, but I didn't pull any punches. I told him, laid the facts out, let him realise that a few of us know this whole place is a sewer of corruption and needs fumigating. I gave him chapter and verse, a few home truths, starting with his local fuzz. I really hit him with that. Because I've had no co-operation whatsoever from them. This place isn't just sunlight and golden beaches, chum: most of the streets are shady on both sides. Lovely for the jolly old tourists and all that, beaux vacances and sur la jolie plage, and you can kiss my arse, but those of us who live here pay through the nose for it . . . I'm convinced this character has the police on his payroll, he's into the rackets. Has to be.'

'But you said he tried to kill you, is that right?'

'Yes, but let me finish. I finally convinced this brass cunt there was a case to answer and he reluctantly promised to get somebody down from the Inspectorate to investigate my complaint, so at least I achieved that much at long last . . . Christ! look at the time. I've got to be on location in just over an hour. Not that I give a flying fart. This film is a wipe-out as far as I'm concerned. So, let me tell you . . . Last night, after we'd wrapped on location, I arranged to pick her up and take her to dinner – somewhere quiet and out of the way. I invented some production meeting for my dear wife's benefit, not that she gives a damn – she had one of her piss-elegant gin-rummy evenings planned . . . I collected my little sweetheart, driving myself for obvious reasons, and when we got up on the Grand Corniche suddenly this car came up alongside and tried to ram us off the road. You can see the dents on my Rolls where he shunted it. Did it twice, so it couldn't have been unintentional . . . Now I didn't actually see his face, because I was too busy holding onto the wheel, but I'm bloody sure it was him. I'm telling you, we were lucky not to have been killed, because we could so easily have gone over the side. My poor darling was terrified, as you can imagine, and I just have to protect her from him. She got involved because

21

she's young, too young to realise what these types are like, and now he's got his claws into her. I'm her only hope, chum, and she's the only one I care about. I don't give a tinker's damn about the rest, nothing matters except her . . . He's obviously desperate now . . . Must be, to have tried a stunt like that.'

I had let him ramble on without interruption, only occasionally making murmurs of amazement. Him, her, them – his scenario was without names, like some screen adaptation of Kafka. It made no sense at all.

'Yes, well, I can tell how worried you are,' I said. 'You sound as though you've really got problems there.'

'What d'you mean, *problems*? I'm not talking about having my fucking teeth capped! I'm talking about a young girl's life! My life, too, come to that. So don't give me *problems*! If that's the best you can come up with when I'm drowning, go fuck yourself!'

'I'm sorry,' I said. 'I didn't mean to sound unsympathetic, Martin, and I'd love to help in some way, but it's a bit difficult when I'm three thousand miles from you.'

There was a long pause, so long in fact that I thought the connection had been broken. He finally said, 'Who is that?'

'Harvey.'

'Harvey?'

'Yes. Harvey Burgess.'

'Oh, Christ!' he said. And again, 'Oh, Christ! What have I been telling you?'

I fumbled. 'Just that you're involved in a tricky personal situation . . . But since I don't know any of the people concerned, and you didn't name them anyway, there's nothing to worry about.'

He took his time before answering. 'And you're Harvey Burgess, right?'

'Yes. You left a message for me to ring you.'

There is something particularly disconcerting about silences over a long-distance phone. It's bad enough when one is searching for ways and means of conveying love or tenderness to articulate the miseries of separation: in the end one usually settles for banalities, triteness – real passion seldom travels well over the airwaves. But in this instance even the mundane did not come easily to my lips.

'I was half asleep when you called,' he said.

'Who did you think you were talking to?'

'Oh, just somebody who . . . You took me on the hop, you see, hence the . . . the misunderstanding.'

'I'm in Connecticut, of course.'

'Yes, course you are. Not your fault, Harvey. I've got my act together now. I did ask you to contact me. I wanted to check on your availability.'

'About a job, is it?'

'Yes, the film I'm shooting. I want some work doing on the script.'

'Well, I won't hold out on you. I'm available. If you want me.'

'Sure I want you, Harvey, that was the reason for calling you. But before you say yes, you'd better listen to what's involved. I mean I'm into it, but from the word go I wasn't happy with the way it plays, so I finally took a stand and insisted on a rewrite. So, don't get too excited, that's all it is, a rewrite. I'm about two weeks into a fourteen-week schedule, so there's just enough time to save the ship. Just about. Chum, you know the way I normally work. Normally I get everything in apple-pie order, because I'm a stickler for professionalism, but this is one of those occasions when I got sucked in against my better judgement. I admit it, I should have known better, but we all make mistakes from time to time.'

He had control of himself by now and I could detect his voice becoming more impersonal as he made the adjustment from embarrassment to his usual tone of authority. From being the intimate confidant I had been quickly recast as the possible employee.

'I thought of you immediately, Harvey, because you're a pro, too. I need a writer of your calibre and experience if I'm going to find a way out of the wood. Now, I'm not trying to flatter you, but when one's desperate one goes for the best, and in my book they don't come any better than you.'

The compliment hovered like a tired gull somewhere mid-way across the Atlantic.

'Nice of you to say so, Martin.' I could trade insincerities with all comers. 'What's the subject matter?'

'Allegedly, the French Revolution, but the way it's

23

written it could just as well be set in the Bronx. I don't know where they got this writer from . . . well, I do, he's a friend of a friend of the fucking producer . . . But just jog my memory. Aren't I right in thinking that you once did a great job on some Napoleon movie?'

'I wrote a script for Warners on Napoleon, yeah.'

'I knew I was right. Great movie.'

'It would have been,' I said. 'Except they never made it. The studio changed hands the day I delivered the script and the new regime stuck it down the john.'

'That's too bad. But I remember the script well.'

'Makes two of us,' I said.

'Anyway, the point is, I know you're an expert on the period.'

'Well, I didn't major in European history, but put it this way, I do know that Marie Antoinette never said, "Let them eat cake." '

'Harvey, I'll let you in on an open secret – she didn't say anything that's in this script. None of the characters in this script bear any resemblance to creatures living or dead, as they say in the disclaimer. I should be making a documentary on Madame Tussaud. Wax, Harvey. I'm in the waxworks business right now, so I'm pleading with you help me out. Get your arse over here and start writing.'

'You wanted it yesterday, right?'

'You said it.'

'Sounds like you need a complete new script. What about the footage you've shot so far?'

'Fuck it. You come up with the goods and I'll throw it out of the window. The moment you say the word I'll put the whole thing into hiatus until we straighten it out.'

'That's possible, is it?'

'It's fucking imperative.'

'And there's a producer lurking around, is there?'

'There is somebody who has the chutzpah to call himself by that title.'

'Anybody I know?'

'If you do, you have my undying sympathy. Does the name Latrough ring any bells?'

'No.'

24

'I congratulate you. Actually I believe it's a misspelling for Latrine. One of the new breed, Harvey, and they're going to put us all away. This one's twenty-eight with the mentality of a baby-seal killer. I'm told he cut his teeth making soft-porn out of Hong Kong using German tax shelter money – all beyond my ken, I'm afraid. The idea of doing bedroom Kung Fu is too bizarre for my taste. Still, I suppose as things go nowadays his credentials are impeccable for our misbegotten industry.'

'How did he get from porn to the French Revolution?'

'You suck, Harvey, nowadays you suck. Still, let's not waste time discussing him. I'll deal with him when the time comes. When can you get here?'

That was the moment when I should have backed off from my own cliff edge. I was being invited into a disaster area, not unfamiliar territory by any means, but this time there were extra warning notices I should have heeded. Maybe I have always been attracted to the wrong people at the wrong time.

Given my way of earning a living, the odds were that I would always be ill at ease whatever choice I made. If not Martin, then inevitably somebody cast from the same mould. Perhaps, that summer, I was ripe for uncertainty. That summer my whole life was rented out.

I heard myself say, 'I can get the first plane from Kennedy in the morning.'

'How marvellous, chum. What a brick you are. And just to show how grateful I am, I'll have my production office cable New York to get you on the Air France Concorde. The studio will squawk at the extra cost, but sod them, chum. What are you now, five or six hours behind us? . . . Okay. Well, by the time you wake up, if you have time to go to bed, my office over there will contact you. I'll also have them get a copy of the existing script to you when they hand you your air ticket. Try and read it on the plane, and I don't care how much caviar you spill on it. Oh, and one last thing. Tell your agent that whatever he asks he'll get.'

'I'm sure he won't hold you to ransom.'

'Chum, be guided by your old pal. Tell him to go in there and screw them. I want you to be happy.'

'Well, thank you.'

'No thanks necessary . . . This round's on me. And about that other thing . . . We'll just forget it, huh?'

'It's already on the cutting room floor,' I said.

The line went dead.

TWO

One always comes back to Baudelaire's dictum: 'The world revolves on misunderstanding.'

That conversation with Martin took place towards the end of the summer of '76, a summer in which most of my dwindling band of friends seemed to be having simultaneous nervous breakdowns. Four couples fell to earth from the marital perch during the month of July alone. All our failures are failures of love.

I was the outsider, being unmarried – a casualty from past wars, safe now in the dressing station. Unlike Martin most of them used me as their chosen confidant, the laundry basket for all their soiled linen. One by one they sought me out to give their reasons, excuses, explanations. They had broken up, separated, divorced because of the cost of living, the drug scene their children were into, the drug scene he or she was into or not into as the case might be. They were going it alone because of the lack of sex, or the sexual demands they could no longer meet; they had had it every which way, you name it, and it was over, it was a turn-off, the earth didn't move, amen. Or maybe it was the extravagance, or the meanness, the stupidity, the lack of political awareness, the sheer bloody boredom. It was the fault of her analyst, the chauvinistic advice of his; it was her habits, his vices, she drank too much, he was smacked out of his mind, gone to lunch until 1984. And then again, all the magic had evaporated, or else there had never been any magic, it was just another ad campaign to get you hooked, she trod it into the ground, it was his doing right from the off, she talks too much, he never speaks, I'm suffocating, I'm liberated, there's no going back, I've been back too many times, if only.

I listened to them all in turn, making the occasional philosophic attempt at wisdom, but in my heart I knew the real reasons: we were all getting older, clinging to the halcyon summers of long ago which were never quite as good as memory would have us believe. In the end I grew weary of being used like some neutered father confessor available for free consultations at any hour of the day or night. The final straw was broken when a gay friend renounced all previous convictions and succumbed to a Jesus complex. The metamorphosis included growing a beard and wearing flannel nightshirts. He regaled me in stultifying detail with accounts of his recurring dreams of crucifixion before buying his ticket for a package tour of the Holy Land – from whence, he confided, he should never have strayed – and from there postcarded me to say he had fallen passionately in love with an Israeli soldier conveniently named Peter. It could be said that he solved his Rubik cube in style, but the divided heterosexuals grew ever more demanding.

There is an easily reached limit to the amount of unbiased sympathy one can muster for those we know too well. It is easier to play God to complete strangers: with strangers one does not have to feign true concern. Not that anybody wants genuine advice in these situations. All they are usually leeching for is confirmation of their own set solutions to insoluble problems.

After a period such sustained efforts produced a kind of emotional anorexia in me. The more I absorbed the spent love of my friends the less I felt inclined to feast again on love myself. Thus it was that at the time Martin made his fatal phone call I could scarcely tip the scales at my old emotional weight.

It had been a lean year all round. I once read something about writers that stuck in my mind, about the need we have for flat, level days, empty days, so empty that even love and friendship would disturb them. I had plenty of flat days that summer, old relationships were crumbling all around me, I should have been climbing the creative peaks, but nothing happened. Have I given up the search for love? was a question I asked myself every time I faced the bathroom mirror, and the answer was always Yes. Yes, I was on a plateau of level emptiness, with time on my hands, free to do as I wished for the first time in a decade. So I put the old theories to the test, I did what we poor cinema hacks are always screaming we need to do in order to gain back self-respect: write the great novel. No more excuses, no more backing away from destiny, establish a routine – Hemingway slugged it out standing up in boxer trunks, Proust wrote in bed, take your pick, Harvey, the dogwood has blossomed, all you have to look at outside is burnt grass and flotsam, you have exhausted all distractions. And so forth and so on. I finally made the effort, laid in a stock of frozen food, several cartons of menthol cigarettes and plugged in the old golfball IBM. I was going to write a painful and grating novel that avoided all the stinking literary fungus, and for a while there it worked.

An old Journal provided the initial fillip, an idea I had begun years before and then abandoned for easier pickings. A frenzied start and then, inevitably, a hiatus – that avenging fullback who blocks us all stood like a colossus on my desk. The greatest affronts to a writer's pride are these times, common to us all, when we cannot find the key to unlock the door to originality. Despite Connolly's admonition from his unquiet grave I wasn't aiming for a masterpiece, just something that would restore a lost faith. I worked at it ten hours a day for the best part of a month, sometimes on the crest, more often struggling for air in the troughs. It is at such times that we test ourselves to the limits: every day we frogmarch ourselves to the interrogation chamber and apply the self-tortures until, at last, a confession is forced from us. I wanted to write passionately for once, a novel purged of compromise, something that violated all the stale shibboleths which enslave those of us who have been seduced by the transient rewards of writing for films. At the end of the month I had a third of the novel in presentable shape and the remainder plotted in my head. I had existed like some demented mole – the landscape of my days and nights littered with worked-over spoil – and now, as I emerged, I was, without knowing it, ripe for disappointment.

It was swift in coming. Some eight years had elapsed since my last published book, but an option for my next hung like an old cardigan on the back of my publisher's door. I drove into New York having retyped the manuscript into pristine beauty and laid it on my editor's desk as a cat brings a dead bird, expectant for praise. That proved to be my only moment of true glory, for a week later his secretary telephoned me to say he had been forced to go out of town and therefore couldn't ring me himself. 'I'm afraid he's going to pass,' she said, briskly, anxious not to prolong the agony. 'He thought there was a great deal to admire, but basically, overall, it just didn't get to him.'

'You said that very nicely,' I told her. 'Were you ever a nurse?'

'No.'

'You reminded me of a nurse who once gave me a lumbar punch when I was in the war.'

There was no reason to give her a bad time, but she was the only one around to hit. The manuscript came back in a Jiffy bag a few days later and I didn't bother to unwrap it. That afternoon I went to see a porn movie, probably on the basis that if you're down go and find out what it's really like at the bottom of the pit. I went from there to a travel agency and booked for a holiday that my accountant insisted I could ill afford and wouldn't enjoy anyway. It only took six days in Miami to prove him right on both counts and I returned home to my rented sauna desperate to be over-whelmed by something. I became acutely conscious of the passing of the years, aware that I was poised to descend to the darker side of life's mountain. The divorced friends started to call again, openly resentful that I had been incommunicado all those weeks, as though my absence from their shattered lives had been the root cause of their discontents.

'You know something, Harv,' one of the most persistent of them said, 'since Shirl and I decided to call it quits, my game has been shot to hell. I can't cut it any more.'

'Game? What game?'

'Golf! What else? I mean, I'm not going to make the team this year. That's what she's done to me.'

'Take her back then.'

'What sort of advice is that?'

'I don't know,' I said. 'Maybe golf was your sex substitute. Maybe hitting that shitty little ball with your ten iron or your wood, or whatever you call those oversized chopsticks you carry around in that Gucci handbag, was your way of getting off your rocks. But that's the best I can offer.'

When he no longer darkened my door, I allowed myself to believe that possibly a golf widow might be receptive to advances from a dedicated non-player. After all, I had already paid the price of admission: both Shirley and spouse had helped themselves to my compassion, I could be venal without conscience. My technique might be rusty, but at least I would go armed with a detailed knowledge of Shirley's sexual peccadilloes. I was out for the quick kill, the old rabbit punch, but at the same time years of walking knee-deep in celluloid slush made it impossible for me to ignore a few romantic trimmings. I wasn't a rewrite man for nothing.

Shirley was surprisingly co-operative, welcoming my suggestion of a mystery tour with an intensity that my weakened libido failed to recognise as a danger signal. I laid my plans with the same care that Hugh Hefner must apply when filling his Jacuzzi with Playmates. The choice of location, I felt, was of prime importance. After much deliberation I selected a quaint New England inn (appropriately called Stonehenge, which doubtless an analyst would trace to a subconscious sacrificial urge), booked a double room, ordered champagne and flowers to be in position on arrival and asked the management to surprise me with a birthday cake. I was rather proud of this last touch, for what could be more guaranteed to make Shirley melt than the sad spectacle of a bachelor's baked offering? In all probability I filched the entire scene from some old Warner Brothers movie of the Thirties: one of those polished tear-jerkers where Miriam Hopkins or Mary Astor carried a doomed torch for Herbert Marshall of blessed memory. I could picture myself as Bart, urbane but bravely concealing a secret sorrow, glancing with just a hint of melancholy across a candlelit table to the accompaniment of a Max Steiner score.

Alas, life seldom imitates the plots of vintage movies, let alone Art, and my attempted illicit weekend proved only that plagiarism in any form does not pay. Shirley didn't cry at the sight of my birthday cake, her tear ducts opened the

31

moment we turned off Route 7 and approached our destination. Apparently I had chosen the one inn on the entire Eastern seaboard that held unbearable memories for her. All unknowing I had lured her back to the scene of her ex-husband's original crime. Stonehenge marked the spot where, as she put it through Kleenex (reverting to her cheer-leader vocabulary), 'I lost my cherry.'

From that lachrymose opening shot, my scenario went resolutely downhill. She ate nothing of the gourmet meal I had so carefully selected in advance, drank the vintage champagne as though it was undated Perrier and gave yet again the hideously familiar history of her six years of splendour in the astro-turf with the golfer. When eventually I got a chance to explain that there could still be life beyond the eighteenth hole, she stunned me with the equivalent of her own ten iron.

'Don't you think neurotic attractions are the biggest turn-on?'

'Always,' I said. At that moment I would have responded to a suggestion that we take a bath together in low-fat yogurt, anything to bring the meal to an end and sample the waiting four-poster bed.

'Since Hal left me I realised that he forced me to become the epitome of average, because he was the epitome of average. Doctor Sainthill has taught me that if only people would let their lives become truly neurotic there would be no average.'

'The good doctor sounds like an original thinker.'

'Oh, he is. I don't make a move without him now. And of course I got my lawyer to write that in the settlement. Hal has to pay for my therapy. I made sure of that.'

'I bet you made neurotically sure of it.'

'You're right. See, I was an emotional virgin, I realise that now. I was only into straight sex. Like, Hal kept me in sexual diapers, know what I mean? I had no idea what went on outside of the missionary position. Until I met Cleo.'

'Cleo?'

'Yeah. See it was all because she gave such great shampoo.'

'I'm sorry, you've lost me for a moment.'

'In the Good Wives Shopping Centre. That's where I get my hair fixed.'

'Of course, now I'm with you,' I said.

'It was her fingers at first. The strength in them, when she massaged conditioner into my scalp, well, I tell you, that's when I began to see what Doctor Sainthill was trying to get across. Like I'd come home, know what I mean?'

'It's an interesting theory, why don't we talk about it more upstairs?'

'Sure. I'll talk about her all night, try and stop me. You've no idea of the power in that beautiful girl's fingers. So it had to happen, there was no way we could avoid it. And Doctor Sainthill approved.'

'I'm being very dense, I guess. What did he approve?'

'Our love. For the first time in my life, I realise that we were destined to act as our bodies dictate.'

I wondered how dear departed Bart Marshall would have handled all this. I raised one eyebrow in what I hoped was a passable impersonation. At the same time I acknowledged that I was licked. Hairdressing and lesbianism are an unbeatable combination.

Yet I don't want to be smart at Shirley's expense. Having sampled Hal, albeit only in the missionary position, I guess she was entitled to wash him out of her hair. In any event, would-be seducers are in no position to criticise. I let her have the double bed to herself that night and moved into another room. We spent the remainder of that endless weekend exchanging those confidences that characterise a relationship that is going nowhere, and then I drove her back to Cleo.

'Just tell me one thing,' I said, 'and believe me, this isn't a trick question, why did you say yes when I asked you for a date?'

'It was a test, Cleo wanted me to test myself. But I got Doctor Sainthill's permission as well.'

'Two head massagers are better than one,' I said, with a rare splash of humour which, like the rest of my endeavours, sank without trace.

That was the night I received Martin's summons, so perhaps Shirley did me a favour by refusing to grant any. Had I displaced Cleo in her affections this story might have been quite different.

THREE

Long before my agent had a chance to flex his flabby muscles on my behalf, Martin's promises were being honoured. A limousine was outside the barn by the time I woke up and I travelled to Kennedy in style. There I was met by no fewer than three members of his New York office, plus a photographer who looked as though he would have been happier covering a funeral. That's one thing about the film industry: condemned men get treated with respect.

Strapped into the most expensive and smallest seat then flying, surrounded by intense-looking businessmen studying computer printouts, I opened Martin's script and began reading in the fond hope that I wouldn't have to use the sick-bag. I was encouraged to find that the author's name on the title page was unknown to me. It is a characteristic of my calling that few of us refuse any opportunity to cannibalise each other's works, and I always feel it is marginally less distasteful to consume strangers.

Rather than attempt to describe the script, I will reproduce the opening page verbatim.

The Bastille Connection

FADE IN:

AFTER MAIN TITLES:

1. INT. BEDROOM – CHATEAU OF MALMAISON – NIGHT – two figures writhing on a large canopied bed. Both are naked and we shall later identify them as Pierre

Duchamp, a titled young nobleman, and Caroline Duprez, a beautiful young courtesan. CAMERA MOVES IN on them as their love-making becomes more frenzied, concentrating on Caroline's exquisite face, contorted now with lust.

2. CUT TO THE DOOR OF THE BEDROOM –
as it burst open, revealing the figure of The Duke de Guise. He looks towards the bed.

> DUKE
> You fool! How can you make love when the whole of France is threatened?!

He strides towards the bed, sword in hand, and flicks the bedclothes aside.

3. CLOSE ON THE TWO LOVERS –
we glimpse Caroline's nubile body. Pierre sits up, outraged.

> PIERRE
> Sir! Have you no feelings for a lady's honour?

> DUKE
> As much, methinks, as you. Come, boy, take your farewells. We ride to Versailles and the King.
>   (he bows to Caroline)
> My apologies, M'mselle.

> CAROLINE
> Oh, Pierre!

She clutches him and the covering slips from her breasts.

CONTINUED:

Page after depressing page followed the same turgid path, and as I read on I cursed myself for ever answering Martin's message. I needed the job – God knows that was true

35

enough – but I had enough experience to know that here I was committed to a collision course. It was one thing to be asked to come up with a few new scenes, that after all had been the story of my professional career. I was known as a 'reliable' hack, somebody who could be depended upon in a crisis. I knew only too well what most people said about me behind my back. 'He's okay, if you just want a quick polish, but don't trust him with a complete script.' The Martins of my world had an attitude of mind I could but admire and wish to emulate. They had no doubts about their own talents. They were God's chosen people, the ones who led the others out of the wilderness. They took the stale loaves and the stinking fish, and fed the multitudes. And how I envied them.

I tried to finish reading the script, since I still had some remnants of conscience and there was always the vague hope that things would improve. But on this occasion there was no last-minute reprieve. It wasn't just that the script went downhill gracefully, it positively zoomed. I could see nothing ahead but trouble: somebody, somewhere, has always paid good money for a script that gets to the starting post, and they never like an outsider telling them that their judgement is at fault.

Fortunately, lunch was served at that point. As I sipped my champagne I pondered what advice a director gives to an actress who is required to make her 'exquisite' face 'contort with lust'. What could have possessed Martin even to contemplate directing such dross? His films were never distinguished by their literate dialogue, but he was experienced enough to recognise pure garbage when he saw it. I could only surmise that he had been offered an enormous fee and had convinced himself, like so many before him, that his talents would triumph over the material.

Whenever I read such a script I am always amazed that some of my colleagues have the temerity to insist that our efforts be regarded as an Art Form. I find it difficult to genuflect before that particular altar given that the majority of us, when employed, are paid a king's ransom compared to the average novelist, to fashion, parodying Oscar Wilde, 'the unspeakable in pursuit of the unread'. Still, screenwriting is more pleasant that digging drains, and that summer, thanks to Martin, it brought me, all expenses paid, to a small village called Valbonne in Le Rouret, and eventually to a full stop in my life.

I drank too much on that flight, but I needed the stimulus of vintage wines to finish reading that puerile script. It was much worse than I had anticipated, historically ludicrous, nodding to the lowest common denominator at every given opportunity. In a sense it was more obscene even than the genuine hard-core movies. It had false pretensions of grandeur, it took itself seriously: in fact, it was pure parody. The French Revolution, according to the unknown author, took place between orgasms.

By the time we landed in Paris I was reviling myself for being such an impulsive whore. There was no connecting flight to Nice at that time of night, so I checked into one of those anonymous hotels that cluster around every major airport. In a perverse way, I actually enjoy them. There is no pretence at real service and provided you never look out of the double-glazed windows you are shielded from the feeling of being in transit. After all, you get the same room whether it's in Hong Kong, Cape Town or Chicago. The menus in the coffee shops are standardised, so one goes from home cooking to home cooking, as it were. Even the sterilised toilet seats impart a certain familiar reassurance and those plastic shower caps are collectors' items.

Because of my misgivings, sleep proved difficult, even though the bed was wired to vibrate at the insertion of a coin. I put in an alarm call for breakfast, denuded my mini-bar of several overpriced miniature bottles of Scotch, then settled down, vibrationless, to study the offending script once again. It depressed me even more on second reading. I realised that I was in desperate need of inspiration if I was to survive the first meeting with Martin. I was inspired to catch the next Concorde home, but that was about all.

The combination of jet-lag, professional fear and Scotch ensured that I was in for a rough night. Thinking about what lay ahead got me thinking about Martin and the other half of that extraordinary telephone conversation. Previous encounters with him had never given me the impression that he was vulnerable in the war between the sexes. If I had

37

given the subject any consideration at all, I had always fixed him as asexual, too pleased with himself and the status quo ever to put himself at risk. On the set he was a tyrant, scathingly sarcastic to any actor who failed to deliver, intolerant of any mistakes made by the crew, or indeed of anybody who hindered the execution of his will. I found it difficult to recast him suddenly as a man 'brought to the brink' by passion. As far as I knew his private life had never been scorched by scandal (he was regarded as poor copy by the gossip columnists for that reason). He had been married to the same hollow woman for over twenty years and they had two grown-up sons, neither of whom had followed their father's career, their futures doubtless decided by Mrs Martin James who made no secret of the fact that she despised everything about the film industry. The most interesting thing I had ever heard said about her was that she played a lethal game of gin rummy for ruinous stakes, but since I had never been invited to any of her intimate gatherings, this had never been tested in fire. Although sexually she was about as exciting as Mrs Khrushchev, and in my book a total justification for adultery, Martin had always given the impression that he was content with his lot. I suppose, to be fair, she was a good hostess and complemented Martin's own snobbishness. Maybe he hadn't been a whited sepulchre throughout his married life, but if ordinary human temptation had occasionally diverted him from his main thrust (which I took to be the glorification of his career) then he had been exquisitely discreet about it, unlike Caroline of *Bastille Connection* fame, his public face had never been contorted by lust.

These and other conjectures finally induced a few hours' fitful sleep. I was jolted awake by the room-service waiter delivering my breakfast twenty minutes early – 'breakfast' consisting of a collection of sealed packages, all of which needed the strength of a fully grown male gorilla to open. An hour or so later I declined an identical plastic offering on the internal flight to Nice and was feeling decidedly grizzled by the time we made our final approach.

The heat outside on the tarmac penetrated the soles of my unsuitable city shoes and as I walked to the passenger terminal I was immediately conscious of being an outsider:

to arrive pale and uninteresting at a holiday resort never fails to induce feelings of inferiority.

I was greeted in the baggage-claim area by a young man wearing the inevitable patched jeans and a T-shirt advertising the title of the film. He identified himself as the Second Assistant, Nigel, and from his accent I took him to be a Cockney. As we shook hands we were joined by a rumpled character with a face the colour and texture of a linen napkin stained with plum juice.

'Harv, good to have you with us.'

Even if he had been the Mayor of Nice bestowing the freedom of the city, I would still have taken an instant dislike to him. Anybody who calls me Harv is automatically crossed off my list. Naturally I knew he wasn't the Mayor of Nice – he had Publicity stamped all over him. The really flip publicists who occupy chintzy offices on Madison and Fifth, with wall to wall Bigelow carpets and secretaries with cute butts, never actually visit film locations. They reserve their energies solely for film festivals. The line publicists share one common characteristic – they exude failure, giving it off with an aura as pungent as stale human sweat. I regard them as I would radioactive waste.

This one called himself Dunbar, Marvin Dunbar, and he had graduated from that school of journalism which trains its students to treat everything that happens on a film set as though the *Hindenburg* is bursting into flames again.

'Harv,' he said, 'I'm Marv, so we'll have to be careful we don't get each other's mail.' This sent him into a choking fit – the plum stains turned ominously darker until he recovered.

'No, seriously, Harv, are we glad to see you. When they told me you were on your way, I could have gone down on the producer.'

Nigel gave me an Arthur Treacher look, except that he was too young to remember Arthur Treacher. He took my baggage tabs and went to the carousel with a porter.

'I've already put a story out,' Dunbar said. 'You know, gave it a little colour, how you came in on their Concorde, they like that, because believe me they're so French here they even shake hands with an open mouth. Know France, do you?'

'I've been before,' I said.

'My first trip. And I'll tell you something, I don't think the food's all it's cracked up to be. You want to have dinner tonight?'

'I imagine Martin will want to see me tonight, thanks all the same.'

'Know the cast, do you?'

'I know very little about anything right now.'

'Great cast. Charles Croze, Suzanne Saphire and a real little sweetheart, even though she is French, Michelle Raye. I got a sensational break with her today. I fixed the cover of *Paris Match*. It's all a question of how you approach people in my job. But it's sure good to see you, Harv. Like, most of the crew is either French or British, and I can take most people, you have to in my job, but I don't go aces on the British or the French. See, I don't kiss ass, I gotta job to do and I do it. I had you put in my hotel, seeing as how you don't know anybody.'

Nigel returned at that point. 'No, that's changed, Marvin.'

'What d'you mean, changed? I fixed it myself.'

'Yeah, well it's been unfixed. Mr Burgess is in the Auberge de Colombier.'

'Who put him there, for Christ's sake? That's away from all the action.'

'The governor, he wanted him there.'

'Oh, shit! Listen, Harv, be guided by me. The Colombier is not where it happens. Where it happens is on the third floor of my hotel.'

'We'd better get cracking,' Nigel said, coming to the rescue.

I followed him outside, with Marvin grumbling behind us. A chauffeur-driven Mercedes drew in and before long we were speeding along the *péage* to Grasse.

'I can't get over them giving you such a bum's rush with the hotel,' Marvin groaned.

'Well, don't worry about it, Marvin. Just keep writing the captions.' Nigel winked back at me in the rear-view mirror.

'How are things in the front line?' I asked.

'Dodgy, I'd say. Très dodgy. This film's been a right cock-up from the word go. Still, all part of Life's rich

40

pageant. Me, I'm not complaining. Bleedin' sight better than the Ball's Pond Road any day. Don't you agree, Marvin?'

'I still can't get over where they put this poor guy.'

'Look, Mr Burgess doesn't like it, we'll move him later on. Ours not to question why. The governor wants him there to begin with, so that's where he's going to be. You're getting him worried. He isn't going to the YMCA, the Auberge is a very fair pad from what I've seen. And I imagine that Mr Burgess has to get cracking on the old rewrite, so he wouldn't have much time for a touch of the other.'

'Am I on my own there?'

'Apart from Michelle. That's Miss Raye. Most of us, most of the cast and English crew that is, we're in Grasse.'

He pronounced it *grass*, as in arse. 'Not bad. I mean Grasse ain't the King's road on a Saturday night. It's where they make all the perfume – well, you probably know that, especially sitting next to Marvin. What're you wearing Marvin?'

'Gigolo.'

'What's that, embalming fluid or antifreeze?'

'Listen, cost me two hundred francs, don't knock it.'

'Gets the birds going, does it? Have to beat them off with clubs, do you?'

'British sense of humour,' Marvin said. 'About as funny as a baby's open grave. But talking of pussy, Harv, you have to get down on those topless beaches. You've never seen so much young tit in all your life.'

'Really?'

'I swear to God. You're gonna blow your brains out.'

'Nigel,' I said,' – and excuse me, Marvin, that's fascinating – Nigel, can I ask you something before we get there. How is our fearless leader?'

'Perhaps not his usual self at the moment. Which is understandable. He's had a lot of aggro on this one, but I'm sure he's going to be pleased to see you.'

'What're the arrangements?'

'Well – and this is up to you – he said for me to tell you that he'd like you to go to his place as soon as you've got settled in.' He flashed a smile at me. He had one gold tooth

41

in the middle of his mouth. I warmed to him. Second Assistants are usually a breed apart.

The world of a film unit on a foreign location is almost impossible to describe to anybody outside the business. We all live, for the duration of the shooting schedule, by the ostrich syndrome: because our heads are buried in the sands of make-believe, we convince ourselves we're immune from most of the rules that govern the lives of others. There is a built-in, shared eroticism, a feeling that excitement – an uncomplicated, no-tears-at-the-end affair – is always on the cards. I'd call it naive rather than cynical, though I'm open to challenge on that. Maybe it stems from the fact that, although we work to very fine limits, time goes backwards, forwards and sideways and that's something very few outsiders can understand: the fact that, for various technical reasons, films aren't shot in continuity. What seems like pure, lunatic chaos is really organised chaos, except when it all screws up and becomes lunatic chaos. And always in the centre of this tiny, isolated archipelago is the director playing God, nursemaid, dictator – ordering day for night, causing water to flow from the rock, passion to flourish where only hate exists. In our case, for God, read Martin James, my mentor, who from all accounts, was not the man he used to be.

FOUR

The moment I first saw the Auberge de Colombier I knew that somebody had made the right choice for me. The action, real or imagined, on the third floor of Dunbar's hotel, receded into the distance, though the action man himself was still outraged on my behalf.

'Jesus!' he said, sweating the moment he stepped out of the air-conditioned car. 'This is a hotel? It's an ancient monument. You're gonna be miserable here, Harv, outa your skull with misery. I bet they don't even have TV in the rooms.'

'Have you ever watched French TV?'

'Sure, I know it'd put you away. But you can get late-night stag movies piped into our place. You know the first day I got here, like I was organised, know what I mean? and I switched on the set in my room and there was Sylvia Kristel getting shafted on a train, her ass in the washbasin. You ever tried that, by the way?'

'Not in living memory.'

'Me, I'm a founder member of the Mile-High Club.' He marched straight up to the desk once we were inside, determined to assert himself.

'Qu'est-ce que c'est the chambre for Mr Burgess? We'd like to see what you've got,' he said to the old concierge who gave off a comfortable scent of garlic at three-feet range.

'Marvin, it's kind of you to be concerned, but I'm sure it's going to be fine, whatever they give me.'

'Listen, don't take the first thing, they'll stick you with a room over the kitchens or something. Maybe they have a bridal suite. D'you have a bridal suite, captain?'

43

'It's all fixed, Marvin,' Nigel said. Even his natural tolerance was wearing thin.

I took a look around and I liked what I saw. The place had probably started life as a farmhouse, then extensions had been added, forming two wings sheltering a paved courtyard. It had an air of studied neglect about it, a deliberate ageing process such as studio painters and set decorators apply, and everything was spotlessly clean. Geraniums trailed from the window boxes and the shutters on the windows, their colours bleached out by the months of sun, were not quite symmetrical. The stonework had the appearance of a water-colour, and as we moved up the cool stairway to inspect my room, white doves lifted themselves from the tiled roof and glided across the courtyard on the thick, hot air.

We were shown to a small suite at the rear of the main block. The windows were open, for the sun was off them by now, and the strong light diffused, giving a distant view of a village with its church spire glimpsed between a row of drooped trees. The bathroom which adjoined the bedroom had an oversized tub standing free in the middle of a tiled floor, stranded, it seemed, like some great white whale on a beach. I felt well content, immediately at home, but Marvin was still not prepared to admit defeat.

'No fridge. Not too much closet space, and a view that'll drive you crazy. That church bell probably goes off all night.'

'It's terrific,' I said. 'Couldn't be better.'

'Well, you've got to live here, but when things get rough, just remember I didn't give you chopped chicken liver . . . Still, at least they sent you some fruit and liquor.'

He pointed to the statutory quota of gifts on the table by the window: the champagne and Chivas Regal and a huge, cellophaned basket of exotic fruit, already wilting from the heat. Women get flowers, men get fruit; if in doubt, send both – somewhere when the rule book was written in stone, it was thus established. There was a card attached to the champagne. It read: *Welcome to the Somme. Martin.* The message was typed and doubtless Martin had phoned it in, if he ever knew he'd sent it.

'Sure it's okay?' Nigel asked.

'Perfect. A room made for a rewrite if ever I saw one. Here.' I handed him the bottle of whisky. 'I take it you're not a teetotaller?'

'I must be honest. I have sometimes rubbed a little round my gums. Just for toothache.'

'How are your teeth?'

'Aching.'

The old concierge staggered in with my baggage. I tipped him lavishly, not from ostentation, but from a general feeling of satisfaction.

'Listen,' Marvin said, calling back into the room while he took a noisy piss. 'I don't want to bug you now, but as soon as you can I'd like to start work on your biog. I got most of it, but I'd like to round it off with a few personal anecdotes, know what I mean? Likewise, if you can come up with anything that happened to you on the fucking Concorde, I can use that too. You know the kinda crap – engine failure, a tyre blowing on take off, that sort of thing always goes over big.'

The idea of telling my life story to Marvin almost made the sun go in.

'Well, there's not much to add,' I said, as Nigel made a masturbatory gesture. 'You go ahead and do what you think.'

'The typewriter should have been waiting for you,' Nigel said. 'I'll check on that. I took a chance and got you an IBM golfball, is that what you're used to?'

'You're a mindreader.'

'And paper, of course. But if there's anything else, just tip me the wink.'

'Yeah, make sure he's comfortable in this museum,' Marvin said. 'Mr Burgess is a very important screenwriter, and American, not one of your Limey mob, so treat him right.'

'Look, no panic, but the governor is anxious to get with you as soon as you're ready. You want to unpack first?'

'Take your time, Harv. Don't let Martin or anybody else push you around. You just got off a plane for Christ'sake!'

'I'm ready when you are.' I ignored him and talked straight to Nigel. 'Let's go jump in the deep end.'

It's amazing how quickly one becomes accustomed to unaccustomed luxury.

I have no hang-ups about accepting hospitality, chauffeur-driven limousines, free board and lodgings or any of the other perks that go with the job. The film industry has perfected double-dealing, double-crosses and double-bookkeeping, the unholy trinity that separates the men from the boys. When I started out I used to have a bright set of illusions which I fondly imagined would last forever, just as I thought the paintwork on the first Chevvy I owned would never rust. Now the only illusion I retain is that next time it can't be as bad.

I sank back into the velour coolness of the Mercedes and we set out for Martin's retreat, which according to Nigel was only ten kilometres or so from my hotel. I would have been more than happy to sit and admire the passing view, but there was no silencing Marvin.

'I gotta find out whether we've parlayed a tie-in with Mercedes. Are we using them in the film?'

'Bit difficult,' Nigel said. 'Unless of course we use them for tumbrils.'

'Yeah, that's right. I was forgetting it's a period job.'

'You just thought the actors were wearing all that drag for fun, did you?'

I suspected that you couldn't insult Marvin and that sarcasm was wasted on him. The boundaries of his world were narrow: he really did believe you had to put fake tinsel on top of the real tinsel.

'What did they use in those days?'

'Guillotines. You could get a good deal with Gillette razors, maybe. Or Swiss army pocket knives.'

Marvin turned to me. 'You're the writer, Harv, can't you come up with something? What the hell did they use a lot of in those days?'

'Toilet water.'

'Toilet water?'

'Yes,' I said. 'It's a bit of a misnomer, because what they didn't use overmuch was toilets and baths. But they made sure they saturated themselves with eau de Cologne and other perfumes.'

'There you are, Marvin! Perfect. We're living in Grasse,

you can go and do your stuff and get us all a couple of gallons of free poncing lotion.'

'Listen, don't knock it. Harv here knows what he's talking about.'

'Only make sure you don't get the stuff you're wearing. With the air conditioning on it's like being upwind of a brothel.'

We were gliding along secondary roads now and while Marvin pondered his paths to glory, I took in the countryside. There was ample evidence that the long hot summer had taken its usual toll: large tracts of forest were charred black, the decapitated trees standing like war-time tank obstacles on the hillsides.

'What would be a terrific idea,' Marvin mused, 'would be to get them to invent a new perfume specially for the film. Revolution? No . . . Wait a minute, I got it. How does Malmaison Mon Amour grab you?'

'Be great as an aerosol,' Nigel said. 'But I can't see the birds spraying it between their bristols.'

'You see what I'm faced with, Harv? We writers are just wasting our talents around characters like him.'

'Too true . . . By the way, don't take offence, but I have a positive loathing of being called Harv.'

'You kidding?'

'No.'

'Gee, I'm sorry. Just that everybody calls me Marv.'

'Marv I can live with. But Harv sets my teeth on edge.'

He rounded on Nigel. 'Why didn't you tip me off?'

'I chalked up a black, Marv. I take all the blame. Look, to make it up to you, I'll give you a great idea. Call the new perfume Marv, short for marvellous, right? Immortalise yourself. Just think, every time a bird gave herself a squirt, you'd have to score.'

The suggestion was not displeasing to him, but before he could elaborate on it we arrived outside the electronically-controlled gates guarding the entrance to Martin's property. The driver got out and spoke into the intercom. Somewhere in the house somebody pressed the right button and the gates began to swing inwards. At regular intervals along the drive there were notices warning intruders that guard dogs patrolled the grounds.

'Don't ask me to get out first,' I said.

Two German shepherds appeared even as I spoke and ran alongside the Mercedes, keeping pace with us as we spattered the gravel on our way to the main entrance. There was no question about it: Martin didn't believe in half measures. The house, although built as a bogus château, was certainly imposing and stood in immaculate grounds. Sprinklers spurted long jets of water through the heat haze and everywhere there was a profusion of colour. As the Mercedes stopped a manservant dressed in a white jacket and black trousers opened the front door. He shouted a command to the two dogs and they stood their ground as I followed Nigel out.

'You sure they're okay?'

'Yeah, they won't move unless he says. Mr James is expecting us, Claude. This is Mr Burgess.'

'Yes, Mr Burgess. If you'd like to follow me?'

'I'm not coming in,' Nigel said. 'For one thing I'm not invited and I've got work to do back at the office. So Marvin and I will scarper, then send the car back to wait for you.'

'I've no idea how long I'll be here.'

'No sweat. The driver's on golden time anyway. He'd love you to stay all night.'

'If you get a chance,' Marvin shouted, 'mention the perfume idea.'

I followed Claude into the house. He led me through a main room paved in marble and furnished in the ornate Italian style. I was fairly certain that some of the pieces had once adorned one of Martin's film sets and had then been borrowed permanently. Such time-honoured practices were democratically applied: I once knew a Teamster Captain who had a modest semi-detached out near La Guardia done over as a plush New Orleans bordello, courtesy of Twentieth Century Fox.

We came, eventually, to a large patio which ran the length of the southern façade and overlooked a monster pool, sculptured from the living rock. Martin was lying on an outside daybed and, a short distance away, shaded by a striped parasol, was a man I had never seen before. The moment he saw me approaching, Martin rose to his feet. As he got closer he made a grimace intended to indicate that certain intimacies were not to be shared with his companion.

'Harvey, dear, you actually made it. I can't tell you how delighted we are to see you, aren't we, David? Come and meet our distinguished producer.'

As a general rule of thumb these days, producers fall into two distinct main categories. Either they are old campaigners who have been beaten into the ground over the years and are now serving out their time, content to be glorified office boys, sad shadows of their former selves, while the studio calls all the shots, or the star dictates. Or else they all resemble the man I was about to meet for the first time: tough, wiry little sons of bitches, often graduates of the pop scene, who change their Rolls Corniches every year, their wives or boy friends every six months, are deeply into real estate, coke and analysis, spend half their waking lives on the radio-telephone, play killer tennis and have only one remaining ambition: to run a studio into the ground. David Latrough was a good example.

He stubbed out a joint as I approached and I caught the flash of one of those solid gold Rolexes that most of us can scarcely lift, let alone wear. He was wearing a pure silk shirt open to the waist, revealing another kilo of gold chains and wall-to-wall chest hair. He didn't get up, but merely waved a hand in my direction. He looked resentful.

'Let me fix you a drink,' Martin said. 'I'm having a beaker of Chablis, but David is into prune juice. It's his month for the health kick. Take your pick. The prune juice is non-vintage.'

'I think I'll sample the poison. I'm sure you trod the grapes yourself.'

I had the feeling that I had interrupted something ugly. Behind the warmth of Martin's greeting, there was a sense of unease, almost as if he, Martin, was the guest and Latrough the owner of all this splendour.

'Has the weather been like this all the time?' I asked, in a conventional attempt to begin a dialogue with Latrough.

'Yeah. Every day. Too bad we weren't getting some of it in the can.'

Martin handed me a generous glass of wine in a goblet

49

that had his initials etched into it. I wouldn't have put it past him to have included a bogus crest.

'David and I were just discussing the sort of changes I want made, but naturally we didn't finalise anything until you got here and had a chance to put your views. I take it you had an opportunity of reading the existing script?'

'Yes.'

'What do I read into that?'

'Can I speak frankly?'

'That's what we're here for, Harvey. Isn't that so, David?'

'We're here to cut the bullshit and get this thing rolling again.'

'Let Harvey say his piece, and then we can discuss it. Go ahead, Harvey, the floor's yours.'

'Well, obviously I came to it totally objectively. After all I didn't know of its existence until you phoned me. I had no idea how far you are in, or what the budget is, who's in the cast, et cetera. So I judged it purely as a script. Cold. And I have to admit I found it fifth rate.'

I looked to Latrough for some reaction, but all I got was a gold-plated freeze.

'Anything specific?' Martin asked.

'No, pretty general. I think there are a few scenes which, doctored, could stand on their own, but overall it's not bad enough to be a parody, it's not exciting enough to hold up as drama, it's just plain boring if you want my honest opinion.'

'Boring?'

'Yes. Ass-paralysingly boring.'

This time we both looked towards Latrough, but he was still the cobra waiting in the basket until he heard the right tune.

'Well,' Martin said, 'I haven't been putting it quite as strong as that, but I'm glad you didn't mince matters, because at this stage of the game there's nothing worse than sitting on the fence. Okay, next question, do you think you can lick it into shape? Bearing in mind that we have a full crew and cast, all costing money, while we sit and debate the question.'

'That depends,' I said.

Latrough spoke for the first time. 'What does it depend on, Mr Burgess?'

'Oh, call him Harvey, David. Don't let's get off on the wrong foot. This isn't a formal Board meeting.'

'It's formal enough for me, when it's costing six grand a day to sit around and chew the fat.'

'David, you know perfectly well, I've never concealed my reservations, about the script. I told you that from day one.'

'Yeah, I remember, but you still started shooting it. If it was such shit, why did you accept?'

'Because you're so persuasive, dear boy. And I take my non-existent hat off to you. You charmed me into it, just as you charmed the studio into putting up the bread. You have an unlimited supply of charm.' He turned back to me. 'David has the sort of charm you can't acquire, you have to be born with it.'

'Let me try some on Mr Harvey Burgess, see if it works with him. See, I don't go ape-shit for message movies, Mr Burgess.'

'What d'you consider a message picture?'

'One that doesn't take money.'

'Interesting new definition, don't you think, Harvey?'

'Look Martin, we all know your opinion. I'm sure you gave it to your rewrite man before he got here. Softened him up, told him what a hard time you've been having pulling down four hundred thousand, plus a piece, plus expenses . . . Now, maybe you'd let me have my shot? Unfortunately the majority of the human race don't happen to share your superior taste in all things. They eat Big Macs in their fingers, they drink beer out of cans, and they've never heard of the fucking French Revolution, because half of them flunked high school and the other half don't give a shit. And do you know why? I do, because I've studied the form. When they pay for their tickets at the box office, they don't want to sit there admiring your fancy camera work and listen to your ideas on why Marie Antoinette blew it. They want to see a little action, they want to see as much tit as we can get away with without being closed down, they want to see Heroes, Martin, big fucking heroes with Magnums in their fists. Now, like it or

51

not, you took the money to make this movie and as far as I know you also read the script. At that time, and correct me if I'm wrong, you had nothing to say except, What's the definition of nett profits after double negative? You managed that without a rewrite.

'Now, going in, we both knew we weren't going to have Clint Eastwood or Charlie Bronson blowing the world apart. What we had, what we got, was a piece of hokum for Joe Public, to be made at a price. Historical? Yeah, sure, nobody was going to wear Calvin Klein jeans. We were going to give them lots of blood and pussy, classy pussy . . .'

'What's all this leading up to, David? I mean, it's a fascinating monologue, but I'm missing the point.'

'The point I'm making, is that suddenly I'm payrolling your ego trip. Suddenly, even for four hundred thousand, plus the piece, plus the expenses, you can't bring yourself to soil your hands or offend your artistic conscience.'

'David, that's a gross exaggeration. All I'm saying, all I've ever said, is that I think this script is lacking in certain elements.'

'So why didn't you find that out before you signed?'

'Yes, you're probably right. I should have spotted it earlier. But I didn't, and for that you're fully entitled to criticise me. However, the moment I realised that I wasn't going to be able to give you what you want, I blew the whistle. Now, we're not in a disaster situation. We've shot a few thousand feet, and some of it we can still use. Your budget can accommodate that?'

'Who says?'

'David, I've been here before, remember? With all due respect I know a padded budget when I see one. You've given yourself plenty of insurance policies, you're covered and you know it. Even with this hiatus, even with the changes I hope Harvey is going to make, I'll still bring it in on schedule. That I guarantee.'

'Okay, well, let's talk about the changes.'

'That's what we're here for. So why not let Harvey get a word in?'

'Are they going to be major?'

'We don't know until Harvey gets to work. Give the poor man a chance. You're double-guessing him before he's even started. Harvey, give us the bottom line. What d'you think needs doing? And forget giving David haemorrhoids, just give it to us straight.'

I had been enjoying the scenery and the Chablis during all this. To tell the truth I had only been listening with half an ear. Their dialogue was not exactly original; every script conference I had ever attended followed the same pattern.

'Well, to begin with the present script is ludicrous, historically – unless of course you want to recast it with the Monty Python team, then you might be sitting on a masterpiece.'

'Wait a minute,' Latrough interrupted. 'I don't want to hear this. Don't give me the historically ludicrous bit, because that makes my balls ache. Show me something that's historically accurate and I'll show you an empty theatre. You think the fucking hunchback of Notre Dame actually swung on those bells? Did Erroll Flynn win the war in Burma? You think Greer Garson discovered a cure for cancer . . . ?'

Martin suddenly hit the arm of his daybed with his fist, knocking his glass of wine off and shattering it. 'David, will you keep your mouth shut for just two seconds! Now, we all know what you think, I happen to be waiting to hear what Harvey thinks. Harvey happens to be a professional screenwriter who's been at it a long time. He's a screenwriter, David, and you, you're just a privileged cunt who got lucky enough to write his name on somebody else's cheques. Go ahead, Harvey.'

Claude appeared on the patio and came forward to clear up the broken glass.

'Leave it! Clear it up later. Just bring me a fresh glass and another bottle.'

I waited until Claude had retreated again. Latrough was fingering his gold chains like a nun who has just been told there was no immaculate conception.

'Well, to begin again . . . let's not talk about it as history, let's just deal with it as a story. As a story I don't know who the hell one is supposed to root for. As it is you've got ten different stories, none of which relate to each other. Consequently, it's confusing, and there's never a chance to develop any real leading roles.'

'That's a valid point,' Martin said. 'And it's something Charles has been moaning about. Well, they all have, in varying degrees. Sorry, Harvey.'

'My feeling is that one should condense some of the subsidiary characters and concentrate on four or five major roles, bringing their separate stories together for the climax. Now without cutting across your views, David, if I may say so, I think there are certain events which actually took place during this period, which are more exciting, more dramatic, and could be better cinema, than the inventions that you've got in the script at the moment. The most obvious example is the execution of the King. Probably *the* most dramatic event of that century. And it's never mentioned in the film, never, not once. Now we don't have to make it a history lesson, because it is what it is and in terms of cinema, horrendous – bloody, literally, and frightening – and could hardly be more visual. Okay, I haven't worked it out in detail, because I've hardly had time, but it seems to me that if you start the film there – play it behind main titles if you like – and show that, show the regicide, and at the same time have one or two of your main characters actually there in the crowd, watching the death of the king, your hero being a Royalist devastated by what he considers is a murder, and your heavy enjoying the spectacle, well then you have – in a few short scenes – not only placed the movie in time, but you've also clearly established the motives for two of your leading players.'

I felt quite pleased with myself at the end of that speech. I not only hadn't worked out that idea in detail, I had only just thought of it. It was, I felt, a creditable ad-lib, one of those rare occasions when inspiration comes to the aid of the party.

'Brilliant!' Martin said. 'Brilliant conception. Makes the whole difference. I can see exactly what Harvey is getting at.'

'Where's it go from there?' Latrough said.

'Well, do you buy that much?'

'Yeah, it's got possibilities. Except it sounds expensive.'

'Forget your pocket calculator for a minute. We're going to make cuts elsewhere and what we save on the cuts we can use for the new scenes. What else, Harvey?'

'I think the dialogue is out of the Ark.'

'You won't find the actors disagreeing with that. Charles has already refused to play one scene, that's really what brought everything to a head.'

'He should read his contract,' Latrough said. 'He has to play what we give him.'

'David, we are not making Kung Fu with a lot of splendid Oriental gentlemen jumping about and grunting. We have a plot and people have to speak lines and those lines have to make some sort of sense. They have to speak English, not some early period Esperanto. Charles may not be Larry Olivier or even Paul Newman, but he does have talent, and he does have a reputation to protect. If he doesn't want to say a certain line he won't say it, and you can hit him with fifteen contracts and twenty-eight lawsuits, and he still won't say it. So let's keep it in the real world, shall we?'

'Yeah.' Latrough consulted his Rolex. 'Okay, so you two have got it all figured out. I'm not going to sit here and trade lines with you. You're both so smart, I'm just the guy who pays for the meal tickets. That's okay. You have your fun. But I just want to leave you with this to think about. Don't be too fucking smart for your own good, Martin. You've got yourself a nice fancy pad here, sprinklers on the lawn, a chintzy butler to put ice cubes in your drinks, and you're the big man locally. But back in Hollywood you're not exactly this year's hottest property. See, back there, they're like me, they don't read Pauline Kael, they read the grosses in *Variety*, they take the returns to bed with them, and when you and your friend Harvey here get through jerking off, you'd better come up with something sensational, and something I like. I may not have your appreciation of Art and all that bullshit, but at least I'm not a turkey farmer. My last three films made money, Martin, your last three didn't even get back prints and advertising. If I were you I'd turn the sprinklers off.'

He got to his feet. 'I'm going to be generous. I'll give you until Sunday to come up with some pages. If I like them, we'll shoot them. If I don't, we go back to the old script. Charles don't want to speak the lines, we'll revoice him. You don't want to direct the old stuff, I'll pay you off.' Then it was my turn. 'Harvey, nothing personal, you understand.

Maybe you're Harold Robbins, and maybe you're not. All you have to be right now is fast. Because come Monday, those cameras are going to roll. Thanks for the prune juice, Martin.'

He walked away into the house. Martin said nothing until we heard the front door slam, then filled his new glass. I could see he was making a considerable effort to stay composed.

'How d'you think we should proceed?' Martin said finally. 'Assuming we have to live by that little man's ultimatum?'

'Up to you. You name it.'

'Well, before the scene you had the misfortune to witness, I had thought up a plan of action, which was . . . we'd go on talking tonight over dinner, arrive at the overall shape of the thing, then tomorrow morning you and I and a couple of the boys – the Art Director, Bernard the First Assistant, and maybe the Production Manager – would take a quick look round at the existing locations, then go to the studio for lunch, where you could see the sets . . . The idea being to give you a feel of the thing before you start writing.'

He went to replenish my glass. I put my hand over it. 'Any more and I'll fall face downwards. I guess the jet-lag finally caught up with me.

'What about a swim then? That might freshen you up.'

'Good idea. Otherwise I don't think I'll last through dinner.'

Martin had kept himself in remarkably good shape. I watched him dive into the pool. Claude appeared, as if on cue, bearing large towelling robes. He waited until Martin had swum his quota of three lengths, then stepped forward to place one of the robes round his shoulders. I was not feeling that energetic, and after getting my hair wet, merely floated in the shallow end.

'Use the Jacuzzi,' Martin said. 'Nothing like it for the tired old muscles. Claude, turn it on, will you?'

I transferred myself into the turbulent waters. Martin came and sat on the edge, dangling his feet in the hot foam.

'We'll eat early. There'll only be the two of us. Alice is out being social, as usual. I can't take too much of the local

56

French high society. They're so bloody grand and conde-
scending.'

'But you're happy here?'

'What's happiness, chum? One misses England, of
course. But not the England of today. What one misses is
what it used to be . . . I meant to ask you, what've you got
in Connecticut?'

'Home, you mean? Nothing. I've been renting a place.'

'How's . . . er . . . Patricia?'

'Pamela.'

'Pamela, sorry.'

'When last heard of, very well. We got divorced.'

'Oh . . . One gets out of touch, living out here. Do I
commiserate or congratulate?'

'Neither. All the stitches were removed two years ago,
there's hardly any scar tissue.'

'Was it friendly or otherwise?'

'The two sets of lawyers were very friendly. As they had
every cause to be.'

'Plays hell with you, doesn't it, any sort of emotional
upheaval like that? Thank God, I've never had to go
through it . . .'

The sun was in my eyes and I couldn't see his face. He
moved away and poured himself another glass of wine.

'Sure I can't tempt you?'

'I'd better not. That's heady stuff. Tell me about the cast.
I know Charles, vaguely, that's to say we've bumped into
each other at parties, but I've never written for him. Is he
behaving himself these days? One hears all sorts of
rumours.'

'He's like every other actor. Insecure, very conscious of
his image, especially since he's showing signs of wear . . .
But I never have any problems with him.'

'I can understand him not wanting to say that dialogue.
Now that our producer has departed, I don't mind telling
you I nearly caught the first plane back. That opening scene
is unreal! Come clean with me . . . Why did you say yes in
the first place? You must have known you were onto a
loser.'

'Yes, I suppose so . . . I suppose like all of us, I thought I
could lick it. And I have to admit that the money was a

consideration. It isn't cheap, living down here, and I'm too set in my ways. I thought . . . that perhaps I could make a really commercial picture out of it. But shit has a habit of remaining shit.'

'How about the women?'

'Well, Suzanne I've worked with before, Michelle is a very talented girl if she's given the chance . . . and they both look good on screen. I mean, Suzanne can be a pain in the arse sometimes, especially if she isn't getting it regularly.'

'And is she?'

'She's between husbands at the moment. The last one, that Egyptian – or was he Saudi? – I don't know, he didn't last long. She said he was very boring in bed. You know the way she loves to give it to you in three-D, she said having it off with him was about as exciting as watching paint dry.'

'Graphic. I must remember that and use it somewhere.'

'On the whole I couldn't have been luckier with the cast I've got.'

'Charles must have had a go at the script, didn't he? I mean, he's no idiot, or did he need the money too?'

'I guess everybody does. We all live beyond our means . . . Yes, Charles has been moaning away ever since he got here, and I made some changes on the floor – I mean, he had some good ideas for his own character, but being an actor, he was only looking out for number one. It's a buggers' mess, I tell you. My own fault.'

'What happens if, in the rewrite, I cut some of the minor characters? Will that present any problems?'

'Have to pay them off, I suppose. We'll go through all that over dinner and then tomorrow you can look at the schedule and decide on the priorities. I must say I feel a lot happier now you're here.'

I crossed my fingers and held them up for him to see.

'Do you think you can break the back of it before the weekend? It's a hell of a pill.'

'I'll have a try.'

'I thought your idea for pre-titles was sensational. It even got our David's attention for a moment.'

'Well, it might work. Give you a better opening than all

that heavy breathing and contorted lust. Who's playing the little courtesan by the way?'

'Which? Oh, the girl in the opening sequence, you mean . . . She's quite talented, I'd like to use her more. She hasn't had all that much experience. I cast her locally, as a matter of fact.'

'She's French, is she?'

'No. Just happens to live down here.'

'What's her name?'

'Laura,' Martin said. 'Laura Taylor . . . See, I cast quite a bit in Paris and then I auditioned down here as well. I had to go through the motions because of the unions, but actually I was pleasantly surprised. I found one or two new faces and Laura was one of them.'

Every director I've ever met can't wait to play Svengali. They like to have at least one Trilby on every picture.

Over an excellent dinner we degutted the existing screenplay, attacking it with the same relish as we consumed the rack of lamb. Martin possessed a good sense of construction and perhaps my presence and the urgency of the situation spurred him on. Rewriting is not a job for the squeamish. In many ways it's a curious experience and the fact that I had travelled the same route many times before made little difference: it's not real writing, it certainly isn't. Art, just surgery without an anaesthetic – you go in with the knife and cut deep, baring the fat and exposing the arteries. Orwell said that at the very bottom of a writer's motives there lies a mystery. I'm not sure that my motives were that mysterious, Orwell was probably talking about kosher authors, not rewrite men. My main motive was to survive the coming week. Latrough hadn't sounded like a man given to idle threats.

I suppose to the ordinary public the mechanics of making a film are nigh incomprehensible. God knows, they are often incomprehensible to those of us who make them. Martin did not seem unduly concerned by the chaos he had created, and yet throughout dinner I got the impression that he was holding himself in check, and more than once my mind went back to that telephone conversation. I sensed it would be a dangerous luxury to try and probe him for further clues, but by the time we had reached the coffee and Calvados we needed a break from the script and it was not unnatural that the conversation should turn to sex and women – the subject is, after all, the universal leveller.

'Did the divorce wipe you out?'

'No, I came away with my underwear and socks.'

'Was it very traumatic?'

'At the time, I suppose it was, yes.'

'What's she doing now?'

'Oh, she remarried. She found immediate comfort with a young man – not quite young enough to be her son, but getting on that way. It's the new fashion, you know.'

'How about you?'

'What about me?'

'Have you found comfort elsewhere?'

'Not really, no.'

'Forgive me asking. I didn't really mean to pry.'

'Please. Nothing to tell really. I've taken a few swings and roundabouts. As a matter of fact the night you rang I'd been making what was for me a fairly heavy frontal attack. I'd scripted a classic dirty weekend, but when we came to shoot it there was too much dialogue and not enough action. Rather like *The Bastille Connection*. We've got to change that title, don't you agree?'

'Yes, not the greatest, is it?'

I had given him the cue, but he didn't pick it up.

'But your weekend was a frost, was it?'

'She turned out to be a dyke.'

'Christ! didn't you suspect anything beforehand?'

'No. She was a recent convert, so she told me, and full of grace. Grace with a small g that is.'

'According to Queen Victoria lesbianism didn't exist, you know. It was never a criminal offence like the poor old buggers. She struck it out of the Act.'

He swirled his Calvados, then drank it down in one go. Pushing the decanter to my side of the table, he said, 'Help yourself, chum, and excuse me for a moment, I just have to make a quick call.'

Left to myself I got up from the table to take a closer look at some of his paintings. He had a Matisse, an early one to my less-than-expert eye, a group of Picasso lithographs from the Vollard Suite and a very engaging Marie Laurencin which had pride of place. I was still standing there, admiring the delicacy of the colours, when Martin returned.

'That's Alice's favourite,' he said. 'Bought it on our first anniversary. Just as well, because I couldn't afford it now.'

'How is Alice?'

'Very chipper. She just came in as a matter of fact. Said she'd join us for a cup of coffee. Then I'll let you get off to bed. I think we've made some progress, don't you? But I'm sure you're shagged out.'

'Fading a little.'

'Small wonder. You've had quite a first day. I think I'll just have another little nip.'

I detected an added nervousness. As he poured himself another Calvados he tipped the decanter awkwardly, spilling some on the elaborate lace tablecloth.

'Oh, Christ! Trust me. That won't please her ladyship.'

'Salt. Put some salt on it.'

He took the salt cellar and covered the stain.

'How does that look?'

'Looks like a stain covered with salt.'

'Let's put a plate over it . . . Ah! darling, there you are.'

The moment his wife entered the room her eyes went straight to the offending mark on the table.

'You remember Harvey, don't you darling? You last met him when he was writing *The Sacred Heart* for me.'

'Yes. How nice to see you again,' she said. 'What's happened there, dear?'

'Where? Oh, here, you mean? Just a slight spill, I'm afraid. Nothing much. I've put salt on it.'

'That never works. It'll have to go away and be expertly treated.'

'Never mind. Only a tablecloth.'

'It's hardly *only* a tablecloth, Martin. It happens to be *the* tablecloth. Why on earth did that stupid man put it on in the first place?'

'Well, don't let's make a Dreyfus case out of it. If it offends you, dear, why don't we take our coffee in the other room?'

I followed Mrs James into the adjoining room which I took to be Martin's den. All the tell-tale signs of an

61

expatriate were dotted about on his large desk – copies of *The Times* and the *Daily Mail*, a stack of *Country Life*, reminders of the umbilical cord that was never completely severed.

'I see you keep in touch,' I said.

'What? Oh, those. Yes . . . More from habit than any-thing else, though Alice couldn't be without her *Times* crossword and obituaries. Not that we have any regrets, do we dear? It all sounds a frightful mess and whenever one goes back for a few days London seems so dreary. It's like war-time again. The streets are filthy and if the sun does shine for a few hours everybody goes into shock, and the entire bloody conversation is about the weather. No, I certainly don't miss it.'

'Are you here on holiday, Mr Burgess?' his wife said. Claude brought in fresh coffee at this point. 'Claude, the tablecloth in there will have to go away and be properly cleaned. Mr James managed to spill something on it. It's a pity you put it on in the first place. You know I keep it for special occasions.'

'Well, it was a special occasion, dear. Harvey came over at a moment's notice to do me a great favour.'

'Oh, so you're not on holiday?'

'Er, no, I wouldn't call it that.'

'Darling, I told you this morning. Harvey's going to rewrite the script for me.'

'Did you? I don't remember.'

'No, well you're not terribly interested in my boring old films, are you? Anyway, that's why he's here, and he's doing me an enormous favour.'

'You're a writer, are you, Mr Burgess?'

'That's what it says on my passport. Some people have been known to cast doubts.'

'Do you know Rosalind Seaton?'

'Seaton? No, can't say I do.'

'She's a writer. Writes such lovely books. I was at school with her.'

'No, I confess I don't know her work.'

'I must lend you one of her books. She always writes about such nice people.'

'I don't know that Harvey will have much time for

reading,' Martin said. At that moment the phone on his desk rang. Before he could get to it his wife picked up the receiver.

'Yes? . . . Who wants him? Just a minute.'

She put her hand over the mouthpiece.

'Are you in to a Laura somebody?'

I watched Martin's face very closely.

'No, I'm not taking any calls.'

'Well, who is she?'

'Just one of the cast, darling. Just tell her I'm in a meeting. Tell her to ring the production office if she's got a problem.'

He bent and poured himself a fresh cup of coffee.

'I'm afraid Mr James isn't available. I suggest the production office if it's anything urgent . . . This is a private number and we don't normally use it for business, certainly not at this time of night.' She put the receiver down. 'Why on earth do you give those people your number?'

'I don't suppose I did, dear. But they have ways and means of finding it out.'

'She's not one of your stars, is she?'

'No, just an actress.'

'Well, it's an impertinence ringing at this hour. We should change the number and then keep it absolutely secret except to very close friends.'

'Yes, well I am making a film, remember. I can't quite live in a nunnery. People do have to contact me from time to time.'

I studied one of the copies of *Country Life* while this exchange was going on. Husband-and-wife scenes are best left undisturbed.

'Don't let's bore poor Harvey with our domestic problems,' Martin said. 'Tell us how your evening went, dear.'

'It was a washout.'

'Oh, didn't you win?'

'I didn't even play. I refuse to sit down at the same table with that ghastly little German character Billy insists on inviting for some reason. He turns very ugly when he loses.'

'So you didn't make the housekeeping money this week?'

If Martin was trying to ease the underlying tension for my

benefit, he failed miserably. His wife was patently not in the mood for family jokes at her expense. Looking at them both, listening to their barbed conversation, it was difficult to imagine what attractions, mental or physical, had brought them together originally. His wife was well preserved facially, though I suspected she had treated herself to a few tucks here and there. Her figure was reasonably held together, though her fleshy arms, pinched at the wrists by the quantity and weight of the bracelets she wore, spoilt the overall effect. Quite unfairly, with typical male cruelty in these matters, I filed her as a ballbreaker who, in the course of married time, had deliberately withheld her sexual favours when it had suited her.

'Where are you staying, Mr Burgess?'

'That auberge, quite close to here . . . What's it called? The Auberge de Colombier.'

'Oh, yes. I hear it's quite pleasant. Of course we don't eat out a great deal. I can't bear eating surrounded by a lot of tourists – and so many foreigners these days. One wonders where they get the money to pay those ridiculous restaurant prices. There's meant to be a depression and yet they seem to flood over here in their thousands. Thank God we're nowhere near the coast. Nice and Cannes are a positive nightmare during the season. Mind you, it appears to be the same the world over. And as for London . . . D'you know, the last time I went back, I went to Harrods, and you'll never believe it, but they actually had notices written in Arabic.'

'You came here, dear. It's the same thing.'

'There's absolutely no comparison, Martin, and you know it. We came here for the climate, the doctor said that I needed to be in a warm climate.'

'Perhaps they went to England for a cold climate.' Again the attempt at joking her out of her mood fell on stony ground.

'Anyway, we must let Harvey get off to bed. He's had a long day and I'm sure he's in need of a bit of shut-eye.'

'You must come and have another meal while you're down here,' his wife said, but there was no warmth in the invitation. 'Do you play gin by any chance?'

'Sad to say, no.'

'Pity. We have a few regulars, but we're always looking for new blood.'

'Freudian slip,' Martin muttered. After I had said my goodbyes he escorted me to the front door. My driver was fast asleep behind the wheel. He woke with a start as Martin rapped on the window.

'I'll pick you up in the morning at your place and we'll set off from there. Nine too early?'

'No, I imagine I shall still be on New York time and wide awake in the middle of the night.'

'Take a pill.'

'I'll read the script. That'll send me off.'

'Don't take any notice of Alice. She means well, but it comes out the wrong way.'

'I didn't notice anything.'

'Good. Good.'

He seemed about to say something else and then thought better of it. Then he said, 'I thought we made some progress, didn't you? I really appreciate your friendship, you know.'

'Listen, I'm grateful for the work. I just hope I can come up with the goods for you.'

'Oh, you will, you will.' I had the feeling that he was urging me to ask him the questions, rather like a boxer who suddenly drops his guard, inviting the knock-out punch. But I couldn't frame the one question I wanted to ask him. We shook hands, formally, and I left him standing there. The two guard dogs bounded out of the darkness and went to his side, and he stroked them both in turn. As my car swung round in the drive our headlights picked out the dogs' eyes. I thought of Gatsby and the eyes of the billboard.

FIVE

Some people boast that they never fail to be given prior notice of impending disasters. Their corns tingle, the pet dog starts to act peculiar, a lone bird flies across the sky: there is no end to the list of oracles from which they draw their premonitions. I don't live by such advance warnings – the major crevasses in my life have always opened up when I least expected them, and I have plunged like some victim of an earthquake. Certainly my wife's defection to a younger and presumably more satisfying lover had not been trailed as a coming attraction on the screen of my subconscious. The first I knew about it was in the gossip columns, ironically enough, since normally I don't merit inclusion in such exalted places. And the funny thing was that single, snide sentence, sandwiched between mentions of Burt Reynolds being romanced for the leading role in a new Fellini movie and Jane Fonda's latest social crusade, had more reality for me than my wife's eventual confession.

It would be dramatically tidier if I could reveal that I accurately predicted the events of that summer; that from the very beginning I saw through Martin's sad self-deceptions and laid my own plans accordingly. It would make the story easier to tell, but it would be a cheat, just a literary device. I went to France at Martin's invitation as a paid spectator, never anticipating that I, too, would become a victim in the triangle that ruined all our lives. Now, of course, reliving those events for the hundredth time, I am fat with hindsight, I can pinpoint every false step we all took, the exact hour of the first betrayal; I can see again that common menu from which we all ordered the special anguish of love. As for premonitions, there were none.

It all began normally enough – normally enough, that is, for a film. One doesn't have to be a soothsayer to chart the expected intrigues. I was sure Latrough had it firmly fixed in his mind that Martin and I were in collusion, that we had engineered the whole thing in order to put him in his place. The real reason – which was that Martin had suddenly got cold feet and needed to take out another insurance policy – would have been too simplistic for Latrough to accept. He needed darker explanations if his own insecurities were to be rationalised. I thought of something dear old Ray Chandler once mumbled to me before collapsing into his soup over a meal at Chasen's. 'It's all an endless contention of tawdry egos' was Ray's verdict. Sammy Glick was still the long-distance runner, wearing a variety of masks though the face never changed. We were all in the same relay race, passing the buck like a baton, bunching together to snatch the inside track.

That first night when I returned to my hotel room, I quickly came to the conclusion that I had been too clever for my own good. It was one thing to ad-lib a new approach when given the stage – just as some actors can give inspired auditions and go resolutely to pieces when handed the role – but now I had to deliver the goods. It was difficult enough to remember what I had invented on the spur of the moment with the old adrenalin pumping, and I cursed my own conceits. Why hadn't I made notes? It was too early in the game to rely on memory. There comes a point in the progress of any novel or script when the characters assume a life of their own and help us over the humps, redirect us from the cul-de-sacs, but I was a long way from that happy stage. The ream of virgin paper sat on my desk waiting to be filled. From habit I took a sheet and fed it into the typewriter just as a junkie prepares the syringe even though he has nothing with which to fill it. Then I sat there, staring at it, as though concentration alone would somehow produce a magic stream of words. I thought, you idiot, you poor misguided idiot, to come all this way just to grapple with familiar panics. The room which a few hours earlier I had been enchanted with became a remembered cell. Inspiration was as securely corked as the bottle of gifted champagne.

I went into the bathroom and stared at myself in the mirror: my beard was ahead of the clock, giving me a haunted look that in some perverse way I found comforting – tangible evidence that I was well cast as a condemned man, moreover a prisoner who had incarcerated myself. I found myself apologising to the gaunt image in the mirror, talking aloud, carrying on a one-sided dialogue. They say that every thought we have is related to past experience, and as I stood there I remembered listening to my father cursing his luck as he shaved. He used an old fashioned cut-throat razor, stropped every morning on a strip of leather shaped like a sticky flycatcher. The association of his muttered anguish and the naked blade applied with such accustomed skill to his stretched cheeks had always terrified me as a child, yet it was this memory that unlocked the first closed door and sent me back to the typewriter. The forged steel no longer stroked my father's drink-mottled skin but began its descent to cleave the King's head from his trunk.

Two hours later when I finally took to my bed, I had roughed out the opening sequence, a more elaborate construction than the one I had, without much thought, outlined to Latrough and Martin. I used the device of the guillotine blade descending in slow motion and then . . . well, I may as well reproduce the actual script for sake of clarity.

FADE IN:

BEFORE MAIN TITLES:

1.   EXT. THE GUILLOTINE BLADE – DAY –
shot against the dull sky. No sound.

2.   EXT. THE FOOT OF THE SCAFFOLD – DAY –
three executioners take the King's hands and tie them behind his back. We see this in Close Shot, never revealing the King's face, nor the faces of his executioners. The King has already been stripped of his jacket. There

should be a brutal urgency about this scene, contrasting with:

3.   INT. A BED CHAMBER — DAY —
the light in the room filtered through closed curtains. Hands caress the naked back of a young girl. As the hands move from her back to cup a breast we

CUT BACK TO:

4.   THE EXECUTIONER'S HANDS —
as the rope securing the King's hands is knotted.

5.   QUICK CUT OF —
the guillotine blade as before.

6.   QUICK CUT OF THE LOVERS —
in the bed. Again we never reveal their faces.

7.   THE KING —
starts to mount the steps to the scaffold. As his body passes through the frame, Camera pans upwards to the guillotine blade yet again.

8.   ANOTHER PAIR OF HANDS —
grasp the bars of a small window in a prison cell. SOUND of a drum roll beginning, heard distantly at first.

9.   THE KING —
steps up into frame and turns to Camera, revealing his face for the first time. He is supported by the Abbé Edgeworth. The drum roll increases in volume.

> LOUIS XVI
> People, I die innocent of all the crimes imputed to me!

The drum roll increases steadily. By the end of the last speech he will ever make, the drums have all but drowned his voice.

LOUIS XVI
I pardon the authors of my death and I pray God that the blood you are about to shed may never fall upon the head of France!

He is suddenly seized by the executioners and propelled towards the plank. There he is quickly bound.

10.   THE LOVERS –
embracing.

11.   THE GUILLOTINE BLADE –
starts its descent in slow motion. During its descent we

CROSS CUT:

12.   TO THE LOVERS –
at least three times, elongating the moment, until finally we use one last shot of the

13.   GUILLOTINE BLADE –
this time at normal speed, so that it falls with terrible speed out of bottom of frame.

14.   THE ABBÉ EDGEWORTH –
kneeling close to the King. His face is suddenly, terribly, spattered with the King's blood.

SHOCK CUT TO:

15.   THE LOVERS –
as the girl suddenly screams and sits up into frame. We shall later identify her by name as Claudine. The camera angle on her should give the impression that she is looking at

16.   THE SEVERED HEAD OF THE KING –
held aloft by its hair.

AND ON THIS
WE BRING UP
THE
MAIN TITLE

17.   CLOSE ON THE CELL WINDOW –
and with the distant sounds of jubilation as the mob
reacts to the regicide, the hands holding the bars slowly
relinquish their hold.

CONTINUING
MAIN
TITLES
OVER

18.   INT. PRISON CELL –
and now a man turns from the cell window, retreating
back into the cell which we now reveal is occupied by
perhaps thirty or forty fellow unfortunates. This is our
central character, Mandat, a royalist officer, who because of his association with the King has joined the
ranks of those awaiting execution.

AS MAIN TITLES
CONTINUE
OVER

He paces the cell, and we see the faces of his fellow
unfortunates. Suddenly he pauses and looks towards:

19.   THE DOOR OF THE CELL –
which is suddenly flung open, revealing a Member of the
Revolutionary Committee flanked by two armed
Guards. The Committee member has a list of those
marked to die on the guillotine. He begins to read out the
names. We see husbands taking their farewells from
wives, lovers from their mistresses. During this Camera
Tracks in to a Close shot of Mandat. He listens impas-
sively as his own name is called out. His eyes go to:

71

20.   A WOMAN –

huddled against the dank walls of the dungeon. She raises her head to look at him.

21.   BACK TO MANDAT –

he makes the slightest of movements with his head – a warning for the woman to betray nothing. Then, along with the half-dozen other selected victims, he is roughly manhandled towards the door of the cell. They disappear outside and as the door is slammed closed:

MAIN TITLES
END

22.   CLOSE SHOT – THE WOMAN –

Elisabeth Lamballe, and like Mandat, whose mistress she is, a member of the old order. Tears stream down her begrimed cheeks.

ELISABETH (whispered)
Goodbye, my dearest dearest . . .

It was a beginning of sorts. Not the opening chapter of Carlyle to be sure, nor a work of towering intellect, but the first steps of a long haul. When I staggered to my bed, burying my unshaven face in the plump pillows, I sank into sleep with the feeling that possibly, given the stamina and the usual required quota of luck, I might be able to justify my existence.

SIX

Such enthusiasms as I had felt the previous night were short lived. When I read through the pages over breakfast in the hotel dining room, I was immediately stricken with doubt. 'Don't panic,' I said as I lit my third cigarette and downed the fourth cup of strong coffee. Then Marvin appeared, slumping down into the spare chair at my table. His face had the appearance of an uneven lawn, mown only in places. I suspected that some half-hearted vanity made him touch up the sides of his hair with one of those preparations that hold back the advancing grey. If I was right, he hadn't studied the wording on the label very closely.

'Mind if I grab a cup of coffee with you?'

'Sure. I'll get a fresh pot.'

'Do you wake up tired, Harvey? I wake up tired. Like I feel I've already done a day's work. Maybe I have. I'd be the last to know.'

He felt in his pocket and brought out a handful of capsules. 'I take these things. Vitamins. Geriatric strength, would you believe?'

When the coffee came he swallowed them one after the other, like a suicide.

'I can't get it up any more, Harvey. All I get to do these days is to eat off the candy counter. Maybe I'm turning into a dyke. You can't win from my seat. No way. There used to be a time when all these pricks were happy as long as you spelt their names right. Now, they want to be written up as human beings. Did I offend you yesterday?'

'I don't think so. Did you?'

'Like, I called you Harv.'

'Oh, that. That's okay. Just a thing I have.'

73

'Listen, you're entitled.' He helped himself to a croissant, buttering it lavishly, then dipping it into his coffee. 'I've gone native,' he said. 'Except I don't think the frogs use butter. You're very quiet.'

'I'm usually quiet at this time in the morning.'

'Likewise . . . I got bumped from my last two jobs. Did they tell you that?'

'No, nobody said a word. None of my business anyway.'

'Somebody'll tell you. The only reason I got this break is because I agreed to work for scale. I had a drink problem. Nothing serious. I was just an alcoholic. I don't have a car, you know. They give a car to the assistant wardrobe, but me I have to thumb rides. On the other hand, I don't have a licence, so why would they give me a car? Well, I can live with it . . . See, the reason I wanted to make sure I didn't offend you, is that we're two of a kind, you and me.'

'We are?'

'Sure. Well, put it this way, there was a time when I was a full-time writer. I started out as a novelist. Know how many novels I wrote?' I shook my head. 'Close on seventy.'

I arranged my face in an expression of amazement.

'What's more every one of them was published.'

'Fantastic.'

'Got you impressed, huh? Well, relax, they were porno paper-backs. One every ten days, not less than eighty-five pages at a dollar a page. Not under my own name. We had house names. Know what my name was? Tessa d'Urberville. The publisher had a classical background. He thought Thomas Hardy was Mickey Rooney's father. Does this heat crease you?'

'No, I like it. Least there's no humidity.'

'Yeah, some guys can take heat. Me – you cold spray cement under my arms and still not stop the deluge. Anyway, let me tell you about Tessa, that is if you're still interested. I don't tell this to many people, because they get the wrong idea, but you being a writer . . . See, this guy who employed us had this theory that the perverts got more of a kick if they thought the stuff was written by a woman. Maybe he had something? Think there's anything in it?'

'Could be.'

'Mind you, today, who cares? We were pioneers – four

of us sharing the same office, knocking them out on the assembly line. Genuine Model T hard cores, every ten days.'

'How on earth did you think up the plots?'

'Plots? What plots? Did you ever read one of those things? They were laid out like a recipe for making pound cake. You just threw in the same ingredients and changed the character names. Get to the head scene by page three, then a couple of really good straight boffs, then into the gang bang, closely followed by anal penetration, a chapter of S and M and finally you baked the whole cake. I specialised in hospital stories – Tessa was very big on enema tricks . . . Am I putting you off your breakfast?'

'No, I've finished.'

'Tell you what will surprise you – one of our team was the genuine article. Miss Parker. Amazing old dame, looked like Eleanor Roosevelt, had the dirtiest imagination I ever came across. She was the house star, made us guys look like we were transcribing the Scriptures.

'What was her speciality?'

'Incest. What's more she could knock one out every three days, then spend the rest of the week knitting sweaters.'

'How old were you, Marvin, when you embarked on this brilliant career?'

'I was just out of the Army. Twenty-three.'

'So how did you drift into publicity?'

'Drift is not the word. There was a guy over at Metro, very into Tessa, bought everything she wrote, even sent her fan letters. Which I answered. Finally he gets so wound up he wants a date. So I strung him along for a bit, you know, penned him some heavy letters . . . then dear old Miss Parker bet me I wouldn't go the distance. Well, that was all I needed – in those days I'd pick up any bet . . . So Tessa sailed forth one night and kept an appointment with destiny. Mind you, I didn't go ape. Like I refused to drag up. In those days I had principles.'

'And?'

'I blackmailed him into giving me a job. From then on it was all downhill . . . Listen, to change the subject let me give you a couple of inside tips. When you get into the

75

rewrite don't give our distinguished leading man too many long speeches. Otherwise they're going to have idiot boards out all over the South of France. He's happier with the big meaningful close-ups. See he always wanted to be Clint Eastwood.'

'That's very useful, thank you.'

'Well, the other's just a hunch. How well do you know Martin?'

'Not that well. Reasonably.'

'I get the feeling he wouldn't object if you built up the part of a certain young actress.'

'You mean Michelle?'

He shook his head. The last of the capsules disappeared. 'You haven't met any of them yet, have you?'

'The cast, you mean? No, not yet.'

'This is a young actress, and I mean young. Not exactly jail bait, but definitely the right side of twenty-one. Name of Miss Laura Taylor.'

'Oh, yes. Martin mentioned her.'

'I bet he did.'

'Why d'you say it like that?'

'Just a Dunbar hunch, of which there aren't too many these days. Wait 'til you meet her. Then you'll get my subtle innuendo.'

He fumbled in one of his pockets and brought out a cheap shorthand notebook. 'But enough of this gossip. Let's talk about you. And don't get worried. This is just to show willing. Nothing I write gets into print. But it makes me look busy. Your biog. I like to be accurate, so let's start from the beginning. Sex, male, race, Caucasian white. Married status . . . ?'

'No.'

'No what?'

'Not married.'

'Ever?'

'Yes.'

'Want to talk about it?'

'No.'

'Children?'

'No.'

'Educated?'

76

'Barely.'

'Okay, let's start again. And give me a break Harvey. Invent some fancy background. Like you once blind-dated Louella Parsons.'

'Marvin,' I said, 'write your own life story, it's got to be more interesting.'

'How about if we just did a straight interview on the state of the world. What's wrong with young people today?'

'They're young.'

'See, you can do it if you try. How d'you feel about the drug scene?'

'Work is the curse of the snorting classes.'

'I like it, I like it! I might get the Pulitzer for this. Any views on wife swopping?'

'Yes. It should start immediately after the wedding ceremony.'

'Harvey, you've been holding out on me. I thought you were just a pretty face. How about sex?'

'What's good for General Motors is good for America.'

'Beautiful. We could put this out in a limited edition.'

He was beginning to exhaust me, but fortunately relief came in the form of Martin who strode into the dining room accompanied by two characters I hadn't seen before.

'Morning, Harvey, did you sleep well? I hope not. I hope you were doing your duty and bending over a hot typewriter all night.'

'I made a start.'

'That's my boy, that's what I like to hear. Sorry, this is Mischa Spoliansky, our Art Director, and Sandy . . . Sandy Banks, Associate Producer.'

I shook hands. Only Mischa acknowledged that Marvin was even in the room.

'We'll go in convoy. You ride with me, we can talk script on the way. Where first, Mischa?'

'The lake. Show him the lake and then work backwards. That's the most important if we're sticking to the present schedule.'

'We may not be. Don't let's get too locked in to the present schedule. Harvey and I ar going to make a lot of changes and we all have to be adaptable.'

'Adaptable, yes, it's the story of my life. But I have to build, so not too many changes, please.'

'Change is the spice of life, Mischa. Keeps you young.'

'I don't want to be young. I was young long enough. I want a nice quiet life.'

'You're in the wrong business,' Martin said. 'Come on, let's get under way.'

As we left Marvin was dunking his second croissant. He winked at me. Once outside, I made a point of looking for signs of damage to the Rolls, but it seemed to be in showroom condition.

Martin's chauffeur drove at a speed that made rational conversation impossible, though Martin appeared not to notice anything out of the ordinary. I handed him the first few pages.

'Is this all?'

'Quality, not quantity,' I said. The car made me feel sick and I could certainly hear more than the ticking of the clock.

Martin scanned through my pages. 'Very good. I like it. What comes next?'

'Well, to get a little action, I thought we could devise a sequence whereby Charles's character is rescued on his way to the guillotine.'

'Scarlet Pimpernel stuff?'

'Not quite, but something like that.'

'Sure, give it a whirl. I had some further thoughts last night, after you'd gone. And by the way, the object of this morning's trip is just to give you some feeling of the locations we'd alredy mapped out. But nothing's sacred.'

'How much change will David buy?'

'Leave David to me. He was flexing his muscles yesterday because he had a new audience. He's all piss and wind when it comes to the crunch.'

After some forty minutes' hard driving, some of it on the old Route Napoleon, climbing all the time, we pulled into a parking area overlooking the man-made Lac de Saint Cassien. Patches of morning mist were still drifting across the flat surface of the lake. There was a solitary fisherman in a rowing boat, wearing a bright red sweater, motionless, the boat seemingly stuck to a mirror, and the scene reminded me of an Impressionist painting.

'*Ondine!*' Mischa exclaimed. 'I have a great idea. We scrap this farce we are making and do *Ondine* instead. It's par-fect, just par-fect. That change I wouldn't mind.'

'We'll do that next,' Martin said. He turned to me. 'I want to use this lot if I can. Simply because it's workable. We can set the love scenes here. I'm all for getting out of the *Last Tango in Paris* interior school of heavy breathing. We've got the locations, let's make use of them.'

'Charles hates exteriors,' Sandy said.

'Who's talking about Charles? That tired old torso is not going to sell tickets. I was talking about the kids, the young lovers.'

'Oh, is that in the script?'

'Sandy, can we all get one thing straight? Harvey is here to rewrite the fucking thing. Forget the old script. Burn it in fact, burn every copy, even the carbons.'

'Just asking. Would be nice to be told before the day.'

'Now let's not get uptight. The man hasn't written it yet. As soon as he has you'll be the first to see it. Then you can make a nice new schedule, and put all those lovely coloured strips of cardboard on your wall, and tell us when we're going wrong. Meantime, just relax will you?'

I began to get sensations of panic once again. I felt very much the new boy being shown round the school. The Head was being gracious and polite to me, but all the senior boys were suspicious, resentful of the intruder. The entourage included other key members of Martin's crew – Gerry, the lighting cameraman, the French First Assistant, Bernard, who drove a Porsche, and the Location Manager, a somewhat lugubrious character named Arnold, with a permanent sinus problem. My presence spelt nothing but trouble for them. At this stage of the game even the smallest change in the script entailed a rethink right down the line. And we were contemplating major surgery. Martin's delight in giving me the conducted tour was not shared by the others. He might well have some inner vision of the finished product, but it wasn't anything that could be passed around like a Polaroid. The function of Mischa and Co. was to try

79

and stay ahead, to anticipate Martin's every whim, and their anchor was the script – without a script they could only flounder. So it all came back to me, my ability to deliver the goods. And the more I was shown that morning, the more anxious I became. Martin was giving me a jigsaw puzzle to solve, but he was only supplying the edges. I needed to find the centre of the puzzle.

After a short coffee break taken in a medieval village square which at least came closer to the mood I hoped to create, our convoy speeded back to Nice and Victorine Studios.

'If we run into some of the cast,' Martin said, 'for Christ'sake don't get into any discussions about the script if you can help it. They'll try and bend your ear, especially our dear Charles – he's always been a frustrated dramatist. Listen by all means, because it's just conceivable that one of them might have an unselfish thought, but don't get into any detail. I really enjoy a good thrash, keeps everybody on edge.'

I had never been inside the Nice studios before, though I knew it by reputation. In happy contrast to Burbank and Culver City, it gave me an immediate impression of a run-down rest home rather than a concrete dream factory. I knew its history went back to the turn of the century, and then presumably it stood in more or less open country-side on that golden coast. Now it was almost engulfed by apartment buildings and seemed something of an anachronism, with Nice airport less than half a mile away. Despite the property speculators' avarice, it had somehow survived – slightly shabby, some of the workshops had the worn look of old-fashioned sepia photographs, their walls overgrown with ivy and briars – but nevertheless a living city-within-a-city, where films continued to be made. The back lot was overgrown, studded with palsied palm trees and the flapping remains of discarded sets. To my passing eye the whole thing looked like an improvisation, some-thing begun but never finished.

We went straight to the terrace restaurant where a mixed crowd of cast and crew were taking an al fresco lunch beneath the plane trees. I noticed Latrough was sitting alone. It was my instinct to join him, but Martin had other ideas and made straight for the large table in the centre of the terrace.

There I was introduced to the three leading members of the cast. They regarded me with understandable suspicion: actors are creatures who feast on uncertainty and being a stranger in their midst I represented yet another unknown quantity, a potential threat to the status quo. I could feel the two actresses, Suzanne and Michelle, sizing me up, while Charles Croze gave me a firm handshake and an even firmer stare. As I took my seat I felt like a soldier advancing into no-man's land in the sure knowledge that the ground ahead had been sown with mines. I don't know why, but I'm always disconcerted at meeting actors for the first time. There was no particular reason for me to be ill-at-ease that day – after all, I had no cause to be on the defensive as most authors are when confronted by their cast, since I had yet to write a single word. But I was immediately conscious of their unease. Until proved otherwise I was automatically one of the enemy.

'You must excuse us,' Charles said. 'Martin has told us so little about you. But then, as I'm sure you know, Martin is an enigma. Had Elgar lived a little longer he would have added another variation. You see we're all huddled in the dark here, the innocent victims of rumour. *'Our nights, and indeed most of our days, have been unruly,'* to do the unspeakable and misquote the Scottish play. Notice I touched wood. Or at least I touched Suzanne's thigh, which is more or less the same thing. That's because, in strict contrast to my public image, I'm really a shy, disorientated, nervous creature.'

'Why are you nervous, Charles?' Martin asked.

'Why? As if you didn't know. Here we all are, my lovely leading ladies, the entire crew, sitting out in the sun, ostensibly having a good time, but riddled with secret fears. Is the picture off? Are we being replaced by Dustin Hoffman and Meryl Streep? Is, God forbid! our talented director on his way out? It has not escaped our notice that at yonder table our noble producer sits lonely as a cloud, incommunicado. What are the ghastly portents? we ask ourselves. Being the humblest of folk, naturally we make no waves, we merely sit and await our fate.'

'Why can't you act like that on screen, Charles? You'd have to get a nomination at least.'

'Don't encourage him,' Suzanne said. 'He's impossible enough as it is.' She had an actress's instinct for capitalising on any given occasion. 'Martin, darling . . .' she began, stroking the back of his hand as one smooths a cat.

'Prenez garde, Martin!' Charles said. 'Whatever she says is going to cost you money.'

'Martin, dear, if this lovely Mr Burgess is going to change the script, do you think you might be persuaded to change some of my costumes at the same time?'

'What's wrong with your costumes, sweetie? You look gorgeous in them.'

'I just don't think they do anything for the character.'

'She's a Method actress, Martin. You know her method? She plays everything for sympathy.'

'Look, dear, I'm not the money man. I don't concern myself with such sordid matters. If you're not happy, why don't you go and speak to David?'

'Yes, go and ask Mr Happiness over there,' Charles said, loud enough for Latrough to have heard. 'And if you really want to clinch it, do a bit of rending asunder, expose your amazing bosom to him, and cry a lot. You know, underplay it.'

'You're perfectly loathsome, Charles. Isn't he loathsome, Michelle?'

'Made a career out of it, darling. Never play nice guys is my motto. Now, I know what's really troubling her. She thinks she looks too young in her present costumes, and I agree, darling. There's a real danger that it'll come across that I'm cradle-snatching.'

He suddenly flashed a smile at me. 'I hope you're noting all this scintillating dialogue, Harvey. It's all for your benefit, you know. We're always on form when we have a new audience to play to. What're you going to do for us? I'm always lost in awe of you writers, since I can only just write my name on a cheque, that's my limit. I mean, how on earth does one start tampering with a masterpiece such as the present script?'

'Carefully,' I said.

82

'I do so admire that sort of dedication to mediocrity. Did you come in from LA?'

'No, Connecticut.'

'I love Los Angeles,' Michelle said. 'Especially the Beverly Wilshire Hotel.'

'What draws you to that, darling?' Is it because Warren Beatty has a permanent suite there?'

'I've never met Warren Beatty.'

'My God! We must get that into the Guinness Book of Records.'

Our food arrived at that moment. More wine was uncorked and it was obvious that most of them intended to make a day of it.

'Do you want me after lunch?' I asked Martin.

'I think the most sensible course is for us to spend a few minutes looking over the schedule with the boys – the existing schedule, that is, because we are locked in to certain locations – and then decide on the priorities. It's a bit arse-about-face as far as you are concerned, I realise that, but I can't think of any other way of doing it. What is today? Tuesday? No, Wednesday. So we've got, or rather you've got, three clear days to block it out and write a few scenes we can shoot next week.'

'That is the most terrifying conversation I've ever listened to,' Charles said. 'And if I can be serious for a moment – through the chair, Martin, as they say at board meetings – we do have to *learn* the new stuff. I just hope it isn't handed to us in make-up on Monday morning. A modest enough request, I hope.' There was an edge to his voice suddenly.

'Charles – and all of you for that matter – we all know the problems. Now I take full responsibility for forcing this hiatus, but I just couldn't allow us to go on as we were. I brought Harvey over and obviously he's been thrown in at the deep end and has to unscramble the existing mess . . . He and I have decided what changes we'd like made and I guarantee that you'll like what we intend to do.'

'Am I still going to be playing the same character?' Suzanne asked.

'Of course.'

'They don't want to break with tradition, dear,' Charles said.

'What about the story?' Michelle asked. 'Is that going to be drastically altered?'

'Well, let's wait and see, shall we? I feel it's grossly unfair to Harvey to put him on the spot. Just trust me.'

'Oh, we do trust you,' Charles said. 'It's not a question of trust, it's a question of having to learn the fucking lines. Excuse my language, Harvey.'

'Oh, thank you, don't apologise to me, will you?' Suzanne said.

'You've heard the word before, darling. Mostly when you were lying down.'

'You should stop drinking at lunchtime, Charles.'

'Now, children, children!' Martin interjected. 'Don't let's squabble. We have to remain one big happy family. It's just a temporary little spanner in the works, but at the end of it all we're going to have a much better picture, and you're all going to come out of it smelling like roses.' He lowered his voice. 'I mean, you're the key people . . . You know how these things infect a unit. If the rest of them see us biting and scratching the whole thing will go to pieces. I realise it's very unsettling, but united we stand. Leave the worrying to me. Just relax, get some sun . . . not too much sun, Suzanne, otherwise we'll have to replace Charles with Sydney Poitier.'

The joke was not to Charles's liking. He sat hunched over the remains of his meal. His moods seemed to fluctuate violently.

'I'm clay,' he said, looking at me with hurt eyes, 'virgin clay, waiting to be moulded. All I ever ask is that you keep it simple, keep it within my limited range.'

'Oh, God, he's going to do his humble bit,' Suzanne said. 'We prefer you arrogant, Charles dear.'

He ignored her. 'You see, Harvey, if you give me anything profound to say I might try and do some face acting which according to Martin is fatal. I have unlimited surface charm – as must be obvious – at my best when I'm staring straight into the camera, preferably not before eleven in the morning, with not a thought in my head. God forbid that I should ever become a scenery chewer like

84

Suzanne. I don't have the figure for it, you see.' He broke off as Latrough approached our table.

'Come and join us, David. The night is young and you're so lovable.'

'No, thank you, Charles. I've got work to do.'

'All this talk of work. Harvey's working, you're working, Suzanne's working up to it, and here I am on full salary plus expenses doing sweet f-all.'

'Yeah, it's tough at the top, Charles . . . Can I see you, Harvey, when you're through with your meal. I'll be in my office.'

He walked away without even acknowledging Martin, but must still have been within earshot when Charles said, 'What it is to be singled out of a crowd. Few are called, Harvey, but you've just had greatness thrust upon you. A word of caution, however. Put some exercise books down the seat of your pants. Just in case the Head gives you six of the best.'

After a plausible interval ('Don't appear too anxious,' Martin said) I went to obey Latrough's summons. Beyond the shadow of the trees the heat was fierce. There was the usual group of hopeful, would-be crowd artists bunched around the entrance to the office block. They seemed to me to be younger on average than their Hollywood counter-parts. I guessed the majority of them were students bum-ming their way along the Coast as best they could, trying to last out the season. Some of the girls smiled at me as I ex-cused myself past them: extras smile at anything that moves.

Latrough had the corner office on the first floor. It was done out in garish, flocked wallpaper and furnished with fake Louis XV, though to be fair he probably inherited the decor from a previous occupant. All he was probably responsible for was the final touch of class – a Coke machine that stood conveniently close to his desk. He was on the phone when I entered the room and waved me to take a seat.

'Shel . . . believe me, I'm on top of it . . . That's what I'm doing now, I'm sitting here doing just that – I *know* the bottom line . . . Look, what d'you want me to do? Deck Charles and put in an insurance claim? . . . Okay, okay, you're right, he's taking us for the moment but when I'm

85

through it's going to be a whole different ball game . . . I'm not giving you the bullshit! . . .' He held the receiver away from his ear and I could hear the voice at the other end of the line shouting something unintelligible. 'Listen, Shel, let me ring you back. I'm just about to go into a meeting with the writer . . . Yeah, yeah, no question . . . Trust me, Shel . . .'

Trust is a favourite word amongst those who make a career of screwing others.

When he had replaced the receiver he poured himself an iced Coke into a plastic cup. He stared at me, taking some crushed ice into his mouth and crunching it noisily.

'So, where are we?'

He picked up a copy of the script and rifled through it as though it was a mail-order catalogue.

'Well, I've roughed out the opening title sequence as discussed.'

'Where are the pages?'

'I gave a copy to Martin.'

Again the long stare. More ice was crunched.

'Who're you working for, Harvey?'

'Who am I working for?'

'Yeah.'

'I assume I'm working for you and Martin.'

'You assume that, huh?'

'Yes.'

'So why didn't I get the pages?'

'I assumed Martin would pass them on to you.'

'You assume a lot, don't you?'

The dialogue was beginning to irritate me.

'Not really. Except I assume I'm working for two grown men who can sort these things out between them. You want the next batch of pages first, you got them. What you do with them is your business.'

'Don't make an enemy of me, Harvey. I was the one who said okay to your deal, not Martin. Your fag agent held a gun to my head, but I still went along with it.'

'I'm suitably grateful. But this was hardly likely to be a picnic, was it? And now that I'm here I can confirm that. It doesn't require much to see that you and Martin are not exactly as close as Funk and Wagnall.'

'We have our differences.'

'So where does that leave me? I'd like to know the ground rules.'

'I paid a lot for this script.'

'I believe you.'

'A lot of bread. See, I didn't have too many problems liking it. I didn't have too many problems getting the money to make it, I didn't have to go down on Charles to get him to play it . . . In fact until last week when our director pulled the plug we were going along just fine.'

He picked up the script again and weighed it in his palm. 'Don't take it personally, but the guy who wrote this has a reputation. He wrote the two top television specials last season. I paid top dollar for him.'

'One gets what one pays for,' I said.

'So I'm not looking for too many changes.'

'Okay. What d'you want me to do? I didn't fly here to pick a fight, you know. I was sitting in Darien minding my own business when the phone rang. Martin wants me to rewrite it, you obviously don't. I'm in the middle. Now, I freely admit I didn't write the two top specials last season. If you want to shoot what you've got, I won't make waves. You're in the catbird seat. I don't happen to think it's the First Folio of *Hamlet*, but that's just a subjective opinion.'

'Harvey . . . I told you, don't make an enemy of me. I'm not looking to go ten rounds with you without a gum shield. I got a problem on my hands here. I got the studio round my neck asking what the fuck's going on, I got sixty crew and a whole lot of actors sitting out there on full salary, the fucking sun is shining and I got no film going through the cameras . . . all because your Limey friend wants to be David Lean all of a sudden. Now, we're not playing Happy Families. We're trying to make a commercial movie here . . .'

He got up from his desk and pulled aside a handful of Venetian blind. The strong sunlight slatted his face.

'So I have to keep my options open . . . My leading man down there, just being helped into his limo that I'm paying for . . . he needs to get back into harness otherwise we're going to have another hiatus while he's dried out . . . I've got to bite on the bullet, Harvey, because come Monday all this bullshit is gonna end.'

'Understood. So, to repeat myself, what d'you want me to do? I'm here, you're going to have to pay me, so you might as well get your pound of flesh. It's just conceivable that I might come up with a few improvements.'

'Yeah.'

'As for what happens between you and Martin, well that's your affair. I'll do what I can and if what I turn in makes you puke, then presumably you'll take your own decisions.'

'Yeah.'

'Meantime, perhaps I should get back to my typewriter. And I'll make sure you get a copy of the pages next time.'

'Yeah, do that.'

'The only other point I'd like to make, and it would seem it needs saying, is that if anything constructive is going to come out of this, you and Martin had better sign a non-aggression pact for the duration. I'm not going to bad-mouth Martin – after all, he offered me the job. But on the other hand, he's not my keeper, or he hasn't been over the years. Curiously enough, I don't have any great hang-ups about my ego. I'm a rewrite man. I don't do heart transplants, but I have been known to remove the odd in-growing toenail. I'll try and give you value for money.'

He nodded. 'Just don't play it too close to the chest . . . Just remember who signs the checks . . . And, for what it's worth, Harvey . . . I did my homework, I looked up your credits . . . You could do with getting your name on a commercial movie.'

Back at my hotel I was immediately button-holed by the ancient concierge. I had difficulty understanding what he was trying to tell me.

'You mean I've got a visitor?'

'Qui, monsieur. Dans la chambre.'

'In my room?'

'Qui, excuse me, Monsieur Burgess, mais . . . I tried, but he said he was a good friend.'

I mounted the stairs wondering what the hell to expect. I thought it had to be either Martin or else a relapsed one-time Tessa d'Urberville. I was wrong on both counts. What confronted me when I opened the door to my suite was a semi-comatose Charles. He was sprawled on my bed.

'Well, hello,' I said.

He opened his eyes and tried to get me in focus.

'It was the heat . . . I got heat prostration, Harvey. Mad dogs and . . . whatever . . . out in the mid-day, noon-day, sun, et-cet-era . . .'

'Fine. You want to sleep it off? Can I get you anything?'

'You could get me Michelle, if you really wanted to be a friend, but otherwise . . . I'll just abuse your hospitality until this petit mal . . . I'm bombed, Harvey, bombed. Got as far as here and couldn't make it any further. Didn't want our director to jump to the right conclusions, so I sought sanctuary . . . Hide me from the Gestapo . . .'

I closed the shutters.

'Put out the light, and then put out the light . . . I knew I could depend on you, Harvey.'

'Listen, I have to work, but you just take it easy.'

'What sort of work do you do, Harvey?'

'That's a good question. You okay? Comfortable? The bathroom is through there should you want it.'

'I want love, Harvey, not a bathroom.'

'Don't we all?'

'And don't worry, I'm not going to make a pass at you.'

I eased off his hand-made Italian loafers. 'I'm relieved to hear it.'

'Where did it all go wrong, Harvey?'

'When I picked up the phone. Now, I'm going to be in the next room hitting the typewriter, so I'll close the door and then I won't disturb you.'

'You just make yourself at home.'

I went into the other room and sat down at my desk. Charles had the right idea. It was too hot to work. The last thing I felt like doing, especially after my meeting with Latrough, was to tackle the remainder of *The Bastille Connection*. My phone rang.

'Harvey? What happened?' It was Martin.

'When?'

'With David?'

'Nothing much. He took exception to the fact that you hadn't shown him my first pages.'

'Oh, fuck him.'

'By all means, but don't let's make life too difficult.'

'What's that meant to signify?'

'Just that I seem to be in no-man's land and getting the crossfire.'

'I'll keep him off your back. You're working for me.'

'That's not his reading of the situation.'

'I'll show him the pages for Christ'sake! Just don't worry about it. All you got to do is keep going. And just one other thing. Charles might be heading in your direction. Don't get involved with him either. Don't get involved with any of them. You've got enough on your plate.'

'You can say that again.'

'I'll give you a ring later to see how it's going.'

'What I would like is a copy of the schedule. We forgot that.'

'That was my fault. I got into a slanging match with Charles after you left. I'll get onto it right away. You just keep at it.'

When he rang off I galvanised myself. I ordered a large pot of coffee and while waiting for it to arrive organised all my talismans: I was programmed like a Pavlovian dog, wired to those legions of Latroughs who, over the years, had trained me to dance to their tunes. Like most writers I had self-hypnotised myself into the belief that I could only work if certain procedures were observed. The coffee had been ordered and now I opened two new packs of cigarettes and placed them to the left of my typewriter with the open ends facing me. Next I made sure that sufficient ashtrays and matches were to hand. The ream of typing paper had to be on the right of the machine. I selected the first sheet, typed the title page, marking it First Revised Draft and adding the date. All meaningless, time-wasting gestures, but necessary.

The hot-shot television writer, last year's hero in the ratings, had doubtless faced his own demons. His past agonies – assuming he shared my own sense of inadequacy whenever faced with a blank sheet of paper – were somewhere concealed in the neatly typed script: mine were still to be released. A writer carries his prison with him.

My problem was: how to flesh out the characters and at the same time devise new scenes that would dovetail into the chosen locations. As far as Latrough was concerned I was a used-car salesman, asking him to trade in his sexual Cadillac for a less phallic model. Without benefit of reference books I needed to dredge my memory for historical facts – pride demanded that at least. And during the next four hours, with Charles still sleeping it off in the adjoining room, I made a concentrated effort to smother a familiar panic and get something tangible down on paper. I was just reaching for the second pack of cigarettes when there was a knock on the door.

'Who is it?'

'Me. Suzanne.'

The interruption was unwelcome – any interruption was unwelcome at that particular moment – and actresses who came uninvited to hotel rooms did not come to discuss the weather. I had been on the verge of solving a very tricky piece of continuity and I knew that with Suzanne's arrival my tenuous thought process would be shattered.

Reluctantly, I let her in.

'Harvey, dear, I know this is terrible of me, and you're right in the middle of everything . . . God! look at all that paper . . . but I just had to see you.'

'That's okay,' I lied. 'What's your problem?'

'Hey! this is such a darling room. Do they have any more like this? I might move in. Get away from the mob.'

'Probably. I haven't enquired . . . What're you worried about?'

'Everything. This whole movie seems like we're on the *Titanic*. I feel like the deck is at an angle and I'm slipping towards the water without a lifejacket. And nobody tells me anything. Our captain is up there on the bridge somewhere giving out with the charm and pretending everything's still beautiful and dandy, but I just know we're going down and it's a horrible feeling.'

I suspected she had rehearsed that speech on the journey over. Despite the heat she was acting out the role of a First Class passenger saving her most precious belongings. She had a mink jacket slung round her shoulders and seemed to have cleaned out Cartier's of all their remaining stock.

'I'm sure it's very unsettling for all the cast.'

'Of course it is. I mean, I take my work very seriously. I know everybody thinks I'm a joke because I've got big tits and I talk too much and fool around with Charles . . . Well, you have to fool around with Charles otherwise you'd blow your stack, because all he wants to talk about is himself and tell his boring jokes which we've all heard fifty times before . . . Look, honey, I've made three pictures with him and on the first one I was dumb enough to get involved for a while . . . It was really from hunger in those days, and now he thinks he can pick up where he left off, and he's got another think coming . . . But that's not what I came here to talk about . . . D'you mind if I park the mink?'

'Please.'

'I've really got to get my head together. Or somebody's got to get my head together and you seemed to be the only one around who might know the score. Martin just smiles and says, 'No problems, darling' – like I'd gone to him to have my bridgework checked – and our producer is off doing his thing whatever that is . . . I just want somebody to tell me what's going on. All I ever hear is rumours. Like I'm being written out.'

'Who said that?'

'I don't know. Yes, I do. Charles hinted at it, and I just thought he was being shitty because I wouldn't let him have it last night . . . You know, I think I will try and move in here, if only to put some air between me and the midnight cowboy.'

I tried not to look in the direction of my bedroom.

'Well, let's get one thing out of the way. Charles was just being shitty. I'm certainly not writing you out. On the contrary.'

'On the what?'

'Time will tell, of course, but I'm trying to improve all the parts, and certainly yours could do with some improvement.'

I don't think she was actually listening to anything I said, or if she was, it wasn't getting through.

'See . . . and you're going to think me just awful, you being a writer, but since we're playing the truth game . . . I never really read the old script. My agent read it for me and sort of, you know, thought I should – and I had tax problems, my last marriage had just gone down the tubes, all the usual pressures . . . And I believe people. Like I don't look for trouble, and if somebody says something I believe them. D'you think that's naive?'

'Happens to us all. If you must know, I wish I'd never read the old script.'

'Change your image, change your luck, my agent said. Say, you've got a great view from here . . . And doves, you've got doves! Did you ever see that television thing where I played a conjurer's assistant? I had to be covered in doves. Well, I was meant to be naked, right? but being television I wore a body stocking and they taped all these live doves to me – they weren't supposed to be taped, but the stupid things kept taking off. You never saw it?'

'No, I must have missed that.'

'It was network. See, that was another disaster my crummy agent parlayed me into . . . and I don't have to act with my tits, I can handle dialogue . . .'

'Suzanne, you don't have to sell yourself to me.'

'Oh, you're sweet. I feel better now I've talked to you . . . Is this it?'

She had wandered over to my desk and picked up some of the pages.

'That's not *it*, exactly . . . mostly just notes.'

'One of these days I'm going to write my life story. Say, can I use the powder room? All that wine. Everybody drinks wine at lunch . . . I never drink when I'm working, of course. Is it through here?'

She moved towards the bedroom door.

'Yeah . . . maybe you'd better use the one downstairs. Mine's a bit untidy.'

'Listen, you should see mine.'

Her hand was on the door handle.

'Well, there's somebody in there. Asleep. Not in the john. In the bedroom. And before another set of rumours start, let me disappoint you . . . I didn't get lucky, I got Charles.'

She stared at me.

'Charles? He's in there?'

'Yeah. This is open house.'

'D'you think he's been listening to what I said about him?'

'I doubt that. When last seen he was feeling no pain.'

'Let me take a peek.'

She opened the door a fraction. 'I'll just tippy-toe past,' she whispered.

'Okay, but for God's sake don't wake him. Otherwise I'll never get any work done.'

'Poor darling. I'll get out of your hair after this, but I just got to go, darling.'

She disappeared into the bedroom and at that moment my phone rang. I rushed to answer it before the second bell. It was Martin.

'How goes it, maestro?'

'It's coming. Slowly, and not necessarily surely.'

'But you've got into it?'

'Yes, in a manner of speaking.'

'Well, look, I'm not going to pressurise you, but when you've got a batch of pages you're happy with, give me a buzz and I'll have Nigel or somebody come over and collect them. Anything you want?'

'Apart from inspiration, you mean?'

'They treating you right there?'

'Yes, fine.'

'Okay, well just checking. Talk to you later.'

By the time I replaced the receiver Charles was standing in the doorway.

'Did I hear voices?'

'Yes, I was on the phone. Sorry if it woke you.'

'What time is it?'

He picked his way to my desk and lifted the coffee pot. 'Is this cold?'

'Yes, it's been there hours. You've been asleep for four hours.'

'Jesus! I must have been dreaming because I could have sworn I heard voices. I really hung one on at lunch. Can we ring down for some fresh coffee?'

'We could, yes, but the fact is, Charles, and don't take this the wrong way, I have to get on with the script.'

He grinned at me.

'Of course, dear heart, and I'm being a fucking nuisance, I know. Just that I feel I've lost a complete day . . . Know what I mean? Where's it gone? that's what I ask myself. Where do all the lost days go? What's that noise?' He went to the open window and stared out. 'Doves . . . Hate bloody birds, they crap over everything. Wonderful setting, though. We should be making Cyrano instead of what we are doing . . . With me as Cyrano . . . and that little French number playing Roxanne. Could be a cheap ride, I don't suppose I would need much make-up.'

With Charles chuntering on and Suzanne still lurking in the bathroom the situation had all the makings of a farce.

'Wonderful stuff, Cyrano.'

Standing at the open window, looking down into the ancient courtyard, the temptation proved too much for him. He suddenly assumed a richer, theatrical voice and began to declaim:

' *"It is a crime to fence with life – I tell you*
There comes one moment, once – and God help those
Who pass that moment by! – when beauty stands
Looking into the soul with grave, sweet eyes
That sicken at pretty words!" '

At that moment, expectant of praise, he turned and found himself face to face with Suzanne.

'Look, darling, I couldn't hide in the john for the rest of the afternoon while you worked your way through Shakespeare.'

'Rostand, you illiterate girl!' With an actor's instinct for the unexpected he had betrayed no surprise at seeing her there, and now advanced on her with outstretched arms.

' *"Love, I love beyond breath, beyond reason, beyond*
one's own power of loving! Your name is like a golden bell
hung in my heart; and when I think of you I tremble, and the
bell swings and rings – Suzanne! Suzanne! . . . along my
veins, Suzanne!" '

She backed away from him.

'Yes, we know you're swinging, but the only stuff in your veins is ninety-per-cent proof.'

'How can you be so unromantic when I'm quoting a great translation of a great play? Of course, I made a slight adjustment to the text to include you, my love. And talking of love, what were you doing in Harvey's bathroom?'

'What d'you think I was doing? You're bombed, Charles.'

'No. Correction. I *was* bombed, but the sight of you has sobered me. *"You may take my happiness to make you happier . . ."* '

'Oh, don't start again.'

'You see how it is, Harvey. Romance is lost on her.'

'Look, we both have to get out of Harvey's hair. He has to work.'

'I wasn't interrupting him. Until you disturbed my rest, I had quietly passed out on yonder couch, sleeping as peacefully as a child.'

'Once a ham, always a ham.'

'All right, we'll go. Let's go back to my room and take Polaroids.'

'That's your idea of a fun evening, is it?'

'No, darling, it's my idea of an erotic evening.'

'What would you do with him, Harvey. He's impossible.'

'Impossible, but adorable. Don't fight it, my sweet. Just give in to your baser instincts.'

'Come on, we must leave Harvey to get on with the script. And another thing, you really are a shit, Charles.'

'What now?'

'You said I was being written out.'

'I said that? It can't be true.'

'Yes, you did. Well, at least you hinted at it.'

'Ah, well that's another matter. My hints should always be disregarded. But you're quite right, we must leave our host in peace. Well, I speak for myself. If you want to go back and hide in the bathroom, darling, don't let me cramp your style. Harvey, dear, on behalf of myself and this lady, I thank you for the use of the bed.'

'You really are a shit, Charles.'

They left together, much to my relief, but when I went back to my typewriter the flow had dried up and tiredness swept over me. I took a quick shower to liven up and then wandered downstairs for dinner. Apart from a couple of businessmen the restaurant was empty. I had no real interest in food, my main concern being to recharge the batteries and get back to my desk. And for the next two days, I scarcely moved outside my room. The pages were collected at regular intervals, but nobody, not even Martin, rang me to say how they were being received and in my race against the clock I was too occupied to worry about their fate. To a layman it must seem incredible that, with several billion dollars riding, such a basic requirement as a coherent script should be cobbled together in this fasion, but it was nothing new to me. In comparison with other scripts I had doctored, this was reasonably smooth going. Some films stagger along on a day-to-day basis – the pink, yellow and blue revised pages churned off the copying machines and delivered to the artists as they sit in the make-up chair. It's never been an industry for the faint-hearted.

I finally lifted my head late afternoon on the Saturday. By then I had completed nearly half the script, doing a scissors-and-paste job, as we say, and had given the production office sufficient material to last the next three weeks. Now it was time to take stock before bracing myself for the next effort.

Feeling in need of some fresh air, I decided to deliver the last batch of pages myself. I started to walk to Valbonne. Half-way there, I met Nigel driving towards my hotel. He reversed his car in the middle of the road and I got in. The seats were littered with maps, laundry, empty beer cans and a half-eaten pizza.

'Sorry about the mess.'

'Looks like the room I've just left. What's happening in the outside world?'

'Well, Charles is under armed guard twenty-four hours a day.'

'Did he go on the lam?'

'Yes, he got a bit restless doing nothing.'

'What a diplomat you are, Nigel. And how are the top brass?'

'Surprisingly docile. All seems to be sweetness and light at the moment, touch wood. They must like what you've written.'

I touched wood. When we arrived at the studio I went straight to the production office and handed in my pages. They had already retyped and Xeroxed the previous batches and while I had a cup of coffee I picked up a copy and began reading. Any feeling of complacency vanished by the time I had gone through the first dozen pages. Much of what I had slaved over had been altered; some of the old dialogue had been put back and the emphasis of many of my scenes changed out of all recognition. Although no stranger to such betrayals, I still felt deflated.

'Is Martin in the studio?'

'I think so,' Nigel said. 'He was in his office when I left.'

I went straight there and entered without knocking.

'Harvey, dear chum. You're back with us in the world of the living. Congratulations, old dear.'

'Oh, I was going to congratulate you.'

I have an idea he knew what was coming, but he covered well. I slapped my copy of the script down in front of him.

'You've done a great job.'

'Oh, you've read the print out, have you?'

'Yes.'

'How does it play for you?'

'I think it's pretty boring. Almost as boring as when I started.'

'No. I think that's just a natural reaction that most writers have. You're too close to it.'

'Why didn't you talk it over with me first?'

'Well, you had enough on your plate, chum. You sound upset. You're not upset, are you?'

'Shouldn't I be?'

I could see his face working as he decided how to handle the situation.

'What's eating you?'

'Just seems a waste of everybody's time to let me go on and on in ignorance, while you – or maybe somebody else, I don't know – are changing everything back again.'

'Oh, now, don't exaggerate. We've made a few changes here and there, but that's our prerogative. You know that.'

'Who's we?'

'David and me.'

'I thought you had the last word. Wasn't that what you said? I thought you and I were going to play Siamese twins on this one.'

'Harvey, one has to play politics. Give a little and take a lot.'

I thought, you idiot, it's the same old mixture – they get you every time.

'David felt strongly about certain things and I couldn't reject all his comments, I had to accommodate him somewhere along the line, throw him a few face-savers.'

'And you think this is an improvement, do you?'

'Course it's an improvement. You've done amazingly in the time.'

'You two haven't done so badly. In most cases you've degutted my stuff, but instead of putting something new back, you've reinstated all the old crap. So you end up with a real crock.'

'I don't agree.'

Old resentments griped me like the stirrings of a duodenal ulcer. I hated myself for immediately going on the defensive. I was old enough and experienced enough to know better. What tattered remnants of pride compelled me to argue the toss about a few pages of script? I rewrite, you rewrite, we rewrite: rewrite (verb, to reduce to the lowest common denominator). It was all such a tawdry game. Maybe a novelist can outlive his critics, but a screenwriter must accept that he is to be judged and condemned before the public have seen his work.

'Harvey, you know the pressures I'm under. I created this hiatus and now I have to shoot to catch up with lost time. Come Monday, we've got to get this thing on the road again. Now, you've done a remarkable job, and we're all grateful . . . I mean, David's really come round to my opinion of your talents . . . The only thing that's happened to your version is that I've taken the best, and then added back those bits and pieces that – probably in your haste to get things down – you perhaps overlooked.'

'But, don't you see,' I said, falling neatly into the flattering trap, 'by doing that you end up with the worst of all possible worlds? Either slug it out with me, go all the way with my ideas, or else settle for what you had. I thought it was lousy, but at least it was consistently lousy. Now you've got something that is spasmodically lousy. I've written in a totally different style. The two don't marry. They can never marry.'

'Harvey . . . we're friends, right? I respect your point of view and all I'm asking is that you respect mine. I have to believe in what I'm shooting or else I lose all contact with reality.'

'We're not talking about reality. We're talking about – at best – a piece of hokum. I've tried to remove the more obvious idiocies. Now, I may not have succeeded, and in that case I'm willing to go back to the old drawing board and work it over yet again . . . But if you're seriously contemplating shooting this, you'd be better off firing the existing cast and hiring a team of comics.'

'I think you're just tired, Harvey, and God knows, chum, you're entitled to be . . .'

'Oh, come on, don't patronise me. Of course I'm fucking tired, what has that got to do with it?'

'Well, I don't think you're doing anybody justice.'

'So you want me to go on as before, do you?'

'Yes, chum.'

'Writing my version which you and David will then chop and change about?'

'Harvey, it was ever thus.'

'You're damn right.'

'Look . . . and believe me, I'm talking as a friend. There's always a chance you're wrong. Don't underestimate me, chum. I do know where to put the cameras. I also know what Suzanne and Charlie are capable of, and I think my knowledge of actors is slightly superior to yours, shall we say? You're exhausted, you haven't given yourself or me the benefit of a good night's sleep. Don't quit on me now, chum. You're my anchor man. I need you. Go out and have a nice relaxing evening . . . And tomorrow – tomorrow is Sunday, isn't it? – I want you to join us all for lunch at the Colombe d'Or. I'm giving a little party for some of the cast and crew.'

'What's that in aid of?'

'Nothing. I just thought it would get us rowing in the same boat . . . just another bit of politics. It's all politics, chum, you know that. You want a drink?'

'Why not?'

'Scotch?'

'Yeah, fine.'

He poured two generous measures.

'Got yourself a date, yet?'

'You have to be kidding.'

'Isn't Michelle staying in your hotel?'

'Martin, it may not look like it, but I've actually been balling the typewriter.'

'D'you fancy Michelle?'

'I don't even fancy myself at the moment . . . Yes, she seems a very attractive girl. Not quite my type, though.'

'What is your type?'

'Well, I married a blonde. Found out they don't have more fun and ever since I've been looking for a bluebird. It's all right for you happily married men, you don't have those problems.'

I looked him straight in the eye when I said that. I felt the need to get my own back.

'Maybe we don't have the same problems,' he said.

'Aren't you ever tempted?'

He turned and added some more ice cubes to his drink. 'In what way?'

'I was brought up to believe that directors had it made. They can take their pick.'

'You've been reading too many bad screenplays.'

'No, I've been writing them.'

Was it possible, I thought, that he had genuinely forgotten our first telephone conversation? Had he been so drunk or drugged that night that he had wiped the slate clean? If not, his blandness did him credit. He was really impressive, but I was still sufficiently angry to want to keep up the pressure.

'Surely, when you're casting, don't you ever cast your eye in the direction of something nubile?'

'It's not worth the candle, chum. Never do it on your own doorstep.'

'Don't hump the staff, you mean?'

'That's the old advice. Good advice, too.'

'But you just told me to try my luck with Michelle.'

'You're different. You don't live here.'

He topped up our glasses. 'You see, chum, and I'd only

tell you this . . . The reason I don't fool around, is because it frightens me.'

'How d'you mean?'

'I went through it once . . . years ago, and never again. I may not have the best marriage in the world, but it suits me . . . I don't want the agony and ecstacy.'

'Well, maybe you're right. In my experience, you seldom get one without the other.'

I finished my drink. In normal circumstances two stiff measures of Scotch on an empty stomach would have put me away, but my smouldering resentment burnt the alcohol before it could do any damage. I hated him on both counts, hated him for his duplicity and his self-assurance.

'Now, chum, we're still mates, are we?'

It was typical of him to employ a word like 'mates' – it reminded me of those mass meetings of the Screenwriters Guild when the great untalented grab the microphone for their big moment of the year and call everybody 'comrades' or 'brothers'. There has always been a separate language for the phonies.

'We're still in business,' I said, smiling. 'I need the bread.'

'Oh, don't say that. You make me feel awful.'

By then I had run out of steam. I couldn't think of a good enough exit line.

'I'll see you at lunch. The Colombe d'Or, you said?'

'Yes. Around twelve-thirty, one o'clock. We'll all relax before the ship sails again.'

I found Nigel hunched over the draft Call Sheet for the resumed shoot on Monday.

'What do Second Assistants do with themselves on a Saturday night?' I said.

'Normally, and with two fingers up to tradition, it's not the loneliest night of the week . . . but unfortunately yours truly has to get this work of fiction round to all the artists and crew before I go to bed.'

'Pity. I thought maybe you would show me a slice of life.'

'I can tell you a few good places to have a good nosh.'

'Yes. Actually, I had something else in mind. Although I wouldn't mind eating as well.'

'Harvey, I'm not your man tonight. I'm lumbered with

this. Otherwise you would have been given the royal tour. We'll do it another night.'

'Ah! but I might not be in the same mood another night.'

While exchanging these pleasantries I had been sorting through a stack of production stills on his desk. They had an artificial gloss to them and the actors looked as wooden as the original dialogue. I was about to leave when one of the photographers caught my eye. I swivelled it round to Nigel. 'Who's this?' I pointed to a girl partially hidden in the background. Nigel peered at it.

'Oh, that's our Laura. Very dolly.'

'What does she do on a Saturday night?'

He seemed to hesitate for once. 'That's one I've never sussed out. Bit out of my price bracket. Don't get me wrong, nice kid.'

'Very beautiful, from what I can see.'

'Yes, she photographs very well.'

'Do you have a number for her?'

'Er . . . well, should be in the cast list, if I can find one.' He fumbled amongst the disorder of his desk top.

'Actually, Harvey, if I can give you a tip, I think she's a non-runner. I don't know for sure, but I have an idea that she's spoken for.'

'Who's the lucky man?'

'Don't know exactly, just a kind of rumour I heard. Word got around that she was off limits.'

'Just my luck,' I said.

'I'll get you fixed next week. We'll go out on a double date and I'll pick you one of my specials.'

I left him to his labours and wandered down the corridor until I came to an empty office. There I found a copy of the Cast List. I looked for Laura's name and wrote down her address and telephone number. If Martin felt free to make changes in my scenario, I could return the favour.

SEVEN

Given the mood I was in when I left the studio, the more I thought about it the more it seemed like a splendid idea. Martin had betrayed me, therefore I would get my own back, ring Laura and try and date her. I had to think up a plausible reason in the first place, but in view of the state of the film and the fact that actors were conditioned to expect the unexpected, I felt I was on a reasonably safe bet. Later I was to look back and marvel at my audacity, but at the time, stoked up with self-righteous anger, I didn't hesitate. The moment I reached the seclusion of my hotel room I dialled the number.

I should have played roulette that night, because my luck held. She was in and answered the phone herself.

'Laura?' – I used the immediate first-name intimacy standard in the film industry – 'This is Harvey. We haven't met, but I've been brought over to do a fast rewrite.'

'Yes,' she said, 'I had heard.'

'One of the things I have to do, and this is good news as far as you're concerned, is build up your role. Did you know that?'

'Martin did mention something.'

'Yes, well Martin also thought I really ought to meet you, because it's a bit difficult to write for somebody you don't know. I had hoped to see you at the studio.'

'I haven't been in since we stopped shooting . . .'

'No, well I don't blame you. Been sunbathing, I expect.'

'Shopping mostly. And a bit of sunbathing. I'm not supposed to get a tan, because of continuity.'

'Well, I think when they restart they're going to shoot

more or less from scratch . . . Anyway, what I wondered was whether you're free for dinner by any chance?'

'Tonight, you mean?'

'Yes. I know it's short notice.'

'Aren't we all supposed to be having lunch tomorrow?'

'At the Colombe d'Or, yes, but I might not be able to get you on your own there – that isn't a hidden threat by the way – so speaking selfishly I'd love to meet you before-hand, because as you can well imagine I'm somewhat under the gun, and I want to do you justice. Are you free by any remote chance?'

'I'd have to get out of something.'

I waited. I felt I had applied enough pressure. The fact that she had not refused point-blank implied that she was wavering. 'Oh, well it's probably too tricky for you. Just a thought.'

'No, it's kind of you. I was just thinking what excuse I could make.'

'Tell the truth, say you have to meet your screenwriter, that your entire career depends upon it. I'll write your dialogue for you if you like.'

She laughed. 'I wish you would. I'm hopeless at getting out of things . . . Yes, I'd love to.'

'You would?'

'Yes. Where shall I meet you?'

'I really ought to meet you, except I don't know my way round. You say.'

'There's meant to be a very good restaurant at the Auberge de Colombier. Do you know where that is?'

'I think so. It's about ten feet below me.'

'What?'

'I'm staying there,' I said. 'That's where I'm phoning you from. I feel as though I'm inviting you home to meet the parents . . . but can't I come and fetch you?'

'No, don't bother. I'll just do what I have to do and I'll be with you . . . what, about eight?'

'Eight is fine. I look forward to it.'

As I put the phone down I had a moment's concern over my own boldness. My thoughts again went to the telephone call that had precipitated me into this situation. If Laura was 'off limits' as Nigel had put it, then all the evidence seemed to point to her being the object of Martin's obsession. Yet ever since my arrival I had looked in vain for any sign of a man fearful of his sanity. On the contrary Martin appeared to be in full command of his emotions. He was either a consummate actor, or else his passion for Laura was pure fantasy, a last-ditch attempt to convince himself that he was still capable of inspiring love. But even if what he had blurted out over the transatlantic air waves were true, at that time I had no serious intentions of attempting to become a rival. I wanted to meet Laura and form my own opinion, to see what lay beyond the beautiful face in the photograph. Her willingness to meet a total stranger at short notice denoted one of two things: either she was secure in Martin's affections and so accepted my invitation at its face value, or else she was willing to explore. Beautiful girls, I have noticed, are seldom unaware of the effect they create when bestowing favours.

She arrived punctually and again I wondered what this signified – was it just a professional actress's disciplined habit? From her photograph I hadn't doubted that she would be beautiful, but I was unprepared for the effect she had on me in the flesh. I would never make a star police witness, for my memory, perhaps with built-in kindness, remains unreliable where those who have wounded me are concerned. Now I can only rely on a few Polaroids which have somehow escaped destruction. As I greeted her in the entrance to the hotel (where I had been waiting since well ahead of time) I was suddenly reminded of a girl I had seen once as a schoolboy – a girl glimpsed at the graduation of my sister, too remote, too rich and too beautiful to be approached, dressed in white mortar-board and gown, surrounded by an admiring throng. Laura seemed that girl, come again to haunt me in the flesh over the long passage of years. She wore a loose-fitting shirt dress of patterned silk which outlined her young breasts as she walked. She walked with that easy grace of those who are accustomed to admiration. Her face was haloed by dense, black hair – a gentle mouth, slightly crooked when she smiled. But even now I can't be certain that I am describing her with any accuracy. All I know is that I was stunned by her beauty, for she seemed somebody singled out and set apart, and the remembered image of the girl at the graduation ceremony leapt into my mind as though I had been programmed to receive it from a satellite I had put into orbit many years before.

Her calmness contrasted with my confusion. I had no idea how I was going to handle my emotions during the rest of the evening.

'Mr Burgess?' she asked, and her eyes searched my face.

'Yes. Harvey. Hello. You're Laura.'

'Yes, hello.'

'It was nice of you to come. Was it difficult for you to get out of your other appointment?'

'No, not really.'

We stood for a moment, both of us feeling awkward. The concierge hovered in the background, and I had that pride of possession we all feel when in the company of a beautiful girl. 'Would you like to go straight in, or have a drink first?'

'Go straight in, shall we? I'm hungry.' She laughed. 'I'm always hungry.'

'You don't have to worry about your figure then?'

'Oh, sometimes.'

The main windows of the restaurant had been opened, and we sat close to one of them, in a corner which I hadn't reserved, but which the Head Waiter, in the best tradition of his calling, had led us to.

'Wasn't it funny you suggesting this place? And me living here. What about you, where are you staying?'

'I live with my parents.'

'But you're not French, are you?'

'My father is, not my mother. I went to school in England though. I took my mother's name when I decided to become an actress. My real name's Tallan.'

'What does your father do?'

'He's a dentist,' she said. I was conscious that I was piling on the questions. Anxious to create a good impression, I was pressing too hard too early.

'I might give him some business while I'm here,' I said. 'Writing, or rather rewriting this script, is like pulling teeth.'

We were handed menus. 'What d'you like eating when you're in one of your hungry moods?'

107

'They've got something I adore,' she said.

'What?'

'Turbot cooked with moules.' She looked up from the menu and caught my expression. 'No?'

'Not for me. If you want me to last through the evening that is. I'm not too good on shellfish.'

'Okay. I'll choose something else.'

'Well, don't let me put you off.'

I paid more attention to her than the menu. I didn't care what I ate, in fact. I was already in the grip of an emotion I hadn't felt for a long time: it was like going to a little-used cupboard and there discovering a favourite jacket one had forgotten and being amazed that it still fitted – I suppose most men are creatures of habit where their love affairs are concerned. Sitting across the small table from her, I willingly surrendered all reason. The menu might just as well have been written in Sanskrit for all it conveyed to me. All my thoughts were concentrated on one thing: I was suddenly, hopelessly consumed with a need to impress her, as though this was a journey's end rather than a beginning, and what had begun as a mere exercise of revenge against Martin, an isolated episode, became a game to be played in earnest. I was totally unprepared for the effect she had on me, and it would be too facile to fall back on the old expression, 'love at first sight'. More truthful to admit that with men it is mostly lust at first encounter. The simple truth was, I was alone with a girl to whom I was instantly attracted. Peacock-like, I wanted to spread my plumage, to preen, to court, to flatter, to do any of those things by which we hope to evoke a little response from those we desire. The curious thing was that despite the difference in our ages – and I guessed that she was in her early twenties – I was the one who felt at a disadvantage, unsure of myself, while she gave the impression of being in command of the situation. I refuse to believe that she was not, from the very beginning, aware of what was taking place. I am not that good an actor and with her infallible female instinct she must have read my heart in my face.

The Head Waiter returned to the table and offered a variety of suggestions, listing the house specialities. Laura discussed her possible choices with him in fluent, colloquial

French, and not for the first time I cursed my parochial education – the fact that I had studied and then neglected to master a foreign language, that typical arrogance of the Anglo-Saxon which we in America have aped.

'What's the verdict?' I asked.

'Well, it all sounds delicious . . . Did you get any of that?'

'Not all of it, no.'

'He says the fish is very good tonight, especially the St Pierre. That's done in a white-wine sauce with grapes and mushrooms.'

'How does that grab you?'

'I'm torn between that and the red mullet baked *en papillote.*'

'I'll have whatever you don't, then we can steal from each other's plates.'

'She gave the order and I chose the wine, a *blanc de blanc* that apparently met with the waiter's approval. I relaxed for the first time.

'Did you think it very odd that I phoned you out of the blue?'

'A bit maybe.'

'You just thought, oh, it's another one of those crazy film people.'

'I'm one of the crazy film people,' she said.

'Shall I be honest?' I said. 'I didn't only want to meet you to discuss the script, that was a white lie. I saw a photograph of you in the office . . .'

She didn't answer that.

'So, you see, I had an ulterior motive. That's your cue to be offended. In some scripts I've worked on, you'd get up and storm out, leaving me with egg on my face.'

'But I'm hungry,' she said. 'So I don't think I'll play that script.'

'You prefer my version, do you?'

'I don't know yet, do I?'

'No, that's true. You don't know anything about me, and all I know about you is that you're very beautiful, and that somehow I've got to write you a very good part . . . I've embarrassed you, haven't I?'

'No.'

Then neither of us said anything. I fumbled for a cigarette. 'Do you?'

'Yes. I try not to.'

'You've got every excuse not to. When I started, nobody had heard of lung cancer. All the ads showed those rugged, outdoor types, just sucking it down into their boots. And they always had a good-looking girl staring at them with admiring eyes. That was my excuse.'

'Have you ever given up?'

'Every morning. Without fail. I did go three weeks once.'

'What happened?'

'I became a raving beast. I guess I'm hooked for life . . . or death.'

'All right, well I won't have one if you won't.'

'I don't think this is the evening for me to quit somehow. I want you to have a nice time.'

'In England, when you go to a proper dinner party, they don't light up until after the loyal toast.'

'What's that?'

'You toast the Queen, and then that character – what's he called? . . . the Master of Ceremonies, no, the Toast Master, I suppose – he says, Ladies and Gentlemen, you may now smoke.'

'Right,' I said. 'Let's have some wine, and I'll toast the Queen.'

I signalled to the waiter to pour our chilled *blanc de blanc*. When the tasting ritual was over, I raised my glass.

'What do I say?'

'The Queen.'

'No, on second thoughts, you'd better say it, you're half British.'

She raised her glass to me.

'Let's just drink to us.'

We touched glasses. Then I lit her cigarette.

'How long have you been acting?' I asked.

'Oh, I haven't done much. Just a few small parts in French television, and once I had a glorified walk-on in a Truffaut movie down here. You could just about recognise me if you were quick enough.'

'Then our Martin discovered you, did he?'

'Well, I met him at a casting session.'

110

'Did he cast you on the spot? I would have done.'

'I had to go back and read for him.'

'What did you think of the old script?'

'I haven't got much to compare it with.'

I was deliberately making small-talk in an effort to discover the exact nature of her relationship with Martin. I had planned the evening in a different mood, starting out in a cold, unemotional frame of mind to get even with Martin. But Laura had changed all that. I was no longer the detached, cynical observer, the tables had been turned. What had begun as a game had backfired.

'You say you went to school in England? Was that fun?'

'Spartan. Cold showers and predatory games mistresses.'

'Which you resisted.'

'You couldn't duck the cold showers. They were meant to build character.'

'How about the games mistresses?'

'Oh, they didn't fancy me. I was a great fat wodge in those days. And anyway I had a mad crush on Mr Anderson, the maths teacher.'

'Unrequited?'

'Oh, yes. He was terrified of us all. I suppose we were fairly horrendous, now I look back.'

'That wasn't in London?'

'No, Sussex. We used to go on school trips to London, to visit museums or the ballet. I liked London.'

'Yes, we all liked London.'

'You don't any more?'

'Maybe I would. I haven't really been back since the war.'

'You were there in the war?'

'Yes,' I said, and I thought, before you were born. It suddenly came home to me how old I was in comparison. Looking at her I could not believe her description of herself as a fat schoolgirl and a great swell of time lost swept over me, a pointless resentment of my own age. All the promiscuous years had ruined me for innocence; I was unprepared for Laura's terrible youthful clarity.

Ever since the break-up of my marriage I had avoided being part of any emotional geometry. In many ways I had deliberately courted a sort of impotence, becoming, for a

111

time, a self-pitying, burnt-out case. Pamela hadn't been much older than Laura when I married her, but there the comparison ended. My ex-wife had been a rich girl who felt the urge to go slumming but who soon revealed the petulance of the rich when her preconceived ideas of *la vie Bohème* proved false. She was in love with an idea, rather than with me. As an escape from the suffocating opulence that had always surrounded her, being the wife of a struggling writer held initial attractions, but they were short-lived. We were not exactly broke, starving or roofless, and I did have my small measure of success, but to some people comparative poverty is harder to take than the breadline. When it was over I never wanted love to come into my life again. Yet within an hour of meeting Laura for the first time I willingly set the whole hideous machinery in motion again, anxious, desperate even, to embrace that unique pain.

I suppose I was lucky I didn't make a bigger fool of myself during that first meal. Perhaps, in retrospect, what saved me was the sudden arrival – unwelcome at the time – of Marvin and Michelle.

'Why, Marvin,' I said, barely concealing my dismay behind the glassy smile I offered to Michelle, 'don't tell me you're still up?'

'Very funny. Hi, Laura. What're you two pussy-cats up to?'

'We're testing the food for Michelin.' I kissed Michelle on both cheeks, since she offered them.

'You two want to be on your own?'

'No,' I lied. Then, 'Why don't you join us?' – since it was difficult to be rude to him without being rude to Michelle, who was, I sensed, embarrassed by Marvin's crassness. The Head Waiter organised another table which was butted up against ours. The only consolation I had was when we rearranged the seating I moved next to Laura. We gallantly volunteered to delay starting our meal until the other two had ordered. I sent for another bottle of wine while Marvin monopolised the conversation. I imagine he didn't feel secure unless he was talking non-stop. Looking back, I think the intrusion hastened the moment when Laura and I became intimate, since it gave us our first common interest.

112

There is nothing like a shared loathing to bring two people together.

'You see this week's *Variety*?' Marvin began. 'There's been another shuffle at Metro. The Abominable Snowman is out and guess who's in? I mean, I just flipped when I read it. They brought back Rhinehart! They must have used chisels to prise him loose from the woodwork.'

'No, his track record is impeccable,' I said. 'He ran Columbia into the ground in seven months flat, then masterminded the worst year in the history of Warners, he was a natural for the job . . . They always land on their feet. You wait, the Snowman won't be out in the cold for long. Anyway, don't let's bore the girls with local Hollywood gossip.'

I could see that both Michelle and Laura were exchanging glances. The evening was already partially ruined for me and I was determined to salvage what remained. Not that Marvin was an easy man to stop in mid-stream; he had no awareness of other people's feelings – probably a lifetime's exposure to the media, a career based on the premise that to say something, however banal, was better than saying nothing, had brought him to this pitch. Such chronic diarrhoea of the mouth was, unfortunately, an occupational disease. Half the trouble was that he mixed almost exclusively with people who didn't listen to words anymore. All that hip philosophy about the message is the media, or maybe it was put the other way round, I never did figure it out. All I know is that most dialogues in the film industry were slanted towards character assassination, spawned from a collective fear: most movie people were basically frightened and therefore had to demand human sacrifices, they had to get the shiv out. In Hollywood, the truth is never told in daylight hours or across a desk. Most of the executives who've ever given me five minutes of their time are like that bird in the old George-Burns-Gracie-Allen routine, the hepplewhite I think they called it, which always flew backwards because it wasn't interested in where it was going, only in where it had been. Tell me the answer, they say, and I'll give you the question.

'I didn't want the two girls to be bored rigid with poor Marvin's second-hand exclusives about what was happen-

113

ing in Culver City and other selected toilets. I wanted to enjoy my dinner, I wanted to fall in love with Laura, both modest ambitions for a man of my advanced years. Attack was my best defence.

'Why d'you think the Snowman is always bad-mouthing you, Marvin, when you speak so well of him?'

'He's bad-mouthing me? Must be jealousy. Can I help it if I've got this sensational body and the face of a Greek god? Get your hand off my thigh, Michelle!'

The second bottle of wine was brought to our table. I was shown the label and then asked to taste it in a clean glass. I went through the routine and nodded my approval.

'You ever sent a bottle back?' Marvin asked.

'Not recently.'

'I did once. I was dating this chick and wanted to impress her, but all I knew about wine was that it cost more than beer. So I chose the most expensive on the list – like it wasn't a class joint, you understand, just classy for me at that particular point in my life. They had three choices, the house white, the house red and the house champagne. So I went for the champagne and when they brought it the waiter had to stick a finger in his cheek to produce the sound effect. I took a little sip and told him it was corked, because I'd seen Paul Henreid do that in a film somewhere, and this chick was very impressionable. When Henreid did it, the waiter did a lot of bowing and scraping and produced another bottle. When I did it, the guy just looked at me. "If it's corked," he said, "you can kiss my ass." He was a real class act. What I hadn't noticed was my bottle had a plastic cap.'

'Marvin,' I said, 'calm down, you're getting too excited too early in the evening. It'll all end up in tears, as mother used to say.'

We turned our attention to the first course. The restaurant was starting to fill up; one half had been taken over by a noisy party of Dutch salesmen intent on a riotous stag night. Their guttural cries silenced even Marvin for a while.

'I thought you'd be bending over that hot typewriter night and day,' he said.

'I've paid my dues for this week. They've got enough to be getting on with.'

'It's so strange, this way of working,' Michelle said. 'I never experienced this before. At least on most French films you *never* have a script, so you know where you are. This way . . .'

'It frightens me too,' Laura said.

'Join the club. Where d'you think it leaves me?'

'Listen,' Marvin said, 'I've worked on movies where the girl-friend of the hairdresser's assistant did rewrites. And they shot the stuff, what's more. At least you girls should feel happy you got Harvey on your side.'

'Are there going to be many changes?'

'Difficult to say. I'm writing one new version which, as far as I can gather, Martin and David are changing back again.'

'But my role, and Laura's, what will happen to them?'

'Harvey's made your role into a transvestite.'

'You serious?'

'Sure. David figures that's gonna be the coming thing next year. He's very big on kinky sex.'

'But I won't play that.'

'He's kidding you,' I said. 'And don't get worried, I'm sure that with a few screaming matches and other hideous manifestations of artistic temperament, you're both going to be taken care of. The way things go, it'll probably be the biggest hit of the season.'

'Over your dead body,' Marvin said. He was a messy eater and his uneven front teeth looked like a market-garden stall.

'Naturally over my dead body. Writers are expendable.'

'Writers and publicity men. But I tell you something girls, whatever else happens, you two are gonna make the papers. That statement comes with a Dunbar guarantee.'

I took the opportunity to nudge Laura with my thigh. She didn't move her leg away, which I took to be an encouraging sign.

'What was your biggest scoop, Marvin?'

'My biggest scoop? Well, I was a leg man on *Cleopatra*.'

'Leg man?' Michelle said, 'what does that mean?'

'Well, it could mean that I fell in love with Cyd Charisse when I was in high school, but in this case it meant that I was

115

doing all the dirty work for Hedda Hopper, to name but three.'

Michelle still looked blank.

'Hedda Hopper,' I explained, 'was a Hollywood institution. She was a hit man for the hat industry. She stuck people with hat pins.'

'Oh, I see. No, I don't, but it doesn't matter. Sorry, Marvin, go on with your story.'

'What was I saying?'

'Your biggest scoop.'

'Oh, yeah. Well, like I said, I was in Rome at the time they were making *Cleopatra*. You remember *Cleopatra*? Come to think of it we were in more or less the same situation as this one, give or take the odd ten million dollars. Joe was writing the script at night, and nobody knew what the hell was going on . . . And, as you recall, Burton was doing his number with Liz. Then we had Eddie Fisher killing her softly with his song, and I got lucky, and got him to give me an exclusive. Which I duly sent back to Hedda. And the exclusive was that Liz and Richard were just good friends.'

'Well, you got it right in the end,' I said.

I found it hard to conceal my impatience, and yet part of me felt sorry for him. My sympathy went out to anybody who had ever been a leg man for Hedda Hopper, a poisonous old broad who was given too much power in her heyday. Marvin was a bore, and he had ruined my evening, but there was no real malice in him. He was like the rest of us on the fringes, and who was to say that his contribution was any less than mine? I had a more exalted title, but like his, it was only on loan. The real power had never rested with the creators, it had always been with the money. Looking at Marvin's veined cheeks, the pores widened by years of solid drinking, I remembered others like him who had started out with such high resolves and then gradually had the enthusiasm bludgeoned out of them. Laura and Michelle listened to his stories with more politeness than me. I doubted whether either of them understood the real sadness behind his forced attempts to remain the life and soul of the party. He was like an athlete on steroids: he could make the pace over a short distance, but he lived in

116

fear of being exposed – the tired old heart was pumping away beneath the frayed Arrow shirt, and the most he could expect at the end of the day would be a couple of column inches tucked away in the pages of *Variety* written by one of the next to go.

The meal itself was excellent, though I ate mine without the pleasure I had previously anticipated. I was too conscious of what was happening to me, too aware of Laura, yet too hemmed in to be able to exploit my new emotions. I was in the process of discovering a simple truth – that I was still capable of love. The perversity of the situation intrigued me, for at that time I had no certain evidence of Martin's involvement, nor did I have any clear idea of how to proceed. Cunning comes quickly to would-be lovers, and as I sat and let Marvin's anecdotes wash over me, I examined all the options. The clever route to take, I argued, was to make friends with those you wish to supplant. I had no further illusions about my contribution to the script. It seemed obvious to me, following the first skirmishes, that Martin was using me: that alone removed any scruples I might have had. Well, two could play that game. I would allow myself to be used in one direction, and use him in another. Quid pro quo.

'What're your views on that, Harvey?'

'Say it again.'

'D'you think French is a better language to act than English?'

'Well, I think it seems to be, to our ears.'

'Why d'you think that?' Laura asked me.

'I don't really. But if you take a really simple phrase – like "I love you" – when we say it, it always seems too short . . . "I love you' . . .' I played it straight to Laura that second time. 'Mind you, I didn't say it very well, but put it in French . . . Well, you say it, Michelle.'

She obliged.

'There! You see, it sounds much more emotional. Mind you, anything Michelle said would sound emotional. I've always been a French-movie buff, maybe that accounts for it. Even their titles sound better than ours. Take that old Gabin movie, *La Bête Humaine*. Translate that into *The Human Beast* and all you've got is a B horror movie.'

'How about *The Bastille Connection*?' Marvin said. 'What would they call that in French, Michelle?'

'Lousy.'

The Dutchmen were in full cry by now, whooping it up, and we had difficulty making ourselves heard.

'Now German, that's a language to act in. And as for singing opera in German!'

'The only language to sing opera in is Italian. A libretto translated into English is absurd.'

'How about the Dutch?' Marvin said. 'They are making more noise than a roomful of Shriners.'

'Who else can we put down?' I said.

'I should have learnt a language,' Marvin said. By now he was verging on the edge of drunkenness. I suspected that the level of alcohol sloshing about in his blood was such that it only needed a few glasses to top him up. I had a horrible feeling he was going to get maudlin as the evening wore on. On the whole I prefer aggressive drunks to the ones who lapse into a crying jag. 'If I'd learnt a language I'd be running a studio now.'

'It's not too late,' I said. 'Buy yourself a Linguaphone course, or go to night school.

'I mean, think how useful it'd be. If I spoke Dutch I could go across to those noisy bastards and tell them to knock it off.'

'Say it a bit louder, Marvin, make sure they hear you.'

I was making the effort, while all the time wanting the meal to end, wanting to be rid of the other two, but there was no escape. Marvin was intent on making a night of it: as soon as the coffee was served he started talking of moving on.

'Let's go to a night club?'

'Night club. You're still living in the Twenties,' I said. 'Nobody goes to night clubs any more.'

'Well, disco, or whatever they call it. What d'you call them, Laura?'

'Discos.'

'Marvin, you go dancing and you're going to be in traction tomorrow.'

'You want to bet? I got Saturday night fever. You girls want to go?'

Michelle looked to Laura. 'Whatever everybody else wants to do,' Laura said.

'Three against one, Harvey.'

'Well, Michelle hasn't said anything yet.'

'Why not?' Michelle answered. 'I can be persuaded to do anything.'

'Anything?' Marvin leered.

'Well, nearly anything.'

'That's my girl. After all, tomorrow we die.'

'No, Monday we die.'

'Okay, let's get a check.'

'Dinner's on me,' I said, since I suspected that Marvin was never in funds. He didn't even make a pretence of fighting for the check. When we left, the entire tableful of Dutchmen got to their feet and applauded the girls. One of them made an attempt to embrace Michelle, but fell over before he reached her.

'See, good idea of mine,' Marvin said. 'We got out just in time.' That gave him a cue for song and he did a tap dance in the car park and croaked out something that was a cross between an Al Jolson impersonation and Tony Bennett after he'd left San Francisco. ' "Just in time, I found you just in time . . ." Anybody want to sign me up?'

'Isn't he funny,' Laura whispered to me as we all piled into the waiting studio car. 'He makes me laugh.' I realised she was looking forward to the rest of the evening. She was still of an age when drunks seemed amusing.

Marvin sang most of the way to Nice, encouraged to stretch his talents by the two girls.

'Do you like dancing?' Laura asked me. I was squeezed in the middle of the back seat between her and Michelle. 'Oh, sure. I was brought up on Chubby Checker,' I said. 'Save me the last waltz.'

There and then I decided to make the best of it: her unconcealed excitement made any other course too churlish. She took over the directions for the driver and guided him to a place behind the Promenade des Anglais called L'Accordéon. The club and dance floor were below ground level and as we entered we were greeted by a noise that went beyond the threshold of pain.

'This is more like it,' Marvin said. 'Order the cham-

119

pagne, Harvey, while I show these natives what it's all about.' He whisked Michelle onto the floor, leaving me to find a table. Once my eyes became accustomed to the gloom we seemed to be in the original Munich beer *keller*, since the entire place had been taken over by what I assumed was a German package tour. They were at least ten drinks ahead of us and sweating well. There were no tables left so we stayed by the bar.

'You want champagne?'

'Later. I'd rather dance,' she said.

'I'm not very good.'

'There isn't room to be good. Come on.'

She led the way into the heaving ranks of next year's Storm Troopers. I almost lost her immediately to a flushed and very blond youth who was actually wearing lederhosen.

'Sorry,' I said. 'But we did win the war.'

As things worked out, I did better than expected. For one thing the dance floor was too small and too crowded for any real dancing – it was rather like Pass The Parcel as we were buffeted around the fringes, and I was spared having to execute any fancy steps. The four-piece band wore shiny gypsy blouses, were long on hair, short on talent and seemed too old for the task.

Conversation was impossible. I guess I had forgotten that the young always take their pleasures noisily – they haven't inherited our hang-ups. Dancing with Laura that night I was reminded of the war years, when for a period we lived only for the moment and just as frenetically.

She mouthed something at me which I couldn't hear.

'What?'

'Isn't this great!' she shouted.

'Great! I may have a heart attack.'

'What?'

'Nothing. Pity they don't turn the sound up,' I said, with a feeble attempt at humour, but she just smiled and swung her body into mine. The standard psychedelic lighting played across her face, so that her features pulsed with the pounding music, rather like a film going in and out of focus. There was something abandoned about her dancing and gradually some of her excitement passed to me: I too cast caution aside like any other middle-aged idiot coming out of hibernation for ulterior motives. Relief only came when the band stopped for their break.

Marvin had succeeded where I had failed: he had got us a table.

'You obviously have influence,' I said, reaching the seat a few seconds before my legs gave way.

'Money talks,' Marvin said. 'I don't speak French, but the French speak my language . . . Present company excepted, Michelle.' He looked like I felt, on the verge of a heart attack. 'Did you see us on the floor? We were terrific. Travolta eat your heart out, baby. Hey! where's the vino I ordered? This is living, Harvey, this is what motion pictures is all about.'

Two bottles of champagne duly arrived at the table.

'Don't look at the label,' Marvin said, 'Otherwise you won't drink it. Last week was a vintage year. Well, here's looking at you, kids.'

It was cold: that was the best you could say about it. On stage it was the turn of the strippers. Two girls appeared, one in black leather and the other covered in sequins, and were greeted with Nuremberg Rally approval by the assembled Germans.

'Go, baby, go!' Marvin shouted.

'This must be a special night,' Laura said. 'I've never seen strippers here before.'

'Listen, Laura, when I take you out for an evening, it's no expense spared,' Marvin helped himself to a second glass of champagne. 'You always travel first class with Dunbar. On the outward journey anyway.' He choked over his own joke.

'How often do you come dancing?' I asked her.

'Oh, whenever I get the chance.'

'Who d'you come with, anybody in particular?'

'No.'

'Does your boyfriend bring you?'

'Which one?'

'Oh, there's more than one, is there?'

Even as I asked the questions, I feared the answers. Perhaps what I feared most was the realisation that she didn't think of me as a possible rival to any of the unspecified young men who had already laid claim. We were packed together so tightly that I could feel the heat of her young body. A single streak of perspiration started at her hairline and travelled down her cheek. For some reason some lines of Auden's came into my mind: 'Lay your sleeping head, my love, human on my faithless arm'. Except that I transposed the crucial word . . . thinking of it as 'faithless on my human arm' because even as I sat there and plotted the start of the affair, I could see how it would end, how it must end.

'How do you girls feel about strippers?' Marvin asked. 'Is it a turn-on or a no-no?'

Michelle shrugged. '*Pas grande chose.* I can take it or leave it.'

'How about you, Laura?'

'It's kind of sad, I suppose.'

'So what turns you girls on? You like grass?'

'Have you got any?' Michelle asked.

'No, have you?'

'Of course.'

She reached for her handbag and produced some expertly rolled joints.

'I thought you'd never ask me,' Marvin said. He took one and sniffed appreciatively. 'Oh, this is the kosher stuff.'

Michelle offered them around.

'I won't, thank you,' Laura said.

'You don't take it?'

'No.'

'Never?'

'I've tried it, but it doesn't do anything for me.'

She held one out to me.

'Not tonight, thanks.'

'What's the matter with you two?' Marvin said. 'You're making me feel guilty.'

Michelle said, 'You object?'

'Not at all.'

By now the strippers were in the closing stages of their act, urged on by an appreciative audience. 'We could be in Berlin, pre-war,' I said to Laura. 'Did you ever see *Cabaret*?'

'Yes, I loved it.'

'You realise it was the film of the musical of the play of

122

the book? Dear old Isherwood really struck gold – little did he know.'

'Oh, this is good,' Marvin exclaimed, inhaling down to his feet. 'Do you get busted over here?'

'No, the flics leave you alone, as long as you're not a pusher.'

On stage the leather top finally came off revealing two incredible breasts pointing straight up.

'Silicone,' Marvin pronounced. 'Have to be. You know, the stuff they inject them with *moves around*! They have to have booster shots all the time.'

'What a fund of information you are Marvin.'

'Yeah, well I once hyped for a joint down in Frisco where Carol Doda did her act. She gave me the info. They pushed her from a 35 to a 44 in a month, eight treatments. She was *unreal*, I tell you, *un-real*! Had to wear special heavy harness, even in bed. I mean, she made this chick look flat-chested. Her boobs were like non-retractable Ferrari headlights.'

'Do men really like them as big as that?' Michelle asked.
'To look at, maybe, but not to live with.'

'Who knows? You only have one life to live, live it big.'

'I think it's gross,' Laura said. 'What d'you mean, it moves around?'

'Like that. One minute it's up here under your chin and the next day it's under your arms.'

'Gross!'

'Tell us more, Marvin. You obviously majored in plastic surgery.'

'Harvey, you know as well as I do, there are broads in Beverly Hills that are made over every year. Guys too.'

'*Men* have it done? You don't mean it?'

'Sure. Not in the chest, but everywhere else. It's big business out on the Coast, honey. If I had the bread they could turn me into Redford.'

'But what sort of men?' Michelle kept at him. 'They must be lunatics.'

'It's the age of the youth cult, honey. Old is ugly. And listen, it happens over here. What about that place in Switzerland where they give you a cocktail of chopped lamb's liver or something? Didn't old Somerset Maugham have a few shots? They tell me he was still trying to drag his boyfriend into the sack the day he snuffed it.'

'You're making all this up!'

'Michelle, where have you been all your life?'

'Well, I don't want to know about those things. I like my men to be what they are.'

'That's why you're so attracted to me, darling. I'm an unrestored ruin. What you see is what you get. Course, I can't speak for Harvey.'

'Oh, everything about me is false,' I said. 'I was cloned years ago, but it didn't take. I'm really a hologram.' All this talk about age was not what I wanted to hear.

The act on stage was building to its sad climax. One last whirl of G-strings, a roll of drums, and then blackout. When the lights came up again the gypsy band were back in place and very soon conversation was obliterated. Before I could make a move, Marvin had asked Laura to dance. I did the polite thing and asked Michelle.

'No, I'll sit this one out, thank you. It's too crowded out there.' Relief must have shown in my face. 'I don't think you like this sort of thing too much?'

'To be honest, the noise makes me feel like my head is going to explode,' I shouted. She smoked her joint elegantly and with obvious relish. Altogether she was a very cool lady, I decided. We sat and watched Marvin being put through his paces by Laura.

'D'you think he'll last the distance?' I said.

'Well, he's enjoying himself. Laura is very good.'

'Yes, isn't she.'

'She photographs very well in the film.'

'Yes. I can believe that, though I haven't seen any of the stuff they shot previously. What was it like?'

'It looked very good. Of course the script was stupid, but what could we do? One gets paid, one does the best one can. You can't take filming too seriously, it's all madness, even on the good films.'

'D' you find Martin easy to work for?'

'He's okay. I like directors to bully me. Then I get angry and then I act better. I think, anyway. Martin is always so polite. To me at any rate. So British, I suppose. It's the first time I've worked for a British director, so it's strange for me.'

Having asked the question, I had rudely looked away from her, my eyes going back to Laura.

'Are you attracted?' Michelle asked.

'Who to?'

'Laura.'

'I don't really know her.'

'That wasn't what I asked you. I'm sorry we disturbed your evening. But there's no stopping Marvin. He doesn't have too much – what d'you call it? – feeling for atmosphere.'

'That's okay. We were just having dinner together. This has been fun.'

'Can I give you a word of advice?'

'Please,' I said.

'About Laura. I have the feeling, and don't ask me why, just instinct I suppose, that maybe somebody was interested before you.'

'Oh, I'm sure.'

'But somebody who might not welcome any competition.'

'Well, it's hardly come to that. I'm not having an affair with her.'

'No, but you'd like to. That's obvious.'

'Is it?'

'Oh, yes. And who could blame you?'

'So who's the competition?'

'Can't you guess?'

'Not a clue,' I said.

'Our director.'

I did my best to look surprised.

'Martin? What gives you that idea?'

'I have eyes in the back of my head when it comes to that sort of thing. And actresses can always tell when another actress is getting special attention.'

'He probably just feels fatherly towards her.'

'Don't you believe it.'

'Well, thanks for mentioning it. Not that I think he has much to worry about where I'm concerned.'

'Don't be silly. If you want her, just be clever about it.

125

After all, Martin is married and you're not. Have you met his wife?'

'Yes.'

'So have I. I think, maybe, he has to be very careful.'

Careful was something I had to be if I had made it that obvious during the course of a meal. Thankfully, Marvin and Laura returned at that point.

'Did you see us?' Marvin said. 'Weren't we something?'

'Amazing.'

'What happened to you two? You chickened out.'

'How could we compete?'

'No, that's true. Isn't this a great evening?'

'Great,' I said. 'You should be in public relations, Marvin.'

As I said that his whole face changed and I had a premonition of what was about to happen. He tore at his collar to loosen it, but there was no strength in his arms – they thrashed the air for a few seconds and then he fell sideways into the next table, scattering glasses. I wasn't quick enough to save him. One moment he was there and the next he had disappeared out of sight. With the help of two startled German tourists we got him back in his chair. I got his shirt open and put a hand over his heart. To my relief it was pumping away quite strongly. His exertions on the dance floor combined with the alcohol and dope had finally pushed him beyond the point of no return.

'Let's get him into the open air, quick,' I said. With the help of one of the tourists we shouldered him through the crowded tables and up the stairs into the street. Fortunately the studio driver was parked nearby and we deposited him in the back seat.

'Is he going to die?' Laura said.

'I doubt it.'

'But it happened so suddenly.'

'No,' I said. 'He's been in training for twenty years. We'll take him back to the hotel and put him to bed.'

'Don't you think we ought to get a doctor?'

'See how he is when we get there. Don't look so worried, darling. He's just drunk, that's all. It was pretty hot down there while he was dancing the light fantastic.'

I went back and paid the bill and then we drove off. I

must say that, after they had got over the first shock, both girls behaved very well. Michelle cradled his head, but he was out cold. There wasn't too much traffic around at that hour of night and our driver put his foot down.

'Your car's at my hotel, of course, isn't it?' I said to Laura. 'We'd better drop you off first. Sorry it's such a dramatic ending to the evening.'

'That's all right. I'm just so worried about him.'

'I dare say he'll sleep it off. I don't think it's all that unusual for dear old Marvin. And I'm not telling tales out of school, but he admitted to me he's an alcoholic.'

'I shouldn't have given him a joint,' Michelle said.

'You weren't to know. Anyway, he's a big boy, he makes his own bed.' She sprayed some cologne onto a handkerchief and wiped his forehead.

I turned to the driver. 'Stop at the Auberge on the way, please.'

'No, I'd like to come with you,' Laura said.

'Really?'

'Yes, I just want to make sure he's all right. I think he ought to have a doctor.'

'Well, let's get him into bed first. I promise he's not going to die. Not tonight anyway.'

We got to Grasse, and happily the driver knew the hotel he was staying at. Several other members of the crew, including Nigel, were still around in the bar when we arrived. Nigel immediately took over.

'I'll see to him,' he said. 'Don't you worry. Come on, me old love, let's have you.' He and the focus puller lifted the unconscious Marvin and took him towards the elevator, oblivious of the stares they attracted from the other guests.

'The girls were wondering whether he ought to see a doctor.'

'No, he'll be all right. He usually ties one on at the end of the week. But I'll sit and watch him for a bit. You get off, take the girls home.'

'We'll keep it to ourselves, shall we?'

'Oh, naturally. Be right as rain by Monday.'

I could see that Laura had been considerably shaken by the episode. On the journey back to the Auberge she kept saying, 'But he looked so awful. I really thought he'd died, poor man.' Certainly the evening had ended on a downer, nothing like I had planned. More and more I was conscious of the age difference between us. I felt convinced that she thought of me in the same way as she thought of the unfortunate Marvin: in her eyes we were probably two of a kind. I thought, quit now, don't try and take it any further, but after we had said goodnight to Michelle and I walked her to the car park that resolve weakened.

'There'll be a full moon in fifteen days,' she said.

'Really? How clever of you to know that.'

'I don't.' She laughed. 'I just guessed.'

'I'll start counting.'

I opened the car door for her. 'Sorry it was all so traumatic this evening.

'Oh, I enjoyed myself. Thank you.'

'So did I. It was just that the last little episode put a bit of a damper on it.'

'Poor Marvin.'

'Poor all of us,' I said, 'come Monday. We've got that to face. Well, you have. I shall just be an onlooker. Do you like going in front of the cameras?'

'No. I get terrible butterflies. I suppose it's because I haven't done very much.'

'I don't think that has anything to do with it. All good actors are scared.'

'Really? You think so?'

'I know so. You're in good company.'

She turned the ignition key but the engine did not fire. She tried several times with the same result.

'Let me have a go. You've probably flooded it.'

I got in and tried all the old tricks, but the engine remained dead.

'You know, you're out of gas,' I said. 'It's registering zero.'

'Oh, no! I knew there was something I should have done. I'm hopeless with anything mechanical.'

'At least this is a switch on the old routine.'

She looked blankly at me.

'The way these scenes usually go is that you're in my car and then, surprise, surprise, I discover I've run out of petrol. We should be on a lonely road, of course, and then I make a pass at you. At least this is original. Don't worry, we'll sort it out. Come back into the hotel and I'll organise a taxi.'

It wasn't quite as simple as I'd imagined, but the old concierge finally managed to locate somebody in Opio willing to turn out. Michelle had disappeared to bed and the bar was long since closed.

'Shall we go up to my room and wait? He'll buzz us when the thing arrives.'

'Is this where you work?' she said, as I showed her into the suite.

'This is where I *try* to work. The whatsit is through there if you want it. I'll ring Nigel in the meantime, see how Marvin's making out.'

I watched with mixed feelings as she disappeared into my bedroom. I got Nigel on the phone, who reported that Marvin was sleeping peacefully, and apparently none the worse for wear. A large spider crawled slowly across my typewriter as I listened to Nigel's medical bulletin. It was still there when Laura reappeared.

'Do you hate spiders?' I said. 'Because if so, I'll perform a supreme act of bravery and put it out of the window.'

'No, they've never frightened me. It's worms I'm terrified of.'

'Worms? How about snakes?'

'They don't bother me. Only worms. They drive me crazy. I saw a great fat worm in the garden today and I couldn't eat lunch.'

She moved to my desk and prodded the spider with a finger. It scurried out of sight.

'Now snakes I could understand – they're the classic Freudian image, or supposed to be – but worms! Do you dream about worms?'

'Not often. Only when I drink red wine. If I drink red wine, I have nightmares.'

'I'll remember that. Don't give the lady red wine.'

All the time we were making this small talk I was desperately thinking of ways and means to steer the conversation towards some tentative declaration. I had lost the knack, it seemed, and again it was the age difference that inhibited me. With somebody like Michelle I would have

129

asked straight questions and doubtless received straight answers. I remembered what Michelle had said and Nigel had hinted at; and then I thought of what Laura herself had told me in the nightclub. There was no possible chance that a girl like her would be unattached. I saw a line of unknown rivals stretching to the horizon, familiar with her likes and dislikes, able to converse on her level, sharing her interests, knowing exactly where they stood.

'Don't worry about your car,' I said. 'I'll get it filled up in the morning and then I'll come and fetch you and take you to Martin's lunch party.'

'Won't that be a bore? I could have my father drive me over to save you the trouble.'

'No trouble.' Then I plunged. 'Have I asked this before . . . Do you have a regular boyfriend?'

'Sort of.'

'He's in love with you, I take it? I really don't have any right to ask you these questions . . . but it's important to me to find out. Yes, of course he's in love with you, he'd be a fool if he wasn't . . . I'm sorry, I'm embarrassing you with all this.'

'No.'

'The point is, you see . . . I could fall in love with you. And that complicates matters, doesn't it?'

'I suppose so.'

'I could, without too much difficulty, fall hopelessly in love with you . . . I'm sure that sounds absurd, just another lunatic aspect of this strange evening . . . You've now been given two prime examples of how the older generation conduct their lives . . . They either pass out drunk, or otherwise make fools of themselves. I apologise.'

'You don't have to apologise,' she said.

'I'm not going to attack you or anything, don't think that. That's not my style . . . It's just that I thought that if you see me again – if you want to see me that is – I ought to reveal my true colours . . . And the only other thing I want to say, so you don't get the wrong idea . . . is, I don't make a habit of falling in love quite so easily, it's as big a shock to me as it must be to you.'

I felt an enormous relief at having confessed, even though I was conscious I hadn't cut a very romantic figure. I

130

might have gone on and said much more, but at that moment the telephone rang and the old concierge announced that her taxi was waiting downstairs.

'Anyway, don't worry. There's nothing you have to do, I just wanted to get it off my chest.'

I made no attempt to touch her, not even when we said goodnight.

'Sleep well,' I said. 'Don't have any nightmares.'

'I won't. We didn't have any red wine.'

'Shall I call for you in the morning? Well, it's practically morning now, isn't it?'

'Yes,' she said. 'Call for me.'

I closed the taxi door and she drove off without looking back at me.

EIGHT

It's astonishing how much hope one can read into the most casual of remarks. The fact that Laura had not rejected me (or worse still, laughed at me) and had not refused my offer to take her to Martin's luncheon party, sustained me through a restless night. Having arranged to be called early I shaved with extra care – shades of the schoolboy returning – selected a brand new shirt which turned out to be the last burial ground of the pin industry. I was bleeding from three fingers by the time I had extracted the last lethal keepsake.

Once dressed for the road I had to attend to Laura's car. I over-tipped one of the staff to fetch a couple of cans of gasoline from the nearest gas station, then after I had got the car started I went and filled the tank and checked the oil and water – something I seldom did for my own vehicles. I needed to ask directions to her home and, in my anxiety to see her again, started out much too early.

Her parents' house was set back from the road, a pleasant if unprepossessing building that seemed to have been designed in a mixture of styles. The gates to the entrance drive were closed and at the last moment I lacked the courage to present myself at the house. Instead I sounded the horn a couple of times. This had the effect of infuriating two hysterical poodles who yapped non-stop at me through the bars of the gate until Laura appeared and silenced them.

'They're idiotic,' she said. 'Get inside both of you. Go on! I would ask you in, but everything's a bit chaotic this morning. We have an aged uncle who suddenly descended on us and promptly collapsed. I shan't be too long.'

'That's okay. The car's all fixed, by the way.'

'Thank you, that was sweet of you. It's a beast to drive, isn't it?'

'It's not the greatest, I admit.'

'I'll be with you shortly.'

I watched her walk back into the house, thinking, how young she looks, younger even than I remembered. I wanted to know all about her, which room she was now entering as I waited; I wanted to pierce the mystery of the life she led, as though by discovering more my chances would increase. I took it as a good sign that she hadn't shown any embarrassment at meeting me again so soon after my blurted confession, but I was wary of reading too much into that – the young today are more self-assured than we ever were. I lit a cigarette and wondered what Martin's reaction would be when I arrived at the restaurant with Laura. Yet it was not Martin I really feared, but all those unknown younger men I had yet to uncover, and in particular the admirer (why did I shy from admitting the word 'lover'?) who fed Martin's own mania.

'What's the news of poor Marvin?' she asked when she rejoined me.

'I have to admit I haven't checked this morning, but I imagine no news is good news.'

She had twisted coloured braids through her thick black hair and now, with the strong sunlight directly on her face, I saw how flawless her skin was. Her body beneath the printed silk shirt-dress had an elastic voluptuousness, all the more disturbing because its gentle outlines were so clearly seen. The perfume she was wearing hinted at the scent of summers past.

For most of the journey to Vence we talked about the coming week on the film. She seemed genuinely concerned about the problems I was having making the script work and I was careful not to badmouth Martin to her, merely confining my comments to generalisations about the hazards of being a rewrite man.

'I envy people who can write, because I can't put two words together. My friends are always complaining that I never write to them. I don't know what it is. I know what I want to say, but I can never get it down on paper. It was the same at school. I was always hopeless at essays.'

'What sort of school was it?'

'A convent.'

'You're Catholic, are you?'

'No. My parents are. Well, I suppose I was baptised a Catholic . . . Are Catholics baptised? . . . But I never go to Mass. Except at Christmas. Are you Catholic?'

'I'm not anything,' I said. 'I don't know what I believe in . . . Just the Minimum Terms Agreement, being cynical. Are your parents happy about you being in this sordid profession?'

'You think it's sordid?'

'I think it's tough, especially on actresses. No, sordid is the wrong word. There are a lot of nice people in the business – the trouble is that they're seldom the ones who employ us. Did you always want to be an actress?'

'No. I think I always thought I'd be a nurse.'

'You wouldn't have lasted long as a nurse.'

'Why?'

'Why? Because the first patient you looked after would have married you. If I woke up in a hospital and found you bending over me with a thermometer, I'd propose on the spot. But then I've always had a thing about nurses . . . So what made you change your mind?'

'I don't know. It just happened. Some photographer took some pictures of me on the beach and they got into the papers. I didn't think much about it until I got offered a part in a film being made down here, and I did it just for a laugh really.'

The Sunday tourist traffic slowed us down as we neared the restaurant and we crawled along in low gear for the last half mile. Two sweating gendarmes were making operatic attempts to sort out the endless flow of cars searching for non-existent parking spaces in the narrow roads. We had to go a considerable distance before we found a spot.

'I've heard a lot about this place,' I said, 'but this is the first time I've eaten here. It's one of the 'in' places, isn't it?'

'Yes. *Très cher*. My father says he has to do a lot of root-canals before he can afford to bring us here. I love food. Don't you love really good food?'

'Depends. It depends on the company I'm with. Eating bores me a lot of the time, it's such an interruption. That

134

goes with being a writer, I think. When I'm on my own I usually eat junk food. I'll make an exception today, though, because I'm with you.'

We arrived outside the restaurant at the same time as Mischa and two or three other members of the crew. They had dressed for the occasion, looking very formal, rather like distant relatives arriving for a smart society wedding.

'You know something,' Mischa said, 'when they give you a party *before* the end of a film it's always a sign that things are going wrong. Hello, Laura, how beautiful you look. Why aren't I forty years younger?'

'Because God pays his debts in less than mysterious ways,' Sandy said. 'He knows what a bloody Jonah you are. Don't be so depressing. Accept gracefully is my motto. Don't you agree, Harvey?'

'Always.'

Just before we entered the vine-shaded terrace I squeezed Laura's hand: 'Whatever else happens, I meant what I said last night.' Then I stood aside and let her go first, and Martin came forward to greet us.

'I was beginning to get anxious.'

'It was the traffic,' I said.

He turned his attention to Laura, ignoring all the others, kissing her on both cheeks.

'Have you missed us all this week?' I heard him say. Then he led us towards the large table set out at the far end of the terrace where the others were waiting, but I noticed that he relinquished his hold on her arm when he was half-way there.

Amazingly, Mrs James had been persuaded to turn out for the occasion, but she didn't look as though she was enjoying it. 'Ah, Mr Burden,' she said, looking past me as she spoke, and I saw that she was staring at Laura. She was wearing a couturier dress that must have eaten into Martin's percentage of the profits. The table had been set with place names and I found myself sitting next to Michelle. Champagne was immediately to hand.

'Isn't this where we left off?' I said, as Michelle and I touched glasses.

'Has anything been heard of the leg man?'

'I don't know. Let's ask Nigel.'

135

'I don't think he's invited,' she said.

'Ah, no! Too far down the pecking order, I expect. We're the privileged ones.'

'I'm a very fragile one.'

She may have felt fragile, but she concealed it well. I don't think I have ever come across anybody who more epitomised typical French beauty. She reminded me of a book of photographs I used to possess. It was called *Judgement of Paris* and from what I remember of the jacket blurb it had been smuggled out of France by the British photographer, John Everard, just as the Germans were at the gates of Paris. The images had stayed with me because the whole *raison d'être* of the book seemed so wonderfully romantic. The photographs of those carefully air-brushed nudes, posed in the dying days of a legendary city I had yet to visit, appealed to my sentimental nature. I thought of the models, with their pert high breasts, left behind to await their fate. Michelle had their look.

The last to arrive, naturally, were Suzanne and Charles. They had two flamboyant young men in tow. As the tourists swivelled in their seats to get a better look, I heard Martin's wife hiss in annoyance, 'Who're those other two, Martin? We haven't got places for them.'

'I've no idea, but don't make a fuss, we'll fit them in,' he answered. Suzanne advanced on him and flung her arms round his neck, doubtless determined to give her public their money's worth from the start.

'What a wonderful idea this is, darling! We should do it every day.'

'Yes, why don't we have this place do the unit catering,' Charles said. 'Alice, you're looking wonderful in your little blue gown. Now, let me introduce two very talented friends of mine . . . Believe it or not, I still have friends, even after my last film. This is Sigmund and Albert.'

'Alfred,' the second man corrected him. He was wearing a topaz ring large enough to receive Cable Television.

'Sorry, Alfred. Mrs James, our hostess, and our beloved director her husband . . . Oh, and of course, not forgetting David Latrough, our generous producer who's paying for this lovely feast out of his own pocket.'

Sigmund bent low and kissed the back of Alice's hand,

which seemed to mollify her a little. Michelle nudged me under the table. 'He's wearing nail varnish,' she whispered. Alfred seemed removed from the whole scene, so I took him to be the boyfriend.

'Alice, dear,' Charles said, plonking himself down in the nearest seat, 'Sigmund will change your whole life if you let him.'

'Really? Charles, you're sitting in the wrong place. I put you over there. Martin, will you organise two extra places, please?'

'Oh, darling, if I sit there I shall have all the peasants staring at me, and fame has never been my spur when I'm eating. Anyway, I'd much rather sit next to you, because I've got something very important to discuss. Sigmund is a genius interior decorator. He'll transform your house.'

'Well, it's kind of you, Charles, but I don't think I want my house transforming.'

'Course you do, darling. I do mine every third year and I've never regretted it. Does wonders for your sex life.'

'Now, Charles, just behave.'

'I'm serious. Sigmund does amazing things with mirrors, don't you dear boy? He's so modest, but everybody's after him. And he plays gin rummy.'

'Oh, really?' She looked interested for the first time. 'Well perhaps we can talk about it later. Let's order, shall we, Martin?' She looked across the table. 'Martin!'

Because the seating arrangements had been altered, Martin had taken the opportunity to sit himself between Laura and Suzanne. 'What, dear?'

'Can we get the menus?'

'Right.'

Waiters were duly summoned and all heads went down for the serious business of the day. It took an age before all tastes were satisfied and the proceedings were interrupted at one point by a somewhat bovine tourist festooned with Nikons who detailed his two equally bovine daughters to stand behind Charles while he focussed on our group.

'Sorry! Thank you! We won't have any of that. I never pose for photos on the Holy Day. Deeply religious. Sundays are reserved exclusively for drinking,' Charles said. 'Fucking fans think they own one,' he added as the man

137

departed, very put out. 'Forgive my language, Alice. Somebody wash my mouth out with more champagne. Are you happy, Alfred? What have you ordered?'

'I'm not eating lunch,' Alfred said. He seemed to have lapsed into a sulk, presumably because Sigmund was not paying him enough attention. 'I'm on a very strict diet this week.'

'What're you talking about?' Sigmund said. 'Since when?'

'Since now.'

I could see that Alice was getting more and more edgy as all her prejudices were confirmed. She was used to dominating her own table, but with the mixture that Martin had assembled, plus Charles's unwelcome additions, she didn't stand a chance. I daresay that Sandy and the rest of the crew felt somewhat ill at ease; they were slightly out of their depth in such mixed company – Charles with his quasi-regal airs, Alice slumming under protest, and the two alien fags hissing at each other. I found it all fascinating in a macabre way. While I filed some of it away for future use, at the same time I despised myself for being part of it. I had attended too many such functions where everybody wore social masks and the jollity was manufactured. The whole event had an air of unreality, because a time bomb was ticking away underneath us all. Some of my resentment stemmed from the fact that I was seated too far away from Laura to be able to carry on any conversation with her. I had taken myself by surprise the evening before in making that unpremeditated declaration and now I had no idea what to do next. The initiative was no longer mine – I had played my trump card first. I was out to conquer and triumph, but I had no weapons to hand with which to fight. Suddenly, I had no faith in myself. All I could see was a young girl who might be willing to accept the flattery of my attentions, but who would ultimately reject me, simply because the age difference between us made rejection inevitable. I had trapped myself. I could not change Laura, nor could I roll back the years. It was as if through that chance phone call Martin had infected me with his own madness, and now I sat at his table and watched him like a fellow sufferer. I could scarcely taste the excellent food set

138

before me, and it took an effort of will to concentrate on anything that Michelle or others said to me. I drank glass after glass of wine and it had as much effect as water, for nothing could dull the ache.

Now, so long after the event, I can see how at the beginning of the affair I dramatised every pitiable intrigue. It seemed – it seems – absurd, ridiculous, that in the space of a few days, prompted first by curiosity, I had committed myself to a young girl I scarcely knew. Starting with that first meal Laura and I took together, I launched my own destruction. It was then that I began to hate Martin for having by chance revealed his secret, hated him for having led me to such unhappiness as only love can bring.

The hatred began at that lunch table under the twisted vine leaves on the terrace overlooking the valley. I saw Laura listening to Martin with a passionate eagerness that she had so far denied me. I saw them all and felt isolated from them. They were like people one travels with on a long-distance bus, with whom, for a period, one is forced to share the same scenery. There are stops along the route and one strikes up spurious friendships which pose no lasting threat, or so it seems.

The meal lasted well into the late afternoon and by then we had the restaurant to ourselves. The other tables had been cleared, most of the waiters had gone off duty. Martin's wife was the first to leave, bestowing glacial farewells on her guests, her smile set as hard as a footprint on Hollywood Boulevard. She made an attempt to persuade Martin to leave with her, but being a co-host he had the perfect reason not to and after her departure he became bolder, ordering a further round of drinks – and, to my sober eyes at least, more openly slavish in his attentions to Laura. When, finally, the party broke up it was he who escorted Laura and Suzanne, announcing that he wanted to discuss the following day's work with them. I suppose I hoped that Laura would somehow include me by making the excuse that I had driven her to the luncheon, but Martin seemed to know about that and forestalled any such move.

'Oh, Harvey, don't worry about Laura's car. I'll have my chauffeur take it back and I'll drive the girls.'

Charles, too far gone to make any coherent contribution,

appeared to have forgotten he had brought Sigmund and the ruffled Alfred. He burped his way out on Mischa's arm without saying goodbye to anybody and his departure signalled the general exodus.

'Looks like I'm taking you home,' Michelle said.

'And I shall accept gratefully.'

We said our thanks to Latrough who had been left to settle the check and walked out into the dusty square where groups of locals were playing *boules*. Much of the heat had gone out of the day, so before getting into Michelle's car we walked up the cobbled ramp and into the old city. I bought her a grotesque Teddy bear in one of the souvenir shops.

'For good luck tomorrow . . .'

'Then I shall buy you one,' she said. 'We'll have one each.'

'Perhaps we should mate them . . . Or maybe I should hole myself up in the hotel, and do a Gabin. You remember that old film he made? It was a classic.'

'*Le Jour Se Lève*, you mean?'

'Yes. Hollywood had the bloody nerve to remake it. I think they even burnt the original negative of the Gabin version . . . Well, there are murders and murders. He had a Teddy bear, remember? With only one ear . . . A Van Gogh bear . . . Great last shot. I'll never forget it. He held it up to the mirror, then he put a hand over one of his own ears.'

'What a memory,' Michelle said.

'Yeah. That's the sort of film I wanted to write when I started out, I saw all the great French films.'

She drove with that consuming, frightening faith which all the French have in the infallibility of the *priorité à droite*, and by the time we arrived back at the Auberge my right leg was rigid from phantom braking.

'I realise I'm only a stand-in, but would you like to have dinner later?' she said.

'Could we face another meal?'

'Maybe not. So? What do we do?'

'Shall we take a raincheck?'

'What's that?'

'It's an Americanism that even I don't really understand. It means, let's think about it and consult later . . . I

140

suppose, hideous though the thought is, I ought to put a little work in on my typewriter.'

'You serious? Can you really do any work after all that?'

'The short, snappy answer is, probably not. But I guess I ought to try, because they're going to be breathing down my neck at any moment.'

'Poor you,' she said. 'I think I shall just collapse. With my bear. Thank you for my bear.'

'Thank you for mine.'

We went upstairs to our separate rooms. Mine was stifling hot, oppressive. In less than a week it had ceased to be a retreat that I got pleasure from returning to: now it was just an hotel room where I forced myself to work. I was hardly in the mood to struggle with the next sequence in the script, but I made the attempt. A large bee crashed around the room, seeming to emulate my own anger. The day had begun with such promise and now lay in ruins. I had fondly imagined that when the luncheon broke up I would spend the rest of the afternoon and perhaps the evening with Laura.

It so happened that I had reached a point in the script where I had to devise a new scene for the character she was playing. I typed a few lines of dialogue, but they were as flat and as devoid of life as I felt. I could think of nothing else but the way she had looked; ugly fantasies of her relationship with Martin – slide after slide passing through my mind's projector like some erotic lecture that only I was watching – deeply disturbing images of lust and the stark act of love. I abandoned all thought of work, drowning myself in a flood of hatred that eventually swept me towards the deeper waters of self-pity. I surprised myself by the intensity of my feelings, for even in the heat of the moment I still retained some sense of the ridiculous. I had talked of 'falling in love' with Laura, using the phrase like some moonfaced schoolboy frenzied with predatory eagerness to possess. I tried to imagine myself in her place, wondering what sort of figure I could possibly cut in her eyes. Women, we men are told, care little for physical beauty; they are not sexually aroused by the same simplistic features of beauty – the male body, despite all efforts by *Playgirl*, has few centrefold attractions to compare with the

141

stimulus most men find in studying the nude female. But if I hoped to find comfort from that, it was short-lived. It seemed all I could offer her was an experience she had already sampled.

The bee was still blundering around the room, lost to view for short periods and then flying dangerously close as, like me, it sought an escape from the room that imprisoned us both. I opened the shutters wide and attempted to push it towards the open air with a rolled newspaper, but this merely confused it more, and suddenly it landed on my shoulder. I struck out in panic. In imagination it seemed as large as a bat, and as I touched it the sting went in. Examining my neck in the bathroom mirror I saw the swelling reddening the skin like a lover's bite. The pain was strangely soothing, it quietened my previous mood and I stood fascinated by the phenomenon of the poison at work. It wasn't for some moments that I came to the realisation that I might be in some danger. The red patch on my neck was now the size of a small saucer and I was conscious of tightening in my throat. I rang Michelle's room.

'Were you asleep?'

'No.'

'I'm sorry to bother you, but I've been stung by a bee. D'you know what one does?'

'Where did it sting you?'

'On my neck.'

'I'll come to your room.'

She arrived armed with a box of tricks. 'Let me see. Yes, that's not good. Is it painful?'

'It's not too pleasant.

She produced some tweezers. 'We have to get the sting out . . . Come nearer the window. Now hold still for a moment . . . I can see it.'

'You've done this before.'

'Hold still . . . You have to get it out whole.'

A few seconds later she claimed victory. 'Now we have to get the swelling down.' She reached into her box for a glass phial which she broke expertly, then soaked a tissue with the liquid contents and applied it to my neck. 'That should start to work in a few minutes. You're lucky, it just missed the vein.'

'How d'you know what to do?'

'I was brought up in the country, and I had three brothers and two sisters . . . One or the other of us was always getting something. And I never travel without my medicine chest.'

'Lucky for me,' I said.

'Is it working? It should work fairly quickly.'

'Yes, I think it is.'

'When I was a little girl, I once swallowed a wasp. It stung me on the tongue and if my father hadn't acted quickly I'd have choked to death. It closes the throat, you see.'

During all her ministrations I had become more and more conscious that she was wearing only a thin silk housecoat. She came closer again and turned my head to the light to see what effect the antidote was having. Her fingers were cool on my skin as she traced a circle round the swelling, pressing it gently. I could feel the soft pressure of her breasts on my arm.

'Will I live to finish the script?'

'I think so.'

'Well, thank you, doctor. What do I owe you?'

'You can have that one on the house.'

Her hand stayed on my neck. I dare say we both had an intimation of what was going to happen. 'Wasn't it fortunate,' I said, 'that I didn't get stung on the lips? Otherwise I wouldn't be able to kiss you.'

'Is that what you want to do?'

'Unless you object.'

'No,' she said. 'I won't object, but I hate to kiss standing up.'

'Then perhaps we should make ourselves more comfortable.'

She studied my face intently for several seconds before answering.

'I think we should both be very sure of what we're doing. We shouldn't have any illusions, don't you agree?'

'I don't know,' I said.

'Because if what I think is going to happen does happen we ought to start off as equals.'

'What does that mean?'

'It means we shouldn't fall in love. For one thing, I don't

143

want that, and if you're honest you don't want it either . . .
So it's better to be honest. If you want to go to bed with me,
that's fine . . .'

'Are doctors allowed to go to bed with their patients?'

'I'm being serious. I'm married, and not unhappily married, but I'm also a woman, and I can't do without sex, and
you attract me . . . which I think you know, otherwise you
wouldn't have done anything to start this . . . Just as long as
we know we're both only here because we're lonely.'

For a moment her calm practically blunted the edge of
my excitement. 'We're not quite equals then . . . I'm not
married,' I said.

'I know that.'

'Why do you say I don't want love?'

'I didn't . . . I said you don't want to fall in love with me,
there's a difference.'

'You're very practical.'

'Yes,' she said. 'People who commit adultery like to
think they have all the answers in advance . . . Don't look
so worried, I'm the only one who should be worrying.' She
went into the bedroom. I locked the door leading to the
corridor before joining her. She had closed the shutters in
the bedroom and I saw her naked body for the first time by
filtered light. There was no need for me to conjure substitute desires and as I quickly shed my clothes to join her a
crushing excitement blotted out all thoughts of Laura.
There is something so unique about embracing a strange
nude body for the first time and as I bent over her to palm
and then kiss her breasts past memories filmed over – it
was as if I had never tasted a woman's flesh before. I moved
to dovetail our bodies and felt the soft heat of her pelt as she
arched into me.

'Tell me what you like,' I said.

In answer she reached down between our bodies, her
hand no longer cool, stroking me, guiding me, her belly
tightening as I entered her. I sensed again that amazement
of doing for the first time what one has done many times
before and yet never fully remembered. I had no sense of
time or place, all my feelings were concentrated on the silky
strangeness of her. The language we both employed (and
she cried out in French) was pain made verbal – a supreme

effort of will, as though separately we needed to convince ourselves that we were not alone as our mounting pleasures blotted out the past and future. It is only when the body dies in the sexual act that the mind starts to live again, and as I tasted the salt of her tears in the aftermath of our shared, slow frenzy, only then did I become aware of my own duplicity. To fuck another person is, like hanging, irrevocable – perhaps that is why more fanciful writers than me have called it 'the little death' – for the trapdoor has been sprung and we must dangle on the rope of conscience. I can't speak for women, but few men ever completely forget their past lusts: we can forget injustice, cruelty, pain, but the act of possessing another body stains us for life.

For minutes after our passions had been slaked we lay still joined. Her damp body fluttered gently beneath me, like a pinned specimen only recently pierced. I had no means of telling what lay beneath her closed lids, and had she opened her eyes at that moment to search my swollen mask she too would have been in ignorance of my thoughts. I sought to place myself, to give myself that small honesty at least, but apart from the familiarity of the room only now coming back into focus, I had no feeling of belonging anywhere. Only the telephone ringing in the other room brought me back to reality. I lifted myself from her, our bodies parting company with wet reluctance, and padded my way from darkness into light.

The sound of the telephone seemed to fill the room. Addicted beyond hope, I reached for a cigarette before lifting the receiver.

'Harvey?'

'Yes.'

'It's me, Laura.'

As I picked up my throwaway lighter I saw the dead bee on top of my pile of manuscript, a faint rim of pollen surrounding its stiffened corpse like a halo. I had a moment's utter panic – what if she was calling from the house phone in the lobby?

'Where are you?' I said.

'Where? I've just got home and I wanted to explain, to apologise for what happened.'

'Apologise? What for?'

'Going off like that. I didn't even say goodbye. It was just that Martin didn't give us a chance.'

'That's okay. I understood.'

'Really? I thought you'd think it so rude.'

'No, I realised Martin wanted to work . . . What have you been doing, rehearsing?'

'Sort of . . . You sure you're not annoyed? You sound odd.'

'Do I? No, I was just lighting a cigarette. And I got stung by a bee.'

'By a bee!'

'Yes. On the neck. You should have been here to take care of me.'

'How awful. Is it all right now?'

'Yes, it was nothing. So how did it go?'

'Bee stings can be dangerous. Have you seen anybody about it?'

'Oh, yes, I had something put on it. Tell me how the rehearsals went. I'm anxious to know how my dialogue played.'

'Well, we didn't actually rehearse much. Just talked about it mostly.'

'You and Suzanne?'

'Well, Suzanne wasn't feeling too good, so Martin drove her back, and then we just talked about it in the car.'

'Good.'

'You're sure you're not annoyed?'

'Absolutely. I'm probably just tired. Apart from the bee sting I've been . . . trying to work some more on the script. Are you on call tomorrow?'

'I'm on stand-by. So I could see you, if you wanted.'

'Tonight you mean?'

'If you wanted.'

'Well, I'd have loved to,' I said, 'but I guess I ought to stay here and work.' I heard Michelle get up from the bed and go into the bathroom. 'Maybe I'll see you tomorrow. I shall probably go out to the location, just to keep tabs on how it goes.'

'I may not be called, of course. They may not pick up my stand-by.'

146

'No. Well, if that's so, I'll give you a ring when I get back. Will you be at home?'

'As far as I know.'

She was silent for a moment and I thought we had been cut off. Then she said, 'I did think about you. What you said last night.'

It was my turn to be silent.

'You still there?'

'Yes.'

'I'm terrible on the phone. I never know what to say.'

'Phones aren't the best means of communication, are they?' I was convinced that at any moment Michelle would appear in the room. 'We'll talk when we meet,' I said. 'Take care of yourself. And thank you for ringing.'

'You too. You take care. Especially after being stung.'

'Bees are like lightning,' I said, 'they never strike twice in the same place.'

I regretted everything the moment the connection was broken. As I exhaled a lungful of smoke the dead bee quivered. I thought how symbolic it was – a corpse lying on top of my attempted hopes. Lifting the top sheet of manuscript, I dropped the dead insect into the wastepaper basket, and at that moment Michelle came into the room. Her hair was wet from the shower and she had a large white bath towel draped round her.

'The assassin has paid the price,' I said. 'He didn't live to boast about it. Strange things, bees. You know that when the Queen mates she flies straight up into the air, out of sight. And all the studs – to call them that – fly after her, and the one that reaches her is given the dubious privilege of having her. He gets one shot, that's all. And that's his swan song – bee song. He falls to earth we know not where . . . You look ravishing like that.'

She came up to me and put her damp, cool arms round my neck. Then she kissed the place on my neck where the bee had stung me.

'I'm not so cruel as the Queen bee,' she said. 'I'll give you another chance.'

'Are we both crazy?'

'Yes.'

'How crazy?'

147

'Oh, only a little bit. Life would be impossible if one didn't do crazy things now and again. Put that awful cigarette out and have one of these. It'll relax you.'

'I am relaxed.'

'Oh, yes? What's this then?' She kneaded my shoulders, pressing her fingers into the muscles. 'You're like iron. Come back into the bedroom and I'll give you a massage.'

'Is there no end to your talents?'

'That's for you to find out.'

I allowed her to lead me to the bed. 'Now lie face downwards,' she said, 'get yourself comfortable. Here, put this pillow under your head. I'm very good at this. I do it for my husband.'

'Lucky guy.'

'Maybe and maybe not.'

'Would he be upset if he found out?'

'Don't talk,' she said. There was a pause while she searched for something in her make-up kit. Then she straddled over me, and poured some oil on my shoulders. As she bent and started the massage I felt the tips of her breasts brush across my back. She had surprisingly strong hands and they quickly found the most painful spots.

'Too hard?'

'Pleasurable pain,' I said, my voice muffled into the pillow.

'You're in bad shape. There! You feel that? That's all knotted up.' She worked up and down my spine, expertly, and despite the occasional pain I found myself drifting into sleep. I've no idea how long she kept it up, nor was I conscious of when she stopped. When I finally woke up she was lying beside me. She put a half-smoked joint between my lips.

'Does that feel better?'

'Amazing. Don't spoil me too much, I might get used to it. What time is it?'

'Oh, I don't know. Around eight o'clock, I guess.'

'You hungry?'

'I'm always hungry after I've made love . . . Your phone went again, by the way, but I didn't answer it for obvious reasons.'

'What it is to be popular,' I said. 'You know who rang me the first time?'

'No.' She took the joint back.

'D'you want to know?'

'If you want to tell me.'

'Laura . . . I'm mad, aren't I? Tell me I'm mad.' I started to tell her the whole story, beginning with Martin's phone call. She lay with her head on my chest and listened without interrupting. 'You've seen them together,' I said, when I'd finished, 'd'you think he's making it all up?'

'Well, I haven't seen them together that much, except on the set . . . But, yes, I think maybe he is infatuated.'

'How about the other part of it, the boyfriend?'

'It'd be odd if a girl like that didn't have a boyfriend.'

'So . . . am I mad?'

'Yes. But then all men are mad. That's normal.'

'If you weren't married, you might cure me.'

'Being married doesn't cure anything.'

'You said you were happy.'

'I am, but I'm still here in bed with you.'

'So does that make you as mad as me?'

'Not quite. I'm not dealing in unknowns.'

'You think I'm being very naive to become . . . to feel this way about a girl I don't even know? . . . Yes, it's ridiculous, really, utterly ridiculous, especially lying here next to you . . . Insulting, too. And I don't mean it that way . . . I should know better at my age.'

'You men always have this thing about age. What are you, an old man? You weren't old with me in bed a few hours ago. Did I ask for your birth certificate before I let you make love to me?'

'You're different.'

'Why am I different?'

'Because you are an extraordinary girl.'

'I'm not extraordinary and I'm not a girl.'

'Then it must be because you're French.'

'Oh, my God! not that . . . That's so American. Look, I give you some advice. You want to have an affair with me while the film lasts, that's great . . . No strings, as you say, no regrets and no guilt. And when it's over we say goodbye and we're still good friends. You want to feel like an old man, you can pretend you're Gabin . . . He didn't do so badly, by the way . . . I won't worry about that. On the other hand, if you want to fall in love with Laura, then you must go and try it. And fuck Martin, fuck the boyfriend, fuck them all. If she wants you, she'll have you. If she doesn't, she won't, it's as simple as that. It's not a script you can write in advance.'

As we lay there, nude, our bodies entwined, and I listened to her listing the choices, I grew more and more confused. It was as if she was describing a complete stranger. I think I must retain a diluted solution of ancestral puritanism in my cholesterol-clogged veins, because part of me was appalled by the man she was describing. Here was this character who less than twenty-four hours before had told a girl young enough to be his daughter that he was in love with her, but who experienced only the mildest hesitation before immediately betraying her and committing adultery. It was difficult to justify either act, for both were so foreign to the person I had always imagined myself to be. I could half-believe that the idiocies and illogicalities of the screenplay were somehow spilling over into my own life, that nothing was real any more. I envied Michelle her calmness, and it was that calmness that evoked new furies. I covered her mouth, smothering my confusions with fresh lusts. Her compliant, soft lips opened to mine and when I took her for the second time that strange Sunday she became at the moment of abandonment my surrogate Laura.

NINE

Early morning on a film location: always the best time of
the day – the cool, lucid period when most temperaments
are quiescent, nothing has had a chance to go wrong and an
air of hopeful expectancy pervades all concerned. Martin
once said to me, 'Every morning I get up prepared, determined to create a masterpiece, nothing less, but by the end
of the day I'm lucky if, in the process of knackering myself,
I've achieved nothing worse than a compromise. My whole
life is an arse-paralysing compromise.'

I recalled that conversation on the Monday that shooting
re-commenced. I had planned to arrive at the same time as
the main unit, but my driver lost his way and when we
finally found the chosen spot – a wooded area between
Valbonne and Opio – the site looked as though a task force
had invaded. It was difficult to see the wood for the
vehicles. With a period film, of course, the twentieth
century has to be totally concealed from any camera angle.
The location manager had marshalled the mass of equipment well away from Martin's first set-up: an array of
artists' trailers, generators, honey wagons (a charming way
of describing the mobile latrines), horse transporters,
camera cars, sound vans, and half a dozen vast pantech-
nicons holding the stock of wardrobe, the props and elec-
trical gear.

I found Charles sitting on the steps of his air-conditioned
trailer, stripped to the waist, having his wig fitted. He had a
small mirror in one hand and a plastic cup of black coffee in
the other.

'Have you any notion of what happened to me after that
lunch yesterday?' was his greeting. 'Those two amazing

151

queens I brought with me – which was a mistake, I now realise – carted me off to some gay bar in Cannes where, I must confess, I indulged myself by drinking too deeply of the evil Calvados. Of course I was drinking to forget. Gay bars are hardly my usual habitat, as the Dowager Lady Mary here will attest.'

He introduced the willowy man attending to his wig.

'I believe you, dear. Millions wouldn't.' The man appeared to take no offence at being called Lady Mary.

'Too macho for me. Queens have changed since my day.'

'Well most of us don't go back that far, dear.'

'You see, Harvey, what I have to put up with at this hour of the day! Help yourself to coffee. It's inside.'

I stepped over and past him into the interior of the trailer. It was an impressive mobile home, large enough to sleep six and containing all creature comforts. I had no doubt that Charles had selected it with tape measure in hand – to ensure that, if but by inches, it was larger than Suzanne's.

'Why do we do it, Harvey?' he shouted after me. 'Can you explain why anybody in their right minds would choose to act at this ungodly hour?'

I joined him again. Without benefit of make-up he looked like some old-time pugilist who had just gone ten rounds and was praying for his seconds to throw in the towel.

'Without the Dowager here and his magic paint box, my career would come to a grinding halt.'

Later I asked him to reveal the origins of the camp nickname. 'She's a treasure,' Charles said, 'I couldn't live without her. She used to be on the halls, what you call vaudeville, that's where the poor old cow started doing what she thought was a class drag act dressed as the late Queen Mary. That was in the days of our censor, the Lord Chamberlain, and the poor thing got carried away one night and went much too far, very *lèse-majesté*, so they pulled the shutters on her – believe it or not, they could in those days. Well, of course, she was distraught. The end of a career and all those lovely frocks. I think it sent her off her head for a time, because after that she granted certain favours to a troop of boy scouts and was asked to spend a few months in one of Her Majesty's penal establishments.'

Despite his hangover, he was in fine form that Monday morning, malice dripped from his lips. 'What d'you think of this period rug I'm being fitted with? Weighs a fucking ton.' He held his hand mirror up and stared at himself. 'On a clear day I could look like Estelle Winwood . . . Oh, Mary, Mary, where did it all go wrong?'

'Well, I told you not to have that last face lift.'

'It's an unnatural way of life, an unnatural way of earning one's living, Harvey, even with your golden words to speak.'

'How *are* the golden words?'

'May I be bluntness itself?'

'I'd expect nothing less,' I said.

'Well, now . . . we both know that we're not about to make Lawrence of Versailles . . . What you have done with your golden words is make life possible. That in the circumstances is a considerable achievement. We're both being paid, dear boy, and we must be suitably grateful.'

'I wish we could be suitably still at the same time,' the Dowager said. 'Otherwise this bugger of a wig is going to go on back to front.'

At that moment Martin appeared from his trailer with Bernard in tow.

'Ah! Caesar comes!' Charles declaimed.

'Good morning, Charles. Morning, Harvey. I trust we're all bushy-tailed and raring to go?'

'It's too early for heartiness, Martin dear. We shall be raring to go when at least four layers of Max Factor have been carefully placed in position . . . but it's doubtful whether we shall ever be, as you put it, bushy-tailed. I had that clause struck out of my contract.'

'Very relieved you're in such good spirits. Rumour has it that you celebrated last night.'

'Rumour is correct for once.'

Martin turned to me. 'Harvey, I've got a little chore for you, so I'm glad you're here early. Do you think you could possibly . . .' He broke off and stared hard at Charles. 'Is that the same wig as you wore last time?'

'The same wig, but probably not the same face under it.'

'I've set it differently,' the Dowager said, immediately on

the defensive, 'since apparently it wasn't to anybody's liking. Of course it only happened to be the authentic period style, but who's counting?'

'Looks odd, that's all.'

'They do look odd before they're fixed into place.'

'All this is so reassuring,' Charles said. He had another look in his mirror. 'Not the fairest of them all this morning. I need a gallon of those life-saving blue eye drops. Paul Newman, where were you when I needed you?'

'How soon will you be ready?'

'Ask the Dowager, not me.'

'Mr Croze will be ready as per Call Sheet. I can't work miracles.'

'Yes, you can!' Charles shouted. 'You can and you *must*!'

'It's just that I've had to change the shooting order. Gerry says the light won't be right for the love scene until just after eleven, so we're starting with . . . What's the scene number, Bernard?'

'Eighteen. Revised page nine.'

'Will that throw you, Charles?'

'Why would a little thing like that throw me? I can read an idiot board with the best of them.'

'Seriously.'

'I shall read it very seriously. What *is* scene eighteen?'

Bernard preferred his copy of the script and Charles peered at it.

'Was that down on the Call Sheet?'

'Yes, it was, Charles. And I want to do it all in one, on a long track. And that's where you come in, Harvey. I need another line for Charles. There should be a reference to the death of the King.'

'There was,' I said, 'but you and David cut it.'

'Really? Must have been a mistake. Can you remember what it was?'

'I think I've still got it in my copy.'

'Well, give it to Elsie, and she'll type up the necessary number of pages.'

The head Prop man called Alf had been hovering in the background during this exchange. He was carrying a dead pigeon.

'Excuse me, governor. Excuse me, Mr Croze. Just wanted to check this is okay.'

'I wanted a wood pigeon, Alf.'

'This is a wood pigeon, governor.'

'Looks more like a dove.'

'No, governor. Definitely your authentic wood pigeon.'

'Am I required to act with that hideous corpse?' Charles asked.

'Yes. It's in Harvey's script. It's symbolic.'

'It's not only symbolic, it's high. The bloody thing stinks.'

'I've got others,' Alf said.

'I'd better see them . . . Bring them over onto the set and we'll decide there. Yes, Mischa?'

'Morning,' Mischa said. 'Could you spare a moment to have a look how we've dressed the woodman's hut? We could have gone too far.'

'I'll be right over,' Martin said. 'Must just have a word with Suzanne.'

'She's still in make-up,' Bernard said.

'Where else would she be?' Charles's mood had changed since the news of the additional dialogue. I excused myself and went in search of the continuity girl. She had set up her 'office' quite close to the first camera set-up. Carpenters were levelling and consolidating a long length of track while the electricians manhandled the mini-arc lamps and reflector boards into position.

'How many copies do they want?' Elsie asked when I had dictated the new dialogue.

'Better do half a dozen, and make sure Charles gets his first, otherwise he'll say he didn't have time to learn it.'

'That's news?'

I was suddenly accosted by another member of the crew. 'Are you the vet?'

'No, I'm not.'

'That fucking horse has gone lame. Sorry, Elsie.'

'Oh, don't mind me.'

'We need it for the first shot. He'll go fucking spare if it can't gallop off into the fucking distance. Who's the vet then? Somebody said you were the vet.'

'No, sorry.'

155

'Fucking amazing, ain't it? Always happens. Just my fucking luck.'

By now groups of extras were drifting towards the shooting area. They looked self-conscious in their period clothes. I guessed that most of them were amateurs, recruited locally, though extras the world over have that look of stateless, displaced persons. Nigel and his two junior assistants started placing them in position; Nigel with his more practised eye sorting out the obvious duds who would ruin a take if allowed too near the camera.

I wandered back in the direction of the artists' trailers. Much of the earlier calm had disappeared as we drew nearer to the time when shooting was due to commence. Now everybody I encountered seemed intent on solving a problem, either real or manufactured. The only people completely at their ease were the drivers: their work was over until the end of the day – now their only concern was to make sure they headed the queue when the meal break was called.

Alf passed me, carrying four dead pigeons this time. 'I don't know what he's going on about,' he said, using me as a convenient sounding board. 'Dead wood pigeons he asked for, and I got him dead wood pigeons. Suppose he wants them in fucking solid oak or something.' He walked on still muttering to himself.

'Do you speak English?' somebody said.

I turned to face a very dignified elderly man.

'Yes.'

'What a relief. Wonder if you could help? See, I'm new to all this. Just down here for a spot of holiday and got talked into doing a bit of this filming business.'

'You're going to be an extra, are you?'

'Am I? Is that what I'm going to be? They told me I was going to be an officer. Point is, people keep telling me to go to wardrobe. Now, that means sweet Fanny Adams to me.'

'I expect they want you to be fitted for a costume.'

'Costume? I imagined I'd be wearing a uniform.'

'Yes, well, same thing.'

'Are you one of the actor chaps?'

'No.'

'I've never seen so many people wandering about doing

156

nothing. Seems extraordinary to me, to have this number of people for something so trivial. Doesn't seem very organised.'

I grabbed at a passing Assistant. 'Where's wardrobe?'

'Over there behind those trees. Any problem?'

'This gentleman is a bit lost, I think.'

'Lost, are you, dad?'

I saw the old boy stiffen at the familiarity.

'What are you? One of the mob or one of the Royals?'

'I'm supposed to be an officer.'

'Okay, I'll get you fixed up. What's your name?'

'Mathews, and I'm here on holiday.'

'Not today you're not, dad.' He was led away to be transformed. I made my way back to Charles's trailer, but by now he had disappeared, presumably to have his make-up completed. I helped myself to another cup of his coffee. He had one of those elaborate leather script-covers which at one time all leading actors sported as a status symbol. Charles's had a facsimile of his signature on the front cover, tooled in gold leaf. Out of curiosity I opened it to see whether he did any homework when preparing for a new role. He had underlined his dialogue in red ink, but apart from a couple of telephone numbers on the title page, he had not given himself a single note. I was still examining it when Michelle appeared in the doorway. She was fully costumed and for a second or two I didn't recognise her.

'You didn't come and say good morning. I've been here for ages.'

'I'm sorry. I would have come and looked for you, but Martin wanted me to write some extra dialogue.'

'I forgive you. How are you?'

'Fine. How are you?'

'I'd like to be back in bed. And preferably yours. Having got me ready for the first shot, now they're not going to use me until lunch-time.'

She took my coffee from me and sipped it.

'You look very fetching,' I said.

'I don't feel it. I can hardly breathe in this costume . . . Oh, God, filming is so boring! Did you sleep well?'

'Well, but not long enough.'

'Did you think about me?'

'Of course.'

'No regrets?'

'No.'

'But now you're worried . . . You're worried, aren't you? Don't look so worried. I meant what I said.'

'I'm not worried.'

'Did you cheat on your wife when you were married?'

'Curiously enough, no I didn't. That isn't any great plus . . . She more than made up for my shortcomings . . . Why did you ask that? Do you have regrets?'

'No. A little guilt, maybe. But that's the kick . . . without that it would just be . . . sordid.'

'You really are a . . . very, very extraordinary character, you know that, don't you? You say such odd things.'

'I don't think so. I just tell the truth.'

'How did you even know I was once married?'

'How? Because you act like a once-married man. You're so formal and correct. It's nice, and it's obvious. Last night you even asked if you could kiss me . . . Let me see your neck.'

She examined me. 'What did I tell you? My cure worked . . . Now it just looks like a love bite.'

'The red badge of courage,' I said.

At that point we were joined by Suzanne. She was wearing the lower half of her costume, but her magnificent and much admired bust was draped with a large towel, and she still had hair-pins stuck in her white wig.

'Isn't it just typical of Martin. Well, not only Martin, all bloody directors are the same. Change their minds at the last moment. Yesterday, when I begged him, pleaded with him, to rehearse, he gave me a big routine about wanting to shoot . . . What's the bloody French name for it, Michelle? Cinema what?'

'*Vérité*.'

'Yeah, what's it mean?'

'It used to mean a lot of amateurs running around with hand-held cameras and not an idea in their heads.'

'Well, that was Martin's line yesterday. He came on very strong that if we over-rehearsed we wouldn't give him the effect he's looking for. I said to him, listen, if this actress doesn't rehearse you'll get some *vérité* all right. You'll get

158

some marvellous footage of me drying stone dead . . . See, my problem is it takes me at least four years to learn anything, and I had somehow learnt the previous crap . . . Not that your stuff's crap, Harvey. It's just that I get confused between the old and the new . . . So be an angel, hear my lines for me, darling . . . Find the page for me while I go to the john. Charles'll be furious if I use his john, but mine has gone on strike or something.'

'So you didn't rehearse at all yesterday?' I said. 'I thought he took you and Laura off for a private session?'

'He might have had a private session with our little ingénue, but not while I was there . . . Oh, God! I can't get through the door with this bloody costume on. How the hell did they manage in those days?'

'They didn't,' Michelle said. 'Their habits were disgusting. Most of them didn't bath, either.'

'Oh, well, Martin's aiming for realism.'

When she emerged she stumbled through her lines a couple of times before we were interrupted by the return of Charles. His transformation was now complete and I had to admit that his faith in the Dowager's skills was fully justified.

'Have they told you what we're starting with, darling? Bloody tracking shot. They'll be farting around all morning with that . . . Plus the fact that I shall give myself a hernia trying to get my leg over that sodding great horse . . .'

When eventually they were called to the set it took the best part of an hour to rehearse the complicated camera movement, get the horse to stand on its mark, make sure that none of the extras impeded Suzanne's and Charles's progress and that the symbolic wood pigeon fell out of the sky and landed on cue at Charles's feet. Because of the length of the track and the angle of the sun it was impossible for the sound crew to get close enough with a conventional microphone on the overhead boom, so both principals had to be wired with radio mikes. On the first take, these picked up a local radio station. I was prepared for temperaments, but everybody kept their cool. Then shooting was halted for a high-flying but very noisy jet.

'Does it pick up?' Martin asked. There was an edge to his voice for the first time.

'Well, I can hear it.' the sound mixer said.

'Have Harvey write in another extra line,' was Charles's contribution. 'You know, just a reference to the inaugural flight of Air Bourbon.'

The sound man stood his ground and refused to give the okay until the plane was but a disintegrating vapour trail. 'If we don't shoot soon,' Charles said, 'I shall have to pee. And with this costume that may mean self-castration.'

'Might do wonders for your voice,' Martin answered.

It took six takes before everything worked to Martin's satisfaction and the entire crew moved to ready the next set-up. Mischa and his team had prepared a pastoral setting a quarter of a mile away, complete with a rustic woodman's hut and a flock of sheep. Charles and Suzanne changed costumes and rehearsed on camera. The scene charmed everybody but the sound man.

'Now what is it?' Martin said.

'We've got to do something about those sheep. Can't we lose them?'

'Lose them? They *make* the shot.'

'Well, they also drown the dialogue.'

'Okay, I'll ask Charles and Suzanne to use more voice.'

'We can't scream at each other, Martin. This is meant to be an intimate scene.'

'Oh, Christ! Animals! Shift them back, Bernard. Take them back as far as that row of trees.'

The sheep proved less than co-operative and although all available hands were mustered to herd them away from the camera, they immediately panicked.

'Watch the equipment, watch the camera somebody!'

One of the crazed animals bolted straight for Suzanne and was only headed off at the last moment, but not before Suzanne had tripped over and fallen into a bed of brambles. She was taken off by the unit nurse for first-aid and it was fully fifteen minutes before order was restored. By then the light did not meet with Gerry's approval. Martin argued with him.

'You did say you wanted this to look like a Fragonard print, didn't you?'

'That was the original conception.'

'Yes, well if you shoot it now with sun directly overhead

160

it'll look more like Frankenstein. This top light is murder on Suzanne.'

'Okay, okay. Bernard! We'll take an early lunch break. When will this be right, Gerry?'

'Three-thirty, four. When the sun gets a bit lower and I can give you some back light.'

'Oh, shit! Fucking sheep. Right, well, let's think . . . Is Laura still on stand-by? You haven't cancelled it?'

'No,' Bernard said. 'I was waiting to see if we got this before lunch.'

'Call her in. We'll do her scene, first shot after lunch. Just make sure she's ready.'

I walked with Martin and Charles to where the dining tables had been set up under canvas awnings.

'Relax,' Charles said. 'Early days yet. I must say, being unkind, I enjoyed dear Suzanne's prat fall. Don't know why she panicked like that. Can't be the first time she's been rammed.'

'Oh, very good, Charlie. Except it wasn't a ram. It was a ewe. Poor darling, I'd better go and see how she is.'

'No, I'll go,' Charles said. 'I was the one who laughed and we don't want her sulking all afternoon. You going to eat in your trailer or mine?'

'Yours. The air-conditioner works in yours.'

When Charles had gone, Martin suddenly said: 'I'd no idea you'd taken Laura out to dinner.'

'Yes. Just thought I ought to meet her before starting to write her role. We had dinner with Michelle and Marvin.'

'So she told me . . . What did you think of her?'

'Nice kid.'

'She's hardly a kid.'

'Comparatively speaking,' I said.

He didn't say anything else until we were inside Charles's trailer. He helped himself to a glass of iced Perrier, then turned and faced me.

'I suppose you've guessed by now?'

'Guessed?'

'Well, you could hardly have forgotten our first conversation. When you phoned me that night.'

'Oh, that.'

'I'm in a mess, Harvey.'

'You mean, Laura's the one?' I wanted to force it out of him. I was enjoying his discomfort.

'Yes,' he said, finally. 'Tell me honestly, do you think I'm mad?'

I took my time before answering. 'You're running a risk, certainly . . . It's a bit near home, isn't it? How perceptive is Alice about these things?'

'I don't know . . . You were there, the night you arrived, when Laura rang the house. What did you think?'

'She seemed a bit needled, but I didn't think anything at the time, because of course, I wasn't in the know then.'

'Did I carry it off?'

'To me you did.'

'I'm obsessed, Harvey. I can't think of anything else.'

'How far has it gone?' As I put the question, I dreaded the answer.

'Too far,' he said. 'Too far to turn back.'

'What about the other business . . . I assume you don't mind me asking these questions? Only, before, you did say forget it.'

'No, I want to talk. I haven't got anybody I can discuss it with, and since you're in on it . . .'

'Just one thing,' I said, 'because obviously I've been puzzled ever since . . . who did you think you were talking to that night?'

'My business manager. His name's Harold, and I guess . . . well, I was shot that night. I'd taken a couple of pills . . . Harold's in New York now, finalising my contract, and I thought it was him. He's the only other person who knows what's going on.'

'Except . . .' I deliberately hesitated.

'What?'

'Well, you know what film units are like. I think one or two people may have got onto it . . . If I may say so, you weren't too subtle at lunch yesterday.'

'No, I know . . . Oh, Christ! you see what a state I'm in.'

'You were going to tell me about the boyfriend. Has he made any other moves?'

'No, he's out of town, so she told me.'

'But what's her attitude, that's the important thing surely?'

'I don't know . . . See, I'm out of my depth. I know that, don't think I don't. I've been too bloody Machiavellian for my own good . . . She's the main reason I pulled the plug on this, you know. Does that shock you?'

'I've heard worse reasons.'

'I had to think of a way to keep her around me . . . And in the old script, her role went nowhere . . . She only had about two weeks' work at the most. I mean, it wasn't the only reason I called a halt . . . the script was junk anyway . . . but I used it as an excuse. That's why you mustn't let me down. Without being too obvious, you and I have got to make sure that her role goes right through to the end . . .'

He broke off as Nigel brought in a tray of food. A moment later Suzanne and Charles joined us. Suzanne was holding an ice pack to one side of her face.

'What's happened?' Martin exclaimed, as professional concern displaced his more personal problems.

'I hit her,' Charles said.

'Don't listen to him, he's being stupid as usual. It's nothing, but when I was getting out of the bloody costume, I caught my foot in the hem and fell against the hair-dryer.'

'Let me see.' Martin took the ice pack away and examined the bruise on her cheek.

'The Dowager says he can fix it after lunch.'

'Well, I don't know. We won't be able to get in close. Is it painful?'

'Not now. Was at the time. Throbs a bit. Let's eat, I'm ravenous.'

'What's on the menu, Nigel?'

'Roast lamb – or, if you prefer cold, there's prawns, avocado salad and chicken.'

'Roast lamb?' Suzanne said. 'On a day like this?'

'Yes, dear,' Charles baited her, 'they killed the one that tried to get you.'

'You know what the sparks are like,' Nigel said, 'they must have the old hot grub.'

'I think cold all round, Nigel. And do we have any beer lager?'

'I'll get some.'

'Quite a first day, darling,' Martin said as we all sat down

163

'What's going to be the third thing? They always go in threes.'

'Oh, cheer us up, Charles, won't you?'

'What happens if you can't shoot on Suzanne this afternoon?'

'I've taken up Laura's stand-by. We'll do her scene instead.'

'Am I in that?'

'No, Charles. You've obviously read the script with your usual care.'

'Dear boy, you know me, the complete professional. I do whatever anybody tells me. But we're all slightly confused at the moment.'

I suspected that neither he nor Suzanne was too dismayed at the prospect of being let off the rest of the day.

During lunch I studied Martin carefully. Despite his inner turmoil, he presented a bland exterior. Whenever Laura's name came up in the conversation he gave no indication of what he was really thinking. Not that the conversation got very personal, it was mostly confined to shop talk, because for all Charles's bombast he cared like any other actor, and he was feeling insecure that day – the morning's shooting hadn't gone that well for anybody, he knew that and probably he was annoyed with himself, wishing he had been sharper, less prone to the nerves he was at such pains to conceal. Suzanne was also putting on a brave front, but no actress likes to feel that she isn't looking her best. All in all, it was an edgy atmosphere – false gaiety being generated, but behind everybody's smiles, the feeling that the film had got off to a bad start.

'When you stop to think about it,' Charles said at one point, 'this whole business is a crock of shit. I mean, we put the same amount of energy, talent, call it what you like, into some half-baked epic as we do when we're acting Shakespeare. I'm not putting you down, Martin, old dear, don't think that, because I'm rowing in the same boat . . . but don't you admit to some feeling of . . . regret is perhaps the wrong word . . . but some feeling of disappointment that we're not all engaged on something more important?'

'You think we ought to be making Shakespeare?'

'No, no, I'm not saying that – the Bard is the Bard, let's

leave him aside . . . leave him to Larry – but I mean, we've all made films we were more excited about, surely?'

'Yes.'

'Well, that's all I'm saying.'

'On the other hand,' Martin said slowly, 'we might surprise ourselves with this. It's early days yet.'

'Harvey, you haven't contributed much. What d'you think?'

'I'm in the hot seat,' I said. 'I've still got to finish the rewrite.'

'Yes, well there you have it. I'm sure you'll turn in something we can all get our teeth into . . . but in the final analysis, wouldn't you rather be working on something with a little more social content?'

'I've done one of those,' Suzanne chimed in. 'For the birds, dear.'

'Was that the title?'

'Ha ha. That thing I did last year, you know, I got a Golden Globe nomination, playing a paraplegic. That had so much social content you wanted to commit suicide afterwards. The three people who saw it did.'

'Yes, but you're quoting a way-out example. I mean films like *The Grapes of Wrath*. I saw it again the other night on the box. Terrific. They just don't make films like that any more. You talk about your last film. What about my last two films? In one I played Om, Lord High Master of some fucking planet I couldn't pronounce, and in the other I came on dressed like Cheetah in the old Tarzan movies, obliterated with hair, and ponced around some plastic Stonehenge . . . blush-making, dear, blush-making. But one has to pay the rent.'

'There's your answer,' Martin said.

On that gloomy note the lunch broke up. I went in Martin's car to the new location for Laura's scene. The Art Department had worked through the meal break in order to have everything ready, but when we arrived the camera and sound equipment had yet to be unloaded. Martin's chauffeur left us alone in the car and once again Martin returned to the subject that was occupying him most.

'There is another way you could help.'

'How's that?'

165

'This may sound ridiculous, but hear me out. All during lunch I was thinking about something you said, about word getting around . . . You know how I'm placed on the domestic scene . . . And there's nothing I can do about that, at least not until the film's finished. Then it might be different, but for the moment I couldn't cope with that upheaval as well. Apart from Harold, you're the only one who knows the full story, and he's not here . . .'

He hesitated, as though unable to frame the right words, and to tell the truth I had no idea what was going through his mind. I was still unable to decide whether his emotions were genuine or merely manufactured for some lost vanity he wished to parade. Was Laura his flickering version of the fire in Humbert Humbert's loins – the final butterfly he hoped to net – or just a fantasy he felt compelled to act out to the end? My reactions were coloured by my own newly-discovered compulsions towards Laura. I had no real compassion for his plight, the mask of concern I showed him concealed a rival. Yet when finally he blurted out his suggestion he again took me by surprise and I was forced to appear reluctant for fear that I would otherwise give myself away.

'Your situation's different . . . You're a free agent, so no one's likely to think it odd if you pay a lot of attention to her. What I was thinking is this. On those occasions when it's impossible for me to see her, could you take care of her? Act as a go-between, as it were? That way, at least I'd be sure she wasn't coming to any harm. Does that seem a crazy idea?'

'I don't know . . . Not crazy, perhaps, but difficult.'

'You mean the fucking boyfriend?'

'No . . . It's just that I'm not quite the free agent you think I am.'

'Oh?'

'I took your previous advice.' I gave him the conspiratorial, we're-all-men-of-the-world expression. 'Regarding Michelle.'

'Well, that's good, that's good. Good for you. God, you were quick off the mark. So that makes it all the more plausible.'

'Does it? How?'

'Well, without wishing to cramp your style, if you also pay a little attention to Laura, people will merely think you're playing the field.'

'What about Michelle? She might not take such a liberal view of things.'

'Yes, well I'm not asking you to have an affair with Laura. I'm just asking you to keep tabs on her.'

'Okay, then, I'll give it a try. I'm rewriting the script, I may as well rewrite your life story as well.'

I actually got him to smile on that. It was then that a unit car arrived, driven by Nigel, bringing Laura to the location. The moment Martin saw her he leapt out of our car and went to greet her. I remained where I was and watched them. He embraced her, and as I watched them kiss all our futures were irrevocably decided.

TEN

Michelle on the ravaged bed. Both of us slaked. Resting, eyes half-closed, the room split down the middle by a single shaft of light. My hand on her soft, spilt breasts. The scent of her mingling with the smells of the inn below, a blend of herbs and garlic and the rural earth-smell of flowers watered in the cool of the evening. Her hand between my legs. Sharp sounds of strangers talking on the terrace below. My mouth against her damp neck, touching a thin chain of gold. Sad thoughts of time lost. And already that sense of familiarity which anticipates boredom.

What was it Scott Fitzgerald wrote? *'A writer's temperament is continually making him do things he can never repair.'* Was that true of me that summer? Is it true now as I try to recall the fateful concatenation of circumstances which brought us all together? I could afford to be generous in my love-making with Michelle because it was purely sexual – there was nothing to repair because nothing had been broken.

While she slept I lay beside her and thought of what Martin had said. Had I betrayed anything by agreeing so readily? I had lived precariously for so many years, accepting secondhand scenarios, courting the destructive element, that Martin's suggestion did not strike me as anything unusual, merely another extension of my normal occupation. It was the season of the cuckoo and we were all intent on plundering alien nests. The more I pondered the more I convinced myself I had a perfect right to deceive him. I had not invited his confidences, he had volunteered them. The rest of his story I now dismissed as fantasy. I could not bring myself to believe in the existence of the would-be murdering boyfriend; that was the sort of sub-plot I automatically deleted. Martin was involved in his own shadow plays, betraying trusts and therefore inviting betrayals.

Michelle stirred beside me. 'Let's have room service,' she said.

'There are some who might say you've already had room service.'

'Are you always witty when you've made love?'

'Especially when I've made love.'

'You're on my arm.'

I shifted my position.

'What did you think of today?'

'Liked her, hated it.'

'No, be serious. Did you think it went well?'

'Filming is a director's medium,' I said. 'Or that's what it says in all those fancy film magazines. So don't ask me, I'm just a writer. Correction. A rewriter.'

'If you were rewriting me, how would you start?'

'I wouldn't change a line on your face. Not that you have any.'

'You're so witty.' She sat up and reached for a cigarette. 'I wouldn't mind rewriting myself one of these days. I'd like to change myself, change the way I live. I'm not ambitious, you see. I only act because of my husband. He likes people to know that he's married to an actress. It does something for him.'

'What would he do if he walked in now?'

'Kill you.'

'Please! Smile when you say that. He's jealous, is he?'

'Aren't all men?'

'I don't know. Are they?'

'All the men I've known. They want to own you. And that's not for me.'

'You don't think I'll want to own you?'

'No. We're just using each other, you and me.'

'Are you always this honest?'

'I'm not always this unfaithful.'

'Well, I'm flattered.'

I felt I had known her for years. It was a curious feeling, something I had never experienced before with any other woman.

Since the conversation with Martin I had made no move towards Laura. The film was easing into a less emotional routine. I continued working on the rewrite of the screenplay, progressing it at the rate of three or four pages a day, and at night Michelle and I usually dined alone and our affair – if one could so dignify it – had settled down into an exchange of needs. I lay myself open to a charge of cynicism, but the truce of love we had signed held, however implausible that may seem. Affection, yes, we had that in plenty, for sex without affection I have always felt to be unspeakable. We were sexually intrigued with each other, and sexually satisfied, discreet as far as the unit were concerned; and, since we had the Auberge to ourselves, I doubt whether, Martin apart, anybody suspected the extent of our relationship.

I surprised myself many times that summer. Prior to meeting Michelle I had never believed it was possible to have a sexual relationship devoid of fears – the fear of failure, of jealousy, ultimate loss. I said earlier that all the mistakes but one were mine and perhaps with Michelle I was too clever, too pleased with the uniqueness of our situation to realise what it was I really desired. I was free and therefore I was unfaithful. In the very act of taking her I constructed treacheries in my heart. It was Laura's body I wanted to enter, Laura's nipples that I longed to suck, Laura's cries I heard when finally Michelle threshed beneath me in that lonely journey of love which women travel.

Throughout it all I had the somnambulistic feeling of living in a dream, the conviction that nothing that transpired between Michelle and me could alter the inevitability of the future I had planned with Laura. The fever for possession never left me. 'Look after her for me,' Martin had said, stamping my visa for deceit. Yet – and in retrospect, I still can't understand this – I was in no hurry to take advantage of his mistaken generosity. If Martin could be devious, so could I.

I let a week pass before I visited the studio again, having convinced myself that my silence would have intrigued her: men have endless conceits. Late on the Saturday afternoon I rented a modest self-drive Renault and drove myself to

Nice. The 'dailies' – our jargon for the processed film – came down in batches from the labs in Paris and were usually screened an hour or so after the unit wrapped. Only the real enthusiasts in the unit bothered to turn up. Charles had told me that he never went to see himself: 'I don't even go and see the finished films, so I'm certainly not going to depress myself with the dailies. God forbid! I like to retain an image of myself looking like the young Robert Taylor, so I don't want to be confronted with Wallace Beery, if you go back that far, dear boy.'

'But doesn't it help you to see yourself the first few days, just to make sure you've set the character?'

'Dear heart, I set my character a hundred years ago and very nasty it was too. Since when I've never varied it. Apart from costume changes and the odd toupee, my dwindling public are never short-changed – they always get exactly the same performance.'

The late afternoon sun was shadowing the ruined sets on the front lot when I arrived at the studios, the perspectives changing as I drove up the crescent drive – now they were real, now they were cardboard. I parked outside the bar and went upstairs to have a beer while waiting for the crew to return from the location. The only occupant at that hour was Mischa. He was playing a manic game of electronic poker on a slot machine.

'If I had a computer brain I could beat this instrument of torture, I'm convinced of it. But I always draw to the wrong cards. Here, you try it.' He put a coin in for me. I hit a full house the first time.

'I don't believe it! I've been playing for an hour and made nothing.'

'I'll buy the drinks,' I said. We took our glasses and sat out under the trees. Clusters of midges circled over our heads. The studio cat picked a delicate path to sit beside our table.

'Only cat I ever knew that drinks beer,' Mischa said. 'Watch.' He poured some of his drink into an ashtray and put it down on the ground. He was right. The cat lapped the ashtray clean. I attempted to stroke it, but it slid from under my hand like a snake and took up a position out of reach.

'What I like about cats,' Mischa said, 'is they're so

171

arrogantly selective when granting their favours. That's why they were worshipped in Egypt. Goddesses. Aloof, disdainful, like beautiful women.'

'Who was that Englishman who wrote, in the dark all cats are grey, speaking of making love to a woman?'

'No idea. But whoever he was, he was stupid. Or queer. Or both maybe. Who wants to make love in the dark anyway? That's typically English. They take their pleasures like they take their beer, lukewarm. Give me fire and ice, and either way not in the dark. Love in the afternoon, ah! those are the memories. That was always the best.'

'Why past tense?'

'Why? he asks. Because . . .' A jet revving up for take-off blotted out the rest of the sentence. Mischa rolled the cold glass against his forehead and then, as the plane thundered into the sky, he suddenly sloshed the dregs of his beer in the direction of the cat. The animal jumped back a foot or so, then turned and walked slowly away.

'See that. She despises humans. Despises our need for affection. She takes it when it suits her, then she doesn't need it. A cat has a good life, I think.'

'We're in a philosophic mood this afternoon, are we?'

'Not really. A mood of contained anger. I was thinking, before you came, what a waste my life has been. When I was a student in Vienna, I wanted to be an artist, to leave something behind . . . and what have I done? I've spent my whole life designing, building sets that exist for a few weeks maybe and then are torn down, or else left to rot unheeded. It's like I've provided endless cities for the Goths to sack . . .'

'We're none of us in the posterity business.'

'You're right, my friend – just another junk movie. You know it and I know it. We are the little whores working for the pimps . . . And it isn't as if I don't have any ambitions left. I have. It's just that the energy isn't there . . . I've reached the point in my life where I have no creative energy any longer, no sexual energy . . . maybe the two are the same. There was a time when I could fuck all night and still put in a day's work at my drawing board. And drink. That too. Now, you see what I'm reduced to – a glass of beer, playing poker with a machine, those are my pleasures.'

'Cheer up,' I said.

'Yes, of course. Cheer up. Soon the great Martin will return from his labours, creating molehills from molehills, and we'll sit there and pretend that he's Picasso, when what he really is, is a faker turning out the second rate . . . That's the only thing that matters, walking down there. Youth! Youth, my friend.'

I turned and there below was Laura. I waved to her. She shielded her eyes to see who it was.

'Come and join us,' I shouted. 'I'll buy you a nice cool drink.'

'Let me get them,' Mischa said when she had climbed to our level. 'What will you have?'

'Oh, just a Perrier.'

'No, no, no! I refuse to give a pretty girl anything but champagne. Harvey and I are feeling sad, we need to be revitalised.'

'Beer and champagne,' I said, 'we'll be in great shape for the dailies.'

'It's the only way to see them.' I noticed he sucked in his stomach as he walked away to the bar.

'Are you sad?' Laura asked.

'Not particularly, and certainly not now . . . So, have you been working hard?'

'Today? No. I had to come in for some wardrobe fittings. Since you wrote the new scenes, I don't have enough changes.'

'What d'you think of them?'

'The clothes?'

'My new scenes.'

'I like them of course.'

'I might end up writing you the best part, you never know.'

'I just hope I can play it, and that Martin's pleased with me.'

'Oh, I don't think you need worry on that score . . . I'm sorry I haven't rung you.'

'Well, you've been busy.'

'Yes,' I said, 'but that wasn't the only reason. I thought maybe I worried you by what I said last time we met.'

Before she could reply Mischa returned carrying an ice

173

bucket and three glasses. He plonked it down on the table. 'There! Now we celebrate. I just thought of something. I know now who you remind me of, young lady . . .'

'Her name's Laura,' I said.

'I know her name. But I prefer to call her young lady. Don't interrupt me . . . I was going to say that walking towards you just now I suddenly remembered who it is she reminds me of. You know who?'

'Your first love in old Vienna.'

'No, not even my last love. I should have been so lucky. She reminds me of the young Hedy Lamarr.'

'Who was she?' Laura said.

Mischa paused in the act of pouring the champagne. 'There you have it, Harvey. I forgive you, my dear, why should you know? Hedy Lamarr was, how shall I put it? She was . . . dazzling. My God! I remember seeing her for the first time when I was working at the old UFA studios . . . She was like a piece of Meissen china, so delicate, so exquisite . . . I would have drunk this out of her slipper, literally, had I been given the opportunity that is, which I wasn't. So let's drink to you and my wasted youth.'

We drank. Mischa continued to stare at Laura.

'Since you haven't the faintest idea what I'm talking about, let me tell you something else . . . Today, nothing is left to the imagination. They wonder why nobody is going to the cinema any more. I'll tell you why . . .'

'Yes, cheer her up,' I said.

'I'm being serious. They're not going because there's no mystery, we've lost the art of suggestion. Take away all the veils and nobody stays for the encore, because that's it, the show's over before it begins. D'you know what I'm talking about? I'm talking about this mania to show everything, every pubic hair . . . No, please don't be offended, but I always have to say things as they are, and in my present state of health, a little champagne loosens the tongue . . . Hedy Lamarr created a great scandal when she was your age, because they photographed her in the nude . . . I mean, if you blinked, you missed it, but everybody went into shock! You'd have thought the world was coming to an end. And they saw nothing, just a few frames, her standing there in the water, her hands covering her breasts . . . pure,

not dirty, just a young girl, glimpsed through trees, naked.
If they made the same film today, you know what would
happen? They would have to put the camera between her
legs, because they have no taste, no talent, only a desire to
bring everybody down to their pathetic level. If I was
younger, if I had the money, you know what I'd do with
you, my dear young lady? I would make sure that you were
always covered from the neck downwards. I'd make you
more mysterious than Garbo. You think Garbo ever stripped for a film? Or Hepburn, or Davis? No, because they
had more class, and that's why they survived. Don't you
agree, Harvey?'

'I'm stunned,' I said. 'You really spark when you get
going, Mischa.'

'I should worry. The only good thing about reaching my
advanced age, is you no longer care what people think of
you. The point is, do you agree with me?'

'Yes, I think I do really.'

'But our little Laura here, what does she think? Look at
her . . . The Gioconda smile, eh? Listening to this boring
old man. What does she care what Hedy Lamarr did sixty
years ago? Times have changed . . . it's just that I haven't
changed with them. So I'll drink to my times and you drink
to yours, my dear.'

If I've given the impression that Mischa was a parody of
the mid-European artist so beloved by those Hollywood
movies, where all mid-Europeans wax lyrically nostalgic
for the Blue Danube (what we in the trade used to call the
Remember-Heidelburg-School-of-Acting), then the fault
is mine. He didn't cry into his non-vintage champagne, and
his diatribe to Laura was delivered with enormous gusto
and enjoyment. Sure, he was disenchanted all right, and I
guess he felt he had never realised whatever dream he
carried away from art college; but at the same time he'd
been around films long enough to pick up a sense of the
dramatic. If the truth were known I think he just liked
having a pretty young girl as an audience. I couldn't blame
him for that. I too wanted to impress Laura that afternoon.
She looked so achingly, yearningly vulnerable, sitting
across from me with the dropping sun haloing her head.
No, my silent quarrel with Mischa was not that he had

monopolised her, monopolised the conversation, but that she would couple me with him in terms of age and attitudes. Maybe in her eyes we were indistinguishable: two relics from another period, stuffed, prejudiced – even the champagne seemed to belong to another era, the age of the stage-door masher. She had asked for Perrier, that was the in-drink for the young set that summer.

I had no further opportunity to advance my own cause, for a few moments later a car pulled up in front of the bar, scattering the gravel and raising the dust. It was the latest Ferrari, bright red, low on the ground. Laura took a last sip of her champagne and stood up.

'You'll have to excuse me,' she said. 'I have to go now. Thank you for the drink.'

We watched her walk down the stairs to the waiting car. A young man got out as she approached and they kissed below us. She must have told him who we were because he glanced up in our direction and I saw him full face for the first time. I guessed him to be in his late twenties, dark, but with too much hair for my middle-aged taste. He had almost as much hair as Laura and when he turned his back to us and opened the passenger door for her he gave the appearance of being her twin sister. He was slim, moulded into his jeans, and he moved with that easy insolence which those who have it made always affect when they have a new audience. He was everything, in fact, that I wasn't and I had a healthy hate for him. I found it difficult to cast him as the dark invader of Martin's life: he didn't look particularly criminal to me, just smart and rich with the sort of face that turns up as the second lead in an episode of *Hart to Hart*.

He reversed the Ferrari in another show-off cloud of dust and accelerated round the corner of one of the sound stages.

'There you have it, Harvey,' Mischa said. 'That is a perfect example of why life is intolerable. After my brilliant comparison with Hedy Lamarr, what does she do? She drives away in a red Ferrari and that young stud reaps all the benefit . . . Of course my speech was all bullshit. If she was mine I'd keep her locked in an attic, I wouldn't let her near this lousy industry of ours. She wouldn't even be

176

allowed a television set. The only late-late show she'd see would be the last reel of my life.'

A certain mistaken euphoria often permeates a film crew viewing their work on the screen for the first time. Whenever I'm invited to see dailies I never cease to be amazed at how easily the third-rate satisfies those who aim for the moon. I'm inured to the fact that any additional dialogue I might have contributed will almost certainly have been changed: if ever my work reaches the screen intact the shock to my system is profound. I'm not accustomed to recognition.

Martin, as I have said, was no Ingmar Bergman. Technically he was proficient, and with the help of a good cameraman could usually find the best angles. His trouble was he had no real sense of the dramatic and invariably pointed his camera at the wrong person at the wrong time. I'm aware that certain of the more flatulent critics – that group who firmly believe that a Sam Fuller movie equals the Second Coming – have laboriously excavated something to admire in Martin's work. Delving into the tomb, they have brought into the light such beauties as *'His work is made more poignant by our awareness of his sceptical sense of humour waiting beyond the horizon'* – which I guess is another way of saying that they wished he had begun the film with the last fade-out. Less perceptive onlookers like me have somehow never appreciated Martin's *'perfect seamlessness'* which apparently stems from *'late Losey and middle Coppola'* though I go along with the suggestion that his films achieve *'a kind of classical distance from reality'*.

Certainly in that batch of dailies he had distanced himself from my rewrite. Between them, he and Latrough had skilfully contrived to end up with the dregs – a little of me, a little of them, and the remainder scooped from the original script. It was now a tale told by four idiots.

My only pleasant surprise that afternoon was when Laura suddenly appeared on the screen. Watching the slate numbers I could see that Martin had taken trouble with her performance. Her nervousness, isolated by a lack of technique, was all too apparent in the earlier takes. But gradually, helped presumably by Martin's uncharacteristic patience, she concealed most of her nerves and what finally became trapped on the celluloid was a hesitancy that was curiously effective. Obviously I viewed her with a biased eye, but even allowing for that, she seemed to be gifted with that indefinable quality no acting school can impose, but which only the camera discovers. With some actors and actresses an alchemy takes place when they face the lens. It is often not discernible on the floor, and yet a subtle transformation takes place when the exposed negative is developed and printed. Monroe, I am told, appeared devoid of talent on the floor and was often the despair of her directors and fellow actors – yet several of her major performances confounded her critics. Don't misunderstand me, I am not classing Laura in the same league as Monroe, but to a degree she did possess the same mixture of innocence and sexuality that the camera photographed. It never hurts for a director to conduct a love affair through the lens, though in Martin's case there was something beyond the normal evidence.

I watched enthralled and yet with a sense of foreboding, the feeling that I was watching a film within a film. I had cast myself for a role I was ill-fitted to play and as if that was not complicated enough I had, in addition, ensured that I was no longer a free agent. I might kid myself that the relationship I had with Michelle was easily severed, but in my heart I knew only too well that sex tangles all our acts. I had aimed to deceive the deceiver, and been trapped by my own cleverness – or was it weakness?

It was the same evening that events took another unexpected turn. For reasons difficult to fathom, Latrough suddenly decided I was the closest thing he had to a friend on the unit. It must be true that it's lonely at the top. He invited me out to dinner at La Bonne Auberge on the coast road between Antibes and Juan-les-Pins, the sort of three-star eating house which demands that you take out a second mortgage before ordering the main course. Not that it was any great problem for me to sample that menu – I have never spurned the bread that others cast upon my waters. The food and service were superb, the wines nectar (since Latrough was sufficiently ignorant to leave the choice to the wine waiter). The only blot on the evening was Latrough's monologue. To hear him talk he had been insulted by or had insulted seventy-five per cent of the population of Beverly Hills.

He took a long time to get to the point.

'The only reason I didn't immediately jump into bed with you, Harvey' – the mental picture terrified me – 'was because I thought you were Martin's man. And anybody who works for me has to be my man, period. But I want you to know, and that's the reason I brought you here, I've revised my opinion of you. I'm thinking ahead now, and I'm planning on various levels. One of these days, and between you and me, it could be sooner rather than later, I'm going to be running one of the major studios. I won't say which one, but the pitch has been made. I got backing, connections, I won't say who with, but I'm not talking chopped chicken liver. I'm talking about backing with a big fucking B. Okay? You take my meaning?'

'I believe you.' There was no good reason not to. Compared to some of the people currently in charge of the studios at that time, he was a Rhodes scholar.

'Like I told you, I'm planning years ahead. When I push the boat out, I want to drown those mothers. But I need someone to be involved, to take some of the load off me. I got a dozen projects under option, and what I need is somebody with the know-how to handle the image. Don't get me wrong, I could handle it myself, but right now I haven't got the time to do that and watch the store. I've got to be out in the market-place putting all the pieces together.'

'Sorry,' I said. 'Image, you said. What image exactly?'

'My fucking image, who else?'

'Ah, yes, I see.' I didn't.

'Take Martin for example. You think this is the start of a great relationship between him and me? Wrong. This is strictly a one-off. I kissed his ass because right now he was all I could afford. But I'll tell you something about Martin. He's a great con artist. He puts up a good front. That fucking great castle he lives in, that wife of his who makes like she never goes to the toilet, the snotty butler, all guaranteed to make you feel he's doing you a favour. Well,

179

listen, I'm the one doing him the favour right now, and only because it suits me. But I do hand him this much: he projects the right image. Maybe it's because he's fucking British or something. I don't know. He's got four ounces of talent and a ton of chutzpah and he's not even Jewish!'

I helped myself to the last of the claret. There was no point in attempting to integrate myself into the conversation.

'So, image-wise, I've got some ground to make up. What I've got to do is make sure everybody knows I'm not just another pretty face. By the way, this guy, this publicity hack we got down here, what's his name . . .?'

'Marvin?'

'That his name? How d'you rate him?'

'He seems keen,' I said.

'Keen? In my book he's a wrist-job. I'm thinking of eighty-sixing him' – he used crew slang denoting the old heave-ho – 'and d'you know why? Because every time he gets me a mention he has to give them my Hong Kong credits.' He fumbled in his wallet and brought out a folded newspaper clipping. 'Look at this in last week's *LA Times*. See the headline? "From Porn to Provence". I need that like I need a bran enema.'

'They love alliteration,' I said.

'Love what?'

'They can be rough sometimes. Maybe it wasn't Marvin's fault.'

'Look, we all have to start somewhere. I raised a little bread with the Chinks and got myself launched, right. Not with porn, just adult movies, a little erotic maybe, I mean you saw a few tits and some soft-focus humping, but nothing you couldn't take your mother to.' He folded the cutting into his wallet, like it was a letter from the White House he wanted to preserve for his memoirs. He caught me looking at him. 'Why do I keep it? That what you're thinking? Just to remind me never to go back. I'm here now and ain't never going back. So that's where you come in. I'll cut you in on the ground floor.'

He snapped his fingers for a waiter. 'Bring us some of your best brandy. Bring the bottle.'

As the waiter retreated he looked past me to one of the other tables.

'Isn't that the chick in our movie?'

I turned. For the second time that day I was surprised at seeing Laura. She was sitting at a corner table with the owner of the red Ferrari. Their heads were close together.

'Yes,' I said.

'Maybe I'm paying her too much if she can afford to eat here.'

'It's always possible that she's not picking up the tab,' I said, knowing as I said it that the sarcasm would go right over his head.

'I've got to get around to some of these chicks. Been too busy to get laid recently. That's unlike me . . . Another part of my image I've neglected.' He gave a leer in Laura's direction. The waiter came back with a newly-opened bottle of brandy and began to warm two glasses over a small burner. 'Jesus! no wonder they charge here, with all the bullshit,' Latrough said. The waiter poured two generous tots, swirling the liquid in the glasses before placing them before us. 'So, let's talk about my image. I want to get your input, Harvey . . . Is this kosher? You know about brandy?'

'I don't know about kosher, but, yes, I'd say this was very good. Two or three of these and we'd feel no pain.'

'See, I don't mind paying, Harvey, just so long as I'm getting what I want. Before I pick your brains, you want to know my idea?'

I nodded, cupping the warm brandy balloon in my hands. Now that I was aware of Laura in the restaurant I found it even more difficult to follow on his rambling dialogue. Jealousy flooded through me, sweeping away concentration.

'I've been bouncing this around in my court – because I think it's got a lot going for it. How'd it be if while we're still down here shooting, I fly in a plane load of media people, put them up in an hotel, show them a bit of the footage, and then have Suzanne host me a dinner?'

I wanted to say: did you think of that yourself or did you read it in a book? 'Terrific, great idea,' I said.

'Wait, that's only half of it. After the dinner I want to

181

make a policy speech. I saw Levine do that once – not that I'm about to make the same spiel as he did – and he really hyped them. See, I don't want to buy space, because that sucks. This way I'd get editorial space. And image-wise, that's class.'

I took a sip of my brandy; it was difficult for me to keep a straight face.

'The way I see it, I wine them and dine them and maybe lay on a few broads for the last course, they ain't gonna knock me, right?'

'If there's any gratitude left in the world, they won't.'

'You're damn right. And that's where you come in.'

Oh, God, I thought, I'm being cast as the universal pimp. 'You want me at the dinner?'

'Sure, sure, you'll get an invite, but that's not it. I want you to write my speech. Like, I could write it myself, but I got so damn many balls in the air at the moment. I'd give you the general line and you could take it from there.'

'You don't think that an important policy speech like that should really be in your own words?'

'It's gonna be in my own words. Once you've delivered, I'll knock it around. I've just got to get a draft. And look, I don't expect you to do it for nothing. You play it right, you've got a meal ticket. I want a class speech. If I wanted a few stag jokes, I'd ask that asshole publicity guy to get out his Bob Hope gag book. I'm talking about a speech that's gonna make headlines . . .'

The more he blathered on, the more depressed I became at the prospect he was offering. The idea of writing a policy statement which embraced his sterile philosophy for the future of the film industry struck me as about as exciting as composing a jacket blurb for a book on terminal cancer.

'. . . an honest speech that for once tells it like it is,' Latrough said, but all I saw in his face was the same old phoniness and greed. 'What d'you say?'

'I'll give it a try . . . You block out the main themes and I'll see what I can contribute after that.'

'Great! This is just the beginning, Harvey. Those mothers are gonna hear a lot of me, and if you're with me now you gonna be travelling first class all the way.'

When the check came he made a point of not looking at

the total, paid with a gold American Express card and left a monstrously large tip – but whether to impress me or because he couldn't count was food for conjecture.

'Tell me the name of that chick again,' he said as we were on our way out.

'Taylor. Laura Taylor.'

He paused by Laura's table.

'Hi, Laura.'

She looked up, startled, her eyes darting from Latrough to me.

'Oh, Mr Latrough . . . Good evening. This is Jean Gelbard . . . David Latrough, the producer, and Harvey Burgess, the writer.'

Gelbard nodded at us, but didn't get up.

'D'you mind if we join you for a few minutes?' Latrough was devoid of sensitivity. I pulled a face at Laura behind his back and she gave me a wan smile.

'Can I buy you a drink?' Latrough said as he sat down.

'No, thank you,' Gelbard said, 'we have something already.'

'So, how're you enjoying the film, Laura?'

'Very much.'

Latrough turned to Gelbard. 'Are you in the business?'

'Which business is that?' He was well-spoken, quietly spoken, though with an edge to his perceptible accent.

'Which business? The movies.'

'No, I'm not.'

'What d'you do?'

'I'm an importer.'

'What d'you import?'

'A variety of things. Electronics mostly.'

'You're making a living, huh?'

'You could say that.'

'So how does it feel to be dating our young star?'

'Perhaps I should ask you how it feels to be employing her,' Gelbard said smoothly. For the first time I caught a glimpse of the menace that Martin had spoken of. Not that I could blame him for taking an immediate dislike to Latrough.

'Harvey here is writing up her role. On my instructions. We treating you right, Laura?'

'No complaints,' she said.

'You got any complaints, come straight to me. I'm the one who signs the checks, remember.'

'If she ever does have any complaints,' Gelbard said, 'I'll make sure you're the first to know.'

Even then Latrough didn't get the message. 'This is a big break for your girlfriend, Jean' – he pronounced it as in Gene Kelly – 'and I'm taking a personal interest in her career. If this one works, I'll have something more for her.'

Gelbard stared him out. I couldn't think of anything to say that would relieve the situation.

'Okay, well I'll leave you two kids to finish your meal. Jean, good to meet you. Stay cool. And don't be late for your call, Laura.'

As we left the dining room, he said: 'I've got to find time to get my act together. That's great pussy.'

I suppressed an urge to push him under the wheels of his chauffeur-driven Mercedes as it glided to receive him. He gave the doorman a 100 franc note.

'What time is it? Think I'll play a little roulette. You want to join me?'

'I'm not a good gambler,' I said. 'Besides I have to get back to my hot typewriter. I'm working for a very tough producer.'

'That's what I like to hear. Stay with it, Harvey. And don't forget, start thinking about the speech.'

'No, of course not. I can't wait.'

It wasn't until he had driven away that I remembered I had left my own car in the studio parking lot. I turned back into the restaurant to have the doorman order me a taxi. He was telephoning for one when Laura and Gelbard walked out. Gelbard paused.

'Where are you trying to get to?'

'Back to the studio. My date left without me.'

'You got lucky,' he said. 'We'll give you a lift.'

'That's very kind. Thank you.'

I accompanied them to where his Ferrari was parked.

'Can you squeeze in the back?'

'Sure. I was admiring it this afternoon. Great looking car.'

'Yeah. It gets me around.'

With the car doors closed Laura's perfume was very disturbing. She turned to me the moment we were under way.

'I was telling Jean he's not well liked by the unit.'

'No, I guess that's a fair statement.'

I caught Gelbard regarding me in his rear-view mirror.

'How can you work for him, a pig like that?'

'Good question. It's marginally better than starving and, fortunately, it's not permanent. As a matter of fact before he so rudely interrupted your dinner I was thinking of committing suicide there at the table. But I suppose I'm used to types like that. I seem to have spent most of my life with them.'

'He wouldn't last with me,' Gelbard said. 'I'd kill him.' He didn't say it with any menace – he just sounded like a young man who didn't care for his girlfriend to be ogled and propositioned.

As soon as we were on the narrow coast road, he put his foot down, weaving in and out of the myriad small Renaults, Fiats and Volkswagens with heart-stopping skill. Was that merely to impress me or Laura I wondered? Obviously she had driven with him before because she seemed relaxed and several times turned to me with a smile, but I could think of nothing to say to her. Perhaps it was my long-standing fear of being driven at such speed that inhibited me that night, or again, perhaps I had the sense that my cause was a lost one. The odds seemed stacked against me. Now that I had finally met Gelbard face to face all my previous confidence vanished. I could deal with Martin as a rival, but it was Gelbard's youth rather than the sinister background which Martin had pinned to him that frightened me. I could come to terms with menace but there is no defence against the years.

When we got to Cagnes he eased his foot from the throttle and passed a joint around. I suppose Martin would have seen that as further evidence of his culpability, and as we eased into the thick traffic along the Promenade des Anglais I thought again of that extraordinary telephone conversation. Was Gelbard the sort of young man to attempt what might have been a fatal accident? He didn't give that impression, although one should always be wary of judging the emotions of others against one's own. He seemed too self-assured, too careful of his own image, and young men of his type who have the run of the South of France in a brand new Ferrari are not usually driven to such desperate acts for the sake of a girl. There are too many pickings to be had during the season, too many equal choices on the topless beaches.

I took the joint from Laura and tasted her lipstick as I inhaled. It seemed, in my confused state that night, achingly erotic and my thoughts winged to those other intimacies which presumably Gelbard and Laura would shortly share. I wondered where he would take her once I had been deposited at my hotel? I would be dropped off like some maiden aunt, somebody who had merely delayed certain pleasures. I had a sudden vision, heightened by the strength of the joint, of Laura spread-eagled beneath him; her black hair webbed on his pillow, her mouth, which I had only sampled by proxy, wetly opened to receive him. Far more than the fear I had experienced during the early part of the drive, these images destroyed me. They were coupled with a terrible envy that knifed through me like colic as some of Martin's hate infected me.

'Have you seen any of the film?' Laura asked. She took back the joint and put it between Gelbard's lips so that he wouldn't have to take his eyes off the road.

'I've seen some of the dailies, not all.'

'Good?'

'I thought you looked good.'

'Did I act it well?'

'I thought so.'

'Martin was very sweet to me. He helped me a lot.'

'That's what directors are for,' I said, watching Gelbard for any reaction to Martin's name. He gave no indication that he was listening to our conversation and I decided to press him. 'Have you met Martin, Jean?'

'Yeah, I think so. I've seen him around when I've been at the studio.'

'He has a very high opinion of this young lady's talents. As do we all, of course.'

'Good. You want the rest of this, chérie?'

186

'No, I've had enough,' Laura said. Gelbard held the joint over his shoulder.

'Me, too,' I said.

He pressed the button and lowered his window. The night air rushed at me as he flicked the remainder of the joint into the darkness. Then he fiddled with the elaborate car radio, stabbing at the controls to find a music programme, but all we heard was a variety of French voices droning intensely. Gelbard settled for a cassette. It was Gheorghe Zamfir playing the music from the film, *Picnic At Hanging Rock*, that haunting theme for Pan-pipes.

'Did you ever see that film?' I said.

'Me? You asking me?' Gelbard said. He shook his head. 'I don't go to the movies much. I run a few video-tapes at home.'

'He likes all the naughty films,' Laura said.

'So? You watch them too.'

'Only because you make me. I think most of them are gross.'

I felt the knife go in again. Martin had told me he wrote poetry and now I believed him – isn't there an element of lunacy in all passions? The new revelation that Laura and Gelbard watched porn video-tapes together filled me with a new sense of loss. I had wanted her to be uncorrupted – not untouched, that would have been asking too much – but uncorrupted. As a rival Martin was acceptable, because at least he granted her the same qualities that I wished to bestow. The noises of panic seemed as loud as the throaty roar of the Ferrari's twelve cylinders. Something I had planted with such expectations had withered. Now, unexpectedly, I longed for the journey to end. I wanted to put myself beyond the reach of their intimacy.

'He probably won't even go and see this film,' Laura was saying. 'Won't you even go and see me?'

'Maybe.'

'I think you're stinking,' she said in a voice mulled with affection. 'You'll come and see me, won't you, Harvey?'

'If they invite me,' I said, hating the self-pity that I could not control. 'The writer's only allowed in under sufferance.' But her question had ignited another fuse, one that would burn long into the nights to come. The first, untouched image of her would always be there on the negative of the film. I could see myself in years to come searching the entertainment columns for some out-of-the-way theatre that might be showing the film, and going there, alone, just to be reminded of her beauty.

When we finally arrived outside the Auberge I could not wait to escape. My thanks and our goodbyes were perfunctory. Laura kissed me on my blank cheek, the way sisters kiss elder brothers.

ELEVEN

'I was just passing by,' Marvin said, 'so I though I'd look in on the off-chance.' He stared at me round the door with hurt eyes. 'Am I disturbing you?'

'Yes,' I said, 'but come on in anyway. You want a cup of coffee. Help yourself to the remains of my pot. It's still vaguely drinkable.'

'You depressed?'

'Not more than usual. Let's say that I'm tired of writing dialogue that nobody ever says. I sometimes get the impression that the film's over but nobody's told me, that I'm still sitting here churning out the pages but the caravan's moved on.'

'Join the club,' Marvin said. 'Listen, you think you've got problems? I just spent the morning with our gifted producer. Know what he laid on me? I gotta organise a junket for him. He wants to fly in the world's Press for a preview, like we're making Proust or something.'

'Why, Marvin,' I said, 'I do believe that somewhere behind that rough exterior there lurks a fugitive from literature.'

'Surprised you, huh? I bet you thought I'd never heard of Proust. Never judge a whorehouse by the entrance.'

'May I use that?'

'Be my guest. Anyway, as if that wasn't enough, I then had Martin giving me a hard time because I wasn't getting the kid enough space.'

'Which kid?'

'Which kid he says! Laura. You know Martin's got the hots for her. He's playing Daddy-Long-Legs or some fucking thing, who knows? So what am I supposed to do? I said.

You want a real revolution on top of everything else? I've got to keep the whole lot of those pampered bastards sweet. Like I plant a story about our leading man, and Suzanne goes into intensive care. I try and get her a mention as a serious actress and all they want is a shot of her chest melons. So naturally they print a shot of her celebrated cantaloups and she carries on like I personally set out to wreck her quote career unquote. How can I win? I can't win.'

Despite the fact that his conversation was a monologue of pain, I welcomed the interruption that day. There is something comforting about discussing a common enemy and at that stage in the proceedings a certain disenchantment with my lot had set in – an old, familiar enemy, to be sure. The rewrite on the script staggered along as I struggled to satisfy at least four different masters. Every since Latrough had claimed me for his own he tended to take my side in any argument with Martin, which in turn hardened Martin's attitude towards any innovations I tried to introduce. Naturally, on the floor, Suzanne and especially Charles threw in their two cents and what finally reached the screen was just above the waterline of the third-rate. Not that anybody seemed to care. Martin was behaving as though he was embarked on nothing less than the definitive film of the French Revolution, and of course he was all the time angling to build up Laura's role, a ploy positively guaranteed to get up Suzanne's nose.

I hadn't seen Laura since the night she and Gelbard gave me a lift home. I don't mind taking my chances, but I stop short of pure masochism. To compensate I still had the home comfort of Michelle. I envied her ability to view Life's battlefield from afar, just as I despised myself for being so craven. So poor, battered old Marvin allowed me to release a little steam – people who have undergone the same surgery love to compare scars.

While Marvin chuntered on, sipping my cold coffee and chain-smoking his way through a packet of Marlboros, the germ of an idea took root in my mind. Like most schemes of its kind it seemed amusing at the time and I made yet another mistake by not thinking it through to its inevitable, logical conclusion. It was intended to be a 'jolly jape' as

190

Charles might have said, the sort of idea he was quite capable of launching himself when in his cups. I didn't have even that justification: the idea came to me when I was reasonably sober, and it was conceived in pure malice. As I said before, most of the mistakes were of my own making that summer, more's the pity, and I've lived to regret them ever since.

Not that Marvin and I stayed sober. We progressed from cold coffee to three bottles of Beaune over a lunch punctuated with anecdotes about why the industry had gone down the tubes. After that I was scarcely in condition to take a shot at a Writers Guild award, so we trundled back to my suite armed with some vintage Calvados and exchanged more racy memoirs. It was during this session that my poisoned dart penetrated Marvin's subconscious.

'The point is, Harvey . . . See, I remembered, I didn't call you Harv . . . you and me, we care. We care like hell.'

'True.'

'That's right, eh? I'm telling it like it is. We care, we fucking care, even though all those bastards out there are screwing us, having always screwed us. I *care* when I sit down at the typewriter and knock out a biog. You care when you sit down at your typewriter and write that beautiful dialogue nobody is ever gonna say. But *why* do we care?'

'Yeah, why do we care?'

'I'll tell you why. We care . . . we care because . . .' Tears started to pour down his cheeks. Then he embarked upon one of his monumental coughing bouts. I lurched across to him and thumped him on the back.

'What happened? Little Calvados go down the wrong way?'

'Everything goes down the wrong way, baby,' he said when he finally recovered. 'You know who I blame? I don't hold it against the fucking Latroughs of this business, or the Martins. I mean, what are they?'

'Nature's noblemen.'

'They get paid more, that's all. They're victims just like you and me. They live better, they eat better, they drive bigger fucking automobiles and they get more pussy . . . Well, maybe not more pussy . . . but they're still victims of

191

the fucking system. It's the system, Harvey, always has been, always will be. Tell you something, the good die young in this business . . . Did you write that?'

'No,' I said.

'You didn't? . . . You should have done. The good die young and the pigs survive. No matter what, they always come up smelling of roses. We can't join 'em, Harvey, and we can't lick 'em. They're fucking bullet proof. If you prick them, do they bleed? Do they fuck. You and me, if we operated like them, we'd be behind bars, but they're still walking tall in the streets, calling the shots. They're the great indestructibles, Harvey. They make Nixon look like a bit player. Like, in the old days they were monsters, all of them monsters – Cohn, Zanuck, Warner, L.B. – and I worked for some of them, I even worked for the daddy of them all, Howard Hughes, he was a crazed monster, but they all had one thing in common that these tight-assed accountants and ex-agents don't have, they actually cared about movies. We used to have fun in those days, because everybody cared in their own way. Sure it was rough because those old monsters played it rough, and you had to stay on your toes . . . Now, what is it? A lot of jumped-up-ten-per-centers, wheeling and fucking dealing us all out of a living. They ain't interested in making movies any more, all they're interested in is seeing how many studios they can shaft before they're found out.'

He ran out of steam at that point, slumped in one of my armchairs, staring into God knows what private future. Watching him was like watching some damaged piece of film: the sprocket holes had been ripped from previous screenings and you knew that it was only a matter of time before the whole thing jammed up for good.

'Why don't we plant a few stories, you and me?'

'Do what?'

'I just had a great idea,' I said. 'You're the one with the connections, Marvin, and I'm the one with the ideas.'

'Stories?'

'Yeah. News items. Hot news items. Nothing that's going to win you the Pulitzer Prize, but stuff that plays them at their own game.'

'Like for instance?'

192

'I don't know, I only just thought of it. But it can go any way you like. You want an example?'

'Lay one on me.'

'Okay. Try this . . . *"Charles Croze is so impressed with the performance being turned in by his co-star Suzanne Saphire that he is insisting he will never make another film without her."* '

'I like it, I like it! Give me another.'

'We switch it . . . *"Suzanne Saphire, currently giving her all in 'The Bastille Connection', is carrying her love scenes over into real life. The Côte d'Azur is alive to the sound of the sweet music being played between her and Charles Croze."* '

'Sensational! Hey, I got one for you. How about, *"David Latrough, who people are talking about as the natural successor to Harry Cohn, only has two things on his mind right now. One is Laura Taylor and the other is Laura Taylor, the rising young star of his latest film."* Now that's vintage Louella, and I should know. She used to pitch one of those every day.'

Looking back, I don't believe either of us had any inkling of the repercussions these gags would produce. Through the Calvados-haze they seemed wildly funny, albeit on a schoolboy level. For my part, having planted the idea, I forgot about it, like one of those letters you compose in your head when riled, and then never write – the contemplation of revenge being sweeter than the execution. But I guess Marvin's wounds were deeper than mine; over the years they had penetrated into the marrow of the bone, and he didn't forget. I often think about that afternoon, for in a way, far more than Martin's original invitation, it determined the events to come.

Not that there was any immediate explosion. I fought my way out of a mother of a hangover and went back to doctoring the script. It had long since ceased to be straightforward rewrite. Every day the production office issued pink, yellow and green Xeroxed pages to the artists. I now thought of it as I would a Lego set. There is an old adage which goes, 'if you attempt to build a horse by committee you end up with a camel.' In the beginning I'd tried to introduce a coherent plot, but the many interpolations had made a mockery of my attempts. Not that anybody seemed too concerned; I suppose we'd all travelled the same dusty road too often to be surprised. Word came back that the dailies, which I no longer bothered to attend, looked ravishing. Great photography hides a multitude of sins.

My relationship with Michelle had fallen into a cosy routine. In some ways, I suppose, we were like an old married couple. I saw little of her during the days because with so many changes the production office were not taking any chances: all the main artists were kept permanently on call, just in case Martin suddenly decided to shoot an unscheduled scene. Very often she was called and made up and then didn't work, a routine that makes some actors exceedingly bolshie. Michelle took it all in her usual sanguine fashion. She read a lot and progressed her needle-point and had enough of the French housewife in her to regard the extra money she was earning as ample compensation for the boredom. My own experience told me that by now the film must have been well over budget – not that I was ever consulted on such matters. I stayed home, turning in my daily quota of pages according to the junta's orders, and dreamed of Laura.

'Jealous?' Michelle said. 'Why on earth should I be jealous?'

'Because I want you to be.'

'That's irrational.'

'I know. I just want somebody to be jealous of me for a change.'

'Okay, I'm jealous, I'm consumed with that fury hell hath no whatever-it-is – that famous saying the British still cling to.'

'Why bring them in? I'm not British.'

'British, American, you're all the same. Now you don't fool me. You're just looking for an excuse to get angry with me, because you've been sitting at your typewriter all day wondering what is happening to your little Laura. You want me to tell you? Our director, who is just as infatuated as you, is throwing the picture to her. You remember that new scene you wrote for me? Well, by some strange

194

coincidence most of my best lines seem to have been given to her.'

'But they wouldn't fit her character.'

'Of course they don't fit, but that doesn't seem to bother our director.'

'Lunatic.'

'Filming is lunatic. I'm a lunatic to be here, you're a lunatic to upset yourself. But it's a nice asylum and they feed us well, they give us cars to ride in, and I can't think of any easier way of earning a living. You know what I do? I sit there and think, well another day, another instalment on the swimming pool. So, don't take it so seriously. Don't take anything seriously . . . Not even your beloved Laura, because she's learning fast, and she's trouble, believe me.'

'I do believe you,' I said.

'So, what d'you want to do? I can give you three choices. You want to go to bed and then eat, or eat and then go to bed, or eat in bed?'

'I'm a gentleman. I always leave the choice to the lady.'

'That's your first mistake.'

'You think the caveman approach is the best?'

'Depends. Sometimes.'

'I'm very bad at swinging from trees. And I'm feeling my age.'

'Oh, poor thing. Okay, I'll decide for us. We have a bath, together if your age will stand it, and then you can take me out to dinner. Somewhere romantic overlooking the sea. I want a great deal to eat and some nice wine. I'm tired of this bloody hotel, tired of their menu, tired of the head waiter's face, in fact tired. But after the meal you are going to give me, I shall be very loving and make you forget all about Laura, the script, your age, Martin, the whole sodding works.'

'Your command of English is improving.'

'I'm an actress, remember?'

'Show me a woman who isn't.'

'How does that plan sound to you?'

'Not bad, not bad at all.'

'So, will you run my bath for me?'

'I'll run *our* bath.'

'So you can be corrupted after all?'

'Oh, I corrupt very easily,' I said.

Then it was Martin's turn to romance me. Much to my amazement I received a formal, printed invitation to dinner – embossed lettering on a gold-edged card, with the words *black tie* in the bottom right hand corner: the works. *Mr and Mrs Martin James Request The Pleasure Of Your Company for Dinner on Friday August 22nd.* I didn't have a black tie, and my first instinct was not to go out and buy one, but the next time I delivered some pages to Martin at the studio he buttonholed me on the subject.

'You haven't replied to Alice's invitation.'

'No, well the truth is I didn't pack a dinner jacket.'

'Oh. Well, I'm sure wardrobe could find one. See, I'm particularly anxious that you should be there.'

'What're you celebrating?'

'Nothing. Alice likes to throw a couple of good dinners during the season. I mean, we get invited out and one has to show the flag in return.'

'What's the cast list?'

'Well obviously a lot of them are Alice's friends more than mine, people she plays gin with, so I need a few chums around to keep my end up.'

'Rentacrowd, huh?'

'No, don't be like that. We've asked Suzanne and Charles, naturally.'

'Since when has Charles ever been natural?'

'Look, I had to ask him. Alice's friends would be mortified if they didn't get to meet him. Don't be so bloody toffy-nosed, just say yes . . .'

'It's not really my scene, with or without a black tie.'

'Well, forget that, do it for me, you owe me one . . . And besides, I want you to bring somebody.'

'Who would that be?'

'Laura, of course. Alice won't smell a rat if she comes with you.'

'Have you asked Michelle?'

'I don't think so. Why?'

196

'Isn't that slightly embarrassing?'

'No, it's an all-British crowd, she'd feel out of place . . . She'll understand. So will you?'

'Who am I to refuse such a favour?'

'Chum, it is a favour, believe me. I see her on the set most days, but of course that's not the same thing. With any luck I can spend some time alone with her after dinner while Alice gets her nose down to the gin table.'

'You don't want me to write you any dialogue, I suppose?'

It took a second or two before he saw the joke.

'Okay,' I said, 'you talked me into it. So, how's it going? Any more threats from the boyfriend?'

'No. It's all been very quiet. I think I must have frightened him off, he doesn't seem to be much in evidence these days.'

'He was in evidence the other night,' I said.

'What d'you mean?'

'I saw them together.'

'Where?'

'Our generous producer took me out to dinner at the second most expensive restaurant in the world, and there they were – *tête à tête,* I believe the expression is.'

'You sure it was him?'

'Gelbard, isn't that the name?' Martin nodded. Disbelief had been replaced by fear in his face. 'We were introduced. As a matter of fact, he gave me a lift home in his very impressive Ferrari.'

'When was this?'

'I don't know, what's today? A week yesterday.'

'Why didn't you tell me?'

'I haven't seen you, have I?'

'You could have got word.'

'Well, I'm sorry, I didn't think.'

'What did you make of him?'

'He was perfectly pleasant to me.' I was enjoying keeping him on the hook. 'Didn't say a great deal, but I have to admit he didn't exactly live up to your lurid description. Just a rich young Joe driving a fast car, not bad looking I suppose.'

'How did she behave?'

'Laura was fine. I thought he behaved very well in the circumstances.'

'What circumstances?'

'Martin, this isn't an episode of *Magnun*. You're grilling me.'

'Sorry. Sorry, chum. Just that I'm anxious to know every detail. What did you mean by "circumstances"?'

'David was his usual tactful self, of course. I mean, don't think I went up to them, it was David, he just barged right in and sat down. I don't think Gelbard took too kindly to that, especially since our producer made no secret of the fact that he fancied our Laura.'

'Little shit! What else?'

'That's about it. We stayed at their table for a bit, then with that inbuilt charm for which he's famous, our David left me stranded on the pavement, and Gelbard offered to drive me home.'

'Did you talk in the car?'

'Course we talked. But not about anything special. We shared a joint.'

'I told you he's into drugs.'

'Martin, come on! Who doesn't smoke a joint these days?'

'I don't.'

'Perhaps you should, it'd relax you.'

'How did she behave towards him?'

'You asked me that. Listen, I didn't spend the night with them. They were having dinner in a public restaurant, she didn't throw the *plat du jour* in his face, nor I imagine did they fornicate on the dessert trolly. At those prices nobody could afford to.'

'But was she friendly to him?'

'Yes.'

'Oh, Christ! You don't know what this has done to me.'

'Well, I'm sorry I mentioned it.'

'No, no. I want to know. I want to know everything . . . See, she told me he was out of town.'

'Perhaps he came back unexpectedly.'

'What day was that again?'

I worked it out for him. He consulted the schedule on his desk. 'She was on call that day, but she finished early as far

198

as I remember . . . I can check on the progress reports.'

'Martin,' I said, 'why crucify yourself? So she still sees him. He's young, he's not married, he drives a fast car . . . You think he's a crook, well, girls go out with crooks.'

'You don't understand.'

'I understand only too well, but just weigh it up for yourself . . . What've you got to offer in exchange? You gonna give up the villa, make a settlement with Alice, take Laura off to Tahiti, live the simple life 'til death do you part? Come on, be realistic. It's not a situation where you can play it fifty-fifty, red or black, you've either got to get out of the game or else put your money on a single number. Aren't I right?'

I didn't expect him to agree with me. Poor sod, he was obsessed, the logic of the situation was not something he wanted spelt out. I could understand it. On the set he could play God and Casanova in full view, act out his fantasies without inhibition – directors were expected to romance their leading ladies, it was nothing out of the ordinary. I daresay Laura was flattered and impressed, the novelty of the situation was enough to turn any young actress's head, but beyond that, when they killed the lights and she went back to real life, then another set of forces took over. God knows I knew what he was going through, but I had no pity to spare. I could stand back and look at his anguish as I might regard a piece of newsreel footage: bang! you see the bomb go off, the house crumbles, the victims run out into the shattered streets, but it isn't happening to you and it doesn't put you off your food for long.

'You think I should tackle her about it?' he asked. 'Face her with it, ask for an explanation?'

'You know her better than me.'

'She might resent it, you mean?'

'I don't know. Let's face it, I don't even know what your relationship is. You've told me some of it, but I've no idea what the bottom line is. Only you can judge that.'

'Do you think she and Gelbard are lovers?'

That was the one question I hoped he wouldn't ask me. 'I don't know,' I said.

'But you must have got some vibes that night you met them together.'

'You obviously haven't asked her?'

'No,' Martin said. ' daren't.'

'Does it matter that much? We can't always go to bed with virgins . . . and in any case, who wants to?'

'It matters to me,' he said. Then, 'I wish to God it was all over, that she'd suddenly do something I could hate her for,' as he picked up the schedule, fixing again the exact moment of her betrayal.

TWELVE

Even though the wardrobe department found me a reasonable dinner jacket and altered the trousers so that I didn't look like a hired waiter, I still felt I'd been cast as the uninvited guest. In a way Martin's ploy reduced my assignment with Laura to the status of a blind date.

As it happened she was working until the unit wrapped the evening of the dinner party and elected to get changed at the studio. 'I won't have time otherwise,' she told me, 'and I can get my hair washed and set. So you get dressed at the hotel and I'll send my car for you.'

'Oh, you have a car now!'

'Yes. Martin arranged it. Since he built up my role.'

'Well, bully for good old Martin. I like being driven. Means I can drink more. Dinner's at eight and I'm told it's rude to arrive late, so what time would you like me?'

'If we leave the studio about twenty after seven . . . that'd be okay, wouldn't it? So I'll have him pick you up at around quarter to seven.'

'You'll recognise me,' I said. 'I'll be the one in the back seat.'

I shaved with unusual care before struggling into my borrowed finery, but it had been a bitch of hot day and by the time the car arrived I felt as though I was modelling a wet suit.

Her chauffeur had graduated from the same driving school as New York cabbies. Where Laura was concerned I seemed doomed to travel in a state of perpetual fear. I was lucky he was the non-talkative variety, because all I could have contributed to any exchange would have been a high-pitched scream.

Somewhat to my surprise Laura was ready by the time we got to the studio. Maybe Martin or even Gelbard had put up the ante for her outfit because otherwise it must have eroded most of her salary. I have a theory that off-the-shoulder dresses cost more than those with straps. You won't find that sort of useful chauvinistic information in any issues of *Vogue*, it's based on some private field studies I conducted during my marriage.

'There's no justice,' I said. 'How come you look cool and ravishing and I look like a geriatric penguin?'

If the dress had been bought for her, she wasn't letting on. 'You really think I look okay? You don't think it's too much?'

'Listen, I gather that apart from us and Suzanne and Charlie our fellow guests are going to be straight out of Mrs Miniver.' She looked blank. 'It's the blue, blue English set tonight, and they've come to watch the actors feed.'

'Well, stay close, don't leave me on my own.'

'How extraordinary. I was just going to say the same to you.'

The Dowager came out of his room to see us off. 'Tell him you think my hair's sensational,' Laura whispered.

'Sensational hair-do,' I said.

'Well, dear, makes a change from gluing down Mrs Croze's remaining strands. Wait a minute, Cinderella, I've left a pin showing. Can't have that. There, darling, perfection, and you shall go to the ball!'

He waved a silk scarf and wiped away an imaginary tear as we drove off.

'He's so sweet,' Laura said. 'He stayed behind specially for me. Where've you been? I haven't seen you in ages.'

'Nine days to be exact.'

'I thought you must be avoiding me.'

'No. Just working hard.'

'I love my part now.'

'Good . . . How's Jean?' I'd promised myself I wouldn't mention his name in the first hour, and there I was blurting it out before we'd passed the studio gate.

'Oh, okay, I guess. He had to go abroad again.'

'He seems a very nice guy.'

'Yes, he's sweet.'

202

'A different sweet from the Dowager, presumably?'

'What? Oh, sure.'

I decided it was not a line of questioning to pursue.

'Do you really think this evening's going to be horrific?'

'We won't let it,' I said. 'All I ask is you slip me the wink about which knife and fork to use.'

'And you tell me if my dress drops any lower.'

'I might not tell you right away. Could be the making of the whole evening.'

'No, promise!'

It was at moments like this that she betrayed her age. I sat next to her in the back of the car feeling like the father of the bride, and it wasn't a good feeling either. You had to be young to get enthusiastic about the prospect of dinner with a bunch of visiting Hooray Henrys and their tiny talk, but some of her excitement infected me.

Maybe I'm being too hard on them: they were well-meaning, though when we first walked in (and as it happens we were the last to arrive) I did get the impression that Martin was remaking *Kind Hearts and Coronets* – everybody, male and female, looked like Alec Guinness to me. The introductions took a lifetime and I immediately forgot everybody's name except one jolly old dame who was actually called a Dame. Those British titles always faze me. I only had time to down one very weak martini before dinner was announced. There were place cards on the elaborately laid table and to my dismay I found that Laura and I had been separated. She was half-way down on the opposite side of the table, sandwiched between two beefy men who had matched complexions, like a pair of garden gnomes. I was flanked by two ladies of indeterminate years wearing conflicting and heady perfumes. The moment I sat down and before I had had time to memorise their names from the place cards, the one on my left who had a curiously strangulated voice asked me if I was one of the actors.

'No. I'm a writer.'

'Oh, really? What do you write?'

'Well, at the moment I'm writing the script for the film that Martin's making.'

'How fascinating,' she said. 'Do you make it up as you go along?'

'More or less.'

'How absolutely fascinating. Did you hear that Betty?' She leaned forward and addressed the woman on my right. 'This gentleman does the words.'

'Please call me Harvey.'

'Harvey. You're not related to the Bristol Harveys, are you?'

'No, Harvey's my first name.'

'How fascinating. Did you hear that Betty? We come from Bristol, you see. Just outside, that is. I wouldn't live in the actual city.'

Then it was Betty's turn. In a stage whisper that must have been heard the length of the table she asked me: 'Which one is Mr Croze?'

'Opposite side, second from the end.'

'*That*'s him?'

'Yes.'

'Of course, they look different, don't they? when they're not on the screen. That's Charles Croze, Ursula.'

'How fascinating,' Ursula said. 'I had a great pash on him when I was at school. I must say it's a great treat to meet all you film people. You must lead such a glamorous life.'

'Twenty-four hours a day,' I said, as the first course was served.

I tried to catch Laura's eye more than once; it was quite obvious that she was an enormous success with the garden gnomes. Martin and his wife sat at opposite ends of the long table, playing the gracious hosts. Martin gave me a conspiratorial smile at one point. I must admit they had both laid it all on with a certain style; the table was decorated with a profusion of fresh flowers and the whole room was candlelit. The food was excellent and the wine abundant. Before long most tongues had been loosened and I was treated to a detailed and highly personal account of Ursula's previous marriage. I thought, it's back to square one, I must have the sort of face that inspires these marital confidences.

'You see, quite apart from the drink, his problem was he had this positively unhealthy fetish about dogs.'

'Dogs?'

'Yes. I breed them, you see. Always have done, it's a sort

204

of family tradition you might say. Mummy was a great breeder.'

'What do you breed?'

'Oh, corgis, naturally.'

'Sorry,' I said, 'I should have known.'

'Are you fond of corgis?'

'I don't think I've ever come across one.'

'Really? Betty, did you hear that? This lovely man has never come across a corgi.'

'I don't believe it!'

'Anyway, you see I like sleeping with at least three on my bed, and my ex simply couldn't understand it. So of course it came down to a simple choice between him and the dogs, and he had to go.'

'Understandable,' I said.

'Now, Harry . . . that's Harry sitting next to that young gel . . . Who is she, by the way? Should I know her?'

'She's an actress. Her name's Laura Taylor.'

'Taylor? Now that's interesting. They're the port people, you know . . . Very brave of her to wear that dress, that will please Harry. He's a great one for the cleavage, but his saving grace is that he adores all my doggies.'

'How many have you got?'

'Betty, how many have I got?'

'What of, dear?'

'Dogs.'

'Well, you've got Algy, Carmen the Second, Prince Albert, Victoria, oh and your favourite, Lord Byron . . .'

By now I was just about ready to fall face forward into my *Beef Wellington*. I looked across to Laura, and Harry, now identified as the gnome on her left, was obviously in the middle of an equally boring set of revelations because she was noticeably glassy-eyed. I had a quick mental picture of Harry in bed smothered by corgis.

Then Ursula dismissed me and it was Betty's turn.

'What's she been telling you?'

'Oh, very interesting. All about her previous marriage.'

Betty lowered her voice to normal conversational level. 'Well, of course she should never have married Rupert. I mean, he was a well-known disaster area, a positive bomb site as far as the ladies were concerned. Very well put together, though, I must say that for him. Not an Adonis but well put together. And Ursula doted on him until that unfortunate episode.'

'What was that?'

'When he poisoned the dogs' food. I thought she'd die, poor dear. She nursed those dogs night and day. Night and day, never left them. The devotion of that friend of mine to her dogs was just nothing short of heartbreaking.'

'Or homebreaking,' I said.

'I beg your pardon?'

'Nothing. This is very good chow.' I had the urge to say things that would shock her, that would shock them both, but my heart wasn't in it. She turned away from me. One thing about the British and about her type in particular, they know exactly how to freeze you out.

When the meal was over the ladies left us to our brandy, port and cigars. Martin urged the men to regroup at his end of the table and I had the benefit of examining the gnomes at close quarters. Harry was a splendid specimen with tufts of hair growing straight out from his cheeks – 'Buggers' grips' I believe they used to call them in the Royal Navy and maybe still do for all I know.

'I say, Martin, you did us proud tonight. Must say I was taken with that little actress girl you sat me next to. She's good value.'

'Amazed she could hold a knife and fork, were you?' Charles said with a smile that I knew to be a danger signal.

Harry was either too polite or too dense to rise to the bait. 'No, absolutely tiptop, I thought. Very good value.'

Martin was quick to head them off. 'Have a cigar, Charlie. And pass the port, Willie. Or have brandy if you prefer.' He shot an anxious glance in my direction.

'How's it been going, Charlie?' I said.

'How's what been going?'

'Come on, you know what I mean.'

'Oh, that . . . Better ask Erich von Stroheim here.'

'You know, I watched some filming once,' the second gnome interrupted. 'Forget what it was called, but it had that very good actor in it. Dead now I think. What was his name? Harry, you remember, you were there with me.'

'Where?'

206

'Got invited for lunch, didn't we? Wanted to tap us for a few sovs. Course, Martin, your chaps always seem to want money. Anyway, point is, we met this actor . . . God, I wish I could remember names. Once married to . . .'

'Oh, that one.'

'Yes. You remember.'

'I can see the face.'

'You're a fat lot of use, Harry. Remember the lunch . . . Was his name Korda?'

'No, he gave the lunch.'

'You're absolutely right, Harry! He wasn't the actor, was he?'

'Is there any point to this boring story?' Charles said. He pushed the port decanter along the table with some force. 'Let me ask you what do you two do for a living?'

Martin stepped in quickly. 'Harry's in property, Charlie.'

'Oh, property. Doing well, are you? Turning over a few sovs?'

'Can't complain, old son.'

'I'm not your old son. Thank God I'm not even your young son. Do you have sons?'

'Two.' Harry was becoming increasingly uneasy, though to his credit he still answered politely.

I could see Martin start to sweat and it was a curious paradox that, whereas he was always fully in command on the set, in his own home playing the gracious host much of that assurance left him. It was as if he was the actor attempting a role for which he was basically miscast.

'Two little property speculators in the making, are they? About to follow in Daddy's shady footsteps.'

Harry turned his back on him. 'This is very good port, Martin. Wasted on some people, I suspect, but not on me.'

'Thank you, Harry, glad you like it. Shall we join the ladies?'

'Oh, are there ladies present as well as actresses?' Charles said.

'Now, Charles, behave yourself,' Martin said.

'Don't bloody patronise me.'

I took him by the arm, but he shook me off.

'And I don't need your help, either. I'm not pissed, not even half-way.'

207

'Nobody's suggesting that, Charles.'

'Good. All I'm trying to do is have a serious discussion about the shortage of houses in the Greater London area, which I understand our landlord here, and his two aspiring sons, are trying to remedy.'

'I don't build houses,' Harry said.

'Oh, you don't build houses. What d'you build?'

'Office blocks mostly.'

'I think we ought to join the ladies, they'll be wondering where we are.'

'Don't kid yourselves,' Charles said, 'they probably don't give a flying fart if they never see any of us again. And I'll tell you something else, having looked round the table, there was only one that I'd want to see again. I thought the rest were terminal ball-breakers.'

'Come on, Charlie,' I said, 'knock it off.'

'Oh, you've joined the enemy, have you, Harvey, gone over to the other side? Well, I don't sing for my supper. And I'm too old, and too successful to submit quietly to being bored rigid. So, I tell you what, you all join the ladies, and I'll take myself off to pastures not necessarily new, but a great deal greener.'

He weaved his way to the door in total silence, pausing only to deposit his brandy glass on a non-existent table. It bounced but did not break on the marble floor. Then he was gone.

'I do apologise,' Martin said. 'Lot of tension, you know. These actors. He's been under a lot of tension lately.'

'Yes,' Harry said.

'Part of the job, I suppose,' the other gnome volunteered.

'I thought it was only actresses that were temperamental.'

'Good thing the glass didn't break,' Willie said.

'Well, I thought it was a bloody good dinner, Martin.'

'Thank you, Harry.'

'These things happen in the best regulated families.'

'What surprised me . . . I mean, the rest was water off a duck's back . . . but what surprised me was he's nothing like he is in real life as he is up there on the screen. That's what surprised me.'

Harry turned to me as we all shuffled out of the dining room. 'Suppose you're used to it, though. Same in my line of business, I suppose. Never does to judge by appearances.'

The women were already gathered in the enormous living room which opened out onto the patio. Flaming torches had been set into the lawns and the entire garden and pool area was floodlit. Extra staff had obviously been recruited for the evening; they moved amongst the guests offering coffee, a variety of liqueurs and salvers of chocolate-covered orange rind. As in the dining room there was a profusion of fresh flowers and the scent of these, mingled with the perfumes worn by the women, was almost overpowering.

I made my way to Laura, who was being cross-examined by one of my dinner companions, the one called Betty.

'How do you diet?' Betty was asking.

'I don't,' Laura said. 'Not seriously, that is, though I shall have to after tonight.'

'Oh, how lucky. Look at her, that's her third piece of chocolate. Do you know each other?'

'Yes,' I said. 'We came together.'

'Oh, well, then you do know each other. We were just talking about diets. I'm on the Wakefield regime, are you familiar with that one?'

Laura and I both shook our heads.

'Well, it's not really something to discuss after dinner . . . Wasn't the food delicious, by the way? Alice is so clever . . . No, I was put on to the Wakefield by a most amazing doctor we met on Mustique. It's a little bit, how shall we say? . . . well, don't be coy Betty, we're all grown up . . . What he does is put you on a course of injections. They inject you with an extract of goat's water. Refined, of course.'

Laura stopped munching on her orange rind.

'Goat's water?'

'Goat's pee-pee.'

'You're joking!'

'No, dear. It's been thoroughly tested and it produces the most amazing results. Well, as you can see.'

She smoothed her dress down over her hips. 'I've had

two courses and the pounds just dropped away. Dropped away . . . Apparently . . .' She looked over her shoulder, as though the next revelation was top security . . . 'Apparently, female goats . . . they have to be female, did I mention that? . . . well, the females produce this extraordinary substance in their pee-pee which works wonders.'

'Well, obviously, you're living proof,' I said.

'I can give you the doctor's address if you like. I mean, he's *besieged*, as you can imagine, but I'm sure he'd fit you in if you mentioned my name.'

Mercifully Martin joined us at that point and we were spared further intimate details.

'Will you excuse me, Betty dear, but Laura here has never seen the garden at night and I want to show her around.'

He led Laura away across the lawns. I could not resist looking across the room to see if Alice had registered his exit. Would she mirror my envy? A shaft of irony lay between us: jealousy of Martin was, at the moment, the only thing we had in common.

'She seems a sweet young thing,' Betty said. 'Of course I'd never let one of my daughters take up the acting profession. Not that they don't have talent. Felicity was quite stunning in her school production of *The Mikado* . . .' I switched off as she gave me a breakdown of her daughters' varied attributes, and as soon as was polite I eased myself away and went in search of Suzanne.

'I've been looking for Charles,' she said.

'Charlie decided he wouldn't stay for the second house.'

'Oh, God! I thought perhaps he was getting a little beady towards the end of dinner. When d'you think we can leave? And of course that selfish sod will have taken the car.'

'I'm sure Martin can arrange transport. I have to stay, I brought Laura . . . She and Martin are wandering lonely as clouds in the paradise garden.'

'How romantic. She'll be bitten rotten by bugs. This lot are heavy going, aren't they? I've just been propositioned by that one over there, the one with a face like an underdone steak.'

'That's a better description than I thought of. I compared him to a garden gnome. Did he make you a decent offer?'

210

'Very prep school stuff. Get me another drink, darling. If I can't leave I may as well tranquillise myself.'

'What's your pleasure?'

'My pleasure, dear, would be to be curled up in bed with a good book. But I'm drinking gin with a dash of it.'

I looked around for a waiter. That was my mistake because I was immediately trapped by Alice.

'Now. I must break up you film people, you always stick together, don't you?'

'It's the herd instinct,' I said. 'We do it for safety.'

She moulded her face into a smile. 'Harry was telling me that Mr Croze left early. Such a pity, because some of the girls were dying to meet him. Come and let me introduce you both to two of my oldest friends.'

Reluctantly we accompanied her to another part of the room.

'This is Gay Hellman, and Commander Salter. Mr Burgess is helping Martin with his script, and I'm sure you know who this lady is . . . Suzanne, dear, are you happy with that, wouldn't you rather have a glass of champagne?'

'No, I'm very happy with gin.'

'Quite right,' the Commander said. 'Shampoo never sits well with me. Very liverish.'

'Well, I'll leave you all to get acquainted.'

I made a valiant attempt to find some common ground with Gay Hellman, whose Christian name was a contradiction. She looked as though she had modelled herself on Virginia Woolf – a reasonable guess on my part as it turned out, because her opening remark was to ask me if I had ever read Katherine Mansfield.

'Not for some years,' I said, 'but I admire her work.'

'We drove through Menton the other day. What is it the French say about it? "You catch le mal at Monte Carlo, you go up into the mountains to recuperate, then you come down to Menton to die!" '

'They say the same thing about Holywood.'

'Do they? The French do?'

'No, just the screenwriters,' I said, but it wasn't the time or place for private jokes, and her thin powdered face, the skin drawn tight over her cheek-bones, betrayed no comprehension.

'What a strange life she and her husband led. Always apart . . . Though I can understand it. I think marriages can only survive if people don't see each other a great deal.'

'Have you put your theory to the test?'

'Well, I was lucky. The Commander was at sea most of the time.'

'I'm sorry, I didn't realise when we were introduced . . .'

'Oh, I kept my maiden name. I paint under that name. It makes me feel I'm still alive.'

'I thought you must be artistic.'

'It's a tiny talent, I'm afraid, but it's all I've got.'

'What do you paint mostly?'

'I paint myself as I always wanted to be. I don't suppose you understand that?'

'Yes,' I said. 'I guess we writers do more or less the same thing.'

I warmed towards her as she suddenly blossomed, anxious to grasp at a shared experience.

'Have you ever been to Menton?'

'No. I don't really know much of this part of the world.'

'It's a fatal place for consumptives . . . or was. Consumption, as it used to be called, seems to have died out, doesn't it? The graveyard there is full of tombstones to the young . . . I sometimes wish I'd died young, when I was really alive, and thought I was full of promise . . .'

'I'd like to see some of your work,' I said.

'Oh, I don't show it to anybody.'

'Not even your husband.'

'Least of all him,' she said. 'Why should I remind him of what he ruined?' She said it with a smile. 'He'd much rather look at the real thing.'

It was at that moment that Laura suddenly reappeared, alone, coming across the lawns like an apparition.

'That girl . . . She's very beautiful. Is she your daughter?'

'No.'

'Oh, dear, have I dropped a brick?'

'Not at all.'

'Don't let her go to Menton,' she said.

Laura came straight towards us. 'Harvey, can I talk to you for a moment? Excuse me.'

She led me outside.

212

'Something's happened.'

'To Martin?'

'Yes . . . but that's not it. Charles has come back.'

'Oh, God, what sort of state's he in?'

'Awful. Come and help.'

I followed her back across the lawns. When we got past the illuminated pool it was difficult to pick our way. Laura took my hand and guided me. I could hear voices, and then a crash and a cry of pain as somebody fell. We ran the last distance. A gazebo stood in a clearing hidden from the house. I could see Charles, but no sign of Martin.

'Don't panic,' Charles said. 'The silly sod's fallen over, that's all.'

It was then that a dishevelled Martin emerged from the screen of conifers.

'I didn't fall over. This stupid bastard pushed me over. I want you out of here, Charles – and if I could finish the film without you, believe me I would.'

'I don't know what all the fuss is about,' Charles said, still addressing us. 'Just a bit unsteady on his pins and he fell over. Shouldn't drink if you can't hold it. Anyway no damage done, you'll live to say "Action" again.'

'Laura, why don't you go inside?' Martin said. 'Otherwise we'll have Alice out here.'

'You sure you're all right?'

'Apart from a ruined dinner jacket, yes.'

She went reluctantly, and not before saying to me, 'Don't let them fight, will you?'

'Nobody's talking about fighting, sweetie,' Charles said. 'Take your fragile innocence somewhere else. As Jack Barrymore said to Fay Compton, I'm tired of your fucking virginity.'

'God, you're an offensive sod when you're drunk, Charles.'

'Going to rewrite my life now, are you, Harvey? Well, let me save you the trouble. I don't want your advice, I don't want anybody's advice.'

'Are you going to leave quietly, Charles, or do I have to have you thrown out?'

'Martin, dear, you're not living in the Middle Ages, despite your pretensions to grandeur. Anyway, you can't

213

even deliver that line properly – you need voice production and a few basic acting lessons before playing East Lynne, you clockwork cunt! If any of your so-called staff attempt to lay a finger on me I'll give you more publicity than this piece of garbage we're making will ever get in the cinemas – if it ever gets to the cinemas, that is. You are not only directing one of the most boring films ever to reach the screen, but if that wasn't enough, you have just given the second most boring dinner party on the Côte d'Azur. You also hold the record for giving the first most boring dinner party on the Côte d'Azur.'

'Come on, Harvey, let's leave him to it. With any luck he'll pass out.'

'I wouldn't be too high and fucking mighty if I were you, darling heart . . . otherwise a little bird might – just might – whisper to the little wifey what you were doing in the gazebo with your favourite ingénue. Oh, your offence was rank. We all know the flesh is weak, though from what I glimpsed in the pale, pale moonlight, yours is weaker than most.'

Martin struck out at him. It was hardly a well-aimed blow and carried little strength with it, but it was sufficient to knock Charles off balance. I put myself between them before the fracas could go any further. There are few sights more pathetic and ludicrous than two middle-aged men, both badly out of condition, having a drunken brawl.

'Come on both of you, for Christ'sake,' I said. 'You're both behaving like lunatics. Go on back to the house, Martin, I'll take care of Charles.'

Martin needed no second bidding, while Charles, dusting himself down, seemed content with his Pyrrhic victory.

'Charlie,' I said, 'be sensible. Call it a night. And for God's sake, when you've slept it off, send him a peace offering, otherwise the rest of the film is going to be a nightmare.'

'They're all nightmares, darling. Every single one. Nightmares.'

'Yes, okay, but you've still got a few weeks to go.'

'What a little diplomat you are, Harvey. The Writers Guild answer to Kissinger. I shall call you Doctor Kissinger from now onwards . . . I don't need to send that pompous

214

fart any peace offering. You were there tonight, helping prop up his social standing on this fabled coast . . . to amuse and entertain those stuffed baboons. We were there, we thespians . . . and I include you as one of the camp followers, branded with the same stigma . . . to add a little gilt to the gingerbread, spice to the feast . . . And I'm too fucking grand to be used, darling. Too grand and too old to be treated like a fucking extra at the banquet. I don't owe Martin anything, certainly not politeness. I don't even have to thank him for the meal . . . That goes down on his expense account, baby, it's in the budget, it comes off the top . . . If I didn't think it would be wasted on them, I'd go back in there and piss in one of Alice's superb flower arrangements. Just to round off the evening and give them something to remember for the rest of their useless lives . . . But I won't, Harvey, out of deference to you, since I know that you're a man of enormous sensitivity . . .'

'So you're going to go quietly?'

'I'm an actor, dear heart. I used to be a bloody good actor, and despite certain misfortunes, I haven't forgotten basic stagecraft . . . I've made one exit, and it's a cardinal rule that one never goes back to tread on one's own laughs. So you needn't concern yourself any more on my behalf.'

'Do you give me your word?'

'What's my fucking word worth, Harvey? I didn't say I didn't *want* to go back, I said my training won't allow me to. That should be good enough for you.'

'How will you get home? D'you want me to arrange for a car?'

'What a splendid idea, Doctor. Now I know how Nixon felt.'

'Come on, then, I'll walk you round to the front.'

'No, don't take my arm. People will begin to talk and the last thing I want is to ruin your reputation as a ladies' man, Doctor.'

We picked our way across the lawns, avoiding the patio, and when we came to the front of the house I tipped his driver to see him safely deposited and then to return for Suzanne. Charles was asleep in the back of the car before the driver had reversed out.

215

I returned to the party by the garden entrance so as not to draw any undue attention and was able to exchange a thumbs-up with Martin. He seemed to have recovered his composure, though I noticed he had distanced himself from Laura. She was talking to Gay Hellman.

'I apologised to Mrs Hellman for dragging you away like that.'

'No need to apologise, my dear.'

'Now it's my turn,' I said. 'I guess we ought to be saying our goodbyes, Laura. You've got to be up early for those publicity photographs.'

She fielded the lie expertly, picking up her cue like a seasoned trouper.

'Yes. Must get my beauty sleep. It was very nice to meet you, Mrs Hellman.'

'I enjoyed meeting both of you.'

We made our way across the room and thanked Alice for having us. She didn't urge us to stay and I dare say Charles was right: we had fulfilled our function.

'You're not leaving already, are you?' Martin said, but he, too, was only going through the motions. To him I made some excuse about having to be back at the hotel for an important phone call. After the recent events I think he was relieved to get off so lightly. Before we left I told Suzanne about the arrangements I had made. 'Brilliant, darling,' she said. 'I owe you one for that.'

'Well,' I said when we were safely in our car, 'quite an evening one way and another. Have you had enough, or do you want to have a quiet drink and compare notes?'

'Not a drink but some coffee, maybe.'

I told the driver to take us back to my hotel. 'And don't break any speed records,' I said. 'We're feeling a little fragile back here.'

'How did you manage with Charles?'

'I got him away.'

'Wasn't it ghastly?'

'Could have been worse I suppose. I'm sorry you were involved. How did it all start?'

'Oh, I'll tell you when we get to the hotel.'

I ordered some coffee from the night porter and we went up to my room.

'Sorry it isn't tidier. Throw all that junk off the chair and put your feet up. Now . . . tell me all.'

'There isn't that much to tell.'

'Well, tell me what there is.'

'Martin and I were just talking when Charles suddenly jumped up from nowhere. You saw what a state he was in, and he just goaded Martin . . .'

'What about?'

'Oh, he said a lot of stupid things that Martin took exception to. Then there was a bit of pushing and shoving . . . and I went to find you.'

'But you said something else when you first found me.'

She looked puzzled. 'Did I?'

'Yes. I asked you if something had happened to Martin and you said, "Yes, but that's not it." '

I waited, but she said nothing.

'Then later Charles seemed to hint at something between you and Martin. Did he make a pass at you, was that it? You don't have to tell me if you don't want to.'

We were interrupted by the night porter bringing the coffee.

'You sure you wouldn't like a drink as well?'

'No, I don't think so.'

I tipped the old boy and told him to take care of our driver.

'We're not going to get much sleep if we drink much of this,' I said. 'Do you want some more cream? Milk, I mean, they don't serve cream with coffee over here, do they?' I watched her closely, the way she sat, the rise and fall of her breasts glimpsed within her party dress.

'So, do you want to tell me?'

'I guess I was taken by surprise, that's all.'

'In what way?'

'Well, Martin's the first really important director I've ever worked for, and I thought he was just being nice to me, I thought perhaps that's how they all behave towards sort of inexperienced people like me . . . I just didn't know any better, I suppose. I just didn't think of him in that way.'

'You mean he did make a pass?'

'Yes . . . You're right about this coffee, it's terribly

217

strong . . . I mean, tell me, am I mad, should I have seen it coming?'

'Well, you haven't told me what happened yet.'

'It was just so embarrassing, because at first I couldn't understand what he was talking about. I really did think he was going to show me his garden . . . I guess I'm really stupid sometimes but it never occurred to me with all those people there and his wife . . . but as soon as we were outside he started on about it . . . How he loved me and couldn't live without me, and how I had to break away from Jean . . . He seems to believe that Jean is some sort of gangster or something.'

'Is he a gangster?'

'Course not. I'm not that stupid. Martin said he was having the police investigate him. He just went on and on – said he had proof, that Jean was going to corrupt me and ruin my life and that I had to promise never to see him again.'

'So how did you reply to that?'

'I didn't know what to say. What could I say? He just got more and more desperate, it was frightening in a way, like he was demented. Then the worst part was he started to cry, and I was terrified that somebody would come out and see him like that . . . You know him better than I do, is he often like that?'

'I've never seen that side of him,' I said, trying to keep my own panic at bay. 'But it sounds a pretty hairy situation for you . . . Is that when Charles made his appearance?'

'No. Martin took me into that summer-house place . . . He was still crying and saying that he'd never felt this way about anybody else ever before, that his marriage was a disaster, and that if I didn't leave Jean he'd do something really desperate . . . And I suppose because he was in such a state I made the mistake of trying to be nice to him . . . I should have just run back to the house . . . Then suddenly he tried to tear my dress open. He said even if it was all hopeless he had to have me once . . . and then he . . . he exposed himself.'

I don't know why, but the way she said it, the use of that slightly old-fashioned expression sounded like something out of a Press report of a court case, a piece of evidence that

218

the key witness had been schooled to repeat, something alien to her.

'And he was like that when Charles appeared.'

'That explains a lot . . . Jesus! what an experience. Not that I think he would have done anything, though maybe he would, I don't know. It's unreal.'

'I suppose now he'll try and write me out of the film . . .'

'No, I doubt that. You're too established. There's a whole sub-plot now, and in any case he doesn't have the last word. He still has to answer to David.'

'But it's bound to make a difference.'

'It seems to me that you hold all the cards.'

'How can I face him again?'

'Well, you won't be alone, there'll always be plenty of other people around on the set. Just do your job as well as you can and let him have the embarrassment.'

'I'm glad I've got you to talk to . . . I couldn't tell any of this to anybody else, my parents or anybody. My father would go spare. He'd be down at the studio and that would be it.'

'Talking of your parents, will they be worried about you being out this late?'

'Yes, I'd better phone them . . . Can I use your phone?'

'Go ahead. Do you want to use the one in the other room?'

'No, that's all right . . . The car's still here, isn't it? Maybe, on second thoughts, I'd better just go, otherwise I'll only disturb the whole house.'

'Whatever you like. Stay if you want to talk some more, I'm easy.'

'You're being very sweet to me.'

'No, I'm not,' I said.

'It's a relief to share it with somebody. I think I ought to go.'

'Well, why don't we see each other tomorrow? That is, unless you've already got a date . . . Are you seeing Jean?'

'No, he's not here. In any case, he's just a friend, there's nothing serious between us . . .'

'Nothing at all?'

'Well, I've known him for a couple of years and we've been out a lot, but he doesn't own me.'

219

'You've been to bed with him, though?'

I hadn't wanted to ask that question, but it was out before I could stop myself.

'Yes.'

'Well, why not?' I said, lightly, trying to retrieve the mistake. 'It's none of my business anyway. Give me a call when you wake up. I'll be here and I'll try and give you a nice day.'

When I had seen her safely in the car and watched her drive away, I went back to my rooms and stared at myself in the mirror over the fireplace. I stared at a stranger, a man with a face disfigured by love.

THIRTEEN

Martin never referred to the incident in the gazebo, but Laura said to me: 'All my boyfriends seem to cry.'

'Have there been that many?'

'No. Just average, I suppose.'

'And what makes them cry?'

'Who knows? . . . Sometimes I hit them.'

'Hit them?'

'Yes.'

'Why?'

'Sometimes I get bored when I see them every day. After a couple of months or so.'

'I'm safe for another month then,' I said. 'Have you made Jean cry?'

She thought for a moment. 'Yes, once. When I wouldn't let him sleep with me.'

'That surprises me. He doesn't seem the crying type.'

'Men are all the same when it comes to sex. Like babies crying for the bottle.'

'Or "the breast"?'

'Yes,' she said, 'that's true. I've never quite understood that.'

'Perhaps we were all deprived in our early years.'

'I never think about my breasts. They're just there.'

'Do you like making love?'

'Yes and no. Depends. It doesn't make me cry if I don't.'

We had that conversation the day after the fateful dinner party. She called me, as promised, and we decided that we would spend the day at the beach. We went to a small private beach on the Nice side of Antibes.

'It's usually clean on that side of the bay,' Laura said,

221

'though one can never be sure. Just a matter of luck really.'

On the drive there she told me that Martin had called her.

'To apologise?'

'Well, he never mentioned that part of it. He just asked whether I had been frightened by Charles's behaviour. I think he was trying to sound me out. Then just before I left an enormous bunch of flowers arrived.'

'I told you he would be the one with the conscience, so you needn't worry about your role in the film. I imagine he's scared witless that Alice might find out.'

'Yes, that must be it.'

The beach was crowded but we managed to secure our allotted space. I rented mattresses for us both and a parasol, for the sun was almost directly overhead and the sand scorched our bare feet. My New England eyes were momentarily dazzled by the variety of naked bodies all around us and perhaps some vestige of ancestral prudery lingered for the first half hour. Laura first opted for a more conservative approach, wearing a bikini that might have done service as three cocktail mats, while I did my middle-aged best to impersonate a Charles Atlas student half-way through the course. We went for an immediate swim to cool ourselves after the car journey and then had a sandwich and a beer at the bar before collapsing on our mattresses. Every time I turned my head I found it was either gazing straight up between the parted legs of some nubile creature, or else being confronted with a mound of glistening red Jello.

Torpid with the heat – for even under the shade of the parasol it pressed down as though the very air had doubled in weight and volume – I tried to disassociate myself from thoughts of venery. If I turned my head to find a cool inch of mattress my mouth was on a level with Laura's half-concealed young breasts. Lizard-like, I could have tongued their pale buds. She was curled inwards, her legs drawn up so that they, too, were shielded from the sun. This posture gave her a strangely childish appearance, as though this was the way she had always slept in her nursery cot. In contrast to the other, entirely naked bodies all around us, she seemed to me to be the more mysterious – without flaw. I think she had the kind of skin that tans evenly without benefit of artificial aids, and the fact that she was flying those three small flags of modesty heightened the eroticism of her pose. I saw with terrible clarity why it was that she made her lovers cry and I wondered when my turn would come.

We swam again later in the afternoon, but by then the sea had lost its brilliance and nameless flotsam scummed the water's edge and clung to our legs as we emerged. Children fractious with exhaustion were being screamed at by lobster parents and the sandcastles had the look of cities laid waste. Before long there would be a general, disgruntled exodus – sun-worship takes its toll – and we decided to leave ahead of the crowd.

'I can't wait to take a bath,' she said. 'The sand's so filthy. Course, none of these are natural beaches, they have to import the sand and renew it every season. Sometimes the winter storms remove it all in a single night.'

When we were in the car park it was Laura who said, 'Let's go back to your hotel. I like it there.' I'm not sure what my feelings were at that precise moment; perhaps most of us have a secret dread at the beginning of any love affair, a desire to pull back from the brink while all illusions are intact.

So it was that when we gained the cool seclusion of my hotel rooms, our roles were reversed. She was relaxed and at home and I was the visiting stranger. She went through into the bathroom and I heard the water start to run into the tub. When she reappeared she was naked to the waist. So unprepared was I for her lack of coquetry that I closed the shutters as she stepped out of jeans and pants, as though to protect her from prying eyes.

'Don't suppose you have any bath oil, do you?'

'No,' I said.

'Men never do. I love bath oil. Lots of it.'

'Duly noted. All I've got is some cologne.'

'Okay. Better than nothing. You going to have one with me?'

'Fine.'

'Or do you prefer having a bath to yourself?'

'Well,' I said, 'it's not a choice I have to make every day.'

As we sat face to face in the cool, cologne-scented water,

some remembered portion of a novel came crowding back – Huxley's *Point Counter Point*, read and stored in my dandelion days. Two of Huxley's characters took a bath together and he wrote, tongue firmly in cheek I expect, '*of such is the Kingdom of Heaven*'. Why did I retain that single image when a thousand other novels had been erased from memory? Was it because the early eroticism of innocence is the more lasting for being beyond comprehension?

'I love these old hotel baths,' Laura said, 'they're so big and comfortable.'

'Yes. I wouldn't recommend mixed bathing in some of the modern hotels I've stayed in.' I smiled at her, for I was still not without a certain amazement. 'Well, here we are.'

'It's so lovely to be cool.'

'Did you mean this to happen?'

'What?'

'This.'

'But nothing has happened,' she said.

'We're just good friends, is that it? Come on, you know what I'm talking about. It isn't every day that I get to share a bath with a Laura Taylor. What do I do if you ask me to soap your back?'

'Soap my back, I guess.'

'But where does that leave me?'

'I don't know.'

'Look, this is a ludicrous conversation and you know it. You know what I'm saying. When we get out of this bath I'm going to want to make love to you. I mean, I haven't taken a vow of celibacy, and I'm not very good at playing guessing games.'

'But I'm not playing a game.'

'The first time I went out with you I told you how I could feel . . . then I saw you with your boyfriend and thought, forget it, because I'm too old to want that sort of nightmare. You have to be very honest with me. Why me suddenly? What happened to all the others?'

'I don't belong to anybody,' she said.

'No, okay, I believe you, but I repeat, why me? I like to know what the odds are before I start gambling. My problem is I don't know how good I'd be at sharing you. You said you don't belong to anybody, but if we started something I might want you to belong to me. How would that sit with you?'

'I don't know, do I, 'til I've tried?'

'That's not an answer. And what about the age difference? We can't ignore that.'

'Why?'

'Because, like Everest, it's there.'

'You're the one who's worrying about that. I don't think about ages. You're just a man.'

'Okay, I'm the one who's worrying about it, and I worry about it because it worries me . . . That sounds like Gertrude Stein.'

'Who's she?'

'There you go! That dates me and that's what I'm talking about . . . Gertrude Stein was a writer, a bull dyke and a mentor to a lot of other writers of promise, in that order probably . . . Anyway, she wasn't my type and you are and here I am sitting in a bath with you, and I don't just want to scrub your back, do I?'

In response she slid her body towards me, sinking herself into the water so that her breasts became like lilies and her soft pubic hair brushed against me. The past itself is perhaps the most potent aphrodisiac and I've never really exorcised first loves. I was being offered what Martin had cried for, that lethal combination of youth and sensuality, the living embodiment of those dark destroying night thoughts some of us carry with us from adolescence to the grave. Her arms came up out of the water to burn my shoulders and almost as in that swirling dream but recently broken, her body moulded itself into mine and what I had many times imagined became a warm reality. Our bodies held slow sway, it was love without urgency (sexual responses, I am told, are more individual than fingerprints) and I had all but forgotten what tenderness there is in the clinging ripeness of a girl. We scarcely moved, joined as we were like sea creatures, though, within, her flesh fluttered against mine and all the time she regarded me with wide, enquiring eyes, as though this was some secret triumph she had rehearsed long ago and was now prepared to share. For my part, I had a sense of wonder and jubilation, yet not entirely divorced from a certain dread of that male ghost

225

who treads across our lusts, trailing the fear of failure in his wake.

Laura had none of Michelle's unguarded frenzy and the comparison was too recent to banish when, with nothing more than the mildest of contractions and a slight drumming of her fingers on my back, she finally surrendered herself. Only now did her eyes close as though, having come to the end of a long journey, she was now free. Her head came to rest on my shoulder and I pressed my lips into the thicket of her damp hair.

'Don't move,' she said, 'don't move just yet. Stay there inside me.'

Nothing I had previously imagined had prepared me for those extraordinary moments. And later, much later, when we stepped from the bath I patted her body dry with the rough hotel towels, then knelt to press my face against her belly and sample the damp heat of her mount, she said for the first time those three words which, no matter how falsely familiar, still have the power to enslave us.

'I love you,' she said and I willed myself to believe her, leading her back into the bedroom and spreading her on the white counterpane, the shuttered light striping her nudeness while I nuzzled between her soft thighs, taking her again with my tongue. I have developed the negative of that first afternoon a hundred times since, print after identical print, every detail in sharp focus. I can recall every inch of that bedroom, where each piece of furniture stood: the chair by the window with the faded needlepoint covering on which she had laid her clothes; the reproduction Fragonard, fly-blown in a pale antique frame, hanging on the wall opposite the bed; the blue vase on the chest of drawers, and the scent of the giant snapdragons and lilies that filled it. I can hear again the soft fluttering of the doves on the sloping roof beneath my window, listen again to the distant church bell telling the hours we shared in such loving disorder. I remember quoting a poem to her (prompted by what remote memory, I wonder?):

' "*A skin as if made of jasmine . . .*
that night in August – was it August? – that night . . .
I can just barely remember the eyes; they were, I think,
blue . . .

Ah, yes, blue" '

'What made you think of that?' she said.

'You, who else?'

'Not somebody from your past?'

'Maybe. You wouldn't expect me not to have a past, would you?'

'Who wrote it?'

'Somebody named Cavafy. The poem was called "Far Off". And that's what my past is, very far off.'

'You always bring everything back to age.'

'Do I? Yes, maybe I do.'

'Who was she?'

'Who was who?'

'The girl you thought of.'

'Questions, questions. Now who's being curious?'

'I'm just interested, that's all. I want to know all about you,'

'Who was she? Nobody and somebody. You. I'd been saving that for you.'

'Liar.'

'How d'you know it's a lie?'

'Men always lie about those things.'

'Oh, you're an authority, are you?'

'Yes.'

'What about women? Don't they lie about love?'

'I want a cigarette, please.'

'Do you smoke these? They're all I've got.'

'I'll try one.'

I lit it for her. She lay supine on the bed, an odalisque. Already the warm evening air was drying the sweat from our bodies, only a thin rivulet, faint as a snail's trail, remained on her smooth belly. She inhaled and then coughed.

'God! what's in these?'

'Just the usual injurious tars,' I said. I took it back from her. It was then, bending over her, taking the damp hair from her forehead strand by strand, that I first noticed she had a scar behind her left ear. I let my hand trace over it down her neck and across her shoulders, then circled a nipple with one finger before cupping my palm over the breast. The fact that she was scarred was strangely comfort-

227

ing. Beauty without any flaws has always intimidated me.

'Did you lie to me?'

'When?' she said.

'A little while ago . . . When you said that you loved me. Did you mean that?'

'I meant it when I said it.'

'Because I made it happen for you?'

'Yes.'

'Only because of that? I tasted your love on my lips.'

Again that searching stare.

'Why are you being so serious all of a sudden. Weren't you happy too?'

'Very.'

'Well, then?'

She suddenly ducked from under me, swinging herself off the bed and going to the window. Opening one of the shutters she stood there, totally nude, taking in great gulps of air. Beyond her the doves took flight. I stifled an urge to tell her to step back from view. I thought, don't, don't be old fashioned. Her mood seemed to have changed so abruptly. I'd forgotten those chameleon qualities that the young parade.

She turned then and loped into the bathroom to use the bidet, shouting to me, 'What're we going to do now?'

'What d'you want to do?'

'Eat.'

'Eat. Right. I'll order something and we'll have it up here.' She said she wanted meat, red meat and prawns to start with and a dessert. She was a healthy girl with a healthy appetite. After the meal she switched on the television. They were showing *Casablanca*, dubbed into French. It was odd hearing Bogie speak in French and Laura translated the bits I couldn't remember by heart. We sat on the floor and watched it, our backs propped against the end of the bed. She had put on one of my shirts when the waiter came up with the food, but the moment he had cleared away she discarded it again. It's difficult to concentrate on a film, even a film as good as that one, with a naked girl lying across your lap and it crossed my mind that it was more a scene for Woody Allen than for me. I suppose I was in a state of shock. I had crossed the Rubicon and nothing

228

would ever be the same again. Even the famous line, 'Play it, Sam', took on a different, more personal meaning.

Laura kept asking me, 'Do they get away in the end?'

'You mean you haven't seen it before?'

'No.'

'My God! I've got to take care of your education.'

'Well, tell me, do they get away?'

'Wait and see.'

'I hate not knowing. It won't spoil it for me, promise.'

'I bet you're the type who turns to the last page of a book first.'

Towards the end, with Ingrid Bergman breaking my heart all over again, I suddenly became conscious that Laura was crying.

'So, you can cry,' I said. 'It isn't just us men.'

'It's so sad . . . Wasn't she beautiful?'

'Yes,' I said, 'we were all in love with her. She made the earth move.'

'What's that mean?'

'Look, you keep telling me not to harp on my great age, and at the same time you keep reminding me of it . . . You've heard of Hemingway, right?'

'Yes.'

'Have you read *For Whom The Bell Tolls*? No? Well, Ingrid played the girl in the film, with Cooper, and she cut her hair off for it which in my day was the equivalent of, say, Mick Jagger suddenly starting to wear grey flannel suits . . . And in the book and in the movie the girl and Robert Jordan, the character played by Cooper, had this terrific love affair. It was during the Spanish Civil War, and they didn't have the advantage of a hotel room, they made love right out there on the bare hillside, very sexy . . . I mean, I'm giving it to you in one-liners, you've got to read the actual book someday . . . because it was considered very daring in its time, the descriptions of their love-making that is, and good old matador Hemingway invented a kind of new language if you like, a sort of English version of Spanish as she is said to be spoken . . . See, you couldn't write fuck in those days . . .'

'You couldn't?'

'Not and become a Book Society choice. So Hemingway

tried to find a way round it, and when they were making love up there on the hillside, he faced, as many of us have faced, the problem of describing what happens when people come. And since this was The Great Love Affair in quotes, they couldn't just come, it had to be something bigger than both of them . . . So, in his words, when they were rutting up there, the earth moved.'

She stared at me.

'End of class for today.'

'Have you ever tried to write about it?'

'Sex? Sure. When I started out as a screenwriter we had the Breen Office looking over our shoulders. On the surface Hollywood was the purest city in the land. Under the skin, of course, it was a seething mass of sexual intrigue . . . none of which was ever allowed on the screen. You won't believe me, but if we tried to show a couple in bed, even a married couple united in the sight of God, they had to keep one foot on the ground. Nobody swore, infidelity couldn't be seen to succeed, crime did not pay, et cetera. And it was more or less the same in books. For years we had to buy Joyce and Lawrence and good old Henry Miller under the counter.'

'But, now, how do you solve it?'

'I don't. And I can't think of anybody who really does, although a lot of us sure are trying. Especially the newly-liberated ladies. They're in there trading fuck for fuck with the guys. It's as if suddenly everybody's been reading the same medical text book and discovered the orgasm. It used to be that if you didn't have a bank account you were one of Life's failures. Now, if you don't experience multiple orgasms you're on the scrap pile. Kinsey and all those other truffle hounds won't even consider you.'

'Will you ever write about us?'

'Could be. In years to come maybe. Every writer steals from his own life. Sometimes you rob yourself consciously, hit and run as it were, and other times you don't realise you've picked your own pockets until after the event. It's a funny old business, being a writer.'

'How will you write about us?'

'You looked about twelve when you said that.' I kissed her. 'How do I know? I don't know whether I'll ever use this, or if I do how it'll come out. One never knows. Anyway, give me time. I haven't got over the first shock yet. And how do I know whether I'm going to get past chapter one with you? I've got a lot of competition.'

'But it fascinates me. I've never met a real writer before.'

'Well, don't get excited because you still haven't.'

'But you've written books. Charles told me.'

'Yes.'

'Can I read one?'

'My darling, they've long since gone to the Great Pulp House In The Sky – you've probably wiped your face on them . . . notice how discreetly I put that? They've been recycled into tissues. My sort of books never make the bestseller lists.'

'Never mind, I'd still like to read one. And you still haven't told me how you'd write about us.'

'Okay, I'd start off with this odd-ball character who comes to the South of France and gets himself hopelessly hooked on a very ugly girl who has never known True Love before. He takes pity on her and lures her back to his hotel room, promising her anything and then not giving her Arpège bath oil. He doesn't see her ugliness, since as we all know from childhood, beauty is in the eye of the beholder . . . He seduces her in the bath . . . No, she seduces him in the bath, that's the switch, because she's a very special ugly girl who confuses him . . . He never understands her, you see, and the less he understands her the more he loves her, since he's never met anybody like her before, and going in he realises that he's going to end up the loser . . . It'll be a sad story with an unhappy ending. Do you think you'll go out and buy that?'

'Why must it have an unhappy ending?'

'Because.'

I took her hands in mine and turned them palm upwards. 'I'll read your hands,' I said.

'Can you?'

'Sure. It's all there. My lusts, your youth, lots of journeys, several dark strangers. Now tell me something. Does Jean love you?'

'He thinks he does.'

'And you? How do you feel?' I thought, a lover's inter-

231

rogation always reverses the traditional roles, we force confessions we don't want to hear.

'I like him a lot,' she said. 'He's a good dancer.'

'Do you tell him you love him? When he's not dancing, that is.'

'Would you rather not see me again?' she said, 'because I can't give up other friends. I don't ask you about sharing.'

'You could. You could ask me not to share you with anybody and I'd do it.'

'Well, I guess we're different.'

It wasn't cruelty I saw in her face, or indifference, just honesty.

FOURTEEN

From that moment onwards I lived like a saboteur dropped behind enemy lines. Having possessed Laura once my every action was directed towards survival. I attacked the script with a renewed zest that perhaps surprised Martin and Latrough, becoming, in many ways, a nicer person, amenable to suggestions, tolerant, gregarious. My visits to the locations and the studio became more frequent, for I studied the Call Sheets as though they were railway time-tables so that I knew to the minute when Laura was on call. When Martin talked about her and his situation I played Best Friend, always ready to commiserate, for there was infinite pleasure in hearing somebody else describe those qualities in her which stoked my own fires. I actually believe that my contributions to the script took on an added dimension, for whereas before, I had laboured from necessity, now I had Laura to impress.

We saw each other often (Gelbard, an unknowing accomplice, continued to absent himself) and I worked out a complicated and in some ways exhausting routine. I was careful never to be seen alone with her in public, nor did I ever leave the studio with her. She would be taken home in her studio car and after an interval I would take the same route in my rented self-drive, parking in the village square a mile or so from her home. By my own choice I was never invited in to meet her parents, for as with any saboteur, I was chary of betrayal.

'What excuse do you give them?' I once asked her. 'Don't they think it strange you going out every night like this?'

'No. They've never been curious. Daddy works so hard

pulling teeth, he's usually exhausted. I doubt if he knows whether I'm in or out.'

'But what about your mother?'

'Oh, I have a very good relationship with my mother,' she said.

I had always been told that the French were curious towards strangers, but maybe the tourist industry cured them of that, because none of the villagers ever gave me a second glance. I would sit in my car, tremored with anticipation, anxiously watching the side road for the first sight of her battered small Renault. If I had any fears at all at the beginning of our affair it was for her driving.

'Are you sure that car's safe? Are the brakes okay? I saw how you took that corner without looking. I worry about you.'

'I'm perfectly safe. You forget, I know all these roads blindfold. Anyway you can always see what's coming at night.

We would meet in the middle of the square – the sort of shot always favoured in those pre-war French movies. Yet we never kissed in the open: I took no chances – saving our first embraces for when we were safely in my car. I bought her gifts, small tokens such as she might have purchased for herself, again so as not to arouse suspicion in others – never anything really expensive, mostly things I thought might amuse her.

Most evenings I drove us into the countryside, selecting some out-of-the-way inn which other members of the crew were unlikely to frequent. Our favourite haunt became a small and unpretentious bistro where the menu was simple and the service unobtrusive. Real lovers shun ostentation; all we wanted was an excuse to be together. We usually drank the house wine, rough but good, and sometimes Laura would share my after-dinner Calvados, always making the same grimace when the liquid first hit the back of her throat. I've no idea what we looked like to other people and to be truthful, except for a Dutch family, guttural and gross, who more or less monopolised the bistro one evening, we never attracted any criticism. The oldest man in the Dutch family – I took him to be the father of the brood – aimed some comments about us in his native language and

234

though neither of us could translate his disapproval was obvious. He had two bovine daughters who must have been roughly the same age as Laura and they emulated his outrage between gulps of sweetbreads. But that incident apart we became, I like to think, part of the furniture, ignored by the other diners who were mostly locals, for it was not an establishment featured in the snob tourist guides. We awarded it our own three stars.

Those were the best times, I don't think there were any better. I was still constantly dazed by my good fortune, by the fact that she gave herself to me so readily and with such grace. Most of the women I'd known and had affairs with had either demanded too much or withheld too much, but Laura seemed devoid of sexual cunning. Her youth, the difference of age between us, frequently pulled me up short and in many ways I had to rethink my ossified attitudes, sometimes dredging my memory to bring discarded opinions to the surface.

'You know what you give me,' I once said. 'You give me life. When I'm with you I see everything differently.' I suppose the only thing about her I found difficult to come to terms with was her style in clothes. 'You look like a pirate,' I said. 'Perhaps I am a pirate,' she answered. 'I like plundering the shops and wearing outrageous clothes.' My previous, conservative taste was often shattered, but that was no great loss. Her peacock finery was always amusing, conflicting colours thrown together, and this was the period when the young were rediscovering the fifties fashions. Sometimes she wore masculine jackets, giving her a rakish look, but never butch. It was a mixture of the old and the new. She coerced me into giving her some of my shirts. 'They're cut better than women's,' she informed me, and of course I could refuse her nothing. They looked better on her – it was strangely erotic to glimpse the outline of her breasts beneath something I had previously worn. She never wore a bra and would often reach across the dinner table and take my hand and place it over a breast. Sometimes the initiative would be mine and I would caress her under the table. It became a sort of dare between us to see what we could get away with in close proximity to other diners.

We searched and found a deserted area on the route back to the village square – a clearing in a small silver-birch forest which concealed my car from passing traffic – and here, after we had made love, we would sometimes give ourselves over to fantasies, our favourite being the one where we were marooned in a log cabin during a snow-storm, making endless love in front of a roaring log fire. We talked of travels we would take together, believing, I suppose, like all lovers, that the affair would never end. She seemed to have forgotten the existence of Gelbard and although we often discussed Martin (I told her parts of the story – how I came to work on the film in the first place), his passion for her seemed part of another age. I worked with her on her role, hearing her lines as I deliberately took the longest route back to her home, delaying the moment when we had to part.

Clever, devious though I might have been with the rest of the cast and crew, there was one person I didn't entirely fool, and that was Michelle. I owed it to her to give some explanation of my absence from her bed. Never before had I had such a choice between two women, so with the predatory instinct for self-preservation, I played the moral-ist, concealing my real reasons. I was never sure whether she believed me or not, but I did at least give her a face-saver. It's always possible that she didn't need one, for all I know she might have had all she wanted from me. At any rate there were no hysterics, no recriminations and we remained on the best of terms. I could not believe my luck.

As far as I was able to tell the film was proceeding smoothly. By now Martin was half-way through the sche-dule and despite the inevitable daily moans about the cost from Latrough, everybody, even the waspish Charles, seemed to have settled into a smooth routine. I found it difficult to judge Martin's state of mind regarding Laura. When we were alone he never missed an opportunity to agonise over his feelings for her. I suppose I should have felt more guilt, but love makes monsters of us all. The humiliation of the episode in the gazebo had obviously had its effect, and he was still concerned that, given a few drinks, Charles might yet betray him.

'I was mad that night, Harvey. Seeing her there sitting at

my own dinner table looking so utterly desirable, something snapped . . . I thought of what might have been, because as you probably realise my marriage is only held together by pity. That and the fact that the boys have always looked up to me, God knows why. Beware of pity, chum.'

I had the feeling that he was acting it out for me, that part of him was enjoying the drama of it all, though perhaps I'm being too cynical. Perhaps the fact that, as he talked about Laura, I could project myself to our next meeting, making his hopes my certainties, renders even my cynicism suspect.

'There are times, chum, when I wish I'd never clapped eyes on her . . . But I did and now I have to live with it somehow . . . Tell me, honestly, do you think I can repair the damage?'

He didn't really crave honesty; he wanted a salve, something to placate the wound, and that is what, with casual generosity, I gave him.

'She's never mentioned it, has she?'

'Not to me,' I said.

'That's something, isn't it? A good sign, wouldn't you say?'

'Definitely.'

'What would you do in my place?'

'I think you can only play it like you are doing. Take care of her on the set, but don't be too obvious about it otherwise Suzanne is going to get her nose out of joint.'

'Oh, I'm careful about that . . . But what's the future, chum? Do you think I've blown it?'

'Well, I think you always had two strikes against you. Not only the boyfriend, but you yourself, your whole set-up here. Let me ask you the fifty-dollar question . . . Let's assume nothing happened that night, there's no competition, no obstacles at all . . . and Laura returns your feelings totally. How would you play it then? Would you throw in your all, make a clean break?'

'I don't know the answer to that, I keep going round in circles . . . Do you think I'm completely dotty, chum?'

'No, I understand completely,' I said.

The only thing to be said in my favour was that Martin would have been incapable of believing that I could be a rival. I'm sure he looked upon me as an employee and staff didn't step out of line in Martin's book. It was true that he regarded me as privileged staff, the old trusted retainer who was aware the Master had a skeleton in the cupboard, somebody to whom he could turn in times of stress, but nevertheless still staff. Beware of pity, he had said, but I had pity to spare for him.

'I don't know what I'd do if I didn't have you to confide in,' he said. 'You've been my only safety valve through all this.'

'You know you can trust me, Martin,' I said.

I don't know how many days passed before the blow fell. Looking at my diary for that year I see that I have circled the date September 7th, but the rest of the page is blank. Now, I can't be sure of anything. Perhaps complete happiness is always an illusion, something that only romantic novelists propogate. I thought I was completely happy, just as all smokers believe that they are the ones who will escape lung cancer.

The day before, which was a Sunday (so perhaps the 7th, being a Monday, *is* the correct date), Laura and I spent the day in the country. I took her far up into the mountains for a picnic lunch. We found a spot overlooking the distant lakes, Napoleon country according to Laura, the route he had taken during the 100 days. There was wild heather everywhere and the constant hum of collecting bees. We ate cheese and fresh crusted bread, peaches and nectarines, washed down with Chablis kept cold on ice. And afterwards, lazily, with more tenderness than passion, we made love. I don't think there had ever been a time in my life when I felt so completely happy.

We stayed there until the sun had gone behind the mountains. The clear air was chilly when we packed and drove back. She had a long scene to play the following morning. 'I'd better go to bed early for once,' she said, 'and learn my lines.' I dropped her outside her home, watching from a distance as she walked into the house, her cartwheeling dogs dancing attendance. When I got back to my own rooms the scent of her was still with me.

I felt too restlessly content to follow her example and

retire early – I knew that I was too hyped-up for sleep – so after a shower and a change of clothes I drove myself into Nice, intending to have a quiet meal at one of the restaurants which line the pedestrian precinct closed to motor traffic. It was always alive: young students working their passage played guitar, others mimed à la Marcel Marceau; there was a distinct flavour of La Vie Bohème about the area, the only discordant note being the inevitable sex shop, black like a funeral parlour, the furtive clientele entering through a beaded doorway. I took a book with me – I seem to remember it was a paperback of Ford's *The Good Soldier*, which I wanted to re-read – and chose a restaurant where the fish specialities, so Michelle had told me, were worth making a detour for. The place was crowded and I had to share the last outside table, my unknown companion being an old man who was solemnly consuming a *bouillabaisse* of monstrous proportions, the mere sight of which dictated that I chose a simple dish of plain grilled sole.

I have always been fascinated by the passing scene, always regretted that I missed living in Paris between the wars when, from all accounts, a whole artistic generation had phoenixed from the boulevard cafés. Most of the strolling population were tourists, their ranks infiltrated by young whores of both sexes, the queens sporting black leather and gypsy earrings: one, a lone transvestite with dyed pink hair, carried a Siamese cat in his arms. The cat had a necklace to match its owner's. I was sitting too far back to be propositioned, and in any case the old man troughing his *bouillabaisse* afforded me unknowing protection.

Perhaps because, paradoxically, she was closest and at the same time furthest from my thoughts, the shock of suddenly seeing Laura almost destroyed my reason. At first I thought, No, it's not her, it couldn't be, just a trick of the imagination, I must be mistaken – there were, after all, any number of young girls parading up and down wearing clothes similar to those she delighted in. Equally, the fact that she was walking hand in hand with a boy of her own age gave me a few seconds false hope. But then they stopped to admire something in a shop window and I had a clearer view. There was no mistake. The boy – he was long-haired, dressed in faded jeans and a T-shirt – was a complete stranger to me. As they lingered outside the shop he put his arm round Laura's shoulders and pulled her to him. I saw them kiss, saw her lips part to receive his kiss. They stood locked together and oblivious, then as the embrace ended she nuzzled at him, her face pushed into his neck the way small children seek contact with those closest to them.

For fully a minute I could do nothing. Bile, the taste of the meal I had just finished, crowded my mouth. There seemed to be no air around me. Then, in new panic, I tried to summon a waiter for the check, but was ignored. I snatched some notes from my pocket and left them under my plate.

'L'addition,' I shouted to the old man, as though, inevitably, he must be deaf as well as old. His head jerked up from his spattered napkin, and he stared at me, understandably bewildered by my sudden frenzy.

'Pay it for me,' I shouted, then left, pushing my way through the crowds in a desperate effort not to lose sight of Laura, but she and the unknown young man had disappeared. I came to the intersection where my choices were four-fold, already out of breath as though I had run a great distance instead of merely a few yards. Blundering around, going first in one direction then in another, my heart loud in my ears, I searched the area for the best part of twenty minutes without ever seeing them again. You fool, you fool, I thought, blaming myself for ever believing in love, at one point even talking out aloud like some madman. And then, suddenly, I found myself almost on top of them as they appeared in the doorway of another shop. She seemed to be buying him a garish T-shirt; she held it against his chest and again he kissed her. I was close enough to touch Laura, and as she turned to go back into the shop we came face to face. Now it was her turn to mirror my panic, staring into my love-blinded face. For a few seconds neither of us moved – the young man was still admiring his gift and unaware – and then I walked quickly away, resisting every urge to look back until I was lost in the unknowing crowd. I have no recollection of how I found my way back to my car, or how long I took to find it; nor do I recall the journey back to the Auberge. I was like a drunken horseman who relies on his mount to see him safely home.

I suppose that when one loves to an extreme it is impossible to comprehend that one is not loved in return. Laura's betrayal seemed all the more inexplicable when only a few hours previously she had given herself to me – then it had been my lips on her welcoming mouth. Gelbard I could have understood, for he had a prior claim, he was somebody I had come to terms with – but the unknown youth was a rival to inspire terror. I made futile comparisons, pacing the bedroom where happiness had begun. I reconstructed everything we had said to each other, as though by the very act of memory I could somehow exorcise the scene I had witnessed. The madman who stared back at me from the bathroom mirror compared his appearance to that of her new lover, since lover he had to be, no other explanation was possible. Yet it appeared inconceivable that she could part from me and a few hours later bestow her favours on somebody else.

For the first time since my arrival in France I began to understand Martin's disintegration. I tortured myself, re-running the sequence on my mind's screen – stopping and starting the footage, examining every frame: the way she had inclined inwards towards his lean body, the look on her face (this in close-up) as she received his kiss, her flash of dismay when I suddenly materialised. Then anger wiped the screen clear of those images, anger fuelled by steady drinking, though the drink never touched me. How twisted we humans are: the deceiver deceived becomes the deceiver outraged. Then my mood fluctuated again. I tried to reason with myself, finding excuses for her, applying a rough logic for her actions, but all the old jealousies returned and with them a pain I swear I had not felt since I was Laura's age. I gave way to a wild hope that perhaps if she could be made to realise the extent of my hurt she would feel some pity – at that moment. I would have settled for pity, for anything but the end of loving.

That night I dreamt that Laura phoned me and said nothing had changed, and I woke to the sound of the telephone ringing but it was Martin's voice I heard on the other end of the line. He immediately launched into a long diatribe I found impossible to follow.

'Where are you?' I finally said, not knowing where I was myself.

'At the studio, where the hell else would I be?'

'Sorry. I hung one on last night.'

I stared at my watch, trying to make out the figures. It seemed to be past ten. Martin was speaking too fast for comprehension, yet there was a note in his voice that made me wary of asking him to repeat himself. I caught the words 'that bloody useless little shit' and then, like a punch under the heart, 'Laura'.

'What's happened?' I said.

'For Christ'sake, haven't you been taking any of it in? I've just spelt it out for you . . . Look, I'm not going to say it all again . . . Get yourself organised and get down here as soon as possible. I've got to talk to you.'

I said, 'Laura's all right, isn't she?', but the line went dead and my mind opened to let panic in again. As I hurriedly shaved, nicking the swollen flesh in several places, I re-lived the previous night's agonies. Sleep is meant to bring relief from pain, but the wound was too recent, the poisons were still at work. I tore off small pieces of toilet paper and stuck them to the cuts on my neck. The blood still oozed as I pulled a clean shirt over my head – specks fouled the collar. I delayed only long enough to gulp a cup of black coffee laced with the remains of the cognac.

On the journey to the studio I rehearsed how I would behave when next I came face to face with Laura. Curiously – or perhaps inevitably – this occupied me more than the reason behind Martin's urgent summons. There was always some new crisis on a film set, actors seem to need a periodic fix of real-life drama to fuel the drama of make-believe. Charles, I thought, must have thrown a temperament in his scene with Laura, that seemed the most likely explanation. On Martin's instructions I had so structured the rewrite as to give Laura the most effective moments. It was a Monday morning, never Charles's best day.

I went straight onto the sound stage, but there was no sign of Martin or any of the artists. Gerry was lighting with the stand-ins and I could detect nothing untoward.

'Where is everybody?' I asked Bernard.

'Who d'you want?'

'Martin. He sent for me in a panic.'

'He's in his office, I think.'

'And watch out,' Gerry said, 'because there's a decided chill in the air.'

'Any idea why?'

'Not a clue.'

'Is it Charlie? Is Charlie playing up?'

'No, haven't seen him, we haven't had a rehearsal yet. Martin stalked onto the set in a right old moody and then stalked off again, didn't even give me a camera angle to be getting on with, so I'm just guessing at the moment. Painting with light though, as always. What've you done to your neck?'

'Attempted suicide,' I said.

As I crossed the lot towards Martin's office I could hear pop music coming from the make-up and hairdressing rooms, then the sound of Suzanne screaming with laughter. The normality of the scene somehow heightened my unease.

Martin was alone, sitting slumped behind his desk. A pose, I thought for my effect, like something out of *Dallas* where the patriarch figure is about to break bad news to an erring scion.

'Excuse my appearance,' I said. 'You caught me on the hop this morning. What's wrong?'

'Read that.'

He swivelled a copy of *The Hollywood Reporter* towards me. 'Inside page, the Hank Grant column.'

Hank Grant has for years collected the social minutia that trickles down from the Beverly Hills canyons like the mud after a heavy rainfall. I knew him to be a non-malicious soul earning an honest crust, but like any columnist with a daily quota to fill he was open to plants from publicists anxious to earn their honest crumbs. I scanned down the text until I spotted Laura's name:

The sun never sets on the Côte d'Azur. Young Laura Taylor is storming her own Bastille in the Latrough–James movie currently lensing in the South of France.

243

Advance reports suggest that not only is Miss Taylor turning in a sizzling performance for her film debut, she is also creating a little private mayhem. The twenty-year-old dazzler appears to have captured David Latrough's heart in some off-screen episodes that would earn an R Rating.

I took my time reading it.

'Well?' Martin said.

'Just the usual stuff. Flattering for our David, I suppose, but harmless enough.'

'What d'you mean, harmless? Don't give me harmless. I'm going to crucify the little sod.'

'Who?'

'That drunken ponce who calls himself a publicity man . . . Hank Grant didn't think that one up for himself. He was handed it.'

'It was probably a dull day,' I said. 'Why get so upset? When you rang me I thought something really hideous had happened.'

'You don't think this is hideous?'

'It's a gossip item, Martin, four days old, by now the whole issue has been recycled into toilet paper. Anyway, how d'you know it was Marvin? Could have been David himself.'

'That makes it worse. You're the one I rely on, and one thing I have learnt about this business, when it's in print the smoke usually turns into fire. Has he been seeing her?'

'Who, David? Maybe, I don't know . . . I mean, I'm not her keeper. But if he has they sure as hell aren't about to announce the wedding bells. You see him more than I do. Has he said anything to you?'

'He's crazy about her.'

'So's the prop man. She's everybody's flavour of the month.'

'Rather Gelbard than him,' Martin said.

'Boy, how soon they forget . . . Not so long ago you were going ape about Gelbard. This means nothing. David probably hasn't even read it.'

'He left it open on my desk this morning.'

'Okay, he's read it. Doesn't make it true. True or false, there's nothing you can do about it.'

'I can do plenty. I can fix that jerk publicity creep for a start.'

'No good blaming him. He doesn't know how you feel about Laura,' I said in a forlorn attempt to make some excuse for poor Marvin. 'David's avid for publicity . . . Did I tell you he wants me to write his speech for the big dinner he's throwing?'

'What dinner?'

'Hasn't he told you?'

'No. What fucking dinner?'

'He's intending to fly in a plane full of media freeloaders, show them a bit of the film, wine and dine them and then make the big speech. Like I said, he's hungry for space.'

'He's not showing any of my film.'

'Well, sorry I mentioned it. I thought he must have discussed it with you.'

'That's all I need . . . Jesus! this whole bloody film has been a nightmare from day one.'

'I heard it's going rather well. Everybody seems very pleased with the stuff, so I've heard.'

'Who's everybody? I'm the only one who counts and I'm not pleased with it. How can you be pleased with basic crap?'

'So what else can I say to cheer you up? You want me to do a handstand, jump out of the window, tell you a few jokes?' I presented a facade of cheerfulness that was far from genuine. I felt some relief that his reason for calling me had nothing to do with the events of the previous evening, but that was all. While he ranted on, all I could think about was my next meeting with Laura. The gossip column item, I knew, had no basis in truth. Or had it? If she could cheat on me so casually with the unknown young man, why not with David Latrough?

'Just keep your ear to the ground, that's all I ask,' Martin said. 'I'll take care of the rest.'

'And keep writing the crap?' I couldn't resist that exit line.

It must have been mental telepathy because on my way out of the studio Latrough buttonholed me.

'Hey, Harvey, just the guy I wanted to see. I've written out a few one-liners for my speech – just to get you started . . . D'you know you're bleeding?'

'Yes,' I said, 'it's the stigmata. If I'm not careful Martin will start to worship me.'

'Why don't you use an electric job?'

'I do. But only on my legs.'

'Listen, save all the jokes for my speech. I'll have my girl type up the notes and get them to you.'

As we stood there outside the sound stage I saw Laura, Charles and Michelle being posed for some publicity shots. Marvin was flapping around giving a somewhat unconvincing performance of a man on top of his job – presumably for Latrough's benefit. While the photographer was reloading, Charles suddenly spotted me. 'Harvey! you old sod, come over here, I've a bone to pick with you.'

Laura turned, shielding her eyes against the sun.

'How long are you going to be around?' Latrough asked.

'I was going back to my hotel to work.'

'Okay, no sweat. I'll have the notes sent over to you. Make a start, will you, because I want to get this thing rolling.'

When he left me I walked over to the group. I heard Marvin say, 'Charles you get in the middle for this one and have the girls on either side. A real close three. Look like you're enjoying it.'

'You want us mounted or just holding hands?'

I waited until the shot had been taken.

'Come and join us,' Charles said. 'Have your holiday snap taken.'

I shook my head.

'Come on, otherwise I'm a single thorn between two roses.'

'Yes, come on,' Michelle said.

'I'm not dressed for it.'

'Don't be so bloody upstage. Anyway, they'll crop you out if they publish it.'

I looked directly at Laura for the first time. She didn't seem too happy about any of it. Charles stepped forward

246

and dragged me into the scene. 'Stand next to Laura. Look like a friend of the bridegroom and say fromage. Go ahead, get it before he changes his mind.'

I posed alongside Laura. Just before the photographer fired his shutter she reached for my dead hand.

'Wearing your red neck this morning, I see,' Charles said. 'Unsteady the hand that wields the razor. Must have been a heavy weekend. We should have got you into make-up. Okay, that's it, Marvin, I've had enough. Never give the public too much of a good thing. I'll have ten copies of the last one, maybe use it as a Christmas card. Is it too early for a drink?'

'Yes, Charlie,' Michelle said. 'We haven't worked yet, remember?'

'No, you're right. What the hell is happening? I had a seven-thirty call, by eight-twenty when the Dowager had worked her magic I looked divine and now all that artistry is fast going to waste. Bernard!'

Bernard appeared on cue.

'What's happening? What sort of call is this?'

'We'll be ready for a full rehearsal in about ten minutes, Mr Croze.'

'When they start calling you Mr Croze you know the rot is setting in. Formality breeds contempt, Bernard. That's my maxim for today. Are you going to stay and watch us stumble through your dialogue, Harvey dear?'

'I'd love to, but duty calls.'

'Oh, do stay,' Laura said. 'Stay and have lunch with us.'

I thought, you're not going to get off that easily. 'I can't,' I said. 'David's just asked me to do something for him in a hurry.'

'Producer's pet,' Charles said. 'Come on girls, if he wants to play hard to get, sod him.' He led them away, but before she left Laura mouthed, 'Please phone me'. I nodded, but without commitment. Then I took Marvin to one side.

'Have you seen Martin this morning?'

'Not yet. Why?'

'A word in your ear. He's out for blood. Your blood in particular.'

'Why, what've I done?' He immediately broke into a sweat, it was like turning on a tap.

247

'A little item in the Hank Grant column. He seems to think it was in your handwriting.'

'Oh, shit! I didn't think he'd use it . . . I just shoved it in with a whole lot of other bits and pieces. Strictly for laughs.'

'Laughs it didn't get. So be prepared.'

I left him standing there. He looked like one of those old comedians who survived to the end of burlesque, coming on between the strip acts, knowing they were going to die but having to go through their routine anyway, because that was show business.

By the time I got back to my hotel there was a message to say that Laura had phoned me. I tried to take stock of the situation, talking out loud to myself – that self-indulgent pursuit of the lonely. It all comes down to pride, I suppose. In love we all think we are unique, God's gift, how could anybody reject us in favour of somebody else? and so forth. I thought back to all the advice I had proffered to others: advice which, repeated to myself, I found cold comfort. You middle-aged dolt, I thought, with your out-dated ideas of romantic love – her generation doesn't think like that. Love is something they pass around like a joint, if you want ordinary home comforts stick to what you understand. What I was suffering from was the sudden withdrawal of the sexual lollipop, just that. There was no need to dress it up in the glad rags of some great poetic romance. All that and more I addressed to myself in a desperate effort to stifle the sense of loss. And all the time I had to resist the urge to return her call, to abase myself, accept whatever consolation prize she cared to offer.

Yet as the day wore on and I struggled to fill my required quota of pages, my resolve weakened like a record player losing speed, so that towards the end of the afternoon I was clock-watching the minutes, waiting for the moment when the shooting would end at the studio. Time passed as slowly as it does on a long flight. I calculated how long it would take her to change out of costume and remove her make-up. Give it another ten minutes, I thought. By then she should be alone in her dressing room, we can talk calmly.

I rang the studio and asked to be put through on her private line.

'Miss Taylor is not answering,' the operator said.

'Well, try make-up please.'

There was a pause and then the Dowager came on the line.

'Is Laura still there?'

'Laura? No, dear, she finished early. She must have gone, oh, a good hour ago . . . I shall see her in the morning. Is there any message?'

'No,' I said. 'No message.'

I had no sooner hung up when my phone went again. It was the concierge.

'Mr Burgess. There is a letter for you. Would you like it brought up?'

'I'll come down,' I said.

But it wasn't from Laura. It was Latrough's notes for his speech. I glanced at them, then made up my mind. A few minutes later I was in my car driving towards Laura's village. I parked outside the local bar and used the telephone kiosk.

Her mother answered.

'Is Laura back from the studio by any chance?'

'Yes.'

'We just want to change her call for tomorrow.'

I heard her shout for Laura and the sound of the dogs yapping in the background. Then Laura came on the line.

'It's me,' I said.

'Oh. Hi.'

'I did call back at the studio, but I missed you.'

'Yes, they let me off early.'

'How did it go?'

'Okay, I think. Slow.'

Her responses were guarded. I tried to keep my own voice matter of fact.

'I was surprised to see you last night.'

'Were you spying on me?'

'No. Why would I do that? I didn't know you were going to be out. You told me you were going to bed early.'

'I was. But an old friend rang me and I changed my mind.'

'I see . . . He seemed like quite an intimate old friend.'

'Not really.'

'It destroyed me,' I said, blurting it out. 'I shouldn't admit that, I suppose, but it did.'

'I'm sorry. I didn't mean to destroy you.'

'You mean, you didn't think I'd ever find out.'

'If that's the way you want to take it.'

'Don't be too cruel,' I said. 'I can't help being jealous.'

'I know about Michelle and I'm not jealous.'

'No . . . well, maybe you don't love me enough to be jealous . . . You still there?'

'Yes.'

'Do you still want to see me?'

'Of course.'

'But on your terms, I suppose?'

'I want to see you. Why do you have to be so serious?'

'Because I am serious. That's my misfortune.'

'Well, I do want to see you.'

'Tonight?'

'Yes.'

'I'm two minutes away, in a call box in the village. That's how stupid and serious I am. I've thought of nothing else all day. How soon can I see you?'

'Give me a chance,' she said. 'I was in the bath when you called.

'How long d'you want? Half an hour?'

'Yes, okay.'

'I'll be outside your house in half an hour. Just tell me one thing . . . Don't see me just to be kind.'

'I'm not.'

'In half an hour then.'

I went into the bar and ordered a Scotch.

'You won't like the whisky I serve,' the proprietor said. He pointed to some nameless brand on the shelf.

'How about a cognac then? Do you recommend that?'

He shrugged and poured me a tot. There were half a dozen locals sitting around regarding me as though I might be a Gestapo officer left over from the Occupation. French village bars don't seem designed for the happy hour. I downed the cognac which tasted like methylated spirit laced with pepper and left before the village elders overwhelmed me with their famed fraternity.

I sat in my car for the next fifteen minutes, spending the

time trying to fathom what I really felt towards Laura. It was like pulling scabs off a wound – a necessary pain. I guess there is no hurt in life equal to that which our lovers can inflict upon us. I was going to meet her again on her terms, there was no point in pretending otherwise. No matter what cards I held back in my hand she could call Gin any time she liked. The long fuse of jealousy had been fired and would smoulder on. I had eaten crow and was Oliver-Twisting it back for more. O the tyranny of a beautiful face and ripe young breasts, forget the belly like a mound of wheat and the navel like a goblet of wine, we feast below with none of the wisdom of Solomon. The elation, the anticipation of masochistic pleasures I felt as I restarted the car engine and drove towards her house belonged to another part of my life . . . And so we preserve all our illusions when the ego has been laid bare.

But, yes, of course, she was worth it, I thought, watching her come from the house and walk towards me.

'Fancy meeting you here,' I said. 'What an amazing piece of luck. Doing anything this evening?'

'Yes, I'm meeting somebody.'

'Pity. I was going to ask you out to dinner.'

'Well, I could be persuaded to change my mind.'

'What would it take?'

'Nothing. I'm persuaded.'

The moment she was in the car she said. 'I'm sorry,' and kissed me.

'You really know how to ruin a man's peace of mind, don't you? After last night I was never going to see you again . . . And here I am, not seeing you again.'

'I can't help the way I am.'

'Can't you?'

'It's just that sometimes I feel I'm being pushed into a corner . . . And then I have to break out.'

'And break hearts,' I said.

'Not deliberately. I'm left as often as I leave.'

'I find that hard to believe. Shall we go to our usual place?' She nodded. I drove slowly, anxious to have my say in private.

'I wish I'd been your first love,' I said. 'But as it is I'll have

251

to settle for you being my last. I've got a terminal case, you know that, don't you?'

She didn't answer.

'So what's the competition? Who have I got to eliminate? I know about Jean and Martin . . .'

'There's nothing to fear from Martin.'

'Nothing? Ever?'

'No, of course not.'

'So what about the boy last night? What's his name?'

'Gerard.'

'Is he a new addition?'

'No. We were at school together,' she said.

'And he's in love with you presumably?'

'I suppose so.'

'What does he do?'

'He's still at college. Studying to be an architect.'

'And you . . . are you in love with him?'

'I've known him since I was sixteen,' she said, and I knew by the way she said it that he had been the first. Far more than the present, the past had the power to empty me. I couldn't bear the thought of those lost years.

'So he must still mean something to have survived?'

'Why d'you want to know all these things? I don't ask you about your other women.'

'That's because you're not the jealous type, or so you tell me. I am. You don't understand that, do you?'

I probed on and on during the meal, as though by pushing the scalpel ever deeper I might perform an operation by which I would be cured of love. None of her answers doused my doubts. I wanted chapter and verse, all the bad news at once – evidence enough to convict her forever. My appetite was muffled with concealed anguish. I presented a cheerful face across the table, but all the while suffering that particular agony which accompanies sexual passion. I could have taken her there at the table, for the knowledge of her simple infidelities only increased my desire. The years that separated us were like a minefield I had to cross, just as otherwise quite rational people are sometimes irresistibly drawn to the live rail in the subway.

'So what's going to happen to us?' I said.

'Nothing. Unless you want it to end.'

'Do any of them want to marry you?'

'I don't want to marry, not yet anyway, not for a long time.'

'What if I asked you?'

'Don't,' she said, 'because you'll only make it worse. Why can't we just go on as we are?'

'That's the deal, is it? I can't have you to myself?'

She looked at me, staring into my eyes; there was tenderness in her expression, but no hope.

'I'm not tough enough,' I said. 'I can't live by those rules, so it's best if we end it now. I've got a couple more weeks on the film and then I'll be out of your life for good and never bother you again.'

'I'll bother you.'

'That's not fair.'

'But I don't want you to stop seeing me.' She reached for my hand, sliding her fingers across my palm and folding them into mine. My body responded, remembering past pleasures, the feel of her skin against mine, the taste of her lips. I knew then that, despite all the brave words, I would never have the courage to break completely – that when it ended, as end it inevitably would, I would still carry the loss forward year after year like a bad debt that will never be honoured.

'What a funny pair we are,' I said.

'Why funny?'

'Don't you think we're funny? I hated you last night, I couldn't bear to see you with that boy, and yet here I am lost again . . . I saw you kiss him and only a few hours before that we'd been making love . . . Have you any idea what that did to me?'

Her hand tightened on mine. 'I never said I was perfect.'

'But you did say you loved me. It's the same old difference, isn't it? Your generation and mine . . . Not that we weren't just as cruel, I suppose. One forgets. When you're in love, as I'm in love, you force those things out of your mind. I love you to distraction.' The phrase, even as it left my mouth, appeared dated, like something out of the bygone age I had been describing. 'So this is where we begin again. But you'll have to live with my jealousy or give me up completely, there isn't any middle course.'

253

Later, when I had parked the car in our secret clearing, her love-making had a new intensity. 'Say it,' I told her, 'say that you love me. Even if you don't mean it, say it now because otherwise I can't do it,' and she moaned the words to me, her body thrashing against mine as that burning release calmed both of us.

FIFTEEN

Perhaps this story would have had a happier ending if we had parted forever that night, but as so often with the making of a film nothing went according to plan or schedule. Martin was virtually on the home stretch with only three weeks remaining when Suzanne suddenly took to her bed with what began as a summer cold. Nobody panicked at that stage since all star artists are heavily insured against everything except being struck by falling UFOs. The production office rescheduled, bringing forward some large crowd scenes that could be shot without the principals being present.

Charles made the expected crude comment on her condition. 'She'll love being fussed over. Curious how French doctors treat everything by shoving bloody suppositories up your arse . . . Case of the moving finger writes and having writ sends you a sodding great bill . . . Have you bombarded her with masses of flowers and peaches, Harvey? I shall be original and send her a copy of *The Joy of Sex*. I always feel so dreadfully erotic whenever I'm forced to take to my bed . . .'

But despite this necessary show of indifference, he was solicitude itself when we all trouped in to see her.

'Camille, dear,' he cooed, 'come back to us soon, life isn't the same without you.'

Like any actress she managed to look glamorous when receiving visitors, but her face had a curious texture under the make-up and I was not entirely surprised when the following day the news was given out that her condition was more serious. The doctors had now diagnosed it as viral pneumonia; the earliest date she could resume filming was three weeks away.

'One's sorry for her, of course,' Martin said, 'but isn't it bloody typical, just as we were in sight of the end!'

We were all assembled for an emergency production meeting. Suzanne had half a dozen scenes remaining before her role was complete, most of them with Charles. Latrough's first thought was to write her out but several of them were key scenes vital to the complicated plot.

After an hour or so of abortive discussion it was inevitable that all eyes turned to me.

'You'll have to come up with something,' Martin said. 'We know we can't entirely dispense with her, but I'm sure that with a little ingenuity, and your usual brilliance, you could revamp some of the stuff and give it to . . .'

I watched his face as he went through the charade of pretending to have mislaid Laura's name.

'Michelle?' I prompted.

'No . . . I think you'd get more value by going for what's-her-name? Laura.'

'Difficult,' I said.

'Yes, well it's difficult for everybody, but we can't just sit around doing fuck-all while madam recovers, can we? We've got the weather to think about. Before very long the bloody leaves will be changing colour.'

'Okay, well obviously I'll try. I can't throw every scene to Laura, otherwise the plot will be total nonsense.'

'What sort of story shall I put out?' Marvin interrupted with his infallible knack of choosing the wrong moment.

'Why do you have to put any story out?' Martin snarled.

'The Press are asking, Martin. I can't keep it under wraps.'

'Just tell them the facts. It's not a State Secret.'

'Tell them she's got pneumonia, right?'

'Yes, pneumonia, and look it up in the dictionary first – we don't want a lawsuit as well as an insurance claim.'

'How long before we get new pages?' Latrough asked. 'I got people flying in.'

'Well, cancel them.'

'How can I cancel them? Don't give me cancel. You want to offend the whole West Coast Press?'

'I offended them years ago, and they've always offended me.'

'Tough! I happen to be the producer and I also happen to believe that this fucking epic you're directing needs all the help it can get. I'm buying you goodwill in advance.'

'Balls! I know what you're buying yourself – all of seven column inches of deathless prose. If you're lucky. The only certain thing you're going to get out of those morons is a drink bill that'll turn you white overnight.'

'You stick to what you know, Martin, and I'll do my thing.'

Neither of them seemed inhibited by having an audience for their slanging match.

'Just don't charge it to the film, that's all.'

'That's great coming from a director who is already over scheduled and over budget! I'll charge what I fucking well like.'

'I'll be in my office, Harvey.' Martin made what he hoped was a dignified exit. The rest of the production crew gathered their papers and shuffled out after him. Latrough motioned for me to hang back.

'Look, screw him. I'm the one who's signing the checks. I want that speech, so get your priorities right. Nothing's gonna change my schedule.'

'What do I tell him when he starts screaming for new pages?'

'Harvey, get wise. You want to be a two-bit rewrite man all your life?'

'Whatever's left of my life, you mean.'

'Play ball with me and your next meal ticket's guaranteed. What d'you owe him, huh? Nothing. You think he'll even send a wreath to your widow?'

'That'd be difficult anyway. I'm not married.'

'You know what I'm talking about. Martin's a fucking has-been. You want a future, row in my boat.'

It was the usual illuminating stuff and I switched off, my thoughts going to Laura, thinking how often a career turned on unforeseen events such as Suzanne's illness. Laura had auditioned for the film as a small-part player, grateful just to get onto the studio lot: Martin had become instantly obsessed, and now she was going to end up with a

257

major role. Some young actresses with fifty times her talent, but lacking her looks, would go a lifetime without ever having such luck. I didn't begrudge her the break, though part of me acknowledged that the more successful she became, the less likely I would keep her. You had to be something of a heartbreaker on and off screen to survive in our business, and she was a heartbreaker. I was in over my head in all sorts of ways.

Of course if I'd had any sense I'd have folded my tent right then, turned in my rented IBM and walked away into one of those good old movie sunsets. But like everybody connected with that sorry mess, I wasn't too heavy on sense that summer. We were all such selfish people and selfishness made us vulnerable, just as we deserved to be. I said at the beginning of this account that most of the mistakes were mine, and that's true. I can't blame anybody but myself.

So, I went back for more, back to Martin's office to listen to him sound off about producers in general and Latrough in particular. To listen to him talk about the girl I was sleeping with and how he was going to change everything and get even with everybody. It was just another of his fantasies, as his original description of Gelbard had been. Maybe our business turns all of us crazy in the end. God knows I've seen enough bright talents burn themselves out. Real talents, not the slick opportunists like Martin. The Martins of my world survive from lack of talent: all they have is a gift for manipulating the talents of others.

That day in his office he ranted on and I feigned interest. I pretended an enthusiasm for a script that had long since been reduced to nonsense. My thoughts went back to that day when the Concorde landed: I could see everything with hideous clarity. To paraphrase old W. C. Fields, those who are sucked in never get an even break. Again – my miscalculation, my conceit, nobody to blame but myself.

When his anger was spent, he turned on the director's voice again, discussing the script changes as though he was translating the Dead Sea Scrolls. He meant me to believe that his ideas for switching some of the old scenes to Laura were purely for the good of the film. At one point he actually had the nerve to suggest that Suzanne's illness was a blessing in disguise. 'One can always improve, Harvey.

258

Well, I don't have to tell you that. The more I think about these changes, the more I'm convinced we got lucky by chance. There's more poignancy in Laura's character playing these scenes. And believe me, I'm not just saying that because.'

'Of course not,' I said.

'We're going to see this through together.' And he gave me another variation on the same theme that Latrough had played. Different instrument, same tune.

So I went back to the hotel room and the first thing I did was ring Laura.

'I was in the papers today,' she said, '*Nice Matin*, they had a picture of me on the front page.' From the way she said it I knew she thought it was important.

'Come on over and show me,' I said. 'I work better when you're here.'

'Oh, I can't.'

'What're you doing?'

'They rang and said I've got three days off, so I'm going to visit some relatives.'

'Where?'

'Just outside, Marseille.'

'You going today?'

'Yes. I'm literally just about to leave and catch the train.'

'Another script change,' I said.

'What?'

'Nothing, just my sense of humour at the moment.' I started to tell her what happened at the studio, but she cut me off.

'Look, I have to run. That sounds great. I'm sorry for Suzanne though.'

'When will you be back?'

'Oh, probably early Tuesday morning. Take care.'

'You take care,' I said. 'Have a good time,' but I didn't mean it. I felt instantly deflated; the only thing that had sustained me through the morning's events at the studio had been the thought of making love in the afternoon.

Such creative energy as remained refused to surface. I looked at the notes I had scribbled down in Martin's office and they depressed me. Then I took out the notes Latrough had given me for his speech: they were headed *Be Sincere*,

259

which was underlined twice. Then he had written in back-ward-sloping handwriting:

> I need a real grabber for openers, not too heavy, but something to make the bastards sit up and take notice. My thoughts here are I should aim for a piece that states the need for the industry to go back to its origins. Where has the family audience gone? Why did it run out on us? Work it round to the wrong people in charge of the front offices, the need for a wind of change (I like that phrase, so try and use it). List a few great old time movies like 'Mr Deeds', Grapes of Wrath', 'Captains Courageous' – I leave that to you – and then go into we got too many captains and not enough courageous.'

I was suddenly too exhausted to read any further, and there was nobody with whom I could share my contempt. I thought, what a long way to come to be a whore. Pouring myself a generous Scotch I lay down on the top of the bed. The doves, which at other times I found soothing and romantic, now irritated. After I had closed the shutters the room became stifling hot and the combination of the heat and the Scotch sent me into one of those daytime sleeps that suffocate. When I came to again it was late afternoon and the sun had moved round off my windows, but the doves were still cooing their monotonous dialogue.

Then the phone rang. I lifted the receiver hoping it would be Laura calling to say she missed me, but instead it was Marvin.

'You working?' he said. 'Did I disturb you?'

'No and no.'

'Listen, you're the only person I can talk to.' He sounded drunk. 'You gotta help me. Can I come up and see you?'

'Why not?' I said wearily. 'Where are you?'

'Down in the lobby.'

'You can come up on one condition. Bring another bottle of Scotch up with you. Charge it to the room.'

He duly appeared and for once I was glad to see him. I broke the seal on the Black Label but before I had poured two measures Marvin started to weep.

'Jesus Christ, Harvey, it's the fucking injustice of it. I

mean, I wouldn't mind being eighty-sixed if I'd screwed up on something important, but that evil mother threw the book at me for nothing! Nothing!'

'Who are we talking about? Latrough?'

'No, Martin! Martin did it.'

'Because of the Hank Grant piece?'

'No, nothing to do with that. How could he do it for that? He's too sharp for that. Like, you know, I've busted my ass on this movie, busted my ass. I got them real space – the cover of *Paris Match*, that spread on Charles in *Town and Country*, you name it. Like today, a picture on the front page of whatever the local fucking rag's called . . . And d'you know what he had the nerve to tell me? He told me I should be concentrating on him. Like who wants to read about him?'

'He does presumably.'

'I showed him what I'd put out. Is it my fault if they don't print it? Like he's not Kubrick, right? He's not Spielberg. Even if he changed sex over the Atlantic flying Pan Am and had a lesbian affair with all ten stewardesses they'd still put him on the back page. What am I, God or something?'

'You're well out of it, Marvin, old sport.'

'What d'you mean I'm out of it? He didn't fire me – that cunning son of a bitch didn't fire me. No way! That would be too simple, wouldn't it? I mean, when he puts the knife in, he really sticks you. Know what he's gonna do? He's gonna bring in somebody over my head, like I'm to stay on and be the office boy.'

'Screw him. Don't stay on.'

'That's great, that's a real comfort. Where would I go? You think they're standing in line out there waiting to give me a job?'

'Have a talk to David then. Tell him your troubles. From what we saw today there's no love lost between those two. Hit him in his pocket book. He's not going to go for paying two guys for the one job.'

'I went to him, already. But Martin's too smart to be caught out on that one. He's bringing in his own people and paying for them.'

'Well, okay, let him. Sit back, take the money and get a sun tan.'

'You still don't understand, do you? Things like that get around. This one was the come-back for me. I blow this and it's the end of the road.'

All the phrases he used were lifted from a dead dictionary. The mediocrity of the life we both shared was there, mirrored in his wasted face. I could see myself in him, the only difference being I was one rung further up the rotted ladder.

'Marvin, I don't want to steal your moment of angst. You're entitled to it. You've earned it and you should savour it. It's about the only thing left to us, the freedom to commiserate with a fellow eunuch.'

'Why can't I put it like that?'

'It's a knack, Marvin. A little party trick I've perfected over the years. Because – and this is in no way an attempt to top your sad story – I have my own burden at this particular moment.'

I replenished our glasses.

'Nothing to be compared with yours, but sad enough from where I sit.'

'Tell me. I want to share it with you. A burden shared is a burden halved.'

'As we all know our well-respected Suzanne, she of the mammoth boobs and limited talent, is lying on her sick bed, even as we speak. Now we wish her no ill. But . . . her untimely malaise has set in motion a chain of events, the outcome of which could well be cataclysmic. The captain of our ship has ordered me to alter course and steer us towards an even bigger fuck-up than presently exists. And that's only part of it . . . Have you even been in love, Marvin?'

'Is the Pope Catholic?'

'I knew you would give me an original answer. Let me repeat the question. Love, Marvin . . . "where many shipwreck and no further get" . . . hopeless love, Marvin, has that ever crept up on you like a thief in the night to steal your reason?'

'Let me think about it.'

'If you need to think about it, then it hasn't – that terrible joy has passed you by, Marvin, and you're the luckier for it. The Scotch is getting to me, let's change the subject before I get maudlin.'

'Pal, I envy your command of language.'

'Don't. That, too, is a curse, old son. Because . . . Sometimes I wish I had no imagination. No urge to turn on the creative tap. It used to gush, Marvin, but now it merely trickles . . . Let me show you something,' I said. I picked up Latrough's notes for his Address to the nation. 'Handle with care, please.' He peered at them.

'What you are looking at with understandable amazement is the blueprint for a speech which our producer intends to stand and deliver in public. There is a slight catch, however . . . I have to write it, he doesn't soil his hands with such matters. You think you have problems. How would you get out of that one?'

'Boy! I knew he was planning this longshoremen's convention, but he never mentioned any speech . . .'

'It's meant to be a closely-kept secret, to be sprung upon an unsuspecting world.'

'They'll piss all over him in print.'

'I think that's a strong probability, but his heart – that big heart of show business – is set on it, Marvin.'

'So you're stuck with it?'

'He wants something sincere, I shall give him sincerity ad nauseam, thick as honey taken from the comb, a speech so glutinously cloying with sincerity that he may well win a Golden Globe Award next time round just for the sheer nerve of delivering it.'

'I can't wait,' Marvin said. Then, abruptly, he succumbed to one of his instantaneous blackouts. I managed to catch him before he fell off his chair and gently lowered him to the floor. Without opening his eyes he curled his body into the foetal position and began to snore. I regarded him with something approaching affection. An evening with an unconscious Marvin was not what I had planned, but stretcher-bearers have a role to play in any war. I loosened his collar and put a cushion under his head. In some curious way his collapse sobered me, or maybe my resentment at the day's happenings had given me a new charge of energy. I went to my desk and fed the typewriter with a clean sheet of paper, intending to attack Latrough's speech. But such are the inexplicable workings of our hearts, I began to write Laura a first love letter.

More than the sexual act itself, the writing of a love letter is the moment of commitment: in translating our physical feelings into words we are forced to acknowledge the extent of our illusions. We seek new ways of expressing the mundane, erotic adjectives to describe ordinary human flesh; we ascribe to the object of our affections qualities which perhaps exist only in our imagination. I find it odd that I can without difficulty project myself into fictitious characters and describe their emotions with great clarity, but when I attempt to convey my own innermost feelings the end result is always blurred. That night – with Laura absent from me – I wanted to seduce her with words so that when she returned and found the letter waiting she would be blinded by the love she had missed. I closed my mind to the outside world; it was as if I had never lived anywhere but those rooms above the courtyard, that my life had always been bounded by the present film. Memories of my existence before Laura – the time I had spent in Connecticut before Martin's call – took a conscious effort to recall.

If I pondered it logically, I knew why I was staying on to further Martin's conceits and Latrough's ambitions. It had nothing to do with my survival in an industry which had long since scraped me bare; nothing to do with the money I was earning – I had already made enough to keep me for a year and my needs were not extravagant. In the normal course of events I would have turned in the requisite number of pages and found some plausible reason to quit the scene. I had done that many times, before disenchantment could set in. Writers are never missed. All the bribes made to me – those golden secure futures which the Martins and Latroughs of my world dangled like Cartier carrots – had all been promised before. Knowing I was being used I had thought I could use them in turn, but it had all backfired. Martin's obsession, so pathetic from a distance, had infected me: what had started out as an exercise in revenge had become my own Nemesis. But no amount of logic cools the blood when we are in the grip of that particular fever – I would have used any means to keep Laura for myself.

Parts of the letter I rewrote twice before sealing the envelope. Marvin still slept on the floor and perhaps I envied him the oblivion. But while I could happily endure his presence as a near-corpse, the thought of finding him alive and boring in the morning lacked a certain enchantment. It took a prolonged effort to rouse him, but he was an amiable drunk and went quietly. I accompanied him downstairs and bundled him into a taxi, then before I could have third thoughts I gave my letter to the concierge to post.

On the principle that one should never leave undone today those tedious chores that will remain to be done tomorrow, I returned to my desk to grapple with the needs of my producer and director. I brought to both tasks that necessary measure of cynicism which gets us screenwriters through the night. It is not to be inferred or imagined that I brooded overmuch about Art or Truth or Integrity. I dare say this indicates a certain shallowness and lack of character, but it was a reasonable bet that nobody would judge my work in artistic terms. Expediency was the name of the game we were all playing. And while I wrote, the presence of Laura was always there in that room. Perhaps what I chose to call love was only another version of Martin's obsession (a belated and in some ways humiliating discovery). I tried to analyse why I had become so enslaved so quickly and completely. Possessing no photographs of Laura I had to rely on remembered images – leaving my desk at one point to go and stare down at the bed, conjuring up memories of her nakedness, reliving those moments when lust had been slaked. But in memory there was no escape from my sad sentimentality towards a girl who had already revealed that I was not the sole object of her affections, nor was there any future in logic or reason: I had put myself beyond all that, for why else would I have dispensed with the available charms of Michelle? I could have asked her to take me back – but I didn't want convenience, I wanted passion, to be engulfed by that drowning of the soul. Ophelia's black waters over my head, blotting out all else.

So it was that I existed during the period Laura was away. I made work the panacea, forcing myself to finish both the additional scenes and Latrough's speech. But even that conscious resolve did not last the course. The evening before she was due to return I weakened and phoned her home, masking my real concerns with a false casualness when her mother answered.

'Has Laura let you know what train she's coming back on?'

Her mother hesitated before answering.

'Oh, I'm not sure . . . I believe she gets in early tomorrow morning, around six, but I could be wrong.'

'That's at Nice, is it?'

'No, Cannes. If she comes in on that one, she'd get off at Cannes. But don't you bother. I'll tell her to call you when she gets in.'

'No bother,' I said.

Before going to bed that night I made doubly sure I would wake up in good time: as well as setting my alarm clock I put in a call with the night porter.

The weather changed during the night and when I left the hotel the following morning rain slashed into my sleeptender face. I wasn't sure where to find Cannes station so had allowed myself plenty of time for errors. The *péage* was deserted and I motored recklessly, leaving twin spumes in my wake. I had a sense of exhilaration, the anticipation of seeing Laura again stifling all other fears.

Luck was with me and I found the station with half an hour to spare. I bought a platform ticket and made repeated anxious enquiries before being convinced that I was standing in the right place for her expected arrival. The only other travellers about at that hour were workmen and students.

At least four other trains came and went before Laura's was signalled. I paced and chain-smoked. The lashing rain had eased off by then, which I took to be a lucky omen, but when finally her train came into view round the curve I had a last-minute panic: I suddenly realised there were two exits from my platform, both leading to subways under the track. I had convinced myself that I would spot her immediately and had already fantasised the aching rewards of catching her by surprise. Stupidly, I had imagined we would be reunited there on the platform.

But it didn't happen like that. At least forty or fifty people alighted from the train and although I scanned the entire length of it, I saw no sign of Laura. Waiting as long as I dared while the crowd thinned, I then sprinted to one of the subway exits, desperate to get ahead of the mob and beat them to the barrier. Once I got there there was still no Laura. It wasn't until fully five minutes after the general exodus that she came into view.

I stood at the top of the subway stairs as she climbed towards me, and the moment I saw the expression on her face I realised I had lost. There was no smile, no welcome, she did not even offer her cheek to be kissed. I had expected weariness, but not this total rejection. During the walk to my car I managed some small-talk to which she scarcely responded.

'Are you all right?' I said. 'You seem very strange.'

'Do I? Probably because I'm tired. I didn't sleep at all.'

'The train seemed crowded. Didn't you get a decent seat?'

'It wasn't that. I was afraid.'

Her answer chilled me.

'Afraid? What of?'

'I don't know. Everything.'

There was no warmth in her voice, no comfort, I might just as well not have been there. It was almost as if I was merely a chauffeur. She yawned continuously, though whether from genuine tiredness or for effect I had no means of telling.

'I thought you'd be pleased that I met you,' I said, laying myself wide open. 'I got up especially early because I wanted to surprise you. Whatever else, this has to be better than a taxi, doesn't it?'

'Yes.'

'Did you have a nice time?'

She nodded.

'How were your relatives?'

I counted the number of times the windscreen wiper arced before she answered.

'You may as well know now, I didn't see any relatives.'

267

She was staring straight ahead. 'I went away with my boyfriend.'

'Your mother's very loyal, very discreet.' I tried to keep my voice normal. 'What made you suddenly decide to do that?'

'He wanted me to. He was sad.'

'Sadder than you've just made me?'

'Oh, I don't know. I'm tired. I don't suppose you have a monopoly on sadness.'

'No, I don't suppose I have. Well, I'm glad you went on an errand of mercy.' I did my best to conceal the sarcasm. 'He didn't travel back with you?'

'No.'

'Why was that?'

'He had to go back to college.'

'Is that the reason for my ecstatic welcome?'

'I said I'm tired.'

'That's right, you did. I guess you didn't sleep much, on or off the train.'

She leaned back against the headrest and closed her eyes. When we arrived outside her house she got out without a thank-you and went through the gate without looking back. I reversed the car too violently, spinning the rear wheels before accelerating away – a pathetic schoolboy gesture, I suppose, in the circumstances, but the only one I could think of. It wasn't until I had gone half a mile down the road that it struck me that she had never identified which boyfriend.

SIXTEEN

There was no improvement in Suzanne's condition and a decision was taken to go ahead and shoot the revamped scenes with Laura taking over much of the plot. I say 'plot', though little approximating to such a thing still existed. By now even I found the story-line incomprehensible, for not only had my rewrites been rewritten but Martin had also allowed Charles to make his own embellishments on the floor. I had a great deal of time for Charles as an actor, but Somerset Maugham he was not.

I kept away from the studio as much as possible and on those occasions when duty demanded that I attend I made a point of avoiding Laura. There's an old Spanish proverb which goes, 'lovers always think that other people have had their eyes put out' – and I tried to convince myself that nobody would notice the change in me. I had changed: I felt dead inside. For those few brief weeks of happiness I had faced every new day with rediscovered enthusiasms; now I found it a physical effort just to get myself together every morning. At night, shunning company, I drank more than was good for me; steady, solitary drinking alone in my room most of the time, though there was one occasion when I cruised the Nice waterfront, ending up amidst the mirrored reflections of fellow prowlers in the bar of the Hyatt Hotel. Perched on high stools, hunched over our potions, we shared only a common desperation. I made a desultory attempt to date one of the waitresses, but it was a lost cause. The other searchers after the same truth exchanged knowing glances – probably they had tried before me. A pianist in the adjoining room played sentimental numbers, distorted through the sound system but still too potent for comfort. He played an Elton John instrumental, 'Song For Guy', which ends with the whispered repetition of 'Life isn't everything' – just the perfect swan-song for my state of mind.

There was another occasion when, semi-bombed, I went to the cutting rooms and spent time looking at some of the assembled reels on the Steinbeck viewing machine. I made the excuse I wanted to see how some of the new scenes were playing, but that wasn't the real reason. The truth was I wanted to torture myself watching those Technicolored images of Laura pass through the film gate at 24 frames a second – that's the speed that reproduces human action accurately. What it doesn't do is reproduce human emotion accurately.

Martin's editor was a bespectacled man of indeterminate age, named George.

'How d'you think it's shaping up?' I asked.

One thing all editors have in common is loyalty to their director. It's in the cutting rooms that the final and bloodiest battles are fought on any film. George was re-solutely non-committal, and I admired him for that. 'Too early to say,' was as far as he would go. 'I think Martin's getting some good performances. Charles seems to be getting back to his old form and the girls are all very good. Shame about poor Suzanne.'

'But does it make any sense? And don't worry, you won't offend me if you say no.

'Well, obviously any film would benefit from having a script that isn't being rewritten as we go along. On the other hand, I've worked on films that went as smooth as clock-work from day one, and they turned out to be disasters. Who knows? Film is a funny commodity.'

'With funny people working on it . . . Have you never wanted to direct yourself?'

'I was offered a film once. Quite a good script and cast, and I thought about it, but I don't have that temperament. I can put the knife in *after* the event, but not during, if you take my meaning.'

I stared at a frozen frame of Laura on the machine. George activated the Steinbeck again and the film went backwards, Laura walked away from me into a building, all her actions reversed. As always it produced a slightly comic effect, a Chaplinesque jerkiness, and then, as George once again advanced the film she came to meet me, just as she had come to meet me on the railway station – only this time she was smiling for the camera, her face was alive with simulated affection, and a few frames later her lips parted to receive her screen lover's kiss. I turned away before I betrayed myself like some rejected adolescent.

Preparations for Latrough's Press jamboree were now well advanced and hardly a day went by without him asking me to make fresh amendments to his speech. I am sure that in his mind it had assumed Gettysburg proportions.

'I've had a hundred-per-cent acceptance,' he told me. 'And I've swung a great deal with the airline. Plus I gotta rate on the champagne.'

'Congratulations,' I said.

'Yeah, I really feel that this is gonna pin a few ears back on the Coast. The only trouble is I'm a bit short on broads.'

'Maybe you should audition?'

'I thought of that, but that's a little tacky. I got somebody working on it in LA. Photographer friend of mine who does a lotta layouts for those girlie magazines. He always has a great list.'

'Well, they'll give it the class you're looking for,' I said. 'And be pretty with it.'

'That's right. Don't want any dogs or party poopers. I'm having printed menus and place cards.'

'It's going to be quite an occasion, I can see.'

'Harvey, I know Martin thinks he shits class, but I'm gonna surprise him. Him and that snotty wife of his. The whole dinner is going to be put on video and when they leave every guest is going to get a copy.'

'Now that's original,' I said.

'You think I've got my speech about right? I don't want to come on too heavy.'

'I think you've struck the right balance.'

'Funny thing, you never know you can write until you try.'

'You've certainly tried.'

'I feel good about it, Harvey. I'm getting good vibes.'

271

The collective madness went some way towards insulating me against total despair over my own situation. I wrote other letters to Laura which I never posted. On two occasions I drove past her house, pride allowing me a chance meeting should it come my way; but each time I drew a blank. I could not bring myself to be the one who first attempted a reconciliation. God knows, I wanted to see her again – the very thought of a permanent separation destroyed me. But her last deception had been too calculated, my pride too blunted by her total rejection. I had no problem in finding all manner of excuses for her – she was young, she had different values, I was no great catch (always the spectre of age difference between us, a ghost that would never be calmed) – but I couldn't face a further rejection.

What decided the issue finally was a pure coincidence. During my solo drinking sessions I seldom took any nourishment other than roasted almonds, bought by the tin when I purchased my quota of liquor in a supermarket (like most serious drinkers I was careful to conceal the extent of my vice from the hotel staff). One night I chipped a molar on a savagely hard almond and toothache was added to my list of pains. I decided I'd better get it attended to, so rang the production office and asked them to get me an early appointment with the nearest dentist. It says a lot for my state of mind that I had forgotten Laura telling me that her father was a dentist. Even when the office phoned back and said that a Doctor Tallan would see me after normal hours that same day, I still didn't make the connection.

'He very kindly made an exception because you're with the film company,' the secretary said.

'Did you also tell him that I'm a craven coward and will probably pass out the moment I sit in the chair?'

I wasn't kidding: visits to the dentist are high on my list of unfavourite events. However, vanity overcame basic fears and I duly presented myself at the surgery at the appointed hour. I was shown straight in.

Doctor Tallan proved to be a pleasant, middle-aged man who spoke good English, albeit with a thick accent, though like most members of his profession he felt compelled to open the proceedings with a joke.

'I understand you have bitten on more than you can chew, Mr Burgess. Let's have a look and see what we can do.'

I suffered the necessary poking and probing investigation, my limbs as rigid as a dead sheep. Then he took an X-ray.

'Yes,' he said, holding the developed film up to the light. 'Quite an interesting mouth. I admire American dentistry. Very good work, and very good prices, too, I understand.'

'You can say that again.'

'We'll do our best and do it a little cheaper. You don't want to lose the tooth, I take it?'

'No.'

'So I think I will give you a root-canal. Have you had one of those before?'

'I don't think so. Is that very painful?'

'You will feel no pain, except when you get my bill, and even then only a little pain.' The number of undiscovered comedians in the dental profession is legion, I've discovered. I resigned myself to the inevitable, but to do him justice he was as good as his word. Anticipation was worse than the actual thing and although I can't say I ever want too many repeat performances, he operated on me with skill and compassion.

'Your film has caused a lot of excitement in my family, Mr Burgess,' Tallan said. 'As you can well imagine.'

It took an effort of will to imagine anything at that moment. I made a gurgling noise by way of reply.

'Yes, a lot of excitement. It's changed our lives.'

I looked up at an egg-shaped reflection of my face in his binocular lenses. 'Iss-that-so?' I gagged.

'You've met my daughter, of course.'

' 'Cuse, me?'

'My daughter, Laura – you know her, I believe.'

All the localised pain left me instantly. It was only then that the penny dropped.

'Yes,' I said. 'Yes, I do.'

He stopped working on me for a moment and I was allowed to rinse out my mouth.

'Is she doing good acting for you?'

'Oh, yes. I think everybody's very pleased with her.'

273

'Oh, that's good. Open wide, please. Not long now, nearly finished. My wife and I don't know much about your profession, I'm afraid . . . We never expected to have a daughter on the films, but children go their own ways these days. Not that we object in her case. If she has talent, then she must give herself the chance.'

For the rest of the treatment I was unaware of any discomfort. Tallan's disclosure had completely thrown me. I became convinced that Laura would think I had deliberately engineered the meeting. And probably despise me for it, I thought. As the cotton-thin nerves in my tooth were painstakingly whittled out I was consumed with old panics which could not be deadened.

From a long way away I heard Tallan say, 'Well, you can relax. That's it for today. You see, you were a better patient than you thought, or maybe I'm a better dentist than you thought . . . I shall need to see you again in about a week when the tooth has settled down a bit . . . I've just packed it for temporary at the moment. How does it feel?'

'Fine.'

'We must make another appointment for you. Let me have a look at my book.'

He went out of the surgery leaving the door open and as I raised my head from the spittoon I saw Laura in the receptionist's office. She had her arms round her father and was kissing him. As she broke from the embrace she saw me. We stared at each other like two people reunited after a war.

'You know my new patient,' her father said.

'Yes. Hello.'

'Hello,' I said.

'Laura came to fetch me home. I'm late for dinner.'

'That's my fault,' I said.

'No, no. And please, if you feel you'd like to, you're very welcome to join us.'

I saw panic flood into Laura's face.

'Oh, I'm sure your wife doesn't want to be bothered with an unexpected guest.'

'Why not? It's our pleasure. My wife is a very good cook, and she likes people to enjoy her cooking. It's better than

274

biting on almonds. Laura, you'd like him to accept, I'm sure?'

'Yes,' she said.

'Well, then, yes, I'd very much like to. Thank you.'

He took off his white coat and donned a golfing jacket. 'Are you driving me, Bobo?'

'Bobo?' I said.

'That's my pet name for her. Because she's such a scatterbrain.'

We all left the surgery and got into Laura's battered Renault. I noticed with satisfaction that she crashed the gears. Once or twice our eyes met in the rear-view mirror, but she did not say anything to me on the journey.

'Your friend Mr Burgess was a good patient, Laura. More than I can say about her, Mr Burgess. My daughter's not too keen on being treated by me.'

'That's often true of doctors' wives, isn't it?' I said. 'I've always been told they prefer not to be treated by their husbands.'

'That's right, yes. It's a family occupational hazard, like my daughter's driving.' He roared with laughter and seemed unaware of the tension between Laura and myself.

The surgery was only a short distance from their home and once again I couldn't believe my stupidity at not having guessed the relationship. Not that I regretted the coincidence: at least the ice was broken and for these moments I had a slight advantage. Apart from my frozen mouth, I began to enjoy the situation.

I could see where Laura got her spirit from. Her mother was quite unlike what I had imagined from her telephone voice: a very vital woman with an oddly beautiful face. I remembered the old adage, 'When you fall in love with the girl, look at the mother.' Madame Tallan must have closely resembled Laura in her youth. She took my chance arrival in her stride and as her husband had boasted, she was a superb cook. The dinner I shared with them was the classic Provencal cuisine, served with an ice-cold bottle of Château de Selle Rose. It was a warm evening and we ate it on the terrace beside their modest pool. After the main course, which was a local fish cooked in paper with a garnish of fresh herbs, we had a chocolate cake that furthered Doctor Tallan's practice with every melting mouthful. I could almost feel the new cavities forming.

The conversation around the dinner table mostly centred on the progress of the film and it was clear that both Tallan and his wife were inordinately proud of Laura. Once they had established that I was, in title at least, responsible for the script, they asked the usual layman's questions and I tried to answer without patronising them. Laura made little or no contribution during the early part of the meal and several times I saw her mother give her a quizzical look, making it clear that she was conscious of Laura's rudeness if not the reason for it. Perhaps in making a good impression on her parents, I thawed her out, because she suddenly came to life again and reverted to her old personality. When we had finished the meal she left the table to make the coffee and it was then that her mother became more confidential with me.

'I'm very grateful to you, Mr Burgess. Well, we both are, and I'm so glad that we've met you at last. Laura has often spoken about you.'

'Really?'

'Oh, yes. You are very important to her little bit of confidence in herself.'

'I never thought of her as lacking confidence,' I said.

'No, well you wouldn't, because she hides it, but she's so secretly sensitive.'

'Well, I'm learning something.'

'She told me she only really comes alive on the set,' Tallan said.

'I think since working on the film – and especially because of the way you've helped her – she's at last begun to get her just sense of her own worth. I mean, obviously as an adoring mother I worry so much about her.' Madame Tallan smiled at me as though excusing herself, and then she said something which I have always remembered. It wasn't a phrase I had ever heard before. She said, 'Laura is in the cup of your hands, Mr Burgess.' I've never forgotten that. It conjures up such tenderness and to this day it returns at odd moments to trouble me.

'That's nice of you to say so.'

'It's true, though you must never let her know I said so, she would be humiliated.'

There wasn't time for any more. Laura returned with the jug of fresh coffee at that moment and we sat in the warm evening glow and savoured the fragrance of the night flowers that grew in such profusion.

'Who's the gardener?' I said.

'My wife's the one with the green fingers,' Tallan said. 'I leave it to her. Me, I've only got to look at flowers and they wither.'

'Oh, Daddy, you're exaggerating. It's just that he's lazy.'

'Why shouldn't I be lazy. I work very hard – you try staring into people's mouths twelve hours a day and you'd be lazy.'

'We work twelve hours too.'

'That isn't work what you do.'

'I don't know that Mr Burgess would agree, dear.'

'Please call me Harvey.'

'Then you must call us Helen and Francois.'

'What Mummy and Daddy never understand is that filming is not as easy as it looks when it comes out on the screen.'

Her use of the terms 'Mummy' and 'Daddy' made her suddenly more vulnerable in my eyes. I felt oddly ill at ease, wondering what her parents would really think of me if they knew the truth about my relationship with their daughter. I had the feeling that Madame Tallan would not disapprove but that Tallan himself might take real offence. Aren't all fathers supposed to have this deep-rooted Freudian thing about their daughters? Especially a daughter as exquisite as Laura.

A moment or so later, when Laura poured me a second cup of coffee she pressed her hand against mine, and gave me a conspiratorial wink behind her parents' backs. We sat there enjoying each other's company until the last rays of sun left the patio. 'You'd better not get a chill in that tooth of yours,' Tallan said. 'How does it feel now?'

'I'd forgotten all about it,' I said, and that was the truth. The sudden surge of renewed hope where Laura and I were concerned had obliterated the dull ache.

'Of course, strictly speaking, I shouldn't have allowed you anything to drink.'

'I won't give you away.'

'I'll drive Harvey home,' Laura said, 'so you needn't worry, Daddy.'

I happily took this as my cue to leave, though I went through the motions of protesting. When I said my thank-yous Madame Tallan whispered to me: 'Don't forget what I told you?' and Laura caught her in the act.

'What're you telling him?'

'Nothing. You mind your own business. And drive carefully.'

Once we were safely alone in her car, Laura returned to the subject. 'I bet my mother said something awful about me.'

'Not at all.'

'What did she say?'

'I'm not telling you.'

'I shan't start the car until you do.'

'Then I'll have to walk home, won't I? Because I'm not going to tell you. It was nothing awful, she only said nice things about you. She's very proud of you. They both are.'

'How embarrassing.'

She started the engine. 'Do you want to go straight home?'

'That's up to you.'

'I can't stay long, I mean if we go to your room.'

'I didn't even know you wanted to come to my room.'

She suddenly leaned over and kissed me, her mouth opening to mine with all her old eagerness.

'What's caused this change of heart?' I said. 'And don't you think we ought to move off? Your parents are going to think it a bit strange if we stay parked here.'

She let in the gear and eased the car out of the driveway.

'You've given me a hard two weeks,' I said.

'I like that! You didn't ever ring me, and I know you've been at the studio and you never came near me.'

'I thought after that morning at the railway station I wasn't too welcome.'

'I wanted to see you and explain.'

'You don't have to explain. I understand.'

'I just felt so guilty.'

'Why guilty particularly?'

'You know why.'

'No, I don't, honestly.'

'Because of my boyfriend. I couldn't come straight from his bed to yours. I just couldn't.'

'And now?'

'Now, I don't feel quite so guilty, I suppose.'

'You're a terrible girl,' I said. 'You know that, don't you? You destroy me.'

'I don't mean to.'

'Let's just park for a while in our usual place. I know you can't stay long, so don't worry.'

'I'm not worried.'

'No, but your parents might be.'

'Oh, they just say that, but they'll be in bed anyway.'

'They're very nice people, especially your mother. You're not unlike her to look at.'

'She's terrific, my mother. She understands me.'

'How much do you tell her? Everything?'

'Not everything, no.'

'Does she ask?'

'No.'

We reached our familiar spot in the clearing. Laura bumped the Renault over the rough grass and then turned off the headlights. It was suddenly very quiet.

'Let's sit in the back,' she said. 'It's more comfortable.'

We got out and rearranged ourselves. It was cramped on the back seat. I had a sudden vision of all those beach-boy films that were the rage with teenagers back in the Sixties; they always included a scene of fumbled sex in the back seat of a borrowed automobile. I reached for Laura and found that she had already unbuttoned her silk blouse. Her bare breasts were cool, almost cold to my touch, and I thought again of her mother's phrase as I cupped my palms over her soft nipples. Our embraces had a new desperation.

'Not here,' I said. 'I want you, don't think I don't, but let's save it for when we can be alone for a long time.'

'Please, I can't wait, please.'

It was as if she wanted to initiate me into a mystery she had only just discovered. I had never known her so pliant or urgent. There on the back seat of the Renault we expunged her guilt and I began to believe in happiness again. And afterwards, as we lay in bundled disorder like two rag dolls, she said, 'Oh, God! I forgot to take my Pill.'

'When?'

'When I was supposed to. Last night. I didn't know I was going to see you. But it'll be all right, I'm sure.'

I heard her with mixed feelings. The recurring cycle of a woman's life is such a mystery to mere men anyway. I had but a hazy idea of the working of the Pill; it was so long since I had enjoyed any sort of prolonged relationship.

'You should be pleased,' she said.

'Why pleased?'

'Probably the reason I forgot was that I didn't intend making love to anybody.'

'That's a very back-handed compliment, miss.'

'No it isn't, it wasn't meant to be. You should be pleased.'

'Grateful for small mercies you mean. Have you ever been pregnant?'

She shook her head.

'No scares?'

'Scares, yes, but they've always worked out in the end. I'm not worried. Are you worried?'

'No. Maybe I'd quite like to be a father, especially if the child was yours.'

She sat up and began to rearrange her clothing. 'It's not going to happen anyway.'

'But what if it did, what would you do? Would you get rid of it?'

'I don't want to talk about it because it's not going to happen.

'I'd marry you,' I said, 'make you an honest woman, give the child a name.' I said it jokingly, but in secret earnest.

'I don't want to get married.'

'Not ever?'

'Oh, sometime, yes, but not yet. How do I look?'

'Very pregnant.'

'No, be serious. Do I look all right?'

'You look like a girl who's just made love on the back seat of a car. No, you look fine.'

'Truly?'

'A bit crumpled maybe, but you said your parents would be in bed. I'm the one who looks terrible, I'm sure. I can hardly see. Good thing I haven't got to walk home because the string has gone in my legs.'

'What a funny expression!'

'Think so? Don't know where I heard it . . . Oh, I think some English actor once said it to me.'

We clambered back into the front seats and she restarted the engine. I put my hand over hers and stopped her engaging the gears.

'I adore you. You know that, don't you?'

'Yes.'

'No matter what happens, I'll never forget you. But I'm not much use to you in the long run, am I?'

'Why do you always say that?'

'Because it's true. And because I'm jealous. When we're together like this you're so warm and tender and I don't think of the other times when you're with somebody else . . . somebody younger who can give you a future.'

'I don't think about your age. You're the only one who thinks about that.'

'Difficult not to . . . Do you love me at all?'

'Of course.'

'Say it then. Even if you only mean it for this moment, say it.'

'I do love you.'

'But not in the same way as I love you?'

'Sometimes. I can't help the other times. That's just me. And I never want to hurt you.'

'Well, that's not your fault. That's my stupidity. I should know better at my age . . .'

'There you go again.'

'Yeah. I'm a hopeless case.'

I kissed her again. 'Good thing you never wear lipstick. The number of handkerchiefs I had to destroy when I was a kid. They looked like butcher's aprons sometimes. The lipsticks used to be bright, bright red and indelible.'

'Yes, I've got an aunt who still wears that kind. When she has a cup of coffee she leaves a thick smear on the rim. It's really gross . . . Why're you looking at me like that?'

'You're so beautiful,' I said. 'Sometimes your beauty blinds me. Go on, drive me home quickly before I really embarrass you.'

She deposited me outside the Auberge.

'I wish I could stay the night,' she said. 'Will I see you tomorrow?'

'If you want to.'

'Of course I want to.'

'It won't make you feel guilty again? No, sorry, that was unfair. I won't come to the studio, but I'll call for you tomorrow evening and we'll go out and have a reunion dinner. How does that grab you?'

'You know me,' she said, 'promise to feed me and I'll do anything.'

'I'll keep you to that.'

The moment she drove away my tooth started to ache again. I welcomed the pain. It kept me awake and I thought about her.

SEVENTEEN

In the two weeks before Latrough's celebrated dinner party I existed in a state of perpetual euphoria. There wasn't a single day when I didn't see Laura and our lovemaking was such that I began to believe nothing would ever change. If she still harboured any guilt towards her student lover she concealed it well, and I was smart enough never to broach the subject again. As for Gelbard, he seemed to be out of the reckoning. The fact that Martin carried on his romance through the lens whenever she was working was something I no longer considered, and so my days and nights passed in a kind of wonder.

Now that I had been introduced to her parents I no longer had to skulk like some private investigator, but could call for her at the house. The morning after that first dinner I sent her mother flowers like any prospective son-in-law anxious to create the right impression, and when next I went for a dental treatment I took Tallan a bottle of very superior cognac by way of saying thank you. That didn't stop him rendering a fairly hefty bill for my root-canal and crown, but it was money I considered well spent. Certainly it was half what I would have paid back in New York: there I might have had to take out a second mortgage for the same work.

Nothing troubled me during that period. I was sweetness itself to all and sundry. Script changes? I did them with a smile and, curiously, with a modicum more originality. It was a pleasure to wake every morning and have the new day stretch out before me, and apart from wine with the meals we shared, I went on the wagon. Left to my own devices once I had cleared all the necessary chores, I started writing my novel once again. I seemed to have found fresh energies, both creative and sexual. I bought a pair of bathroom scales and surveyed myself in the mirror willing my abused flesh to shrink. Of such, I suppose, is the power of love, the fillip we receive when love is returned.

And Laura? Was her love for me feigned or genuine at that time? I like to believe it was genuine, because if not then everything that followed was a mockery. Yes, I'm sure it was, and God knows I've had enough time since to go over every single moment of that summer. At night my mind is like a Xerox machine, endlessly spilling out the same pages as I relive the past.

On the rest days we went shopping together and I bombarded her with gifts. If she admired something in a shop window I would return later, alone, and purchase it for her. There is some element in all of us, I suspect, which believes that to sustain love we must make frequent offerings. Probably, if I ever break a lifelong vow and place myself on an analyst's sacrificial altar, he will explain that as a sub-conscious insecurity. Well, I don't need to spend good money to be told that. I knew I was insecure at the time – and of my own free will and with the balance of my mind splendidly disturbed, I happily paid the danegeld. To her credit Laura never asked for anything from me and had no predatory craving for expensive jewellery; she liked wild, flamboyant junk trinkets, necklaces of many colours, and outlandish clothes which, had I not been in love with her, I would have found slightly embarrassing. In so many ways she made me change my conservative attitudes, for she often questioned statements I made as a senior citizen educating the younger generation. I began to see the world through her eyes.

'I wish I'd met you twenty years earlier,' I said.

'You'd have been arrested.'

'Well, you know what I mean.'

'I like you as you are.'

'Now maybe.'

'Don't start on your "I'm so much older than you" routine,' she said. 'You always come back to that.'

She liked eating the most sickly desserts: Black Forest cake topped with cream and containing probably a million calories, or else ten scoops of different flavoured ices. Perhaps one of the most irritating things about the young is that they can abuse their systems without punishment. No matter how heartily she ate the meals I shared with her she never seemed to put on a single ounce, whereas in order to keep her company I had to starve myself out of her sight. What she liked best was to have me serve her champagne while she was luxuriating in my bath. 'Isn't it decadent?' she used to say. 'I feel really depraved.'

'You are depraved.'

I could spend hours watching her braid her thick, black hair and I was never more content than when she padded about the room stark naked learning her lines for the following day's scenes. Her body seemed to me perfection, unflawed, the skin supple and coffee-tanned, her breasts firm on her torso, the nipples so delicately shaded. And unlike so many girls who walk in beauty, she was genuinely unconceited about her body, thinking herself too thin, and her breasts not large enough.

'You should be happy about that,' I told her.

'But aren't men supposed to go for great big titties? What about all those magazines you read?'

'I don't read too many any more.'

'But isn't that true?'

'Yes, maybe for some.'

'I bet you wish I had bigger ones. Be honest.'

'I'm very content,' I said, kissing them in turn. 'Big boobs are great when you're your age, but come the deluge and watch out! You're lucky, because you're never going to have two hammocks swinging low.'

'How can you be sure?'

'Because I've made a life-long study, that's why. Doctor Burgess, screenwriter and breast expert.'

Just as I had been desperate to learn more about her boyfriends, now she questioned me about my past affairs and especially about my marriage. That was the curious paradox about her. She was at pains never to commit herself totally, always holding back some part of herself, and yet at the same time she needed the assurance that she was not alone. Sometimes our love-making was one-sided; she would lie passively beneath me as though a long way away and nothing I did could break that mood in her. Only that one night in the car did she give herself to me completely. But such were my own desperations that I thought of little else but giving pleasure to her, learning for the first time to be unselfish. I could spend an endless time bringing her slowly to a climax, holding back my own orgasm until, with her head pendulating on the pillow, she would beg me to join her. 'Say it,' I would urge, 'say you love me, say it.' And only when she whispered the words I craved more than anything else, did I complete the circle.

It said much for her nubile resilience that she was able to carry on our love affair and spend long hours in front of the cameras without any apparent ill effects. As part of his preparations for the coming Press visit Latrough had insisted that George, the editor, assemble a representative reel of finished film to run half an hour or so. This was all part of his master plan to woo the visiting firemen. I was allowed to see the first rough cut of this footage and I had to admit that Martin's technical expertise disguised many of the cracks in the proverbial wallpaper. Obviously I was biased where Laura's performance was concerned, but even allowing for that her physical presence on the screen was so compelling that her lack of acting experience was relatively unimportant. Gerry had photographed her with loving care and under Martin's direction she gave a creditable account of herself against the superior talents of Charles and Michelle. It was a curious experience for me to watch two women with whom I had been intimate, up there on the screen. I still had a certain conscience where Michelle was concerned, but love makes us callous. I could look at Michelle objectively, but not Laura. There were secret pleasures in watching her move. I was the unknown voyeur reliving old lusts. And when Martin or Latrough commented on her beauty I could sit in the darkness of the viewing room feeling smug, for they did so without my intimate knowledge.

The only person I felt sorry for was poor Suzanne. Although she was making a slow recovery she was still under medical orders not to resume work. Those script changes forced on me by her unfortunate illness had worked reasonably well, and of course much to Laura's advantage. The cruel truth about film-making is that any performance can be made or marred in the cutting room. The audience only sees what is up there on the screen in the finished version: it has no knowledge of the dramas which were fought out on the floor – no film actor forgets his lines at the premiere. Suzanne's original role had of necessity been heavily truncated in order to integrate Laura's new scenes into the story.

Even though I had been responsible for reshaping the script I was still pleasantly surprised to find that between them Martin and George had discovered ways and means of making the changes dramatically palatable. I don't want to give the impression that I was witness to a masterpiece – at best it was only a pot-boiler, but it had a certain old-fashioned gloss.

Laura had never been allowed to see herself in any of the dailies. Martin was adamant on that point. 'Big mistake to let her see herself. She'll become self-conscious either way – either she'll think she's the cat's whiskers and start acting up a storm, or else more probably she'll hate herself and go into a depression. That's always the way with beginners.'

Naturally Laura close-questioned me in bed.

'Frightening,' I said. 'You've no idea how ugly you are on the screen.' She punched me.

'No, tell me the truth, and not about how I look. Did I act it well?'

'You gave a reasonable account of yourself,' I teased.

'Was Martin pleased?'

'You know he is. He's been slavering over you ever since day one.'

'But you really thought I wasn't too bad?'

'I thought you were very good. It's just a pity that you've got such a hideous face . . .' and I blocked her arm as she went to punch me again, and held her down, stopping her mouth with kisses.

I suppose if it was true that she gave me a new lease of life, in return I opened her eyes to some parts of the world I inhabited. I think what intrigued her most about me was the mystery of how people write. It was not a subject upon which I could throw much light, although it flattered me to have her interest. Most women of my acquaintance have been at some pains to point out that writers are usually a disappointment in the flesh. I tried to guide her towards some of the authors I thought she would benefit from reading. In that respect her education was sadly lacking, and I gently chided her for it.

'There's never time,' she said, 'but I will one day. Make a list for me.' I appointed myself that night (shades of Scott Fitzgerald), and in so doing gave myself the greater pleasure. I tried to obtain some of the books I listed, but few of them were available on the French coast. Most of the bookshops that stocked English books concentrated on today's forgettable bestsellers.

'I shall send them to you,' I said, 'when I get back to the States.'

It was the first time I had openly admitted to myself that there had to be an end to loving. The film had gone on so long that my once and future life scarcely came into my reckoning. It was only in the vaguest terms that I thought about returning home, and where Laura was concerned I deliberately lived from day to day, rationing happiness.

Just as when she addressed her parents as Mummy and Daddy, I saw other aspects of her which reminded me that she had but recently passed from adolescence to young womanhood. I remember her joy when she bought the new dress she intended to wear for Latrough's party. Only those who are too rich or too spoilt derive no pleasure from new clothes, but Laura's peculiar excitement on this occasion stemmed partly, I am sure, from the fact that this was the first time she was buying something expensive with her own money. I thought her choice a bad one, for it detracted from rather than enhanced her natural beauty, being too fussy and overblown – but nothing would have induced me to say so. She modelled it for me the moment she returned from the shop, and I said all the things she wanted to hear. To Laura the party was to be the signal that she had arrived and was being accepted as an actress. I recalled how innocently pleased she had been the day her photograph first appeared in a local newspaper, and I despised myself for being so jaded. I had seen it all before, but she couldn't have known that she was just another pawn in Latrough's social ambitions and the whole performance provoked nothing but amazed wonder from her.

'Marvin tells me that a whole plane-load of people are coming in, all the top newspaper people.'

'La crème de la crème,' I said. 'They won't walk off the plane, they'll be poured off it.'

'And a television crew, he said.'

'Every moment preserved for posterity.'

She whirled around my room as though the festivities had already begun. There is something about a pretty girl in a ball gown that provokes thoughts of lechery, and when she slipped it from her shoulders the eroticism proved irresistible. She stood beside my bed, a naked Venus stepping from a sea of silk, smiling as women often smile when they know they have us at their mercy and are willing to bestow an act of sexual charity. I tumbled her on the bed's edge, frenzied to taste her, to trace with my tongue that familiar route from lips to breasts to her sweet cunt.

Maybe only Charles, with his actor's radar for detecting any threat to his position, suspected the truth of my relationship with Laura. There was a part of me that clamoured for a confidant and had it not been for Martin's involvement I dare say I would have openly paraded my conquest. The male animal always likes to strut. I feared not so much for myself but for Laura and my own instincts told me that if Martin became aware of our relationship he would take it out on her. I had not forgotten his frenzy in the gazebo the night of the dinner party, not could I dismiss the memory of his paranoia about Gelbard. Equally, in some perverse way, I had no wish to prick his sexual ego further; after all, it was he who had led me to Laura. But Charles was another kettle of fish altogether. He was too old a hand at the game not to be aware that Laura's elevation through the ranks from small-part player to virtual star had not come about purely because of Suzanne's illness – that had merely been a contributing factor.

I'm sure he suspected, but in the beginning most of his arrows were aimed in Martin's direction. I was the long shot.

'I don't blame Martin,' he said. 'If I was married to Alice I'd want to flee from wonderland and creep through the keyhole into Laura's bedchamber. Course, it takes a lot of men that way at his age, you know. Not only film directors, but poor boring little bank managers and the like who suddenly get a perpetual hard-on for the new girl in the computer room. Without such real-life human dramas, where would the dear old *News of the World* be?'

'Is that an English newspaper?'

'Not *just* a newspaper, chum, it's the very rock on which our civilization is built. Not being familiar with the English Sabbath you wouldn't understand, but for whole sections of our moral population that news-sheet represents all that is finest in our land – defrocked clergymen on grave charges, milkmen who deflower whole housing estates, axe murderers and child molesters, the very cream of our egalitarian society . . . No, no, Sunday without the *News of The World* would be unthinkable.'

Behind his banter lurked a more cunning line of investigation.

'Of course where old Martin is concerned, I suppose it's always necessary to oil the Svengali mechanism . . . and she's a pretty little Trilby, isn't she, our Laura? Does she attract you? I mean, I don't suppose you'd object if she sat on your face for the odd hour or so, would you?'

'Chance would be a fine thing,' I said.

'The only thing that bothers me when they're that young is they have no conversation. Very sweet and all that, but a trifle boring I've always found. Post coitus, that is. Do you think old Martin's ever got there?'

'I doubt it.'

'Do you? Now that's interesting. Why?'

'Well, he could have done, I suppose. Seems unlikely. As you say, the formidable Alice keeps him on a pretty tight rein.'

'Still, she never visits the studio. There's always time for a quick knee-trembler during the lunch-break. Ah! if only my caravan could talk. I bet he's tried . . . Well, we know he's tried, don't we? There was that charming little episode in the summer-house when I disgraced myself. You took her home that night, didn't you?'

'Yes, I did.'

'Did she reveal all?'

'She said he flashed it.'

'Oh, poor darling. Only of interest to an archaeologist I would have thought . . .'

And there for the moment he left it, but I knew him well enough to realise that he was sniffing around like a truffle hound, and I didn't trust him.

The other potential fly in the ointment was Latrough. I didn't think of him as a real threat because Laura and I had discussed him on several occasions and I knew she found him physically repellent. He was merely nuisance value, but I didn't discount him entirely. Ambition is a curious beast, and Laura was ambitious. Without in any way approaching my present level of involvement I had charted quite a few Lauras in my time. Back in the days when I was a contract writer on the Fox lot during the elder Zanuck's regime, I had seen them come and briefly conquer – nice, comely girls who had won some beauty contest in their home towns and been immediately shipped out West like so much cattle. Once signed to a term deal they were re-modelled, given drama lessons and taught the basic rules for survival. Some of them were passed around like cards from a deck, but once the cellophane had been broken they soon lost their shine. Since few of them had any real talent their stay was limited and afterwards one caught glimpses of them serving in some fashionable eatery until, inevitably, they were swallowed up in the nowhere city. Those who did have a modicum of talent found that a price still had to be paid if their contracts were to be renewed. I hoped I wasn't putting Laura into that category, but one could never discount the lure of fame and she had taken the first sip. Equally, I was not blameless, for love led me to heap exaggerated compliments and encourage her to the belief that she was on her way. It is through kindness that we so often prepare the way for our own rejections.

What made me wary of Latrough was the fact that from the moment he started to plan the seating arrangements for his dinner party, he made it quite clear that Laura would be his official date for the evening.

'Supposing Suzanne has recovered sufficiently by the night?' I asked. 'Won't that put her nose out of joint?'

'Why should it?'

'Just because she'll think it's her rightful place.'

'Listen, you can bet your ass she's going to recover – even if she has to get there on crutches there's no way she's going to miss that dinner. And she won't want to talk to me, she'll want to set the record straight and tell the world what a trouper she is, give them a bellyful of that "the show must go on" crap. You think she'd pass that up? No way, baby, no way!'

I immediately, but casually, told Laura to be on her guard. 'It won't be like Cinderella,' I said. 'There's no chance of you turning into a pumpkin at midnight, but I guarantee that our David will become Frankenstein on the stroke.'

'But won't you be there to look after me?'

'Fisticuffs aren't my style really, though naturally I should do my level best to protect your honour.'

'I bet I can manage him.'

'Don't even try,' I said, 'save all your loving for me, Beatles-wise.'

Martin took a jaundiced view of the whole thing. I imagine he was peeved at not having been consulted before the event and was determined not to show any enthusiasm. 'What worries me,' he said, 'is that David's devoid of taste. Barren, totally barren. I'm sure he's chosen some ghastly menu and inferior wines and everybody will come down with dysentery. It'll be quite frightful. Charles will get pissed, I expect, and insult all and sundry as he did at my party. I might have to have a diplomatic illness on the night. Alice positively hates that sort of thing and she's bound to be po-faced. For one thing she hates the way Americans eat everything with a fork, that really offends her . . . Nothing personal, chum, but you know what I mean . . . Oh, God! just directing this bloody film is quite enough without having to get involved in this sort of nightmare.'

I think it was mostly said for effect, because Martin was as avid for publicity as the next man, providing of course that he was the centre of attraction. His films usually carried the possessive credit – it was a 'Martin James Film' on the posters. All writers are supposed to take to the barricades at such effrontery, but frankly I've never been able to work up much steam – it's usually been a profound relief for me to share the blame.

The Press gang flew in en masse on the appointed day and at David's request I formed part of the welcoming committee at the airport. It was made up of myself, Marvin and Michelle – hardly a four-gun salute, but everybody else was working. At least it gave Marvin a brief moment of glory.

I recognised a few faces – the old hands who had seen it all before and who stepped off the plane with wary expressions, like whores who have been paid in advance and are determined not to give value for money. *Les girls* who had been recruited by David's resourceful photographer friend looked as though they were still stapled to the centrefolds; like imported wine, they didn't seem to have travelled well and, in contrast to the hardened jet set, stumbled out into the fierce Mediterranean sun in some disarray, needing repairs and maintenance.

There was the usual scramble and panic with the baggage before all heads had been counted and everybody safely accommodated in the waiting coach.

I overheard one member of the élite corps mutter: 'Jesus! no limousines. Whenever they bus you, you know you're in for a down-market trip.'

David had taken two floors at one of the flashier hotels on the seafront at the busier end of Nice, close to the Place Massena. I soon realised why he had given Marvin the honour of receiving them: sorting out the rooms proved a lengthy and acrimonious nightmare. For members of a profession that prides itself on reporting the human condition in all its many facets, they showed a marked reluctance to share double rooms. The procedure was further complicated by the fact that the arrival of our party coincided with the departure of a package tour. The crowded lobby sounded like a demented aviary and, since half the rooms allocated to us had yet to be made up, there was a lot of aggressive dialogue flying around.

It was Marvin's instinct to take care of the girls before anybody else, but I knew my public and persuaded him otherwise. 'Go for the obvious drunks,' I whispered. 'Get them upstairs and out of sight, Michelle and I'll take the girls for a cup of coffee. Bribe heavily, because this is the moment of truth. Survive this and the rest will be downhill.

I think he acted on my advice and eventually order was restored. The assorted girls proved pleasant enough; for many of them it was their first trip abroad and charmingly they had but a hazy idea of what was in store. Michelle surprised me yet again by revealing herself as one of Nature's den mothers, dispensing cogent and useful information which they drank in open-mouthed. They were vastly impressed by the fact that she could order coffee and croissants in her native tongue.

'Somebody told me you call waiters *cochon*,' one of the girls said. She was from West Covina, an unnatural blonde of stunning proportions.

'*Garcon*,' Michelle quickly corrected.

'Oh, did I pronounce it wrong?'

'Slightly.'

There was nothing planned until later in the afternoon, and once the rooms had finally been sorted out they were all left to their own devices. Michelle and I felt we had provided service above and beyond the call of duty, and made our exit. Marvin – with an eye for the sure thing which I could only admire – had already selected the girl with whom he was most likely to succeed.

'I'll hang around just in case anybody needs me,' he said as he escorted the girls to the elevator. 'See you later.'

Michelle took her own car and went shopping. I had to report to David at the studio.

'How were they?' I noticed he had a folder on his desk containing eight by ten glossies of the girls. 'My friend doesn't miss a trick. These arrived right on the nail. What are they like in the flesh? . . . This little chick, for example.' He pushed one of the photographs to my side of his desk.

'They weren't exactly wearing their war-paint when they got off, but they all have great potential I'm sure.'

'So, I can wait. And the others?'

'The heavy mob? Well, I guess it was a long trip. They gave the impression they'd come to re-open Harry Cohn's tomb rather than have a good time . . . Just relax, David. They're here, we shoe-horned them into their rooms, and when they've had a sleep I'm sure they'll revert to their true personalities. Which is to say they'll find fault with everything.'

'Don't give me a heart attack . . . Did Marvin perform?'

'How can you describe perfection? Marvin was great, he did you proud and he's still there looking after the shop.'

'Well, maybe I misjudged him. I'll give the creep another chance. Soon as he gets back here I want to have him put my speech on cards and then get it Xeroxed. I guess most of them will ask for a copy.'

'Bound to,' I said. 'It's well known that most of them collect limited editions.' He was too hyped up to notice the pearls I was casting in his direction.

'See, I need it on cards. I tried learning it, and then I thought, what the hell? Know something? I gotta little more respect for actors. Learning lines ain't that easy.'

'David, you teach me something every day.'

He consulted his itinerary. 'I've told Martin to wrap half an hour early today, to give the cast time to freshen up. We got a cocktail party here at the studio at six, then I'm gonna show them the exploitation reel of film and afterwards we bus them all back to the hotel for the dinner.'

'You think show them the film before the dinner?'

'Sure. Why not?'

I grimaced. 'Well, you're running the show, it's your decision . . . Just make sure they go in a good mood. You know what that bunch is like. All hand-picked knockers.'

'That's why I'm laying on the cocktails. To get 'em nicely oiled.'

'Course. I knew you had it under control.'

'Don't do that! I've planned this thing like fucking D-Day.'

'Sorry, I spoke out of turn.'

He looked at the photographs again, flipped one of them to read the vital statistics pasted on the back. 'Betsy Anne Beattie. My friend has given her three stars, his highest award. You sure you didn't pick her out?'

'I failed you,' I said. 'But I thought our Laura was your date for the evening?'

'She's my official date. This is the one I'm gonna hump. Go ahead, look at the rest, you're entitled.'

'Can you spare one?'

'Harvey, you're on my team. You think I'd leave you on the touchline?'

'Well, it's more than generous of you, David, but I don't have your confidence.'

'What're you talking about? You think these chicks have come over here to sell Girl Guide cookies? They know the score.'

'I'll take a raincheck. Let's make sure the guests get enough to eat first.'

I went onto the set and watched a couple of scenes being shot. Martin was being brusque and unhelpful to a small-part French actor who had a few lines with Charles.

'I thought you told me you could speak English,' Martin said as he cut the fifth take before it had run its course.

'I speak not bad English, not perfect, naturally.'

'You don't have to tell me it's not perfect. I'm not deaf, you know. Just give him the cue once again, Charles.'

Charles obliged. I had previously noticed that he saved his outbursts of temperament for members of the hierarchy rather than those who were in no position to answer back, and I liked him for that.

'No, no no! The word is "arduous"!' Martin shouted. 'The way you say it, it sounds like "adieu".'

'Let me just go over it quietly,' Charles said.

'I haven't got time, Charles. Just change the fucking line.'

'Change it to "laborious",' I volunteered. Martin turned to see me.

'Thank you. For once you're here when we need you. Okay, d'you think you can manage to say "lab-bor-re-us"? Say it.'

Tha hapless actor repeated it several times.

'Yes, well it's marginally better. All right, let's go again.' He came and stood beside me as the clapper board went in. 'Useless French cunt! Okay. Are we turning?'

'Yes, governor.'

'Right, action!'

The actor struggled through it.

'Cut! Well, it's not going to get any better so we'd better print it. Print the last one only, Elsie darling. Then let's move around and get a close shot of Charles.'

The French actor made himself scarce as the camera crew trundled the dolly to the new set-up and Charles's stand-in took over his position.

'Pity you didn't get here earlier,' Martin said to me. 'We could have rewritten the whole bloody scene.'

'I had to be at the airport to greet our distinguished visitors. David's orders.'

'Oh, God, we've got that to go through tonight, haven't we? Don't for God'sake let any of them come onto the set. They're not around are they?'

'No, they're all sleeping off jet-lag I suspect.'

'Fucking waste of money. Here am I strapped down for a few extra quid, having to cast useless sods like that one because that's all I can afford, but he can afford to schlep in plane-loads just to satisfy his ego. Pisses me off! Are we ready?'

'Five minutes, sir. Just moving a few lamps.'

'I shall want Laura after this next shot.'

'Standing by, sir.'

'I'll just go and apologise to her for keeping her waiting,' Martin said. He strode off in the direction of her trailer. Sprawled in his canvas chair, Charles beckoned to me to join him.

'I chose a good day,' I said.

'Oh, Mrs James is charm itself today. I think it must be the time of month. I fancy a nice cup of tea to steady my nerves.' He waved in Nigel's direction. 'Dear boy, any chance of a cuppa for your aged leading man?'

'Right away, sir.'

'Harvey, you want to join me?'

'Wouldn't mind a cup of coffee if there's one going.'

'And a coffee for Mr Burgess! Be my turn next, I expect. He's had his knickers in a twist all morning, and that poor French fucker got the brunt of it. Course we know the reason why.'

'Because of the dinner party, you mean?'

'No . . . He's annoyed because he's had to keep his little darling waiting. That's where he's gone now. To beg forgiveness.'

I sensed it was better not to comment.

297

'The news about Suzanne's better, isn't it?'

'Depends which way you look at it . . . No, I'm being cruel. It'll be nice to have the old bag back again. Then we'll see the sparks fly . . . Our Suzanne is not going to take too kindly to the fact that our director's pet has been given some of her scenes.'

'Well, in fairness Martin didn't have any option.'

'We're not talking about fairness, dear boy. We're talking about bitchiness. Ah! thank you, Nigel, what a saintly boy you are.'

He sipped his tea and made a face. 'Gnat's piss, of course, but at least it's hot. They can't make tea, the French. What was I saying? Oh, yes, I've an idea that our little Laura is in for a few surprises in the near future.'

'How has she done?'

'Well, she's not Edith Evans, shall we say, but keen, anxious to please, and she's done her best. Martin's delighted, naturally. I will say one thing though, he reverts to his own lovable nature whenever she's on the set, so I must be grateful for that.'

Martin returned at that point and I had no idea from his expression whether his black mood had passed or not, but judged it politic not to outstay my welcome.

'See you later, Charles.'

'Yes, we've got to get tarted up, haven't we? And then be on our best behaviour.' He smiled at me over the rim of his teacup.

I poked my head into Laura's trailer on the way out. She was sitting there in costume, reading one of the books I had recommended.

'Not going to stay,' I whispered. 'Just wanted to tell you you're safe tonight. Not from me, naturally, but your producer. Relief forces have arrived, so all's well.'

'Here am I trying to improve my mind and all you can think of is sex.'

'Yes, I know, it's disgusting. I love you. See you at the party.'

EIGHTEEN

It doesn't take any great effort to work up a healthy dislike of those ladies and gentlemen of the Press who shape our destinies. Over the years I have suffered their often insufferable opinions, brushed aside their snide asides, ignored the fact that they have ignored me, eaten the varieties of crow they have set before me; I have been slated by them, misquoted by them, damned with faint praise by them and generally been made to feel insignificant by them. It has been a somewhat one-sided relationship: most of the time I have been the cow waiting to be served by the odd stray bull. Such pleasures as they have given me have been momentary. Now with the passing of time I have evolved a good working arrangement: they don't know who I am and I make a point of trying not to find out who they are.

So it was that I drifted anonymously through the crush at the cocktail party, attaching myself to odd groups with a pleasant but vacuous expression – a useful ploy which convinced most of the guests that we had already been introduced. The majority of the small-talk was not about our film, but about the latest box-office failures and which studio was likely to go broke next. They were like professional mourners going from wake to wake.

I saw Charles holding forth in one corner, and at least he was making sure that he got in with his insults first. In fact he was immunised against their verbal and written toxins: for one thing he genuinely didn't give a damn any longer, and for another there was no longer any fun to be had out of knocking him – by sheer staying power he had beaten their raps.

Martin didn't put in an appearance until the festivities

were well under way, and I dare say his absence suited Latrough. For the first half an hour he had the floor to himself and you could see he was enjoying having a paid and captive audience. I noted he had already made the pitch to Betsy Anne Beattie – she laughed before he finished his jokes. As for the rest of the girls they were behaving as though every male journalist was an unmarried member of the British Royal Family. I guess it was fairly heady stuff for most of them to be air-lifted straight out of a casting office and dropped into your actual South of France. They were dressed to impress, or, more accurately, undressed to impress. But I didn't begrudge anybody their quota of fun and games that night. I was at peace with the world and determined to savour every embarrassing moment. That's one thing about being in love: it makes you nicer.

When Martin finally made his carefully staged late entrance he came armed with Suzanne, Michelle and Laura. Latrough immediately detached himself from Betsy Anne and went to claim his share of the reflected glory. Our three girls certainly knew how to put their best foot forward. With that sure instinct for knowing that in the presence of the real thing it's fatal to appear as mutton masquerading as lamb, Suzanne had put on a quite stunningly conservative number. She had obviously decided that her role for the evening was Camille. Michelle was daring couturier-chic and as for Laura . . . well, we had made a pact that I would only admire her from afar, an arrangement which had its drawbacks since the flash-bulbs immediately began to pop and she was surrounded by Press. I glimpsed her excited face through the crush – one learns to watch for the warning signs of that familiar disease, early success. At that time I still felt reasonably secure, but I wouldn't say I was complacent.

'Hey! guess what – Latrough actually said something nice to me.' It was Marvin by my side. He was holding two glasses of champagne. 'Who did I get these for?' he said. 'I don't know, maybe it was me. I'll drink them anyway . . . Yeah, I must have done something right for a change. Mind you, the night is young, a lot can happen yet.' He gave a broad wink and downed both glasses.

'You're looking guilty.'

'I always look guilty, because I usually am. Now then, do your duty, Marvin,' he said. 'Break 'em up. There are too many people round our Laura and not enough round yesterday's enemy.'

He weaved his way through the crowd, gathering stray members of the Press as he went, a prophet in his own land. I found Charles, who had also been abandoned the moment our three girls arrived on the scene.

'Are you going to break your vow and go to the screening?'

'No way, old darling,' he said. 'I've already given them a glimpse of my genius and they must be satisfied with that. I shall stay here and do what I can to assist the French wine industry. We also serve who only drink and wait.'

'But you are coming to the dinner? You mustn't miss David's speech.'

'He's making a *speech*? You mean he's going to bury these Caesars?'

'On closed-circuit TV yet.'

'Oi vay! the courage of the man! Well, I must stay sober for that. Well, perhaps not sober, but reasonably upright . . . which reminds me, I haven't yet paid my respects to me leading lady. And don't say, Which one? Just point me in the direction of our late invalid.'

'Over there,' I said.

'How fragile she looks. I'm surrounded by courage tonight.'

A short while later Latrough banged on a table for silence and announced that the screening was about to start. He led the way across the studio lot towards the viewing theatre. I worked my way alongside Laura.

'Good evening,' I said. 'What a pretty dress. Is it new?'

'Yes. Do you like it?'

'Very disturbing.'

The small theatre was crowded and latecomers were forced to stand in the aisle. Somebody shouted: 'David, you've got a smash on your hands!' and at least the drinks seemed to have induced a general air of goodwill. I had to admit that George had done his stuff; what we were looking at was not so much an assembly as a glorified trailer. He had carefully chosen all the best sequences and if I hadn't known the truth I might have believed we had the makings of a decent film. Laura came out of it very well, as did all the cast in fact. Charles was giving one of his intense, moody performances, slightly hesitant, bringing himself down to Laura's low-key level in the scenes they played together, which I thought was generous of him. Whatever the cause the effect was impressive. Half-way through I heard Suzanne say, 'They should put this out instead of the film' – which got a laugh from the Press, but didn't exactly bring a smile to Martin's lips. Gerry's camera-work was stunning throughout and, since George had found some stock music and dubbed this onto the track, there was no doubt that the overall impression was creditable. Here and there I detected snatches of my dialogue, sacred and profane remains, as it were, of my midnight marathons. I couldn't help thinking that with a little more thought and less engineered chaos we might have come up with something really unusual. The period of the French Revolution still holds a pertinent fascination, for we can still hear echoes of the same unrest in our own times. Shot as our film was in real locations, the actors authentically costumed, even the confusion of the storyline could not destroy the sense of brooding terror.

When the lights went up there was a genuine murmur of approval and, whether or not they had been topped up with charity by the free drinks, quite a few of the visitors volunteered friendly opinions. I saw Martin thaw visibly, and not surprisingly David was in his element. Despite all the omens his plan had survived the first and major hurdle. I hated to admit it, but there was even a chance, given the mentality of most of those present, that his speech might be well received – at least on the night. My permanent cynicism questioned whether the goodwill would extend beyond the actual trip: once these particular captains and kings had departed to their normal hunting grounds they would probably revert to type. They prided themselves on being such honourable people, any hint of bribery sent them scurrying for the ink of vitriol.

I looked around for Marvin but he had disappeared. The thought that he might have joined Charles and embarked on a shared blind seemed a pity in the circumstances; since the compliments were flying, he might have received his share for once.

The bus was waiting to take the entire party to the venue for the dinner. Charles duly appeared but there was still no sign of Marvin and the bus left without him. He wasn't at the hotel to greet us either. It was very odd.

Martin's misgivings about the menu proved unfounded. I suppose the answer is that we were in France and the French have to try very hard before they serve you a really bad meal. I found myself sitting between the lady film critic of one of the Valley newspapers and another female colleague who wrote social notes for some Pasadena weekly. We quickly dispensed with who I was and the conversation was immediately steered towards Laura. Both ladies were avid to learn more about her. Where had Martin found her, did she have any boyfriends, was she fun on the set? and so forth. I resisted giving them some choice answers, and it was a curious experience for me trying to see Laura through their eyes. They scribbled away on the backs of their menus and seemed happy enough with what I invented. Then they quizzed me about the local shops and where could they get the best rate of exchange. I guess that was the really important business of the evening as far as they were concerned. The one who was a film critic didn't seem to have enjoyed anything since *Gone With The Wind*, though she did wax lyrical about some obscure Polish epic which had apparently changed her life. Her companion confessed that she never went to the movies any more because she was terrified of getting mugged in the parking lot. Both of them thought there was too much sex in films nowadays. The lady from Pasadena thought *Fear of Flying* the greatest book she had ever read, while the one who came from the Valley of the Dolls told me that she had it from a very intimate source that Hemingway had always been a closet queen. They were both heavily into diets, though naturally they were taking a sabbatical this trip, and weren't the French fries something else? They sang their songs like linnets in both my ears. One asked me why I continued to live in the East when California was there for the asking, and the other gave me ten minutes on the way the smog had affected her

303

son's grades. It was like tuning a radio non-stop and never finding a station you wanted to listen to. Only Latrough's speech saved me from a nervous breakdown.

He began with a joke, a very mild joke denuded of any ethnic references at my insistence, an old chestnut I had dredged from memory and revamped for the occasion. He killed it stone dead by getting the tag line in the wrong place, though Charles continued to laugh for nearly half a minute. My two companions whispered for me to explain it and I sensed that our leader was going to have an uphill task holding his audience. I caught Laura looking down the table in my direction and rolled my eyes at her. She lifted her napkin to conceal her return smile.

I guess the poor sod had no real inkling of what he was embarked upon. Watching him face that jaundiced mob was like watching a vegetarian make his pitch to a bunch of Chigago meat-packers. Somebody like him had always been there, of course, right from the days when the glove-salesmen came West. They had the inside track in the rat race to gain the only prize that Hollywood respected, and which was only awarded behind closed doors: the power to screw anybody who got in your way. There was a hint of old man Zanuck about Latrough that night, the Zanuck who prowled the lot in jodhpurs and carried a riding whip; a touch of Harry Cohn, the Cohn who enjoyed clipping the wings of any talent that tried to flee his nest; and more than a *soupçon* of Jack Warner, the brother famed for his social gaffes. They were all there in embryo, just waiting to burst out of his tuxedo like the monster in *Alien*. Except that Latrough didn't come from outer space. He was a street fighter if ever I saw one and if the film industry could be said to have been made for him, it was equally true that he was made for the film industry.

Recovering from the flat joke, he began the rest of his speech confidently enough, and I wish I could remember every word verbatim. It was the sort of quasi-patriotic garbage that could have secured Spiro Agnew a term in the White House. He hit them with a string of clichés which had all the impact of a feather-duster. I saw the heads start to go down – Martin slumped in his seat in an attitude of prayer – and those around started to mutter into their

304

brandies and B and Bs. I do remember that when he said something like, '. . . what this great industry of ours needs more than anything else is men of integrity,' somebody close to me let go with an audible 'Holy shit!'. Maybe he was totally unaware that his act was dying; he was using a microphone and probably listening to the sound of his own voice. At any rate he gave no sign of losing his nerve, but what he did do was to mix the order of his cards. Or that's what I thought at first. He was in the middle of a long and rambling anecdote about his suitability for the task ahead when he turned over the next card and made the evening one for the history books. Lacking my knowledge of what had been prepared, it's quite possible that the majority of the audience thought that what came next was an inspired put-down. I exclude Martin and his wife, of course, and I'm quite sure Charles had his doubts. That particular section of his speech I have retained, and dined out on it many times.

He was saying, '. . . so in all humbleness and in the words of our greatest President, I ask not what the movie business can do for me, but what I can do for the movie business . . .' – turned his next card and continued – 'because you need to be a real prick to succeed.' He got as far as that before faltering. After the first stunned silence there was a ripple of laughter starting at the back of the room and a few people applauded. Latrough's face at that moment was immortalised into one of the great moments on home video: I still have a copy of the unexpurgated tape. He moved to his next card and, amazingly, picked up the threads. 'That is why, ladies and gentlemen of the Press, I have put my money where my mouth is, and placed my bets for the future . . . because I believe that somebody has to renew the faith. It has been my pleasure to greet you here tonight and to announce a programme of films . . .' – it was time to turn a card again – 'that are guaranteed to empty theatres across America.' A greater panic now transformed him. I suppose I was the only person in the room to guess who had doctored the cards: the reason for Marvin's disappearance became clear – the rabbit had finally turned on the snake.

This time the audience fell apart.

'Is he kidding?' the lady from Pasadena asked me.

'I don't think so,' I said. 'I think it's meant to be a very honest speech.'

They wanted more, and with good old Marvin's help, they got more. Latrough found his continuity again and somehow managed to make himself heard above the uproar, even finding sufficient nerve to restart with: 'Let me recap on that . . . I want you good people to be the first to know about my programme. At this very moment in time I have, in active preparation, no fewer than sixteen projects which I am certain will attract major stars and major talent. There has never been any lack of talent in our industry, what has been lacking in recent years are phonies like . . . What the fuck is going on here?'

That was all it needed for Alice to leave the proceedings. Martin made a feeble attempt to persuade her to remain but she brushed him aside and swept out. The microphone was still live and the room heard Latrough scream, 'Kill those cameras, I want it all wiped.' This provoked a fresh round of applause. The irony of it was he was a success of a kind: instead of being bored rigid, his audience had been gifted the sort of copy they craved for. He was guaranteed big space and like it or not he had put himself on the map.

Maybe Betsy Anne employed her labial skills to restore his damaged ego later that night, and if so I guess that was the only comfort he got from the whole episode. The dinner party broke up in some disarray shortly afterwards. My two companions were scribbling furiously when I excused myself and went to find Laura. Latrough was surrounded by a group of journalists and still trying to talk his way out of it. Only Betsy Anne and Charles remained seated at the tables. I suspect Charles was too far gone to realise the festivities had finished, and the girl was just bewildered by the sudden turn of events. Nobody noticed Laura and me leaving together and we managed to keep straight faces until we were outside on the pavement.

'Well, we won't top that in a hurry,' I said.

'Wasn't it amazing? Why d'you think it all went wrong?'

'Can you keep a secret? I have a hunch that our present and soon-to-be-ex publicity man arranged it as his parting gift.'

'Really? D'you think he did it deliberately?'

'It has his stamp on it.'

We made ourselves near hysterical during the drive back to my hotel reliving every golden moment. Quite apart from the climax to the evening, Laura had apparently had a fairly gruesome time coping with an intense middle-aged queen who wrote a regular column for one of the gay magazines. How he got on the invitation list was anybody's guess, though again that might have been Marvin's handiwork.

'He kept telling me that he ran a pirate copy of *Death in Venice* at least once a week, and that he had an orgasm every time. Isn't that gross? He said, "I can't *look* at a deckchair, even a striped awning turns me on." '

'What did he think of our epic?'

'The only thing he mentioned was he thought the young soldier who does that scene with Charles had wonderful thighs.'

'Well, I told you I'd take care of your education. What did you think of yourself in the film?'

'Embarrassing. I'd no idea I looked like that.'

'Ugly, you mean?'

'No, I'm serious. And I've got such a funny voice. Not a bit like I imagined it was. Do I really sound like that?'

'You're just looking for compliments.'

'I'm not, truly I'm not. I thought I was just awful. Be honest with me, didn't you think I was awful?'

'No.'

'You have to say that.'

'I don't *have* to say it. And I'm not flattering you. I think you're still rough at the edges, but you've got the looks and a personality which comes across on the screen like gangbusters. If I ever get the chance I'll write you a really good part, tailor-make it for you.'

'I thought Michelle was terrific.'

'Yes. She's been at it longer than you. How about Charles?'

'I thought they were all good except me.'

'Well, do you believe me at all?'

'I suppose so.'

'You believe I love you?'

'There you are, you're biased.'

'Okay, I'm biased, but at the same time I wouldn't kid you about this. I haven't said you're going to get an Academy Award the first time out, now have I?'

'No.'

'What I said – and it's true, so listen to the voice of experience – is that you give a very good account of yourself up against some old hands at the game. You photograph like a dream, and you're going to get other offers when this comes out. You wait and see. Now then, Miss Modesty, what time d'you have to be in tonight?'

'Oh, I said I'd be very late, because I imagined it would go on forever, never having been to one of these things.'

There was a new night porter on duty who gave me an old-fashioned look as we mounted the stairs.

The moment we entered my rooms Laura said, 'Tell me something. You're always so interested in my boy-friends . . .'

'Not interested, just jealous.'

'Well, you tell me something for a change. Out of all the women you've had, how do I compare? First of all, how many women have you had?'

'God! what a question.'

'So many you can't remember, I suppose?'

'Not that many, as a matter of fact. I've always been the faithful type.'

'Twenty?'

'Just a minute. I'm not that good at mental arithmetic . . . Allowing for errors and failing memory I'd say around a baker's dozen, including my wife. Not an auspicious tally.'

'Quite a lot though.'

'I don't know. Works out at an average of one every three years.'

'Did you start early?'

'I tried to start early, but I think I must have been a late developer.'

'Were you in love with them all?'

'Was I in love with them all . . . ? Put it this way, I never went the distance with anybody for whom I felt no affection . . . What's all this leading up to?'

'I want you to love me more than any of the others.'

'How d'you know I don't? I told you, you're my last love, for as long as you will have me. Aren't you funny, my precious? You're in a funny mood tonight, aren't you?'

'No.'

'What is it then? What made you suddenly want to know?'

'Nothing. Just because.'

'I love you right now. And I've wanted you from the moment you walked in tonight. You're lucky I didn't run amok and attack you during the dinner.'

'I'd have liked that.'

'We'd have topped his speech, that's for sure. Take your beautiful dress off, I don't want to spoil it.'

'I'm dying to have a pee. All that wine.'

She left me and went through into the bathroom. I heard her turn on the light and then she gave a cry.

'What have you done?'

'Oh, God!' she said. 'Oh, my God!'

I rushed to the bathroom. She was standing in one corner and her hands were half covering her eyes.

'What, darling? What is it?'

Then I saw Marvin. He was lying between the bidet and the edge of the bath, face downwards on the tiled floor. One arm was thrown across the bidet and the other stretched out as though he had been reaching for something. There was an empty bottle of Scotch close to him and in the basin of the bidet a small pill bottle. I leant down and turned him over. I know you are supposed to deduce something from the last expression on a suicide's face, but Marvin's was just a blank mask – neither peaceful nor anguished, just a blank. I did all the usual things, massaged his heart, applied mouth-to-mouth resuscitation, in-expertly and with no great conviction. He was as dead as you ever are.

Laura did nothing. She just pressed herself into the corner of the room. When it became obvious that there was no sign of life, I took her by the hand and led her into the bedroom and sat her on the bed.

'Why?' was all she said.

'Don't upset yourself, my darling. D'you want a drink?' She shook her head.

'It was just such a shock, wasn't it? I know, I know. You just sit there for a moment while I think what I have to do, and then as soon as I can I'll get you home.'

I went back into the bathroom. He had left a note. It was clutched in his right hand and addressed to me. It said:

I hope I gave you a few laughs earlier in the evening to make up for this. I'm sorry to do this to you, but I know you're a buddy I can trust. Let my sister know, she's the only one who cares, and see she gets what's left. Not unhappy, just tired of it all.

Scribbled underneath was the address of a Miss Dunbar in Detroit.

I read the note a second time before folding it and putting it in my pocket. Then I retrieved the pill bottle. I thought, well he died in character. The first time I met him he'd said all the action he ever got was on the third floor of an hotel. You poor sod, I said aloud, at least you left them something to remember you by.

I closed the door on him and went back into the bedroom to cradle Laura in my arms. She was trembling from the shock.

'I've never seen anybody dead before.'

'Yes, well don't think about it, sweetheart. I must make some phone calls.' I covered her with a blanket.

The first person I telephoned was Martin. His wife answered and from the tone of her voice she was still on her dignity.

'Could I speak to Martin please?'

'Who is that?'

'Harvey. Harvey Burgess.'

'Well, it's very late, Mr Burgess. My husband's already gone to bed.'

'Yes, I'm sorry, but it is important.'

'Well, I hope so, because it's most inconsiderate to ring at this hour. Wait a minute. I'll just see if he's still awake.'

They must have slept in separate rooms because I heard her buzz an extension and then the line went dead for a period.

'Harvey?'

'Yes, Martin. I apologise for disturbing you, but I've got some bad news, I'm afraid.'

'What now?'

'Marvin's killed himself.'

'He's done what?'

'Committed suicide.'

'Who did you say?'

'Marvin, our publicity man. He took an overdose, in my bathroom as it happens. I found him a few minutes ago when I got back from the dinner party.'

'Just a minute. Let me put a light on . . . You say Marvin topped himself in your bathroom? Jesus Christ! Why was he in your bathroom?'

'I've no idea. He wasn't at the party, as you probably noticed, and presumably he came to my place because . . . oh, who knows why? that's unimportant. The point is we have to notify the authorities I take it and I rang you first because, being a resident, I thought you might know somebody in the police department. I seem to remember you once said you had contacts.'

'That's all I need at this time of night, and I have to work in the morning.'

'Yeah, well I'll take care of everything, but I just wanted to check with you first. If you have got a contact it might be useful. I'm sure you're not keen to have too much publicity.'

'Damn right, especially with that mob of David's right on the doorstep. What a fucking thing to happen, as if that bloody fiasco of a dinner wasn't enough. Okay, give me a few moments and I'll see who I can raise. Where are you now?'

'I'm at the hotel.'

'Give me that number and wait there. And Harvey . . .'

'Yes?'

'Don't touch anything.'

'There's nothing to touch,' I said, 'it's not the movies.'

Laura was still shivering. 'Come on, sweetheart,' I said, 'let's get you home. You don't want to be around here when the police arrive.'

'Why?' she said again.

'Maybe he didn't mean it.' I said gently.

311

'But people only do that when they're desperately unhappy. He didn't seem unhappy.'

I took her down to the lobby and slapped a 100 franc note into the porter's hand. 'Get a taxi for this young lady. Quickly.' The sight of the money galvanised him and he rang a local number.

'Ten minutes,' he said.

'Poor Marvin,' Laura kept saying. I put my coat round her shoulders and walked her up and down, ever more conscious of the difference in our ages: the death of somebody is a great divider.

'You go back and get a good night's sleep. I'll ring you in the morning. Are you on early call?'

'On stand-by.'

'Then you can sleep late.'

'I won't sleep at all. Will they take him away tonight.'

'I imagine so.'

'Promise you won't stay there if they don't.'

'I'll be okay. You just take care of yourself.'

The taxi arrived and I paid the driver in advance. I watched it out of sight and then went back into the hotel and questioned the porter. 'Did you show a gentleman to my room earlier on?'

'Gentleman? No.'

'What time did you come on duty?'

'The usual. Ten o'clock.'

'Well, something has happened and you may as well know now. Your colleague must have shown a friend of mine up to my room and unfortunately he's met with an accident. I've phoned the police and I'm expecting them to arrive any moment.'

'Police? What sort of accident?'

'I think my friend took an overdose of drugs.'

He stared at me. I could see his mind working. My arrival with Laura, then her hurried departure and now the news I had just given him. For some irrational reason I began to feel guilty.

'Is your friend seriously ill?'

'He's dead.'

He moved a little way away from me, as though suddenly threatened. At that moment the phone rang. He went to the small switchboard and keyed the call to his headphones.

'You're Mr Burgess, yes?'

'Yes.'

'It's for you.'

I picked up the desk extension. It was Martin.

'They're on their way. I did what I could, but the man I know wasn't on duty, so for God's sake be careful what you tell them. Whatever you do, try and play it down.'

'I'll do my best. There's bound to be a post-mortem, I suppose, or is it different over here?'

'I imagine it's the same anywhere with suicide. Did he leave a note?'

'No.' I lied. 'Nothing.'

'I always thought he was unstable. The thought occurred to me, you don't think he had anything to do with that business tonight, do you?'

'David's speech? It's possible, I suppose.'

'More likely to have been Charles. I never thought that Marvin had a sense of humour.'

'No,' I said. 'But then very few of us have.'

A short while afterwards the police and ambulance arrived. I hadn't realised that the paramedics come under the fire brigade in France. They rushed in like firemen, but of course there was nothing for them to do but eventually remove the body. The police were something else. I guess I had anticipated somebody looking like Claude Rains in that smart Foreign-Legion-type uniform, but what I got was a weedy-looking individual in civilian clothes and sporting a moustache which looked as though it had been drawn on with an eyebrow pencil. He was accompanied by a young woman, who proved to be the one who spoke English and seemed to be his superior in rank. They viewed the body and took away the two bottles. I told them as much as I knew and after a cursory examination of my rooms they allowed the paramedics to remove poor Marvin to the mortuary.

'You will have to make a statement,' the young woman said.

'Tonight?'

'No, that's not necessary. You are living here, yes?'

'I'm staying in this hotel until my work's finished.'

313

'Ah, yes, the filming. But you didn't live with this man?' I couldn't quite make up my mind whether she meant just that, or whether it was just that she was speaking in a foreign language.

'No, he was staying in a hotel in Grasse.'

'He was an actor, yes?'

'Publicity man,' I said.

'Do you know which hotel in Grasse?'

'I'm not sure. But the office at the studio could tell you when they get there in the morning.'

'And when was the last time you saw him?'

I began to get that uneasy feeling that always creeps in whenever I talk to anybody in authority. She seemed to be asking a lot of questions.

'Earlier this evening, around six o'clock.'

'Here?'

'No, at the studio. We had a party there.'

'Did you notice anything different about him?'

'No. He seemed happier than usual, if anything.'

'And then what?'

'Then I went on to a dinner party, which he didn't attend, and I came back here and found him almost immediately. I tried to revive him, but it wasn't any use.'

'The pills he presumably took – were those yours or his?'

'His. I do have some of my own, but they're in a different bottle.'

'Show me, please.'

I went into the bathroom and produced them.

'Did he take other drugs?'

'Maybe. I wouldn't know. Does it matter now?'

'Perhaps,' she said. 'That's what we're here to find out, aren't we?'

I wished Martin had been able to locate his friendly contact. That is if he ever had one. There were so many things about Martin that didn't add up.

'So what did you do after you found him? What time was that, by the way?'

'What time is it now? Twelve-twenty . . . Well, I didn't look at my watch, but I made one phone call to the director of the film, Mr James, who's lived down here for some years . . . I'd say about forty minutes ago, about twenty to

314

midnight . . . And Mr James said he'd call you, and that's about it.'

She nodded. 'Could you just wait for a moment, please?' She left the room, but the man stayed where he was.

'Drink?' I picked up a bottle and showed it to him. He shook his head.

'Do you mind if I do? I feel in need of one. It was a great shock. He was a friend of mine.'

He ran his finger across his moustache as if to check that it was still there, but gave no indication that he had understood anything I'd said. I poured myself a stiff drink and knocked it back. Then the young woman detective returned.

'The concierge said that when you returned you had a young lady with you.'

'That's right.'

'You didn't mention that.'

'Well, you didn't ask me.'

'Who was she?'

'Look,' I said, 'this isn't a murder investigation, is it? The young lady is a member of the cast. She was at the same dinner party and we came back here for a nightcap. Finding our friend dead was a great shock to her, so I sent her home in a taxi.'

'Can I have her name please?'

'Taylor,' I said, and defiantly poured myself a second drink. 'A Miss Taylor. Her father is a local dentist, Doctor Tallan. He's in the telephone book, a respected citizen. And French. The difference being that Taylor is a stage nom de plume.'

'Thank you. Now is there anything else you have forgotten, Mr Burgess?'

I hesitated just a fraction too long before producing Marvin's note from my pocket. She took it from me.

'Why didn't you show me this before?'

'No sinister reason. It seemed kind of personal and of no great importance to anybody else.'

'When a person dies in unusual circumstances, Mr Burgess, everything is important until proved otherwise.'

I suddenly felt very weary. 'Yes, of course, but I guess I'm in shock too.'

'Does the letter signify anything to you?'

'Only that he wanted out.'

'I'm sorry, I don't understand.'

'I think my friend felt he didn't have much to live for – isn't that the usual reason why people kill themselves? Doesn't he say that? "Not unhappy, just tired of it all."'

She consulted the note again, then spoke to her companion at some length, and naturally this time I didn't understand a word.

'I think perhaps on second thoughts it would be best if you made your statement tonight. While it's still fresh.'

I found myself wishing I was dealing with a man; there was something very intimidating about her – her appearance didn't marry up with her attitude. I was sure she was a black belt at judo or something like that, a little too liberated for my taste.

'Fine,' I said. 'Let's get it over.'

She sat beside me in my car and I tailed the police vehicle to the old part of Nice. There I really caught up with my past: the police station, although reasonably presentable from the outside, looked exactly like the set of every French film inside. I followed them both up some unswept stairs to the first floor and the female Maigret showed me into the charge room. There were five or six hookers sitting on wooden benches in the corridor and she closed the door on them before sitting down at an ancient typewriter. She fed in some headed report sheets – I counted five, with carbons in between – and hit the keys, typing on in silence for several minutes.

'Right,' she began. 'Your name, present address, home address and occupation.'

I went through it all again. She might have been good at her job, but she was what I call a hit-and-rub-out typist and the statement took the best part of an hour. At one point another woman brought her a cup of coffee, but nobody offered me one. When it was over, I signed the bottom of each page and obtained her permission to leave. The hookers were still waiting in the corridor, and not for the first time in my life I felt a certain affinity with them.

NINETEEN

'Why the bloody hell did you have to drag Laura into it?' Martin shouted at me. I had never seen him quite so angry. 'And what was she doing going back to your hotel at that hour?'

'You were at the same party,' I said. 'You must remember that it didn't exactly end on a high note. She was David's date, not mine. He dumped her and I offered to take her home. We stopped by at my hotel on the way to have a nightcap. End of story.'

'So? You didn't have to tell the police that. You should have kept her out of it.'

'I didn't volunteer the information. Your friends wheedled it out of the night porter. Don't give me a hard time, Martin. I didn't feed Marvin the pills, and I didn't rehearse his death scene.'

'I'm not interested in fucking Marvin, I'm only interested in Laura, her reputation.'

'She didn't kill him either. She just had the misfortune to find him. Look, screw you! I was up half the night giving my life story to a female-flatfoot, and that wasn't any fun, believe me. So don't think you have a monopoly of concern for Laura. I tried to protect her! Until the goddamn porter put his two cents in, I hadn't mentioned her. As it happens that was a mistake. It's always a mistake not to come clean. You should know that, you've directed enough whodunnits. They treated me like a suspect.'

He calmed down a little after that.

'Well, all right, I'll accept it wasn't your fault, but you do realise that we're now sitting on an unexploded bomb. We've got half the world's Press on our doorstep, thanks to

317

David, and already they've got wind of it. His speech was bad enough, and now they've got this to pick over, and don't think they won't.'

'Martin,' I said, 'he's dead. They're going to have an inquest and Laura and me are the only material witnesses. Now unless you've got a direct line to the President, it's got to run its course. You don't like it, I don't like it, but that's the way it is.'

'That stupid, bloody man! He was nothing but trouble when he was alive, and he's still trouble.'

'Boy! you're really big on compassion, aren't you?'

He stopped pacing up and down his office and stared at me. 'What was he to you, then?'

'Friendly,' I said. 'We need all the friends we can get, or so I'm told.'

'You've always got a smart answer, haven't you? It's a pity some of that scintillating dialogue doesn't find its way into your scripts.'

'You took the words right out of my mouth.'

'Just remember who brought you here, Harvey. You're not that much in demand.'

'No. It's nice of you to remind me.'

'I trusted you with Laura, and you've let me down.'

'Oh, come on, Martin,' I said. 'Be your age. You want to trade insults, go ahead . . . You think I planned this whole thing? That Marvin and I were in cahoots? That he told me in advance and I said, well don't do it in your hotel, come and use mine? The fact that I invited Laura back for a drink was purely fortuitous.'

'But you are playing a double game, aren't you, Harvey?'

That pulled me up short.

'Am I? In what way?'

'You haven't told me the whole story, have you? You see, I checked with my friend at police headquarters this morning and he told me an interesting fact . . . There was a suicide note. Yet when I asked you last night, you denied it.'

'Oh, Christ! you're in the wrong business, Martin, you should have become a policeman yourself.' The relief I felt that he had not found out about my relationship with Laura gave me the courage to bluff it out. 'I don't know what I said

318

last night. Yes, there was a note. Addressed to me. A sad note from a guy who had made up his mind to swallow the pills. Now, he wasn't an atom spy, or a mass murderer, he was just a poor hack working for scale. His death isn't important to you, Martin, it's just a temporary inconvenience . . . a hair in the gate. What d'you care?'

'You'll be finished soon, won't you?' he said. 'There's only that one other scene to rewrite for Suzanne and then you're through. You haven't done badly out of it, considering it was only meant to be a few weeks in the first place.'

'Yes, I got lucky. It's mostly been a pleasure,' I said. 'When would you like me to go?'

'Oh, there's no particular hurry. Once you've turned in the last pages, that's up to you. I'll tell the production office to issue a week's notice. I don't want to be ungenerous. What you do after that is your business.'

'That's fine. I'll have to stay on for the inquest or whatever they call them over here. No regrets, I've enjoyed it.'

I left his office and went to Laura's dressing-room, but it was empty and her costumes were still on their hangers. Then I went to the bar and used the public telephone to call her. Madame Tallan answered.

'Is Laura awake yet?'

'No. She was so upset last night.'

'Yes, it was a nasty shock for her, I'm sorry.'

'Whatever possessed the poor man? I never met him of course, though he did ring here a few times, and he always seemed cheerful enough. Anyway thank you for taking care of Laura as you did.'

'I'm very fond of her,' I said. I don't know why, but I found myself crying, and had to keep the emotion out of my voice. 'When she does wake, perhaps she'll be good enough to call me. I'll be at my hotel. She knows the number.'

'I'll tell her. How's the tooth?'

'The tooth? Oh, the tooth! Fine, no trouble, your husband did a great job.'

I blundered down the steps leading from the bar and drove out to avoid meeting anybody else. The reality of Marvin's death had suddenly hit me. I wasn't depressed that Martin had terminated my contract. In a way it removed any lingering obligation. In a week's time I would be a free agent again. But as I drove past the airport I thought back to the day of my arrival, and Marvin's genuine if irritating concern for my comfort; and I was sorry I hadn't been nicer to him. It seemed a sad summing up of his life that in the end he had nobody to write to except a man he had known only for two or three months.

Once back at the hotel I occupied myself with writing the last remaining scene. When inspiration flagged I stared at the familiar view, waiting for the only voice I wanted to hear. When the maid came in to make the bed and clean the room I noticed she didn't linger over the bathroom. When I used it myself I thought perhaps I'd still feel Marvin's presence, but it was just a bare, functional place: it didn't even contain anything of me, let alone Marvin.

Laura finally rang just after lunch. Her voice sounded normal enough, but I sensed that something was still worrying her.

'Well, dormouse, you finally came out of hibernation.'

'I had nightmares all night,' she said. 'Awful ones, where he was lying on the floor covered in worms.'

'Try not to think about it. Have they picked up your call?'

'No, they just cancelled it. Martin rang to say he wouldn't get to my scene.'

'He rang you himself, did he? You're honoured. Look, if you can face it after last night I'd like to take you out for a really super meal. Wherever you like, you choose.'

There was a pause, then she said, 'I can't tonight.'

'Oh. Why not?'

'I have to go to Martin's. He invited me just now.'

'I see. I should have got in first. You have to go, I suppose?'

'I don't want to particularly, but he is the director.'

'That's right, always keep in with the director. By the way, to get rid of all the good news, I got notice today. I finish on the film in a week.'

'But we've still got another three weeks, they told me.'

'You have, yes, but not me.'

'That's awful.'

'I'm not taking the next plane out. I'll still be here, it's just that I'm off the payroll. You won't get rid of me that easily . . . Tell me, did Martin ask you anything about last night?'

'Yes.'

'What did he want to know?'

'Why I was in your hotel.'

'And what did you tell him?'

'The truth. That we just went back for a drink. That wasn't a lie, was it?'

'As it happens, no . . . Well, good luck this evening. I shall miss you.'

'What will you do? Don't stay in, will you? Why don't you move to another hotel?'

'It worries you, doesn't it?'

'I can't ever go back there,' she said.

'Looks like I'll have to move, then.'

'Am I being silly?'

'No, darling. I understand. Will I see you tomorrow?'

'I think so. I'm working tomorrow, so come to the studio. Depends what time we finish.'

Perhaps I detected a certain lack of enthusiasm in her voice, but I chose to ignore it. It was quite obvious that Marvin's suicide had affected her deeply.

'Okay. I'll get there for lunch. Don't have any more nightmares. Marvin isn't a ghost you need to fear.'

'No,' she said, but there was still a note of doubt.

The police had kept Marvin's note to me, but I remembered the address of his sister and put a call in to the Detroit operator. The efficiency of our American telephone system takes some beating: I had no sooner given the name and address of Miss Dunbar than the enquiry operator reeled off her number.

I waited until I felt sure she would be up and about before placing the call. Over the years I have been lucky that there have been few times I've had to break bad news, and I've always felt relieved that I'm not a doctor or a policeman. I could probably stomach the blood and the danger to a degree, but I doubt if I could ever become reconciled to daily contact with grief.

The number rang for ages before anybody answered. The voice that spoke to me at the other end of the line was

321

unmistakably that of an old woman – slightly querulous, with a hint of alarm in it: I could imagine her receiving strangers at her front door in just the same way. It was a voice that instantly conveyed the daily uncertainty of inner-city life; the double security bolts on the door, the fear of being on the streets after dark, the anonymous occupants of the next apartment who come and go as the neighbourhood slips into decay.

'Hello. Yes?'

'Miss Dunbar?'

I was committed to the conversation before I had really thought it through, and now I had no idea how to begin.

'Miss Dunbar, this is Harvey Burgess. You don't know me, I'm afraid, and I'm ringing you from France.'

'From where?'

'France.'

'Oh, yes?' The uncertainty in her voice was now more pronounced.

'I've been working on a film with your brother, Marvin.'

'That's nice.'

'Yes.'

'He's my brother, you know.'

'I know, yes . . .'

'Who is that again?'

'Harvey Burgess.'

'Do I know you?'

'No, but I was a friend of Marvin's.'

'He has lots of friends, but of course I don't meet them.'

'Miss Dunbar,' I said, beginning again, 'the reason I'm calling you is that I'm afraid I haven't got good news . . . Are you still there?'

'Yes, I'm still listening.'

'Marvin hasn't been too well.'

'No, well he never looks after himself, that's what I've always told him.'

I was lost by then. It was a scene I could have written, had written more than once, but in real life I couldn't play it.

'The news I have to tell you is . . . and I hope you'll forgive me for telling you like this, is that Marvin met with an accident last night.'

There was another pause.

'What sort of accident?'

'A serious one, and he asked me to let you know, you being his closest relative . . .'

'Is he all right?'

'No, and I know this going to be a big shock to you . . . I'm afraid he died.'

I waited. It's curious how, on transatlantic calls, distance seems shortened: I could feel that old woman's shock as though she was sitting a few feet from me.

'Marvin's dead?' she finally said.

'Yes. I'm very sorry.' And then, with no warning, I found I knew what I had to do. 'I shall take care of everything over here and bring him home to be buried. I'm sure that's what you would want, and what would have pleased Marvin . . . Miss Dunbar?'

Grief takes many forms, but her reply, when it came, took me off guard. I'm quite certain I could never have invented such a line, or had I by chance stumbled upon it and put it into a script, it would have been struck out as unreal. Yet she said it, and I heard it, and I can remember it to this day. She said, 'I think I'll go and eat some chocolate,' and then she hung up.

I found myself sweating from the agony of the last few minutes. I could visualise that unknown old woman leaving the phone and wandering about her apartment, going to wherever she kept her store of chocolate and breaking the wrapper. I could see her sitting by a window, for my mind worked like a camera. Click, and there was grief. Click and the old jaws munched on the Hersey bar. Click and a tear was frozen on her cheek. Or maybe not even a tear. Just a negative dropped into the developer, and what the chemical bath produced was just the image of a human being suddenly cut off from hope.

It was guilt by association. The fact that Marvin had chosen my bathroom in which to end his life made me suspect in certain people's eyes. Martin's reaction, once he learnt that Laura had been with me, had not been unexpected but I found that others started to act as though what Marvin died of was contagious and I was the carrier. In particular, Suzanne surprised me. When I visited the studio the following day I was naturally buttonholed to give further details. It was only now when he had gone that the other members of the unit seemed to recall what a great character he had been (though I except Nigel from the rest: he alone expressed genuine grief).

'I've no patience with people who commit suicide,' Suzanne said. 'We've all felt like it, but you just don't give in. It's a very selfish way to go. No thought for other people.'

'What other people?' I said. 'He didn't have anybody except an old maiden sister.'

'Well, what about you, and poor Laura? She was the one who found him. She's very upset.'

'Yes, I know that, but Marvin couldn't have guessed that. That was pure coincidence.'

'Okay, well you then. He did it in your bathroom, so presumably he guessed you'd find him.'

'Oh, Suzanne,' I said, 'what does it matter now?'

'It matters because it's selfish and unfeeling, and he left us in the lurch. It's made me feel quite ill again.'

As it happened, Martin's fears about any adverse publicity were never realised. The visiting Los Angeles group showed little interest in reporting the event. I saw a small paragraph in one of the trades which merely gave the bare facts:

PUBLICIST TAKES OVERDOSE

Marvin Dunbar, 63, who entered the industry as fan-magger scribe in '48, was discovered dead of a drug overdose in French hotel. Dead man was freelancing on *The Bastille Connection*, currently lensing at Victorine Studios, Nice.

Latrough retrieved part of his losses by offering the vacant position to one of the visitors. Naturally he was his usual forgiving self where Marvin was concerned.

'He saved me the trouble,' was his first comment to me. 'You know he was the one who switched my cards? What a loser! I tell you something, he's well out of it, and we're better off without him. This new guy I've inked for the job is gonna get us some space for a change. Do me a favour and just play it down at the inquest.'

I still had the inquest to face, of course, and I was concerned at Laura having to be involved. But there again I hadn't reckoned with Martin's influence. Way back he had made much of the corruption on the coast, but he used it when it suited him.

When I saw Laura at lunch that day she was understandably subdued. I tried to steer around the subject as much as possible though it wasn't easy with a constant stream of people coming to the table and asking questions.

'When we're called to the inquest,' I said, 'let me do all the talking. I can say I was the one who first found him, it's only a white lie.'

'I don't have to go.'

'Well, I think you will have to, darling.'

'No,' she said, 'Martin's got me out of it. He talked to somebody and explained about my being needed every day in the film, and they agreed I needn't attend.'

Without looking at her I said, 'I'm glad.'

'It's still awful for you.'

'Not really.'

'Have they told you when?'

'Not yet . . . I've been thinking. When it's over, I think I shall take his body back to Detroit.'

She stared at me.

'To Detroit?'

'Yes. The only relative he had was a sister, a little older than him, though I'm only guessing from the sound of her voice . . . She lives there. I called her and broke the news.'

'But why do you have to take him back?'

'I don't have to. I just thought somebody ought, and nobody else seems to give a damn.'

'Will you come back?'

'That depends on you. Whether you want me to come back. Do you?'

'Of course I do.'

'You seem odd today.'

'No I'm not . . . I still haven't got over finding him there like that.'

'You sure there's nothing else?'

325

'No.'

'What else did Martin tell you?'

'Tell me?'

'Yes. Did he grill you about me?'

'He asked how often I'd seen you.'

'There you are, you see. That's the price you pay for being such a popular girl. And what did you tell him?'

'Just that I'd seen you a couple of times.'

'He thinks he's in love with you.'

'That's stupid.'

'No. Takes all sorts. He's entitled. Just that he's mean with it. So take care of yourself when I'm away.'

'When d'you think you'll go?'

'As soon as I fix the formalities. There's bound to be a lot of red tape, or maybe not, I don't know.'

I soon found out that the Byzantine ways of officialdom are the same the world over. There's a great deal to be said for the Indian way of disposing of the dead – to burn them garlanded with flowers on a bed of cedar wood. We have made death as complicated as life.

The inquest wasn't as hideous as I had imagined. I guess nobody was that interested in the fate of Marvin Dunbar, alive or dead. I gave my evidence, the police and medical authorities gave theirs and the expected verdict was duly delivered. It was what came after that proved the most irksome. I went from office to office, signing document after document, before his body was released to me. After that I had a further round of frustration, finding an airline prepared to take the casket, buying the necessary tickets, hiring the necessary transport, and all conducted in my halting French which in turn led to frequent misunderstandings on both sides.

The night before I left, Laura and I had a farewell dinner. The first chill of winter was in the air and leaves were falling from the trees when I drove to her house. It was as if, with Marvin's death, the season of love had come to an end.

I had a drink with her parents while waiting for Laura to come down from her room. They were sympathetic about Marvin and their concern was the more touching since he was a complete stranger to them.

'It must be sad to die like that so far from home,' Madame Tallan said.

'I don't know that he had a home. In his sort of job you live most of your life out of suitcases, going from location to location, hotel to hotel.'

'Laura tells me that you're taking his body home to be buried.'

'Yes.'

'That's kind of you. Laura's going to miss you.'

'I hope so,' I said. 'I shall certainly miss her.'

'Well, I'm sure you'll be back,' her father said. 'Come back and see us again, if only for a dental check-up.' He had opened champagne in my honour. 'Safe journey.'

'Yes, safe journey,' his wife echoed.

There was a photograph on the mantelpiece of Laura as a young girl, taken, I guessed, when she was fourteen or so. I moved to examine it more closely.

'That was her confirmation,' her mother said. 'But she's a naughty girl, she hasn't kept up with her religion. The young don't seem to need it like we did, do they?'

'Did we need it?' I asked.

'I think so. The values were all there, you didn't have to think twice about them. Not that I'm the one to speak. I don't go to Mass as often as I should. Are you religious?'

'No.'

'Were you ever?'

'I seem to remember I passed through a manic period when I read the Bible from cover to cover and thought I'd be a missionary.'

'How old were you when that happened?'

'Oh, eight or thereabouts.'

'Were you brought up a Catholic?'

'No. My parents were Baptists. I thought that was frightening, I remember, being dunked under the water. They went in for full immersion. It was a heavy scene.'

Then Laura came down the stairs. I never ceased to be freshly amazed by her beauty.

We went back to our favourite haunt. The nights were drawing in and most of the tourists had gone home, so we had the place more or less to ourselves and were able to sit at our usual table in the corner. There was a hesitancy

327

about our conversation as we both skirted around thoughts of the future. I'm not very good at farewell scenes, and I dare say my determination not to show my gnawing despair made me over-flippant. The jokes fell flat and when the main course came we lapsed into silence for a while.

'I wonder when the film will come out?' she said.

'They usually take three or four months after shooting.'

'As long as that?'

'Well, they have to edit, then score the music, make the titles and dub it.'

'What's that?'

'Dubbing? That's the last process. It's taking all the sound tracks – dialogue, effects, music – and mixing them all together, so that you get a clean sound track. Then that's striped onto the edge of the picture to produce what is known as a "married" print.'

'Sounds very complicated.'

'Yes, I guess it is really . . . Like you and me. We're complicated, aren't we? A very funny pair, don't you think so?'

'Yes.'

'They ought to invent a process for us. Take my dialogue, your effect on me, a little romantic music – but whether it would produce a marriage is another thing . . . Smile, that's a joke. Not a very good one, but worth a faint smile. That's better . . . Would you ever marry me?'

'You haven't asked me,' she said.

'Not recently, you mean? Okay. I'll ask you now: will you?'

'I don't want to get married to anybody just yet,' she said gently enough.

'I can wait. Are you going to give me any hope at all?'

'I wouldn't be any good to you.'

'Oh, they all say that. And don't look so worried. You don't have to give a definite answer right now . . . we haven't decided on the music yet, and there are a lot more effects to be added, plenty of time . . . before I'm in the wheelchair.'

The dialogue seemed to depress her, and I hardly dared guess at the reason why. There was a thread of masochism in my decision to take poor old Marvin's body back to the

States. My Jack Armstrong gesture had come more from a sense of outrage than anything else. At the time I had imagined it might make a few ashamed of their behaviour towards him, but that had been but wishful thinking. They'd forgotten him already, and my gesture was going to cost me a painful separation from Laura. Painful and foolish, I thought, sitting across from her at that corner table, my hand on hers. Why should she be faithful to me? I had no real claim on her except a love she did not, or could not, fully return.

Yes, I believed she loved me, but sporadically. I'd once joked to her, 'I'm your sporadic lover', in the aftermath of the time when she went to Marseille with her student boyfriend. She had smothered her guilt then, but for how long? I had no great faith in the absence-makes-the-heart-grow-fonder theory. Maybe at my age there was some truth in it for me, but not for her, and I couldn't blame her for that. I was grateful for the small mercies of love – the revelation of her body, the memories of those times we had shared.

'One thing I do want,' I said. 'I want a photo of you to take with me.'

'I'll have to send you one.'

'You could give me one tonight when I take you home.'

She reached down by the side of her chair for her handbag and rummaged in it.

'I did bring you something to remember me by. It's not new, it belonged to my grandfather, but it's real silver.' She opened her palm and revealed an old Zippo lighter – the original inner core had been given an engraved silver case.

'It does work. I tried it.'

'But don't you want to keep it?'

'No, it's for you.'

I flicked it and as it flamed I was reminded of my time in the army during the war – the solace of a cigarette during the lulls, taken gratefully without the burden of today's social and medical pressures. Everybody used a Zippo then.

'I'll treasure it,' I said. 'Thank you, darling . . . I haven't got a going-away present for you.'

'You've given me enough already.'

She ordered her usual calorie-saturated dessert, *tarte aux pommes* this time, with thick cream and Calvados poured over it. I accepted a mouthful from her, fed to me as you feed babies. We lingered over our coffee.

'What time is your plane tomorrow?'

'I have to be at the airport at eleven.'

'Where do they put the . . . coffin?'

'In the cargo hold.'

'With the baggage?'

'I guess so.'

'I can't bear it,' she said, and suddenly she was crying. 'I don't like to think of him there.'

I handed her my handkerchief – women never seem to have handkerchiefs, I've noticed.

'He's out of it, it makes no difference to him.'

'I know, I know, but I still think it's sad. I wish I believed more in something. I won't come and see you off, because I'd only cry like this.'

'If you cry, I shall start. Be like all your other boyfriends.' It was the first time that evening I'd acknowledged their existence, but of course they were uppermost in my thoughts. 'I'll wave to you,' I said, trying to repair the damage. 'I expect I'll pass right over your house.'

'I might be at the studio, if they call me.'

'Then I'll ruin a take, won't I?' The sound stages were not proof against the roar of a 747 on take-off. 'Even if you don't see me, you'll certainly hear me.'

'I wish we didn't have to talk about it.'

I paid the bill and we left and walked with our arms around each other to the car park. She was shivering and I took my jacket off and put it around her shoulders, but she still shivered. In the narrow street three dogs, two German shepherds and a ragged Chow, fretted and moaned at each other as they strutted about prior to a territorial fight. We gave them a wide berth.

'It must be lonely here in the winter,' I said.

'Yes. I shan't stay here forever. I want to get away and travel.'

'Where particularly?'

'Africa.'

'You've left it a bit late. Africa isn't too friendly these days.'

'I don't think that's true,' she said. 'There are still places.'

'How about America, and in particular Connecticut? You could travel to me. I'd send you a ticket. First class . . . but only one way.'

'That would be nice.'

'So when? Name the date.'

She tightened her grip on my arm but did not answer.

'You can't say I don't try,' I said.

We reached the car. The windscreen had a faint patina of frost on it.

'Where shall we go? Oh, I'm sorry, I forgot. We don't have a choice any more, do we? You can't face my hotel, I suppose?'

'It's stupid of me, but I can't.'

I started the engine and turned the heater on.

'Back to our forest clearing then. Are you very cold?'

'No, I feel better now.'

As we drove away there was an old woman – or was it a priest? – watching us from a nearby doorway. I drove slowly, wanting to make every minute count. When we reached our usual clearing I killed the engine and switched off the headlamps. It was very quiet. After a while my eyes became accustomed to the darkness and I could make out the silver outlines of the surrounding birch trees. There was almost a full moon.

'Don't you want to make one of your predictions?'

'What about?' Laura said.

'Aren't you the moon expert? The first time I met you, you predicted a full moon. We've got one tonight.'

She rubbed away a circle of condensation on her window and looked out. 'It's sort of spooky here tonight,' she said.

'I'll lock us in. Come here.'

I put my arm around her and let her head fall on my shoulder.

'I hate goodbyes.'

'We won't prolong it,' I said.

'But I will see you again.'

'Promise?'

'Of course.'

'Well, even if you don't, I shall always remember this summer.'

331

'Why do you say that?'

'Why? Because for once I'm being realistic. A little late in the day perhaps. I'm sure you mean it, but things change, we all change, we can't help ourselves. See, I didn't know I would fall in love with you as I have done . . . and I should have known better. You've got your boyfriend . . . And what's happened to Martin's *bête noire*, the Ferrari owner? He seems to have dropped out of the running lately.'

'Oh, he rings now and again. But he was never what you thought.'

'So who are my rivals? Who am I leaving you to?'

'You make me sound awful.'

'I don't mean to . . . Will you feel guilty about me when next you see your other boyfriend, the one in college?'

'I expect so.'

'Has he asked you to marry him?'

'Yes. All the time.'

'And?'

'I told you, I don't want to get married to anybody until I've done lots of things.'

'What happens if you get pregnant?'

'Why do you say that?'

'Normal question. It's always a possibility. Would you have it?'

'I don't know, do I? It hasn't happened.'

'But if it did?' I pressed.

She traced a finger picture on the frosted window. 'I wouldn't have an abortion,' she said slowly. 'But why are you asking me that?'

'No sinister reason . . . I'd like to give you babies, I'd like to marry you, to stay here and never leave, never share you, all those things that aren't going to happen . . .'

'They might . . .'

'I'm being dreary, aren't I? Boring you with my jealousy . . . I didn't plan it that way, but I can't help myself. I wanted our last night to be perfect, and I've ruined it, haven't I?'

'No. And it isn't our last night . . . it doesn't have to be . . . I know we'll see each other again.'

Her lips opened to mine, and as we kissed I suddenly caught sight of my face in the rear-view mirror: it was the

332

face of a stranger. I thought, is that what love looks like? I had wanted to say such tender, wise things to her, to imprint myself on her like a stain, marking her so that others who came after would know some of the pain I felt. I couldn't bear the thought of others touching the breasts I now shaped in my hands. We kissed with sad caution as though passion, too, was a rival.

'I shall write to you. I shall write every day. That's the penalty you pay for having a writer fall in love with you. Will you write to me?'

'I'm not very good at writing things, not to anybody.'

'Anything. I don't care. Just a postcard with your name on it, I'll settle for that . . . Just so I'll know you haven't forgotten me.'

'I won't ever forget you. Anyway, I shall see you again. You'll come back or we'll meet somewhere else.'

'Yes, that's right. Let's believe that.'

I restarted the engine and we bumped our way across the rutted grass and back onto the road. Laura didn't talk, but she reached across and gripped my hand on the steering wheel. I thought, in a few minutes the agony of living without her begins.

When we got to her house she stopped me from getting out.

'Take care.'

'You take care. I'll try and ring you in the morning before I leave.'

I watched her unlock the gates and walk up the short drive. Half-way there she turned back.

'One last kiss,' she said, and our mouths touched through the open window. Then she was gone. I reversed and drove back along the way we had come. I had gone a mile or so when my headlamps picked up an object lying in the road. I braked and took a closer look, thinking it to be some small night animal. I didn't want to kill anything else that night. But it was only a single black rubber glove, such as workmen use, the bloated fingers pointing upwards as though indicating the route which, with complete freedom of choice, I had determined to take.

TWENTY

I said all the other mistakes were mine, and that's true enough. Leaving Laura when I did, and how I did, now seems the biggest mistake of all. Now, I can't conceive why it was that I took it upon myself to bury Marvin. With hindsight it seems more the act of a madman than one of charity.

The night I parted from Laura I hardly slept at all. Once I had packed I sat down to write her the first of many love letters: a long rambling affair such as we compose in panic, fearful we have left too many things unsaid. I suppose I believed I could persuade her to faithfulness by my pen alone.

Love makes us careless of friendships, though apart from Michelle and Nigel there were few on the crew I would miss or who would miss me. I woke early and drove to the flower market in the old part of Antibes. There I arranged for a mass of red roses to be delivered to Laura later in the day. I also bought a smaller bunch for Michelle and left these with a note for the concierge to give her. Back at the Auberge I busied myself destroying all the various discarded versions of the script; I felt like a member of an embassy staff burning the files as enemy forces drew closer. Then I rang Martin, judging my moment so as to catch him before he left for the studio.

'Oh, you're going today, are you? Nobody told me. Thought perhaps you'd stay on a bit and take a holiday. Perhaps you think you've had a holiday.'

'I was intending to,' I said, 'until the Marvin business. But I'm flying to Detroit for the funeral.'

'Dear chum, that's very noble. Hope somebody'll do that for me.'

'Anytime you want to be buried in Detroit, give me a bell.'

We both played out the scene of counterfeit friendship.

'Well, safe landings and here's to the next time, eh? I think we might have a winner here.'

'Let's hope so.'

'Cheers then.'

'Remember me to Laura,' I said, unable to resist it, but the phone was already dead.

Once at the airport I checked in and confirmed that Marvin's coffin had been cleared and was on the same plane. I went through Passport Control, suffered the perfunctory security search, bought a carton of duty-free cigarettes, then went to find a phone booth. I phoned Laura's home: her mother told me I had just missed her, she was on her way to the studio. I called there but she hadn't arrived. I had a coffee at the bar and kept looking at my watch. For some reason it seems that clocks go slower at airports. The economy passengers started boarding and I rang again. This time I was told she was in make-up and I finally got through there. Once again I'd missed her. I had the call transferred through to the stage, but the shooting bell was up and all calls were blocked. I heard my name announced in barely discernible English over the airport public address system: apparently I was keeping the plane waiting, but I still made one last attempt to get through. This time, with time running out, I found her. She was still on the set and couldn't talk.

'Then I'll say it for us,' I said, waving away an airline official who had come to claim me. 'I love you, try to remember me.'

'I will, of course I will.'

'I can't stay because the plane's just about to take off, but I've written, you should get a letter tomorrow. And I'll ring when I arrive. Take care of yourself.' I heard the shooting bell sound in the background. 'Don't dream about worms,' I said and then we were cut off.

The official hurried me towards the Boarding Gate and I stepped out into bright sunlight and ran across the burning

335

tarmac to be greeted like a delinquent by the stewardess at the top of the stairs. The moment I was inside they closed the hatches and started the engines. It wasn't until I had fastened my safety belt that I realised I was still carrying the letter.

I had a window seat on the port side of the aircraft and as we lifted off the runway I could just see the cluster of buildings that make up the Victorine Studios. The big plane lurched in the hot air, seeming to claw its way slowly into the sky, like a man going hand over hand up a ladder. I'm never too relaxed on take-offs, although reasonably fatalistic – I guess it's quicker than cancer – but this time I closed my eyes and, like the hypocrite I am, I prayed.

Once the seat-belt signs had gone off and the plane had done a U-turn over the sea, gaining height to clear the mountains as it recrossed the coast and set course, I tried to distinguish landmarks below. I knew that we must be passing over the Valbonne area and that somewhere down there was a life I might never see again. But I couldn't make out any familiar reference points, just the lighthouse-like flares as the sun struck terraced greenhouses dotting the unreal patterned symmetry of the countryside below.

I opened my own letter and re-read it. It said none of the things I wanted to say, so I went to the toilet and flushed it away. When I returned to my seat I began again, berating myself for many foolishnesses. There was a short stop-over in Paris and then began the long haul to New York. I thought back to the speed of my arrival, that rushing towards the chaos of love.

By contrast with Nice, Detroit seemed like something out of the Ice Age. My plane finally touched down some eleven hours later in a hailstorm. Once I was through the baggage hall I tried a direct-dial call to the studios. I ran out of change before I could speak to Laura, since inevitably they had to ring various extensions to try and locate her. I left the phone with the feeling that the distance between us could never be bridged again.

I then had a depressing hour with a man from the mortician's. He brought back memories of a famous Hollywood landmark that used to stand at the beginning of the Strip on Sunset Boulevard. This was a funeral parlour with the joyous name of Utter McKinley, and their sign over the entrance was a huge clock with no hands. I hadn't had that much experience with the funeral trade, but I guess Evelyn Waugh wrote the last, unexaggerated word. Death be not proud and have your check-book handy. Some of the questions put to me I couldn't answer – I had no idea whether Marvin had left a Will with instructions, or, failing that, what his sister's wishes in the matter would be. Some people have a thing about cremation, and others don't relish the cold, cold earth.

'Do you wish a lying-in period?' was one of the questions the man put to me.

'What does that entail?'

'Well, a little cosmetics.' He never met my eyes, but looked past me all the time as though taking instructions from the Grim Reaper himself.

'No . . . well, I doubt that will be called for, but until I've discussed it with the deceased's sister I can't give you a decision.'

'Then there's the casket. If you'd care to study this beautiful brochure, Mr Burgess, I'm sure you'll find something appropriate. None of your compressed cardboard jobs. We've just introduced our latest nuclear-age model, guaranteed to survive a ten-megaton blast. It's proving very popular.'

'My friend survived quite a few of those,' I murmured, but he didn't react.

Pressing me further as to the numbers likely to attend the funeral, he then offered to supply professional mourners – 'It looks better,' he said – and I thought how Marvin would have appreciated that irony. The Last Call Sheet, as it were. I wondered if they had casting sessions in the trade to weed out the bad criers. I finally persuaded him to wait until the following day for final instructions and he went off to arrange the removal of the body from the Cargo section to his own private chapel of remembrance, but not before he had taken a check off me on account.

I took a taxi and booked into the nearest hotel. Already the jet-lag was taking effect but I still had things to do. I

337

phoned Miss Dunbar again, and once more the same fragile voice answered.

'Miss Dunbar, this is Harvey Burgess again. You remember I phoned you from France with the news about poor Marvin?'

'Yes. It's Mr Burgess, isn't it?'

'That's right. I'm here now, in Detroit.'

'Where are you?'

'Well, pretty close. I've just got off a plane and I've come here to see you and help you arrange the funeral. I brought Marvin with me.' I hoped that was the right way of expressing it.

'Poor Marvin. He died, you know. He had an accident.'

'Yes, that's right, and now I've brought him back so that you could see he was buried properly at home.'

'This wasn't his home,' she said. 'He never lived here.'

'Well, I thought you'd like to be at the funeral, that was my reason.'

'I don't think I'll go. I don't go out much.'

'Fine, whatever you decide of course . . . but maybe it'd be better if I came to see you, rather than talk on the phone. Then you can tell me exactly what you want done. How would that be?'

'All the photographs are still here. He used to send me photographs and I kept every one. Had them all framed. I expect a lot of the people in the photographs will want to be at the funeral, but I shan't go . . . I went to my mother's but not to my father's.'

'Really? . . . So, shall I come and see you?'

'It seems a long way to come all the way from France.'

'No. I've already come from France. I'm here, you see, in Detroit.'

'Oh, you're here, are you?'

The conversation went round in the same circle for another five minutes before I managed to convince her that I was now back on American soil and she agreed to receive me. I took a hurried club sandwich and a pot of coffee to keep awake, then got a taxi to her address.

As I had guessed she lived in a fairly run-down neighbourhood. Her apartment was on the second floor of an old tenement building. The ground floor was occupied by a

338

chiropractor, a Doctor Osmani. The entrance hall looked as though it had never seen the services of a janitor and was piled high with empty cartons. I looked at the inscription on one of them as I climbed to the second floor: it said, NOVELTY HALLOWEEN MASKS By the side of Miss Dunbar's door there were the inevitable graffiti scrawls. Hers read: FOR MOTHERS DAY I'M GOING TO GIVE HER SHIT

I rang what I took to be the doorbell, but it produced no sound that I could hear. I knocked on the door and after an appreciable wait detected signs of life on the other side. There was a security peep-hole bored into the centre panel and I had no doubt that I was being observed through it.

'It's Mr Burgess,' I said loudly. 'I phoned and said I was coming, remember?'

Somewhere above a door opened and a blast of heavy rock music cannoned down.

Finally she drew the bolts and unlocked the door, but it was still secured on a chain. I could just make out her face in the crack.

'It's quite all right, Miss Dunbar. Only me, Mr Burgess, Marvin's friend.'

Are the others there?' she said.

'No, I'm quite alone.'

'I thought I heard others.'

'No. Just the music, I think it must have been.'

She closed the door again to release the chain and then I was admitted. I was prepared for squalor, but the interior of her small, dingy apartment was sharp as hen's teeth, as the saying goes down south – a faded replica of a bygone age when most people cared about appearances. She led me down a short corridor into the main room, a room crammed with furniture and bric-a-brac. What immediately took my eye were the framed photographs occupying every available flat surface. It was like walking into a museum of the golden age of movies. They were mostly studio publicity shots – Gable, Turner, Bogart, Davis, Crawford, Astaire, Cooper, Tracy, Rooney, Hepburn, Garland, you name them. Some of them included a younger Marvin, and all were signed. I went closer, recognising a more recent face and there, on the side table next to what was obviously her favourite chair, was a black-and-white glossy of Laura.

And because it was now part of the museum it seemed to place her in the past, intensifying my feeling that it was a chapter closed forever.

'That only arrived last week,' she said. 'He never forgets. He's a good brother to me, and of course all his friends think the world of him. You can see what they've written. Lovely words.'

'Yes, I can see. You must be very proud of your collection.'

'I watch all Marvin's old films on television. Never miss one. I keep a list in this book.' She picked up a child's school notebook from the same table and offered it to me. I opened it and read a few pages. She had neat, almost copperplate writing and sure enough she had carefully listed page after page of old movies that presumably Marvin had once worked on.

'He made some lovely films, you know.' She suddenly looked at me as though seeing me for the first time. 'I haven't got your photo, have I?'

'No, I don't think so.'

'That's funny. Perhaps it'll come later. Mustn't be without that.'

I suddenly felt very tired, but there didn't seem to be anywhere to sit down.

'I wish this was a happier occasion,' I started to say, but she had left the room. I heard the sound of crockery and a short while later she returned with a tray of tea and some cookies. 'These are my brownies,' she said. 'I always bake brownies on a Thursday, just enough to last the week. Mustn't overdo it. But I couldn't be without my brownies.'

I took one. They were thick and glutinous, utterly delicious, but they sat heavily on the club sandwich.

'I hope you like tea?'

'Yes, thank you.'

'Marvin liked iced tea. He never touched any spirits, you know . . . That was because of father. Father wouldn't have spirits in the house. I'm giving you father's cup. I always keep that for guests.'

'It's very kind of you.'

She had a curiously period face, early American, the sort

340

of Rockwell old lady who used to grace the covers of the *Saturday Evening Post*. There was a hint of camphor mixed with plain eau de Cologne about her, spiced mustiness. I noticed that she wore a black velvet band round her crinkled neck and her fine white hair was neatly arranged in a bun. She nibbled on her own brownie like a mouse – and indeed, as with many old people, there was a sort of rodent quality about her movements.

I began again. 'I hope I did the right thing by bringing Marvin's body back here. It just didn't seem right to have him buried in a foreign country.'

'I haven't got anything black, you see. That's why I can't go. I don't like black. It's the wrong colour for me. My mother always wore black and I never liked it.'

I nodded. The brownie stuck to my teeth. 'I don't suppose Marvin ever left you any instructions, did he?'

'What sort of instructions?'

'Well, I wondered, if he ever discussed . . . What religion was he?'

'We aren't Catholic. My father had no time for them.'

'No, I meant, did he ever mention he wanted to be cremated for instance? Or perhaps he left a Will?'

She put down her teacup and again left the room without a word. To pass the time I took up Laura's photograph. In the usual manner of these things she was smiling straight into the camera, a manufactured smile which I knew had masked her nervousness. I recognised the location and could just make out Michelle in the background. It seemed a long way to come to catch up with past loves.

When Miss Dunbar returned she was carrying a black security tin, the kind shopkeepers used to have for the daily take. She handed it to me.

'All his letters,' she said. 'I kept them all. Right from the first one.'

I opened the tin. It was filled with letters as she had said, each one still in the original envelope.

'They make lovely reading. You read one.'

I took the top one and extracted the thin air-mail paper. It was dated 1950 and written from the Super Chief. '*Hi, Sis,*' it began, '*well here we are again hot-footing it towards the windy city . . .*' It was like a schoolboy's letter to his mother and I went through the pretence of reading it to the end.

'He certainly knew how to express himself,' I said. 'I don't suppose there's a Will amongst these, is there?'

'You do it,' she said. 'You do it all. I trust you. I don't want to think about it. If I think about it, he won't ever come back. So you do it, you know what Marvin wanted. Just make sure all his friends know.' She indicated the photographs. 'They're bound to send flowers. His friends are people who know how to behave. Such wonderful friends. They thought the world of him.'

'Yes, I'm sure they did.'

I lingered for perhaps a further twenty minutes, letting her ramble on, until I could decently take my leave. The subject of the funeral was never mentioned again. She saw me to the door and thanked me. 'Be sure and tell Mr Cooper,' were her last words. 'Such a gent. Just like Marvin. He never used a dirty word. Not like some of them today. I switch off when they use those words.'

As I retreated down the dusty stairs I heard the bolts being shot and the chain rattled as the museum was secured once again.

I imagine I must have proved a major disappointment to the mortician. I declined the nuclear-proof casket, the embalming and the professional mourners. The cremation service took place on the outskirts of town. The priest *in situ* delivered the minimum rites and the basic wooden casket duly disappeared through the plastic curtains on its way to the furnace. I took a wreath with me and wrote on the card, '*To Marvin with love from Sis and all your many friends*'. Then I settled the account and took a taxi back into town. In a funny way the whole episode helped me get my own situation into some sort of perspective.

That same day I checked out of the hotel and caught a shuttle back to New York. And so it was, almost three months to the day, that I unlocked the door to my rented barn and stepped back into another charnel house. Apart from a threatening note from the telephone company, and a reminder that my subscription to the Writers Guild was overdue, I had received no mail in my absence. I tried the telephone but it was dead – so that, for the moment, solved that problem. I couldn't call Laura.

The neglected garden looked like the set for *Suddenly Last Summer* and the pool water had been stained black by rotting leaves. Naturally there was no food in the house, but I managed to locate half a bottle of Scotch and drank that straight before falling into a crevasse of oblivion.

I must have slept a full twelve hours or more and woke not knowing what country I was in. I lay there, my eyes rheumed, listening for the sound of the doves outside the window, completely disorientated. I badly needed a cup of coffee, but there was no room service and not even a stale jar of Nescafé in the kitchen. I felt and looked like a tramp. The previous night I had even forgotten to switch on the water heater – not that it would have served any purpose for, like the telephone, the electricity also had been disconnected. I washed and shaved in cold water, then drove into Darien to get myself organised.

The first priority was to pay a visit to the bank. Naturally none of the tellers remembered me, and I had to prove I was a non Communist, all-American white Caucasian with a credit rating roughly on a par with the Rockerfellers before the computer spewed out an okay and they allowed me to draw out some of my own money. Not that the coffers were full. I had earned good money and spent most of it, living high on the hog in France. Allowing for my agent's commission, withholding and welfare taxes and union dues, I realised I needed to look for another job.

I then set about getting the telephone and utilities reinstated and paid a visit to the local supermarket to stock up on essentials. By the end of the morning I felt like one of the Pilgrim Fathers straight off the boat. I knew nobody and the whole experience was unnerving. It was as if I had to start again from the beginning and learn the mechanics of existing on my own. Going the rounds, I constantly thought of the life I had left behind and found myself plotting Laura's progress through the day in that other country. Now she's just coming off the set, now she'll be having her shampoo in hairdressing, now she's leaving the studio – seeing the house she lived in, the hysterical welcome from her dogs . . . and then, doubt. How would she spent her

343

evening? In my absence, who had moved in to fill my place?

It wasn't until the following day that the phone company cleared my request and the phone was reinstated. I had busied myself getting the barn straight; it appeared to have become a breeding ground for a monstrous species of spider the size of Suzanne's false eyelashes. Making a half-hearted attempt to drain the pool I found the accumulation of leaves had blocked the filter outlet. That second night I had hardly slept at all, my body protesting at being shuttled around the world at top speed. But the moment the phone was in working order again I dialled that familiar number. This time Laura's father picked up.

'Ah, Doctor Tallan, it's Harvey here, ringing from the States.'

'Oh, you've arrived safely, have you? We were wondering.'

'Yes, I'm just about in one piece. Is Laura around?'

'No, I'm afraid not. You're unlucky. They apparently didn't need her for a few days so she's gone off with some friends for a skiing trip into the mountains.'

'Skiing? This time of year?'

'Well, there've been very early falls in some places, so they've gone looking for it. The weather's changed since you left.'

'Did she leave any number where I could reach her?'

'Wait a minute, I'll ask my wife. They don't tell me anything.'

I hung on and eventually he returned to the phone.

'No, sorry. Apparently they took off in a hurry and we've no idea where they'll land up. But I expect she'll ring us in due course.'

'Well, when she does, would you tell her to ring me on this number collect?' I passed it over. 'And any time of the day, doesn't matter, I'll be here.'

'Yes, there's a time difference, of course.'

'Six hours I believe.'

'Not so long now and we'll be putting the clocks back. How's your mouth by the way?'

'Fine, just fine. You'll give that message then?'

'The moment she rings.'

'Thank you, and please give my best regards to your wife.'

'Thank you, I will, and hers to you, I'm sure.'

When I broke the connection I felt sickened. There and then, like some drug addict reaching for a fix, I began another letter to her, but although I tried to smother my real feelings the pages of the first draft were saturated in self-pity. Once a rewrite man, always a rewrite man. The second attempt was an improvement. I went out and posted it immediately. I had no idea how long a letter would take to reach her and the local office in the Good Wives Shopping Centre was predictably vague on the subject. I bought a few new books to read, catching up on the mysteries of American publishing, and as I stepped out of the bookshop I noticed a hairdressing salon which triggered off memories of my abortive weekend with Shirley, the golfing widow. For no real reason except that I was desperate for some contact with another human being, I entered the salon.

The black-rooted blonde behind the reception desk gave me a curious look.

'Sir, we're not unisex,' she said.

'I just wanted to enquire about somebody.' Amazingly the name jumped into my mind. 'Do you have an assitant called Cleo working here?'

'Cleo? No, I don't think so. Mr André, do we have anybody called Cleo?'

The proprietor drifted across to us in a cloud of Grey Flannel cologne. He looked as though the Dowager Lady Mary had worked him over for about ten hours.

'What's the problem?'

'No problem,' I said. 'It's just that I've been abroad for a few months and I was anxious to contact a girl called Cleo. I was told she worked here.

'Oh, that Cleo! Yeah, well she did, but she left.' He turned to the receptionist. 'You remember Cleo, Marilyn.'

'Do I?'

'Sure. She made it big. Got herself fixed up with you-know-who.'

'Oh, yeah, yeah, now I remember.'

He turned back to me. 'Can't help you, sorry.'

345

By now I'd gone off the whole idea anyway.

'That's okay, thanks anyway.'

'My pleasure. Have a good day now.'

From his dialogue I guessed that Cleo had set up house, or possibly a massage parlour, with our mutual friend Shirley. Well, good luck, I thought, I'm all for spreading it around.

Back at the house I put a call in to my agent on the Coast. He was out at a breakfast meeting, naturally. I've often thought that Kellogg's should sponsor the entire agency business. 'Have him return my call,' I asked the switchboard girl.

'What's it in connection with?'

'Bankruptcy,' I said. 'I'm a client. Don't send money, send food parcels.'

The joke went sour before the connection was broken. Judging from the state of my finances, I wasn't exaggerating that much. I'm a lousy housekeeper, I never know where the money goes to. The trouble with being a freelance is that, when you're in work, the dough comes in sizeable chunks, inducing a spendthrift mentality. I didn't need to be an honours graduate in accountancy to read the writing on the wall. There it was writ in letters large: Father Hubbard, the larder is bare. It required somebody to remind the outside world that I was alive. A quick television script seemed the best bet, and I got out my little black book and studied the contacts. It was like reading the guest list for a Mafia wedding.

Considering that I withheld 90% of his income I was pleasantly surprised that Manny, my agent, returned the call within the same working day.

'So how's the world treating you, darling?'

'Well, darling,' I said, 'the world could well have forgotten me.'

'You back from Krautland?'

'France, actually.'

'How'd it go? That could be a useful credit. I hear the film's terrific and you did a terrific job.'

'Your loyalty knows no bounds, Manny.'

'Who were you sthupping out there, darling?'

'I was sthupped. Stitched up as usual.'

'Listen, you got paid, right? So quit complaining. It's when you *don't* get sthupped. Then you complain. So what else is new?'

'You tell me. Who's beating you over the head to employ me?'

'Darling, this place is like a fucking morgue. I've never known it so bad.'

'So who's paying for your breakfasts?'

'Listen, sweetheart, I'm busting my ass for you, believe me.'

'I need a job, Manny. Anything. How about an episode, a quickie?'

'What d'you want to go back to those for? You just came off a feature. I want you to stay in features.'

'What features?'

'You're right, what features? Nothing did any business this summer except that fucking *Moonbeams*. All the rest went straight down the tubes. I'm telling you, this town is dead, people are walking around with their fingers up their ass. All those morons running the studios.'

'Well, do what you can, huh? Go down on somebody.'

'Darling, once they know you need them, they shaft you.'

'Darling,' I said, 'right now I don't care. Just get me a job.'

Despite his lack of couth, I was attached to him. Previously I had been with the junior echelon of one of the big agencies, shunted between a variety of daunting young fledglings who had only one aim in life, and it wasn't me. Their main concern was to get their hands on a virgin script and further their own ambitions. Manny was a comfortable old phoney – in his own haphazard way he did care about his clients, and he was always good for a small loan when times got really bad. The main drawback to my career was that I had never been able to stomach the Beverly Hills-Palm Springs social rounds. To get into the big time you have to qualify for the 'A' List, and I had never graduated beyond the letter M. I knew writers pulling down a steady $300,000 a year who couldn't write copy for a beer commercial, but they knew which hostess to romance, whom to lose to at tennis, the 'in' health club to frequent. Not that it gave

347

me sour grapes. I knew the ground rules, it just bored me to play by them.

If I was in bad shape financially, emotionally I was also overdrawn. Sitting alone in that rented barn, eating my frozen curds and whey, I tried to take stock of myself. Middle-aged men who fall for young girls are at best objects of scorn, not pity. If only there was a transplant by which we could be cured of loving, how many would stampede to be first in the queue? I sat there and gave myself all the usual advice, but the truth of the matter was all I could think about was that neat little triangle of pubic hair, that body unmarked by cellulite, those assuaging lips. There was a sort of madness in my emptiness. Laura seemed utterly set apart from all the other women in my life. Was it merely because of her youth? Had I fallen into the ageless trap of bestowing perfection on somebody who, reason urged, could only be human? Yes and yes and yes again. And yet.

Help of a kind came unexpectedly. My landlord suddenly arrived back, knocking at his own front door in the middle of the night. I'd known Howard for about twenty years. It was one of those on and off relationships that maybe are the best kind to have. Sometimes we hadn't seen each other for months, but when our paths crossed again we could pick up the threads easily enough. Perhaps the reason our friendship had survived so long was that we had never been in competition. Howard was one of 'democracy's para-sites', to use his own phrase – a natural drifter, devoid of any particular ambition and with very few hang-ups. His only failing, which I had often shared at one remove, was that he invariably fell hopelessly in love with the wrong women. And invariably married them. He had money – how much I never enquired, but certainly enough to sustain four alimony payments at the last count. He was the same age as me, easy-going, generous to his friends, an obsessive romantic and mostly good company. His taste in women was on a level with the decor of the barn, that is to say he bought the first thing he saw in the shop window.

I staggered down in my pyjamas to open the door to him.

'Oh, Christ!' he said. 'Harvey! I knew I'd rented it out to somebody, but I couldn't for the life of me remember who. Is it convenient?'

'Don't be stupid, come on in.'

'No seriously. See, I got somebody with me.'

'Let me guess. Blonde: about five-feet-four in her stocking feet: takes a 35B cup: loves you, Mick Jagger and Jack Nicolson in that order: takes Tiger's Milk mixed with wheatgerm and is great in the sack. Am I warm?'

'Jackpot!'

'Name?'

'Priscilla.'

'Have you bought the ring?'

'It's away being made smaller.'

'And when do I meet her?'

'She's gone for a walk in the garden. She's into Nature.'

'Oh, that's a switch. Likes to feel the dew on her bare feet, eh?'

'You got it, Bonzo.'

I helped him off-load his station wagon. He seemed to have accumulated the entire year's output of Louis Vuitton. In the middle of all this Priscilla made her first appearance. Priscilla Model Five, that is. She bore an uncanny resemblance to the four who had preceded her, the only difference being that she was younger than the rest and, at first glance, less shop-soiled.

'Honey, this is my old friend, Harvey. Harvey, meet Priscilla.'

'Hi, Harvey.'

'I apologise for the pyjamas, but that's the landlord's fault for not warning me.'

'Remember what I said on the way here, honey. I said I had the feeling that I'd rented the place out, but I couldn't remember who to.'

Priscilla padded past us as we moved the last of the suitcases into the barn. She left a trail of wet footprints and the bottoms of her snug-fitting jeans were sodden.

'Listen, Bonzo,' Howard whispered, 'if it's too heavy a scene we can shift tail to a motel for the night. Just say the word. You flying solo these days?'

'Grounded. Lost my licence.'

He stood in the doorway and looked at his own habitat as though visiting it for the first time. 'You done some re-

349

modelling? Was that window always there? I mean, no sweat, I like it.'

'Just as you left it,' I said. 'Welcome home, Miss Havisham.'

'God, I don't know, I can't remember anything these days. Must be love.

Priscilla came back into view.

'It's so chic,' she said. 'I mean, this is really old, right?'

'Part of our heritage, honey. Harvey Burgess slept here.'

'Not too often,' I said. 'So how was your trip?'

'Well, for the first month it was a wipe-out, Bonzo.'

'What's with this Bonzo all of a sudden?'

'It's his new, favourite word,' Priscilla said.

'Then, I met this little Bonzo here, and found happiness. I just happened alone on this beach intent on furthering my anthropological studies, and lo and behold there she was naked as a jay bird. Believing her to have been washed up from a shipwreck I immediately rushed to her aid, and the rest is written in the sand.'

'What a touching story,' I said. 'I'd like to set it to music. And where did this strange encounter of the fifth kind take place?'

'St Tropez. Little old St Tropez, gateway to the beast.'

'You were in the South of France?'

'Never moved.'

'But I was in the South of France. All summer.'

'So you just rented my pad as a front, huh?'

'No, I suddenly got offered a job. I only got back a couple of days ago, that's why, when you examine the old plantation in the light of day you will doubtless notice that the jungle has crept up to us.'

'I like wild, primitive gardens,' Priscilla said.

'She's a very basic girl, Bonzo. She eats raw mushrooms, and they don't come more primitive than that.'

'And while we're on the subject, don't take a swim in the pool. I'm sorry to say I haven't been a model tenant. But all will be restored, have no fear.'

'Bonzo, if you weren't here you have to have a refund. Too bad we didn't meet up.'

'Listen,' I said, 'landlord's privileges, you take the bedroom. I'll just curl up down here with the man-eating spiders.'

'I love spiders,' Priscilla said. 'You don't kill them, do you?'

'Not with my bare hands,' I said.

'You should never kill them, it's unlucky.'

'Isn't she something?' Howard said. He swept her up in his arms. The spectacle of teenage love being demonstrated by a man who had made four journeys to the marriage altar was hard to take in the middle of the night.

'Why don't you take her upstairs, Rhett?' I said. 'Because after all, tomorrow may not be another day.'

'Didn't I tell you, honey? Didn't I tell you that my old buddy Harvey was a great wit? A great writer, and a great best man. Bonzo, I want you to do me the honours when I lead this noble little savage up the aisle.'

'Are you married, Harvey?' Priscilla said between kisses.

'Not in the eyes of God.'

'Oh, I love that. That's neat.'

'No, I wouldn't go that far. Definitely not neat.'

'I can't get over the fact that we were all in the South of France and I didn't know . . . We've got a lot to talk about, Bonzo. But first I think I'll get this little lady to bed before she goes off the boil. I feel just dreadful turning you out of your room.'

'Landlords are like that, Howard. No scruples. You're just behaving true to type.'

'Okay, I can't deny it. Onwards and upwards, honey.'

Priscilla came and put her arms round me. Her hair still smelt of the sea, or so it seemed. 'I think Howard's right. You're our sort of people.' She kissed me full on the lips. 'Promise you won't sleep on any spiders and in the morning I'll make you one of my specials for breakfast.'

'Wait 'til you taste it, Bonzo! Priscilla's Pecker Perker – guaranteed to make the heart grow fonder.'

I noticed he didn't attempt to carry her upstairs. It was the only piece of comfort I had.

Howard was as good as his word and applied for a wedding licence the following day. Part of me was appalled and part was envious. I could watch their antics with a certain

351

detachment, yet at the same time I yearned to have Howard's freedom of choice.

As with Laura and me, there was an age gap between Howard and Priscilla; not such a chasm as ours, but sufficient to have given most men pause for thought. I suppose the answer was that Howard was emotionally fearless, sexually fatalistic.

'I never expect it to *last,* Bonzo. Good God, that way lies chaos. Marriage is always Howard's end – note you are not the only one who can make literary puns – not his beginning. It's a funny thing with me. No trouble getting them into the sack – "piece of cake, Skipper," as they say in those British war films. And if it works I just *have* to marry them. One last lingering worm of Puritanism I guess. And then you see, I move on to the next stage. Once I've got over the first flush of married bliss, it starts to go downhill. No particular time schedule. Couple of times it's been whoosh! and I'm at the bottom of the slope before I know where I am, but then on the other two occasions it was a gradual descent . . . there's no set pattern. But I always know I'm on the downward path when I start looking at fresh pussy. Ghastly admission, I know, really shameful, but I can be honest with you, Bonzo. Never grown up, I suppose, that's what the old shrinks would say. Had it too easy, never had to bother about earning a living . . . well, you know what I've always thought of myself, a bloody parasite . . . but harmless, don't you think? I mean, I don't go around exploiting the poor, I'm not racist, very liberal when it comes to the vote, give to charity, kind to dumb animals, and cunt-struck. That about sums me up.'

'Can't you just live with them instead of marrying them? Wouldn't it be cheaper for one thing?'

'Doesn't work, Bonzo. Tried it. Disaster. Can't perform for some extraordinary reason. So one pays the price and looks cheerful. Course you're so much more sensible than me.'

'Am I?'

'Well, aren't you?'

'Not really. Not at the moment anyway.'

'Ah! do I detect a touch of hidden heartbreak?'

'Obviously not all that well hidden.'

I was superstitious about telling anybody about my real feelings for Laura. The fact that at any given moment of the day I was likely to come across Howard and Priscilla locked in some turgid embrace, and that Priscilla was in the disturbing habit of wandering about the place semi-naked, had done little to ease my own anxieties. I had received no word from Laura. I felt I couldn't ring her parents again, I just had to sweat it out and hope for the best. It was a very exacting time, for in the space of ten days I had attended a funeral and been recruited as best man for a wedding. In between I nursed my own wounds. My fantasies about Laura embraced everything from death in an avalanche to that other death of her unfaithfulness. I imagined all manner of erotic infidelities: after all, the log cabin in the mountains had been one of our private dreams. As the days passed I became more and more convinced that my cause was lost. So when Howard pressed me to give him a blow by blow account, I hedged.

'For a while there I had a certain thing going in the South of France,' I told him.

Fortunately for me, like most people in the throes of a sexual fever, he wasn't that interested in my personal affairs.

'It's the place, Bonzo. I defy anybody not to be seduced by the atmosphere out there. It changes us, it's a return to living with a capital L, my friend. The moment I stepped off the plane I knew I was going to be liberated. Christ! I was shot when I left here. The previous Mrs Howard Turner had really worked me over. If I wasn't exactly down the toilet, I sure as hell was half-way through the bathroom door.'

'Which makes your present courage all the more remarkable,' I said.

'It's not courage, Bonzo. It's a death wish. But who could resist this sort of death? Look at her, Bonzo. Isn't she worth a prostrate operation?'

This was in response to one of Priscilla's celebrated entrances. Bare-footed as usual, she was wearing one of Howard's T-shirts over a bikini bottom. The effect, let us not mince matters, would have made me faint from certain hungers in normal circumstances. They went into an immediate clinch, and I realised that my days at the barn had to be numbered. I couldn't stand the strain. Happiness in others is not always contagious.

The legal formalities for the marriage having been completed, Howard named the day. Never one to do things by half measures, he took her into New York and prized loose a piece of forever from Harry Winston's emporium. It wasn't so much a wedding ring as a way of life. I made all the appropriate noises when Priscilla flashed it at me. And then Howard sprang another of his Puritan surprises.

'Do you mind if I sleep downstairs tonight, Bonzo?'

'Are you offering me the best man's privileges?'

'No, but d'you know something? If it had to be anybody, you'd be my first choice. Now don't laugh, but, revealing all, I can admit to you that although I can perform wonders during the lead-up, the actual night before is a no-no.'

'Of course, you're not complicated, are you? Take an overdose of Vitamin E.'

'It's not physical, Bonzo. Purely mental. Something gets blocked in the old grey matter.'

'So are we bedding down together?'

'Never tried it. Had a few advances made to me in my gilded youth, always declined gracefully. Mother taught me, never forget your manners.'

As it happens neither of us slept much that night. We reviewed our respective lives until birdsong deafened us.

'It's a fallacy that our feathered friends greet the dawn,' Howard remarked. 'The little fuckers are at it all night if you ask me.'

He had probed a little deeper concerning my summer in Valbonne. I regaled him with suitably embroidered anecdotes about Charles and Latrough's disastrous dinner party, but skirted around the Laura situation. I felt the need for an insurance policy: I had convinced myself that talking about her would tempt fate. I had forgiven her once, swallowed what remained of my pride, and I was determined to do it again if necessary. I could stomach anything except her total rejection.

The wedding ceremony in its perfunctory swiftness had certain similarities with Marvin's funeral. My warped sense of humour produced a sudden vision of Howard's naked

354

body being drawn towards the fires of lust. I couldn't believe all the things that were happening to me in such a short space of time.

Just to emphasise the point, the Justice of the Peace who performed the rites had a speech impediment: he couldn't say his 'r's. This induced in Howard and me choked hysteria at the critical stage of the proceedings. Priscilla cried throughout, presumably overcome by the lack of atmosphere. When pronounced man and wife they practically had each other there and then.

We returned to the old barn which, in our brief absence, had been transformed. Howard had hired a three-piece gypsy band of dubious authenticity, and a firm of outside caterers. There was food enough for twenty, complete with a wedding cake in the shape of a mushroom. This started to wilt from the heat before it could be cut. The band played Viennese waltzes in the style of Laurence Welk, and a good time was had by two. I felt somewhat removed from the festivities.

When the strains of 'The Blue Danube' were but a hideous memory, and the last of the debris had been removed (Howard donated the remains of the feast to the local hospital for retarded children), it became increasingly obvious that my continued presence was a social embarrassment.

'Let's not have any arguments,' I said. 'I shall emulate the good Captain Oates and retire to a motel for the night and in the morning make arrangements to leave these hallowed walls forever.'

'Bonzo, what can I say? It wouldn't have been the same without you.'

'Wasn't it all just perfect?' Priscilla said.

She kissed me in a way that Emily Post would not have approved of in a young bride. Her perfume still lingered when I turned down the sheets at the nearby motel, where there was still no escape from the human condition. Like a corpse in some cheap casket I was sandwiched between the thin cardboard walls, forced to listen to the rutting noises of consummation. No soothing lullabies, just those echoes of past joys. I dreamt of Laura that night, but she was somehow mixed up with Priscilla and a wedding ceremony, with the grinning face of Martin replacing Howard's. I woke feeling exhausted as though I had run a race and come in last. I staggered out into the dismal foyer and bought my breakfast from the machines: technology may be convenient and efficient, but it sure as hell doesn't do anything for the spirits. When I had cut my way through the plastic wrapping on the donut and spilt the scalding liquid masquerading as coffee, I knew I had to do something drastic.

I paid one last visit to the barn to collect the rest of my belongings. The newly-weds were nowhere to be seen, so I left a note for Howard with an address where I could be contacted. '*I might get a call from France,*' I wrote. '*Whatever else you do on the downward slopes be sure and pass on my whereabouts.*' During the night I had decided on a plan of action. Hollywood was where the work was and it was to Hollywood I was going. The address I gave was the good old Beverly Wilshire, where from long custom I always got a special rate.

Leaving Darien I drove straight to Kennedy and managed to get a seat on American Flight No. 3 with about eight minutes to spare. The in-flight entertainment was the celebrated *Moonbeams* that Manny had mentioned. It was just another variation of the space wars, the twist this time being that The Things looked like a mutated corps de ballet.

The endless counterpane of Los Angeles appeared grubbier than ever in the smog haze as we began our descent. On the ground it wasn't so noticeable, but the heat pressed down – not the heat of the South of France with its scent of flower blossoms, but a hot air laden with automobile fumes. I hadn't been out to the Coast in a couple of years, but in that short space of time at least a dozen familiar landmarks had been bulldozed. Wilshire Boulevard looked more or less the same, except for the huge new Neiman Marcus building where the new millionaires of Beverly Hills could now purchase His and Her mink coats for their poodles. The hotel's old doorman was still there, but he looked a little frail humping my bags and typewriter into the lobby. There was no room in the new block at the rear, so I took a double in the original building, known in the business as the Warren Beatty Intensive Care Unit.

I've always had a love-hate relationship with Los Angeles. There is none of the immediate excitement of New York, but lotus-eating has its merits for a while. I liked the Beverly Wilshire better than the Bel Air or the Beverly Hills; it was handier for the restaurants and had the added attraction of a bookshop on the premises. Most of the deals were still made over breakfast and lunch in the Polo Lounge of the Hills, but I wasn't in that league.

The first thing I did when I got to the room was to ring down and tell the operator to be sure and take messages. 'I'm expecting an important call from France,' I said, 'so if you don't get me in the room make sure you take a number. It'll be a Miss Taylor calling. Not your Miss Taylor, but my Miss Taylor.'

Then it was time to let Manny know that I was in town and hungry for work.

'I've got some feelers out, darling. How does a trip to downtown Burbank grab you?'

'I'll take it.'

'You seen that new series called *Going Half The Way*?'

'No.'

'Well, it's a crock of shit, but it's Number Two. They're looking for a new writer to make the star happy. Star! Six months ago he couldn't get himself arrested, now he has script approval.'

'What is the name of this threat?'

'Don't ask me. If you're interested I'll push it.'

'I'm interested,' I said.

'Where are you?'

'At the Wilshire. Room 423.'

'I'll get back.'

I went down to the Pink Turtle coffee shop and bought all the trades – those mail-order catalogues for the hopeful. The menu hadn't changed, but I liked that, it made me feel at home. I needed some stability in my life. Adding another three thousand miles between myself and Laura had some-how eased part of the anguish. Or maybe my mood had changed. The fact that she hadn't bothered to get in touch since my return to Howard's barn had hardened me to the realities of the situation. I imagined she was with her own group of young friends having a great time – there was no real reason why she should concern herself overmuch with me. Then again, she was probably nowhere near a phone. I made every excuse for her, but I couldn't help thinking back to those times when everything seemed possible.

Returning to my room I saw the message light was flashing. Manny had called back as promised. I had an appointment over in Burbank the following morning. I lay on top of the bed and read the trades. Nothing had changed in those. The same pack had been shuffled, the same claims were still being made; the only discernible difference that I could see was that the price of houses had doubled. You could now get a five-bedroom, five-bath, pool and jacuzzi for a two-million steal.

I got out my contracts book again and started ringing a few numbers. The trouble with LA is that nobody ever stays anywhere longer than a year; I sometimes get the impression that the entire population is constantly on the move, like an army of ants. I rang a writer named Garfield and his daughter said he was in Honolulu. Then I rang another writer chum, Bob Herbert, and his ex-wife gave me ten minutes of pure hate. A couple of other numbers merely responded with a recorded message from the operator: 'The number you are trying to reach is no longer in service. Please check your phone-book.' The girl had quite a sexy voice, I thought, and I listened to her repeat the same message a few times. I thought, you might as well report yourself out of service.

Having drawn 100% blanks, I wandered down to the Pink Turtle again. Hotel life on your own is lonelier than a bachelor pad. Everybody else seems to be meeting somebody. This time I ordered the home-made apple pie with a scoop of frozen yoghurt. The pie didn't remind me of anybody's home. I tried to talk to a couple of cops sitting up at the counter, but they weren't what you would call sociable types. A policewoman joined them, and that started me wondering what it would be like to be married to a girl who packed a gun and had been trained in ju-jitsu. That was something that not even Howard had sampled. Then it was back to Brentano's bookshop and a closer study of the paperback racks. I came to the conclusion that I must be one of the few unknown screenwriters who hadn't written a book on *How To Write A Screenplay*. There was quite a variety to choose from. I opened one at the first page, anxious to share the secret of his success theory. The chapter was headed THINK OF A STORY. Now why hadn't I thought of that?

I tried paying for my purchases with my American Express card only to find that it had gone out of date while I was in Europe. The girl behind the counter looked at me as though I had a social disease when I proffered cash.

Feeling the need to assert myself somehow I crossed the road against the lights, noticed that one of the last remaining cinemas in Beverly Hills had now become a fashion house, and did some window-shopping along Rodeo. Gucci had a few thousand-dollar bargains, like metal-and-leather photograph frames and other such essentials of modern life, and the art gallery which stayed open late was exhibiting a collection of nudes in fluorescent colours bright enough to shave by. I did enter one of these establishments to enquire the price of a trenchcoat. The assistant looked at me with disdain: only peasants asked the prices.

'Seventeen hundred fifty,' he lisped.

'You don't happen to have the number of the Beverly Hills police, do you?'

'What for?'

'I'd like to make a citizen's arrest for extortion,' I said.

Outside, a procession of Mercedes and Porsches cruised ceaselessly round the blocks as though their occupants were flatly determined to be seen by somebody. The more opulent the cars the more their owners seemed determined to look like junkies. I could sniff revolution in the air.

And all the time I was thinking, when I get back to the room she'll have rung. I even played the childhood game of not stepping on the cracks between the paving stones, willing Laura to call me. But the message light was dark when I returned. I wrote her another letter and posted it in the chute outside my bedroom door. That's always an adventure on a dull night, like putting a message in a bottle and floating it out to sea. And so, like Pepys, to bed.

TWENTY-ONE

Even for money it was difficult to wax enthusiastic about writing an episode of *Going Half The Way*. The series was shooting for the second season, having climbed the dizzy heights in its first. I studied some of the story-lines they handed me and then ran a few video-tapes of the earlier episodes.

'Just soak up the flavour,' one of the three producers said. The female-person story editor sat by my elbow in the viewing room and dutifully laughed at all the jokes. It was as if she had been selected from a multitude of applicants to major in necrophilia.

I guess to survive in television you have to believe in the product, but to sustain a belief in a long-running situation comedy requires the dedication of a Trappist monk. *Going Half The Way* was based on the unlikely premise that a used-car salesman could have a wife running for President.

'There's something for everybody,' the female person informed. 'We're reaching across the board, getting the young housewives in the AB bracket as well as those lower down the scale. We give them hope, and it's just beautiful the way this has taken off. Don't you just love him? He's so dreadful he's marvellous. And she comes over gangbusters. We're even pulling in the Libbers on this one. You should see the mail, it's coming in by the sackful, and all of it good.'

I had been given an office for the duration of my stay which bore all the marks of a charge room. Incarcerated with the allocated storyline I now had to flesh out the skeleton, using old scripts as guidelines for the characters – all of whom had long since been set in concrete.

360

'We do have a little problem with Jim,' the female person said confidentially. Jim was the male star currently flexing his muscles. 'Jim is a lovely human being, but he's going through an identity crisis at the moment, and this makes him a little difficult to deal with when it comes to the script conferences. Now we want to keep him happy. So when you write be sure and write him some really ring-a-ding dialogue.'

My working knowledge of real-life used-car salesmen was sketchy to say the least, and since Jim's character had gradually undergone a metamorphosis since the earlier episodes, the prospect before me was daunting. I introduced one innovation which, in my innocence, I imagined would curry favour: I had him lose the franchise for General Motors and move over to Datsun, which in turn – my imagination at full stretch – allowed some humour with a Japanese car executive. This precipitated a major identity crisis for me.

'This a put-on?' one of the producers said when I turned in my first batch of pages.

'You don't like the idea?'

'We're locked in to General Motors. They give us all the cars. Didn't you see the video? And another thing, Jim hates anything ethnic. Lose the Jap. Lose the whole fucking idea.'

I went back to my cell and did a crib job on some of the old scripts, a ruse which surprisingly went undetected. I was immediately embraced as one of the team. 'Keep this up, Harvey,' the female person said, 'and you're going to stick around. Now you've really got the flavour. There's just one thing I know they won't buy. Not that I wouldn't, because I'm with you, I like subtle touches . . . but the line where he says, 'May my heart never grow fonder' – that could spell trouble.

I stared at her.

'What's wrong with it?'

'Well, of course, I know what you intended and like I said, I really dig innuendo. But Harvey . . . !'

Since I had never intended any subtlety her reaction continued to puzzle me.

'Fonder?' the female person said with a knowing smile

361

'Jane Fonda maybe? Come on, Harvey, you're trying to slip one under the door.'

I pretended guilt. 'Clever of you to spot it,' I said.

'That's what I'm here for. But nice try.'

As I worked, the phone on my desk constantly baited me. By now I had convinced myself that something terrible had happened to Laura. She had been involved in a skiing accident, she was ill, the car had crashed on the way back from the mountains. My imagination, which plodded through the mechanics of the script, worked overtime on my own affairs.

It was now nearly three weeks since I'd had any word of her. I made good and bad resolutions. Back in the hotel room I started talking to myself, asking the questions and answering them. She had such a hold over me and though every bit of reason urged me to accept her silence, my resolve finally broke and I rang her home.

This time Madame Tallan came to the phone. I tried to keep my voice flat.

'I rang to see if Laura was back.'

'No, Laura isn't here at the moment.'

'But she got back safely from her skiing trip, did she?'

'Oh, yes.'

The telephone is a funny instrument. The intonations one hears over the air waves are capable of many interpretations. There is no face to go with the voice. No expressions. Like a blind man, you rely on the ear alone, but unlike the blind you are not trained to translate the small hesitations.

'I was wondering why I hadn't heard from her. Maybe she rang my old number and didn't get a reply. Because I've moved you see. I'm in Los Angeles now, working on a television series . . . D'you think she perhaps tried and didn't get anywhere?'

'I really couldn't say.'

'Well, perhaps you'd like my new number. It's a hotel, the Beverly Wilshire.' I gave her the number, but she didn't repeat it and I had the feeling that she hadn't bothered to write it down. 'I've written to her, of course. D'you know if she's had my letters?'

'I think a letter did come, yes.'

'Only one? I've written several times.'

'Yes, well I don't always see the post,' Madame Tallan said.

'But she's okay, is she?'

'Yes, thank you.'

'Will she be in later on? I could ring again.'

'No, she's gone away again.'

'Oh . . . Is the film finished now?'

'She finished her part, yes.'

I could make no headway and her reluctance to tell me anything helpful was painfully obvious. I continued to try and sound casual.

'Well, fine. Give her that number when she does come back. I shall be here for a while and if I do move on, I'll ring, or write, and give the new address. I hope you and Doctor Tallan are well . . .'

'Thank you. We're very well.'

'Good. Well, nice talking to you.'

'Goodbye, Mr Burgess.'

More than anything else in the one-sided conversation the formality of her last words chilled me. I couldn't unravel any of the knots and I was filled with dread. I rang Howard. He seemed in great form, full of the joys of married life, but he had no news for me. Then I spent an hour tracking down Nigel in the South of France. I felt I could rely on him to tell me the truth. I finally located him in his hotel in Grasse, but even with Nigel I felt the need to conceal the real purpose of my call.

'Not many of us left,' he said. 'We're on the last knockings, just picking up a few inserts and shooting backgrounds for the titles. Not having much luck with the weather at the moment, we've had a mistral for the best part of a week.'

'How did the last lot of stuff go?'

'Seemed to go okay.'

'Did Charles behave himself?'

'We had one tricky day, but he was all right most of the time.'

'Suzanne . . . did she manage to shoot her remaining scenes?'

'Yes. She's a pro.'

'What about your fearless leader?'

'Even he seemed to mellow towards the end. You say you're in LA now? Working?'

'If you can call it that.'

'David went to LA. You might bump into him. That is, if you want to.'

'So what else is new? Oh, I went to poor old Marvin's funeral.'

'Ah, that was nice. Still think about him.'

'Who else is there?'

'Just a skeleton crew really. The Dowager's gone home. I hear she got done in Customs, trying to smuggle in a mink wrap.'

'Well give everybody my regards . . . Oh, particularly Michelle and Laura if you see them. Are they still around?'

'I haven't seen either of them since the end-of-picture party.'

'How were they?'

'Great,'

'It's just that Laura asked me to get something for her over here . . . some special make-up you can't get in France, and I sent it to her, but I haven't heard back and just wondered if she got it. Then . . . I don't know . . . somebody said she hadn't been well or something. Did you hear that?'

'No. I'll give her a buzz if you like.'

'Would you? I'm at the Beverly Wilshire. So if you do contact her ask her to call me. Because if she didn't get the first lot I sent her I'll send her some more. And take care of yourself.'

'Same to you, Harvey. Let's hope we meet up again.'

My despair first urged me to believe in a conspiracy – but a conspiracy by whom, and for what? The most rational explanation I next thought of was that, somehow (perhaps Laura herself had let slip the truth of her relationship with me?), her parents had learnt of our affair. They were middle-class and Catholic, it stood to reason they would be shocked and offended. After all I was hardly the season's catch for their only and beautiful daughter. In all probability the fact that they had accepted me into their home would have further offended their sense of morality. I had deceived them to their faces, under their own roof while accepting their hospitality. And the reason (I argued with myself) that Madame Tallan had made no reference to it during the telephone conversation was equally in character. She could not bring herself to admit anything to me. No, they had chosen the most effective weapon to kill the affair, denying me any knowledge of Laura, doubtless preventing her from contacting me, destroying my letters before she could see them. It all seemed to fit into place.

But what of Laura during all this? She had never struck me as being under her parent's thumb. I knew she had a will of her own. And if they objected to me, why did they allow her those other ample freedoms? She wasn't kept under lock and key, they had allowed her to pursue a career as an actress without protest or restraint. They could hardly be so blinkered as not to know she would be subject to all the usual temptations . . . As soon as I persuaded myself of one set of arguments, I rejected it for another. I could think of nobody to whom I could turn to discover the truth. It was obviously out of the question to ask Martin. I was lost, and cursed my stupidity at ever having left her. While I was still there I had a chance.

For the next week I was like a caged beast. I went to the television studio every day and in many ways the cell I occupied there was a kind of sanctuary, the only place where I felt safe. Coming back to that empty, impersonal hotel room every night, I was instantly reminded of her. I wrote other letters; some I destroyed and some I posted. Waking or sleeping the fever never left me. Whether others noticed any change in me I neither knew nor cared. I suppose the chances are I appeared no different from the other writers on the series – everybody operated in a kind of frenzied isolation, fighting the clock, the creative block, the endless demands put upon us. Ironically, because I was totally indifferent to outside influences, because I was so withdrawn into my shell, the work I turned in every day not only acted as a salve but also found favour with my employers. I was asked to stay on and write a further episode. I could not contemplate being left to my own devices and so accepted.

Now, with the mystery of those lost months explained, I realise that this was the ultimate mistake I made. But the long fuse of despair had been set alight and I lacked the will to extinguish it. I had no saving beliefs, no other faith to turn to, I was paralysed by love.

As week succeeded week and no word came, I slowly adopted a different personality, becoming less concerned with my personal appearance, not caring what I ate (sometimes I would order the same dish for two or three meals running), turning myself into a recluse. At weekends I hardly left my room except to journey downwards for the papers and cigarettes. I spurned room service because it meant using the telephone, it involved contact with waiters, unwelcome intrusions into my self-imposed exile. At the studio my behaviour was interpreted as diligence, a welcome attribute for a writer. I gave them value for their money, the pages were delivered on time, the petty revisions expedited without protest. If anything the only reaction I got was veiled scorn from some of the other hacks on the series: presumably they felt I was letting the side down. Once I had established a routine the actual writing proved less of a chore than many a previous assignment. True, one had to attend the weekly script conference and listen to a dozen different opinions – but I had smothered dissent: now I performed to order. The agreed story line would be handed to me and, with the characters now locked into a formula, it was merely a matter of writing the dialogue, something I had never found difficult. I cannot pretend that it was the sort of existence that would have commended itself to Flaubert, but the rewards were substantial.

Anyone connected with a successful television series, networked and then sold across the world, gets a share in a pot of gold. There were repeat fees and residuals flowing to me at regular intervals and for the first time in my life I accumulated a healthy bank balance. Because I knew where the next check was coming from I was able to plan ahead, a luxury hitherto unknown. I was aware of the dangers, the slow erosion of all genuine creative ambition, for no artist can surrender the basic freedoms without cost to himself.

After three months or so, the room at the Beverly Wilshire began to pall; at night the walls seemed to be closing in like that Edgar Allan Poe horror story. I scanned the small ads in the back of the trades and eventually came across a pleasant furnished apartment in a house on North Doheny, above the Strip. I took it for a year and paid the rent in advance. I had the use of a small pool, there was a janitor for the building and a maid who came in twice a week to dust and sweep up. It wasn't high-style living, but infinitely preferable to hotel life, and I gradually began to emerge from my self-imposed exile and pull myself together, although Christmas alone was a test.

From time to time there were snippets in the trade press regarding *The Bastille Connection*. Reading them I experienced mixed emotions. Latrough was back on the Coast wheeling and dealing, and on one occasion I chanced upon him lunching in the studio commissary. He told me the film was now finished and delivered, due for an Easter release, but made no further mention of the rosy future he had once outlined to me. Although my madness had subsided, I had one temporary relapse when the first ads appeared and the art work montage included a shot of Laura. They had given her feature billing under the title and I stared at her name and the face above it for several minutes: it was like suddenly chancing upon a much-loved object one has misplaced and thought lost forever.

During all this time I had been completely asexual, as detached and torpid as a neutered tom cat. The past had indeed become a foreign country, deliberately buried at the back of my mind. I won't say that my work sublimated all else, but I had settled into a new phase.

Chance had played such an important part in the events of the previous year and once again chance surprised me. I took to going out more and acquired a few new friends with whom I occasionally spent an evening. Two of them, a married couple who both worked on the series. Sonya and Larry Edwards, seduced me into sampling their latest high-fibre vegetarian diet which they insisted had changed their lives. We used to eat at a newly opened health-food restaurant on Olympic Boulevard. Like all converts we became obsessed with our beliefs and every day compared the findings of the bathroom scales.

'The world is divided into two classes,' Larry was fond of saying. 'Those who have haemorrhoids and those who are about to get them.' In general our conversations were spiced with scatological details. I have often noticed that people who embrace health fads betray an unhealthy tendency to concentrate on the study of coprolites. We convinced ourselves that the diet was working wonders, that we three had found the truth while the rest of our fellows were poisoning themselves with white bread, refined sugar and steroid-packed broiler chickens and the like. I was forced to beg off their invitations at least once a week to slip off on my own for a rare T-bone steak and French fries. Then, replete with harmful toxins, I would puff away on a forbidden cigarette.

It was on one such occasion, a week or so after New Year, dining alone in joyous style, that the past caught up with me again. Lifting my head from a particularly succulent cut of corn-fed Angus beef, I saw Charles sitting across the restaurant in the company of two presentable young ladies. He saw me at the same time and roared his greeting.

'Harvey, you old sod! What the hell are you doing here?'

He insisted that I join his table for the remainder of my meal. I was introduced to his two companions, though he seemed a little vague as to their names. 'This is Marigold, and this is Lucy.'

'The other way round,' Lucy said.

Charles shrugged this off. 'The great Harvey here spent last summer with me on the Côte d'Azur, where we both gave our all for a little number which shall be nameless. Any news of our epic, chum?'

'I bumped into the great David a while back and he seemed to think they were saving it for Easter.'

'Ah! yes, and on the third day David Latrough rose from his bed and ascended into the box office . . . Harvey here wrote the words and I spoke them with my usual authority, girls.'

'Are you both in the business?' I asked.

'Course they're not in the bloody business,' Charles shouted. 'They've got more sense.'

'We're air hostesses,' Marigold said.

'Don't you read the ads?' Charles thundered. 'British Airways take more care of you. These two decided that I needed taking great care of.'

'I thought I detected British accents.'

'I'm Scottish,' Lucy said.

'What brings you out here, Charles?'

'You may well ask. It has been suggested that I should appear in yet another revival of *My Fair Lady*. So I'm here to find out if my producer, who is as gay as Dick's hatband, will tell me the reason why a woman can't be more like a man. But for God's sake don't let's talk about that. I'm delighted to see you, old chum, because for one thing I was sitting here wondering how I was going to keep these two little darlings amused. Aren't they a credit to the old country, dear boy? Look at their skins. English roses.'

'I'm Scottish,' Lucy repeated.

'Are you girls on stopover?' I asked.

'Yes, we have four days this trip.'

'Where do they put you?'

'Down at Santa Monica.'

'Decent hotel?'

'Not bad.'

'I was telling them how this place has changed since I was first here. Used to be a paradise, Santa Monica and Malibu. None of those five-million-dollar wooden shacks and bloody joggers. Hollywood had style then. And you travelled here in style. Five days on the old Mary from Southampton, then the train across country. Pissed the entire time. Sorry girls! Watch your language, Charles.'

As the meal progressed it became apparent to me that, although they were obviously flattered and amused by Charles's attention, it was by no means certain that they wished to sample his hospitality beyond bedtime. The wine flowed as it always did when Charles was the host and he seemed quietly confident that he was onto two sure bets. When eventually the girls excused themselves to go to the ladies' room, he offered me the choice.

'Which one d'you fancy, old son?'

'Charles, I'm not at all sure that the girls have the same thought in mind.'

'Course they do. It's a well-known fact that air hostesses can't wait to get at it.'

'I have to work in the morning anyway.'

'We all have to work in the morning. But we're not talking about the fucking morning, are we? We're talking about the hours of darkness. What's the matter with you? You gone chicken all of a sudden?'

'No. I'm just not in the market right now.'

'Oh, Christ! now he tells me. Not still carrying a torch for our little Laura, are you?'

I tried to conceal my shock.

'Laura?'

'Yes, dear. You didn't pull the wool over these tired old eyes. Though, of course, as always, I was discretion itself. Not that I blame you. She was no hardship to behold, our Laura.'

'I don't know what you're talking about.'

'Yes, you do. It's a good try, and I'm all for behaving like a gentleman, but your look of innocence doesn't fool me . . . I know what went on between you and the delectable Laura.'

Why did I deny it? There was a part of me that longed to confess all, as though by confessing I could exorcise the last remnants of love. I was spared for the moment when the two girls returned to the table. I guessed they had devised an escape strategy in the ladies' room and perhaps, if Charles had not raised the ghost of Laura, I might have lent my persuasion to his cause. When we finished the meal and Charles suggested going somewhere both of them pleaded exhaustion.

'It was a lovely dinner,' Lucy said.

'Yes, terrific. I'm sorry we have to crash out, but I guess we're both still on London time.'

'Where's your stamina?' Charles said. He winked at me behind their backs. 'I thought you had to fly the flag?'

'No, really, we have to get our beauty sleep.'

'Well, Harvey and I'll drive you back to your hotel anyway, and we'll talk about it.'

I was none too sanguine about Charles's ability to steer us in the dirction of Malibu, but with one or two hairy moments he drove the rented Cadillac with reasonable care. I dare say he was still convinced that the night held promise of further delights, but those were two very knowing young ladies. When we arrived at their hotel and

Charles made his final pitch, they deflected his aim with practised skill.

'Aren't you going to invite us up for a nightcap?' he said.

'We can't, alas. This hotel's very sticky. Got to keep up appearances, but it was a lovely evening,' Marigold said.

'Yes, we enjoyed it tremendously,' Lucy echoed.

'Do you mean to say you're going to leave me and Harvey stranded on the pavement?'

'Oh, I don't think you'll be stranded for long.'

'It was a big thrill to meet you both,' Lucy said. 'And we'll certainly watch out for the film now that we've met you. Good luck with *My Fair Lady*.'

'I was rather hoping for a little luck tonight,' Charles said. A certain edge had crept into his voice.

'Yes, well, another time perhaps.'

'Goodnight, Harvey,' Marigold said.

They shook hands and walked into the lobby. We saw them meet up with other crew members.

'Well, sod that!' Charles said.

'I told you.'

'Must be losing my touch. I could have sworn they were two certainties. Ah, well! Back to the old drawing board, I suppose. What shall we do? I can't face going back to my bloody hotel, much too early. Let's trundle along the coast and find a suitable place in which to drown our recent sorrows.'

I had no alternative but to fall in with his suggestion since I was without my own transport. We drove on down the Pacific Coast Highway until Charles spotted a bar that was to his liking.

'Actually, I'm relieved we didn't have to go through with it,' he said once he had a glass of brandy in his hand. 'I don't know about you, chum, but it's the thought that counts these days. The actual performance is a bit of a strain. Do you find that?'

'I've retired completely. Given it all up for my Art,' I said, sensing I was once again on dangerous ground.

'Since when?'

'I've decided the thrill of the chase is overrated.'

'She's just a faded memory, is she?'

'Who?'

'Who? he says! Who were we talking about a little while back? Your Laura.

'Why d'you keep saying my Laura?'

'Well, wasn't she? I have to hand it to you, you were a cagey sod. Suppose you had to be really with old Martin pawing the ground like a rutting camel. He was mad about her, you know.'

'Was he?'

'Oh, fuck off! Course he was. You knew that, don't pretend you didn't. Why else d'you think you were told to build up her part? Martin had a bad case. Not that she wanted to know, I'm sure. Had more taste.'

'I think she had quite a few admirers. David was sniffing around for a time.'

'That little shit. D'you know at the end of the film he had the bloody nerve to ask me if I'd do all my post-syncing for free? Said I owed it to him . . .'

I thought for a moment he had let me off the hook, but once Charles latched on to something he never let go. 'Listen, chum, it's none of my business and if you don't want to talk about it, fair enough. I just thought you might be interested in knowing what became of her.'

'How d'you mean, what became of her?'

'Well, my constant source of information is the Dowager Lady Mary. She has her pierced ears very close to the ground at all times. I was in London a week or so ago doing some ghastly television chat show, and I always insist they get in Mary to tart up the old face. She was the one who told me. Where she gets all her information from I've no idea, but she's usually right about most things.'

'Something about Laura, you mean?'

'Yes, and listen, I hope I'm not dropping bricks, chum, but according to Mother Mary, our little Laura went and got herself pregnant. Which has probably blighted a promising career.'

I prayed that I would betray nothing.

'I hope you're not in line for a paternity case, chum.'

'No such luck,' I said.

'Course there's always a chance that our Mary is just repeating malicious gossip. They love nothing better, all those queens . . . But from what he said it's apparently true. Now, who could be the father, we ask ourselves?'

'She had a boyfriend I believe. I saw him at the studio once or twice.'

'The news has shocked you, hasn't it?'

'It was a surprise, yes.'

'No, I know it's shocked you. Sorry, chum.'

'No need to be sorry.'

'Well, I should learn to keep my trap shut. I'm as bad as that silly old Mary.'

I stared down at the ashtray and studied the wording of the advertisement around the rim. I could hardly distinguish anything.

'Sorry, chum,' he repeated.

'That's okay.'

He made a rather obvious effort to change the subject and I tried hard to keep up some sort of front and listen to him. But all the while I was desperate for the evening to come to an end. The news he had given me, true or false, made ordinary conversation impossible. Love, as well as light, thickens when we receive ill tidings. I needed time and I needed solitude to get my emotions in order. Perhaps Charles, in a rare moment of sensitivity, understood this, because after one further drink he called it a night. We drove back to Beverly Hills and when he dropped me off at my house he made no attempt to invite himself in. I had the feeling that he was just as vulnerable as myself. He had more money, a public image, but behind the successful facade there was the same emptiness.

It's difficult to describe what my real feelings were. There were so many questions that remained incapable of being answered. I convinced myself that the news was correct, since it would offer an explanation for Laura's otherwise inexplicable silence and her mother's reluctance to give me a clue as to her whereabouts. And if it was correct, what was to be the outcome? I tried to remember everything that Laura had ever said to me, everything that had ever passed between us. My most vivid memory was of the night I had been invited to dinner at her home and we made love in the back of the car. Was it on that occasion that she suddenly confessed she had forgotten to take the Pill? I couldn't pinpoint the actual moment and anyway I had but a hazy

373

knowledge of how those things worked. I imagine that some married couples sleeping in the same bed every night may keep a mutual check, but an affair has no such continuity.

Nothing made much sense that night. Unable to sleep, I went over it again and again in my mind, then searched through an old diary to see if that would reveal any clues. What had she once said about abortion? How many times did we make love after that occasion? Had it happened during her stay with her boyfriend in Marseille, and when was that, before or after the time in the car? Before, I thought, it must have been before, because that was our reconciliation, the only time I had felt her love equalled my own.

The next day at the studio I could not bring myself to concentrate on anything else. I sat for hours in front of my typewriter, staring at the blank sheet of paper – considering and rejecting half a dozen plans of action. Without breaking my contract there was no way I could take off for at least another month. The series still had three episodes to shoot before it went into hiatus and whatever I finally decided I would need as much cash in the bank as I could get. I suppose what anguished me most was the possibility that Laura might think *I* was the one who had callously abandoned *her*. If none of my letters had reached her, if my various messages had never been passed on, what else could she believe? In the confused state I was in it took little to convince me that this was the most plausible explanation for her silence. There and then I dialled her number. The connection was made – the slow, definite French ringing tone, so different from any other, sounded at the other end. I let it ring for fully five minutes, but there was no answer. Throughout the afternoon I dialled every fifteen minutes or so, finally asking the international operator to check whether there was any fault on the line. I was assured that the phone was working normally.

Do these things now read like the actions of a madman? I think for a time I did return to a sort of madness. I tried to recall everything we had ever said to each other, but in the end I could no longer distinguish between hope and reality. Had she really ever told me, 'If I did get pregnant, I'd never

374

make it hard for you?' or was that something I imagined? I remembered her views on marriage well enough, but wasn't it true that women, most women, change their tune once pregnant? I had no yardstick by which to judge. My wife had never risked the vagaries of chance – with her it was always the double lock on the door, the trusty diaphragm and for good measure the Pill as well, but never discussed, discussion would have clouded an already decided issue. Or lack of issue.

Then my mind opened to embrace worse terrors. All the abortion stories I had ever heard came crowding back, legal and illegal, clandestine, clinical, secret deeds that men can scarcely take in, the last mystery that women retain. Laura had said she would never contemplate abortion, but that was said in innocence. In the event, it wasn't one's own morality that decided such things: others transplanted fear, a grafting on of sin – how many foetuses had perished because of what the neighbours might think? There was no limit to human hypocrisy when life was forfeit.

There and then I made plane bookings to travel back to Europe, setting myself a definite deadline. I would finish up my remaining two scripts as soon as possible, then shut up the apartment and take off. The decision, once made, had the effect of calming me. In the meantime I would continue to explore every means of discovering Laura's present whereabouts. I rang Charles at his hotel.

'You were right about me last night, so there's no point in denying it.'

'It was still pretty crass of me, chum.'

'Well, there it is. You guessed the truth and the other news did shake me. What I rang about was to ask if you happen to have a number for the Dowager. I want to find out what I can.'

'Sure, of course. Hold on. He should still be there. I think he said he was starting a new film fairly shortly, but I don't think it was on location. I've an idea he said he was going to be at Pinewood for a few weeks. Here it is. It's a London number.'

He passed it to me.

'Thanks. Just one other thing,' I said. 'What's his real name?'

'Joseph. Hence Mary, I suppose.'

It was the middle of the night in England by then, so I had to wait until the following day. Luck was with me for once and I got through the first time.

'Well, dear,' he said, 'I can't tell you a great deal more than the bare facts. I went back to France for a few days to renew acquaintance with a certain little amour I met while we were down there filming, and during the course of my visit I dropped in at the studio just to say hello . . . And that nice old biddy who worked in wardrobe told me. Now how she got to know, I really couldn't say. But I mean she wasn't being malicious or anything. On the contrary. Just said what a pity it was. I don't know how these girls get themselves in such a state . . . well, of course, I know *how*. I meant why? I thought that was all taken care of these days.'

'Mistakes do happen.'

'Yes. Well, we have our problems too, but the patter of tiny feet mercifully isn't one of them.'

'But did this wardrobe woman . . . did she know where Laura is? I can't find out anything, you see. Her phone doesn't answer, and I've no idea where to start looking.'

'Oh. I don't think I can help you there. All I've got is the old Cast List, but I suppose you've got that. Let me think, who else might know? Bernard?'

'Yes, that's a good idea. I've still got his number.'

'Dare I ask – I mean, do you have a special reason for wanting to find her?'

'Yes,' I said. It no longer seemed important to keep it secret, my only concern was to locate her.

'Didn't mind me being nosy?'

'No, not at all.'

'She was a pretty little thing. Lovely hair.'

'Well, you've been a big help. Hope your new film goes well.'

'Oh, it's one of those dreary space epics, dear. Everybody poncing about in frocks made of cooking foil.'

I did as he suggested and rang Bernard, but there the trail ended. He had no new address to give me and said he hadn't seen or heard of Laura since the film had finished. I almost got as far as dialling Martin, but thought better of it

At irregular times over the next week I continued to ring Laura's old number, but there was never a reply. It was as if she and her parents had disappeared off the face of the earth. In one of my blackest moods – they came on without warning – I seriously considered hiring a private detective agency, but even in my muddled state that seemed a little too bizarre.

In the days that remained before I was free to leave I can't pretend that I lived a normal existence. All I could think was, let her be alive, let me see her again, let me have a chance – praying to a God who, even as I pleaded, remained a stranger.

TWENTY-TWO

There was no repeat Concorde flight when I began the first leg of my journey back to France. I went economy, indifferent to the lack of comfort, on the long haul over the Pole. In a way I welcomed being part of the crowded rear section of the Jumbo: people aren't so gregarious there as they are in first class and in my mood I wanted isolation. It was a bumpy flight with turbulence most of the night, but at least we had a tail wind. The plane landed on time and enabled me to make the connection to Nice.

I had reserved a hire car in advance. This was waiting for me when I stepped out into the thin sunlight on shaky traveller's legs. The moment I had signed for it I headed for the *péage*, taking a route I knew by heart. At that point I still believed that fortune must favour me.

At the last moment, I changed direction and decided to drive to Tallan's surgery first: perhaps I thought I might get a more sympathetic hearing from him than from his wife. I had it fixed in my mind that she was the one who disapproved of me for some reason. The first doubts crept back when I noticed that his nameplate was no longer on the surgery door. Instead a shining new plate gave the name and credentials of a Doctor Chavrier. I went inside and the receptionist told me the doctor was at the local hospital extracting wisdom teeth under a general anaesthetic. I asked her if she could give me any information about Tallan.

'I'm afraid I don't know,' she said warily. 'That's something you'd have to ask Doctor Chavrier. He should be back in just over an hour.

Rather than sit around I drove back along the road to

378

their old house. I guess I knew what I would find. The place was shuttered, the garden neglected and overgrown. No excited poodles sounded the alarm. I considered climbing over the locked gate to look through the windows, but I was being observed by two local farm helpers and abandoned the idea. Still with time to kill I went in search of past landmarks, visiting the car park where sometimes we had met, the small *tabac* where she bought her cigarettes, the antique shop where I had once bought her a gift: they were all exactly as I remembered them, the only difference was that Laura was no longer there.

Chavrier had returned by the time I got back to the surgery and after a short wait I was shown into his office. He was a man in his late thirties, I suppose, with a boyish appearance – quietly spoken, the way some dentists cultivate a deliberately reassuring personality. I began by explaining that the Tallans were old friends and that I had lost touch, but he could tell me little.

'I never actually met Doctor Tallan. The practice was for sale and I conducted the negotiations through his lawyer. The house I didn't buy because we already had a place quite close to here . . . But as to why he went or where he went, I've no idea. I could certainly give you the name of his lawyer, if that's any use.'

'Yes, if you would be so kind.'

He asked his receptionist to look up the file.

'All I can tell you – from what some of his old patients have told me – is that they appeared to pack up and leave without saying goodbye to anybody. Seems odd, but lucky for me I suppose, because this is a very busy practice and, touch wood, the local people have accepted me. It's always difficult at first and he was much respected, Doctor Tallan. A good dentist. I've seen his work.'

'I've got some of it in my mouth,' I said. 'They're a nice family altogether. That's why I'm anxious to trace them.'

I took a note of the lawyer's address, which was in Cannes. Having thanked him, I decided I might as well book into an hotel in Cannes; I couldn't face going back to the old Auberge. By the time I had checked in it was too late to achieve anything else that day. I took a couple of sleeping pills and dropped into a familiar bottomless pit.

The next morning I presented myself at the lawyer's office, having first telephoned for an appointment. The building was in the older part of town, away from the seafront. I entered the building through a shaded court-yard. A concierge was sluicing down the cobbles.

Maître Blandinot received me at the appointed time. In appearance he was not unlike that fine old French actor, the late Michel Simon: wobbly jowls and a paunch which suggested good living. He spoke with an advocate's measured delivery as though addressing an unseen jury who needed to be cajoled to his way of thinking. From the very beginning of the interview I formed the impression that he had foreseen and anticipated my visit and the enquiries I was about to make – but perhaps that was just an experienced lawyer's trick, his party piece, as it were. He offered me a cup of excellent coffee, freshly brewed, served in thin Limoges cups. I came straight to the point. He listened intently, his hands brought together and resting under his nose in an attitude of prayer. Curiously enough the first question he put to me was the same one that the Dowager Mary had posed.

'You have a special reason, do you, Mr Burgess, for wishing to contact the Tallans?'

'Well, special in that they were close friends and it's always sad to lose touch with friends . . . the more so as one gets older.'

'I understand.' He waited for me to continue.

I went on to explain something about the film and my function, and how I was greatly interested in Laura's career and believed she had a unique talent which I hoped to further. I suppose I did exaggerate my own influence in the industry, even to the extent of inventing a new script which I told him was awaiting production. 'There's a very good role in it which I think Laura could play.'

'I understand,' he repeated. He took his coffee black and sipped at it as a bird takes water, pursing his lips and raising his head to stare up at the ornate ceiling. 'I would like to help you, Mr Burgess, but unfortunately my hands are tied. As a professional man I am bound to observe the instructions of my clients until such time as they see fit to release me from them. Now, I am not unsympathetic to your

enquiry – your name and credentials are not entirely unknown to me, and I realise that your motives are entirely
genuine. However, ethically I am obliged to carry out my
client's wishes . . . and regrettably, Doctor Tallan was
emphatic in this regard. He wished to sever all connections
and instructed me not to divulge his present whereabouts. I
have a power of attorney to conduct his remaining business
in this country, but for the rest I am not at liberty to give you
the information you seek.'

'Can I ask you this, then?' Are they . . . is the family still
in this area?'

'The answer to that is, no, sir.'

Something he had just let slip prompted me to press him
further.

'If I can turn the tables on you and conduct my own
cross-examination . . . Are you permitted to tell me
whether they're still in France?'

He pondered this for a moment. 'I think I can – without betraying a confidence – say that they are not in
France.'

'None of them?'

'Their new home is not in this country.'

'And again, without breaking your professional code of
conduct, d'you think it would be any use my trying to trace
them through other sources?'

'Such as?'

'Well, I'm not sure. Being a foreigner I'm not *au fait* with
your laws and regulations . . . Back home there are various
agencies, departments, to which one can go for this sort of
information. The Missing Persons Bureau, for example.'

'But they are not "missing", Mr Burgess.'

'As far as I'm concerned, they are.'

'Point taken, but I'm sorry I have to remain neutral. You
are, of course, at liberty to make any enquiries you wish.
It's just that, as far as I am concerned, I'm powerless to help
you any more.'

'Do you think it's worth my while to go on trying?'

'That's entirely your choice and your right.'

'Can you answer me this then? . . . Nothing awful happened, did it? I mean, nothing sinister?'

'No,' he said slowly, 'certainly nothing sinister.'

'I brought a letter with me. To Laura. Would you be kind enough to forward it on?'

I slid it across his desk. He did not pick it up.

'Presumably you're allowed to do that?'

He took his time before replying.

'I'll certainly see that it reaches them at their present address.' He poured himself a second cup of coffee. 'Excuse me, can I give you another cup?'

'Thank you.'

'We lawyers often have curious tasks to perform. Priests hear confessions from murderers, we have to defend them . . . That's at one end of the scale. You see, one has to set aside any questions of morality and only act according to the strict letter of the law. I know in this case, because we are merely talking about a private, civil affair, no laws have been broken that I know of . . .'

'What about hearts?'

His hands came up under his chin again and he regarded me across the wide desk.

'I would be right in saying, would I not, that your relationship with the Tallan's daughter went beyond a purely professional friendship?'

'Yes.'

He nodded. 'Then, as a man, I'm sorry for you, Mr Burgess.'

'In what way sorry?'

'That I can't be of more assistance. I can only wish you well and hope that whatever you eventually discover will put your mind at rest.'

He stood up and held out his hand.

'Forgive me, but I am due in court.'

'You've been more than kind. Just tell me one more thing, though . . . D'you think I'll be lucky and find them?'

'Lucky?' he said. 'I don't know. There are so many variations of luck, Mr Burgess.'

Afterwards I sat in the sun at the seafront café and had a sandwich and a beer. The first of the new season's tourists were strolling up and down. Some of the young girls reminded me of Laura, just by the way they walked or wore their hair.

I went over what Blandinot had told me – or not told me

in many cases – and tried to unravel new puzzles. The only direct answer he had given me was when he had admitted they were no longer in France. I derived some comfort from his denial that there had been anything sinister about their sudden flight – yet a successful dentist, happily married, a respected member of the community, did not disappear without good cause. I had used the word 'sinister'; but what if, instead, I had chosen to say 'scandal'? Would his answer, or the change of expression on his face, have told me more? It wasn't too far-fetched to believe that the Tallans' bourgeois sense of morality could well have played a vital role. Given their Catholicism, given such a close-knit community, and Tallan's standing in that community, it was clear to me that they must have been appalled to find their only daughter was carrying an illegitimate child. In my tawdry world one forgets the existence of ordinary people. We choose to ignore most of the values by which the majority still try to live. The fact that we consider it chic and liberal to promote the so-called 'permissive' society in our films and glossy magazines – with their loaded emphasis on transient materialism, their obscene insistence that our civilisation can only persist by the dictum of 'anything goes' – would mean little or nothing to those who live quietly outside the mainstream.

It was there, at that café table, that the idea that I could have been the father of Laura's child took root for the first time. I suppose, in a sense, I wanted that added burden as a vindication of all my past actions and future intents. Until then the thought had been swept to the back of my mind, perhaps deliberately, perhaps subconsciously. A sudden, vivid picture of Laura pregnant came into focus. I visualised that body I had worshipped grown fecund, the small breasts she had once mocked ripening, the skin on her smooth belly stretching to accommodate the life within. There and then I was seized with an unbearable longing to find her again, but the options open to me were few. I had little or no idea where or how to proceed next, for in real life it is a mistake to think that we can all transform ourselves into detectives. That is the stuff of romantic novels. I had glibly mentioned a Missing Persons Bureau to Blandinot, and perhaps if I had been on my home territory I could have bulldozed my way through officialdom, for we Americans make it a matter of principle not to be overawed by our institutional processes. As it was, as a foreigner, unable to speak the language fluently, I started with a dozen strikes against me. How, for instance, did one check which country they had gone to? The world might have shrunk in the last two decades, but it was still a vast haystack in which to find a needle. The airlines? Yes, one could ask for, but not necessarily be granted, permission to examine all the passenger indents – if they existed. Passport Control was another obvious avenue to explore, but did the French authorities keep a record of departing citizens, or only those returning?

I had set aside sufficient funds to stake me for a couple of months while I pursued my search, and that was the course of action I followed. It did not take me long to discover that life today is closer to Kafka than Saroyan: there is not such an abundance of goodwill towards strangers that we can afford to take it for granted. I followed a score of false trails, only to come up against the same blank walls of an indifferent bureaucracy. For days on end I hunted through volume after volume in the Central Registry, searching for birth certificates, marriage certificates, and, with much foreboding, death certificates. Going back to the Valbonne area I questioned the locals – shopkeepers, bartenders and the like – becoming in the process an object of some suspicion. At one point my enquiries attracted the attention of the police and it was with some difficulty that I managed to persuade them that my motives were innocent. They knew of Tallan's hurried departure, of course, but he had broken no laws, left no debts and they had but a passing interest in the matter. The only fact I ever gleaned came from the local pharmacist, who recollected that Doctor Tallan had once mentioned a desire to visit Brazil before he died.

My growing frustration and despair now led me to do something against my better judgement. I decided that, after all, I would contact Martin. Through Mischa, who was still working at the Victorine Studio, I found out that Martin was in residence. Rather than give him prior notice and thus an easier excuse to snub me, I drove straight to the villa one morning. The gardens were as pristine as ever, the house freshly painted with new shutters and awnings to shield against the coming hot weather. I was admitted by the same man-servant and made to feel uneasy by the same two guard dogs. Little had changed inside the house and as I was shown through the main rooms to where Martin sat on the terrace, I had a vivid memory of that earlier occasion when all our lives first became entangled.

Martin was reading his latest copy of *Country Life*. Whatever his real feelings at being disturbed without warning, he greeted me warmly enough and immediately saw to it that I was offered a drink.

'Surprise, surprise,' he said. 'I'd no idea you were back on this side of the pond. How long have you been here?'

'Oh, quite a while, but I've been driving around, sightseeing mostly. I needed a break. I've had my nose down for months writing a television series. I don't think you get it over here, but that's no loss. We're in hiatus at the moment, so I took off for a trip down memory lane.'

'Where's the series being shot?'

'LA.'

'God! I'm so relieved I haven't been asked back lately. Hate the place, chum. I suppose it's just as ghastly as ever? Matter of fact, I was talking to Bobby Palumbo the other day . . . D'you know him, by the way?'

'Don't think so.'

'He's an old chum. We used to belong to the MCC together . . . Rich as paint and dabbles in all sorts of things. He's invested in movies, I believe, though being a chum I've never tapped him . . . Anyway, he and his wife moved over to Beverly Hills a few years back. I bumped into them over at Monte the other day and he said they'd had enough. Sold his place to an Arab for an absolute fortune. He said the bloody Arab was welcome to it. I gather the violence is quite awful now. Do you find that?'

'Nobody's attacked me,' I said. 'Except the IRS.'

'Is that a terrorist group?'

'In a manner of speaking. They terrify me. The Internal Revenue Service.'

'Oh, I see. Yes, I'd forgotten. Thought you meant something like the IRA.'

He served the white wine which his man-servant had brought out with impeccable discreetness.

'Word is that the film's due out this coming Easter,' I said.

'Yes, I believe so. Expect they'll fuck it up as usual.'

'You happy with it?'

'One's never happy with one's own work, do you think? It's got something, but whether they'll go for it is anybody's guess these days. They seem to want – well, God knows what they do want.'

'I saw Charles a little while back.'

'The Great Charlie? How was he? Sober or barking?'

'Mellow. Trying to make it with two air hostesses.'

'Isn't it amazing? Chap in his position still chasing after scrubbers.'

'They were British,' I said. Then, after a pause, 'Have you seen anybody, anybody from the cast or crew, I mean?'

'No, thank goodness. One doesn't, you know. Once a film ends everybody gets scattered. That hideous dwarf we had as producer rang and tried to invite himself here, but I soon put him off.'

'David? He wasn't a dwarf.'

'Prototype mental pygmy. I shall never forget that hot-making speech he made. Still I dare say he'll end up running a studio like the rest . . . No, I try and avoid everybody. Don't encourage visitors. Let one in and the flood gates are open. Not that you're not very welcome, chum, don't think I was referring to you.'

'No, I can quite see . . . but I thought perhaps you might have some news to tell me about Laura,' I said, not looking at him, sipping the chilled wine.

'No.'

He got to his feet and went and closed the sliding glass doors.

'Glass walls have ears, chum. No, haven't pursued that. Tell the truth, towards the end of the film it was getting a little dodgy. I saw the writing on the bathroom mirror just in time . . . Course, I did go through a patch there for a time, and you were a brick, chum, and I haven't forgotten. I'm always suggesting you for scripts whenever anybody asks me to recommend a writer. Always put your name forward.'

'Well, that's nice of you.'

'Not at all. You were there when I needed you. I don't mind admitting now that I really thought seriously of taking to the hills with our little Laura . . . I was in a bad way. Bad way. Funny isn't it, how those little darlings get under your skin? When that little beaver of theirs is staring you in the face . . . Remember that great line of Nicolson's, in *Cuckoo's Nest*?'

'No, remind me.'

'Well, I can't remember it exactly, but you know how he gives everything that manic quality of his? It was something about how that little hairy nest between their legs drives us mad . . . That and their bloody youth, that firm skin – the works . . . I was mad, deranged . . . Well, I should tell you.'

He pushed himself back into his reclining deckchair and surveyed his domain. 'That view's quite something, isn't it? . . . But I actually did think of chucking it in . . . pulled back from the brink just in the nick of time . . . ravishing though she was. She was ravishing, wasn't she?'

'Yes,' I said.

'You could see why I got myself in such a state?'

'Oh, sure.'

'I'd never seen such beauty. Bowled me over.'

'How d'you think she came out in the film?'

'Put it this way . . . as good as she'll ever be, I suspect. I'm not sure that there's a great deal more to come. Very effective . . . Of course, I really worked on her.'

'Yes, I know . . . And she hasn't pestered you since?'

He looked back towards the house.

'No, thank God. See, I could just about get away with it while we were shooting, but after that, no way. She did ring once, but I didn't take the call . . .'

'Somebody . . . somebody at the studio, told me that she and her family had moved away from here. Had you heard that?'

'No, but I'm relieved if it's true. It's a closed book, chum. I'm over it . . . It's odd being a director really. In a way you have to fall in love with them to get the performance.'

'I never thought of it in that way,' I said.

I have always envied those born without imagination, who seldom feel guilt or remorse – terrorists in the art of love who can plant the bomb of anguish and then walk away with never a thought for those they will maim.

He laughed. 'Happy days, eh?'

I came close to wasting hatred on him at that moment, but real hatred should be saved for greater causes. I suffered his intolerable conceit for one reason only: I would have feasted with hyenas for any news of Laura. Martin's deceits and postures had led me to this point in my life, and now I despised him.

I think at that moment I despised us all – all of us who used the Lauras of our world, urging them to believe in our distorted, selfish visions that were as transient as fame itself. I had met her by chance, and by chance and without malice aforethought she had destroyed me, but the real incubus was that impulse which makes us worship success. I had employed my age and experience to impress her and further my own ends, but I had neglected to warn her that the visions were only ever on loan. Looking at Martin's self-satisfied face I saw a partial reflection of myself, and the image chilled me. Martin had made me a fellow conspirator and now, listening to his awful dismissal of her, I felt tainted by this dull human thing we call trust.

'But that's enough of my troubles,' he was saying. 'Apart from your series, what else has been happening to you?'

'Not a great deal.'

'What about your love life? Have you seen Michelle this trip?'

'No.'

'Thought you were well in there?'

'We had our moments.'

'Quite right. Keeps us young, chum . . . You're a sly old sod on the quiet, if you ask me. You know, I can say this now, there was a moment when I suspected you fancied Laura yourself.'

'Really? What gave you that idea?'

'I don't know. I got certain vibes. Good thing I trusted you.'

I finished my drink and got to my feet.

'Good seeing you again, Martin. Thanks for the hospitality.'

'My dear chum, you're very welcome. Stay for lunch.'

'No, I've got to meet some people in Antibes.'

He didn't press me. He didn't even get up from his chair when I left. I guess the view fascinated him more than I did.

I checked out of the hotel that afternoon, drove to the airport and turned in the rented car. Then I took the first available plane to Paris and began the journey back to what, I suppose, was home of a sort.

TWENTY-THREE

It's a sad reflection on my character that my old notebooks and diaries, which record so many trivial events, contain scarcely a mention of Laura and those anguished days five years ago. I did come across her phone number the other week, tucked into one of the pockets of an old wallet. It was written on a scrap torn from a Call Sheet. I stared at it for quite some time before its significance dawned on me, yet once it was as firmly engraved on my memory as my Army serial number.

The Bastille Connection did eventually get into the cinemas, but under a different title, and not at Easter as originally announced. Those faceless creatures who decide such things renamed it, *Under The Shadow of The Knife*. I received a credit for Additional Dialogue. I made the pilgrimage one August night to Westwood where it had a limited premier run, joining a sparse and mainly indifferent audience. The critics hadn't been generous to it, though Gerry's cinephotography drew justified praise and he received a nomination that year. I suppose the best one could say about it was that it was competent. The final version betrayed the fact that quite a number of soiled hands had disposed of the afterbirth. The print I saw, hideously colour-graded, was hardly a triumph for modern technology: at one moment, Charles appeared with a bright violet face which I hope the Dowager Lady Mary never had the misfortune to witness – the poor thing would have gone into an immediate decline. As to the story, well, that was virtually impossible even for me to follow, so God knows what the general public made of it. I sat isolated among the restless popcorn eaters watching a time that would never come again. There was my love up there on the screen, illuminating the darkness with her beauty, and I wept unashamedly.

Now the passing years have blunted the edges of regret, but there is no real escape: the film crops up at regular intervals on late-night television. I try not to watch, but my resolve frequently weakens. I can just about bear to see it alone when appearances don't matter but in company I find it impossible. I guess the human heart is a very mysterious thing.

After my return empty-handed from France I struggled to get back into the old routine. The series was picked up for a third and fourth and fifth season, and by then I had become a fixture. Within the parochial confines of the television world I achieved a certain measure of respectability: never in the top echelon, but known as a reliable asset to the team. You can't knock success, as the saying stupidly goes. It wasn't the kind of success I had once yearned for, and the Great American Novel gathered dust on my desk.

Yet it would be dishonest, indeed ungrateful, to pretend that there weren't other compensations. If my once precious integrity had been tarnished, at least my bank balance prospered. I moved out of the rented apartment at the end of the lease and put the down payment on a smart little pad on the crest of Laurel Way. I had a better view of the smog up there and nobody got mugged on my actual doorstep. I bought a dog, and kept a loaded gun by my bed. Just an average Beverly Hills citizen in fact. My circle of drinking companions gradually increased and I lived what the magazines describe as the good life, on the surface at least becoming something like the sort of man who is supposed to read *Playboy*. Not that my modest pool was ever filled to overflowing with naked, nubile talent. I had my allotted moments, but the affairs were short-lived and spaced apart. Laura had cured me of love. I could have changed for her, I had wanted her for a lifetime; but now all that remained was a networked memory of a girl I once knew in another country.

I wrote at the start of this account that most of the mistakes were mine and I went to some pains never to repeat them. There is an often repeated maxim in my trade that a story seldom has a true beginning or an end, something is always left ragged, inconclusive – that we write more by chance than by design. Not that I'm much to go by; most of the time I've only rewritten the labours of others.

There is a kind of ending to this story, just as there is a kind of end to loving. The child's dream – all those fairy tales we tell ourselves before we attempt to live them – can't be sustained forever, no matter how hard we try. I used to believe that writing was the panacea, that when I began to set all this down on paper I would somehow be cured and Laura would cease to torment me. Did I once mock at Martin's obsession? If so, I take it all back: I even forgive him the conceit that filled out his days. At least he gave me somebody to blame – yet, without him, I would never have known her. So I will write what I know, the little I know.

I have never believed in the existence of a benign, all-powerful God watching over our every action, just as I have never believed that anybody outside the business ever bothers to read the technical credits on television. It's doubtless in the worst of taste to mention God and Mammon in the same breath, but it was Mammon rather than the Almighty who had the last word where Laura was concerned.

In my present, if temporary, exalted state I am entitled to a large office and the services of a secretary. A few weeks ago I was surprised when she informed me that a Mr Castaldi wished to see me. Normally nobody wishes to see me; I am summoned to see others.

'Who is he?' I asked over the intercom.

'No idea, Mr Burgess.'

From her voice I gathered he was standing beside her in the outside office. I lowered my own voice a fraction.

'What is it, d'you think? Somebody trying to peddle a script?'

'No, I asked that.'

'What then?'

'He says it's a personal matter, Mr Burgess.'

My next reaction was to think I had defaulted on the mortgage.

'Find out more,' I said.

I waited. She came back on the line.

'This gentleman says you once had a mutual friend in Valbonne. That's in France.'

'Valbonne?'

'Yes, Mr Burgess.'

'Okay,' I said. 'Show him in . . . and, Betty, no calls.'

I got up from behind my desk to greet him. The young man she ushered into my office was a complete stranger. Twenty-three or four maybe, neatly dressed, pressed jeans and a golfing jacket; hair long but trimmed; a somewhat surly face, though perhaps guarded would be a better description.

'Mr Burgess?'

'Yes.'

'Please forgive me for interrupting your work like this . . .' There was no real warmth in his apology. 'My name is Gerard Castaldi, but you don't know me.' His English was good, but I could detect the remains of a European accent. 'This is an imposition on my part, I'm afraid.'

'Not at all. What can I do for you?'

'We did nearly meet once. In Nice. About five years ago.'

'Did we?'

'Yes . . . You knew my wife, I think.'

Perhaps it was then that I had the first small premonition of disaster, but even so I still didn't suspect the truth.

'You were there making a film.'

'That's right, yes. Yes, I was.'

'My wife also.'

I thought, here it comes, the touch. There was something vaguely unpleasant about him, a certain arrogance that usually signals a favour that is going to be asked.

'I think you knew her as Laura Taylor,' he said, and never took his eyes off me.

'Yes,' I said, 'yes, I did know Laura.'

I sat down again. The effect on me was the same as if he had been a doctor informing me I had a terminal disease. I tried not to look at him, but busied myself attempting to

393

open a packet of cigarettes. I wanted my voice to sound normal when I spoke.

'Laura's your wife, is she?'

'Was,' he said. And then I looked up at him again. There was no change in his expression. I suppose for a few seconds I lived with hope of a kind.

'You're no longer married?'

'Laura's dead,' he said. 'She died four years ago.'

The cellophane on the cigarette packet refused to come apart. He offered me a Gauloise. My hands shook so violently I couldn't light it. Castaldi leaned over the desk and lit it for me.

'You must forgive me,' I said. 'I'm sorry, but your news, what you've just told me, was so unexpected. I'm very sad to hear of your wife's death . . . More sad than I can say . . . Look, please sit down.' The cigarette stuck to my lip. 'As a matter of fact, I often wondered what had become of . . . your wife.' There was no way of finding the right words. I began again. 'As a matter of fact I tried to keep in touch,' but shock made me lose the thread of what I wanted to say and I ended, 'Your wife had a promising career ahead of her . . . Everybody thought very highly of her.'

'Yes, I believe so.'

There was a long pause. 'Are you here on a visit?'

'No, I live here now. I practise, I work here.'

'Ah, you work here. What do you practise?'

'I'm an architect.'

There was a clue there and I struggled to decipher it. Recovering a little, I said, 'I'm being very rude. Can I offer you a drink?'

'Yes, I will have a drink. A beer would be fine.'

I went to my small fridge, glad of the opportunity to turn my back on him for a few moments.

'What made you find me?' I said. 'Or rather, how did you find me?'

'I saw your name on television.'

I handed him his beer. Then as we raised our glasses, I found myself saying. 'Can I ask how your wife died?' but the words seemed blurred.

'She died in childbirth.'

Once again the words reached me as though from a great

distance. I had the same sensation as one gets during the descent after a long plane journey. He stared at me but it was impossible to read his thoughts.

'Poor Laura,' I said, and even her name sounded dead as the enormity of his flat statement hit me. For the first time his features softened; I had the feeling that he had originally come to gloat, and now regretted it.

'I thought perhaps you would have guessed,' he said.

'No.'

He seemed to anticipate my next question.

'I'm sure you're wondering why I came here to see you . . . It wasn't just that, I have something for you. This was the real reason.' Fumbling inside the pocket of his golfing jacket he produced an envelope. I saw that it bore a Brazilian stamp and had already been opened. 'I apologise for the fact that I opened it, but I had no idea what it contained.'

Inside were perhaps half a dozen letters still in their original envelopes. They were all addressed to Laura and I recognised my own handwriting.

'They are yours, aren't they?' he said.

'Yes.'

I put them down on the desk.

'How did you come by them?'

'They were sent to me just like that, about a year ago. From her parents. Laura never saw them. They must have kept them from her.'

'With no explanation?'

'Did you know her parents?'

'Yes and no. I met them on a few occasions. They seemed very pleasant, very ordinary.'

'Ordinary. Yes, that's a good word for them,' he said. 'So ordinary, it took them five years to feel guilt. No, there was no explanation.'

'Did you read them?' I said.

'I read one of them.'

'Then you know I loved her?'

'I always knew that,' he said.

'Well, at least we don't have to go on pretending then, do we? You say these came a year ago, so what made you suddenly decide to return them now? You could have destroyed them at any time, I'd have been none the wiser.'

In some curious way the sight of my old letters had given me an advantage over him for the first time since he entered the room.

'Yes, that's true, and I did think about it, and then I thought of what Laura would have wanted. I used to hate you, you see, but she was very fond of you, and I owed it to her.'

He had hesitated on the word "fond".

'Can I ask you something else, something that always puzzled me? . . . Why did her parents up and suddenly leave like that? I may as well tell you that I went back, I tried to find Laura, but I got nowhere. Now I know part of it, but not about why they left like that.'

'Laura didn't want to have the baby at first, she was going to get rid of it . . . but then her mother and father found out, I don't know how but they did and they turned on her. They turned on her, that's the only way to describe it. Like they were suddenly living a hundred years ago. And that changed Laura, too. Because of them, because of their attitude, she became determined to have the baby, just to spite them I think . . . And they just left her. Washed their hands. They left her and went. Her father closed the practice and they went, left the country.

'Oh, Christ!' I said. 'Dear Christ!' As if I had suddenly started believing in Him and His mercies.

'Laura came to me . . . You see, we grew up together, we were in school, I was her first . . . We were always in love. Even though she sometimes felt unsure, she always came back . . . She came back to me this time. I was still in Marseille, studying for my exams, and she came there and we lived in my room. As a student I didn't have any money, but she had saved a little from the film, and I took a job at nights in a bar, and we managed. And I married her.'

He looked at me defiantly and then I remembered the face of somebody much younger, and I saw him as he had been that awful evening in Nice when, by chance, I came upon them both walking arm-in-arm, so obviously lovers.

'You said she died in childbirth . . . Did the baby live?'

'Yes, she lived, thank God. She was premature, seven months, but she lived . . . And later, because of the baby, I married again. An American girl, that was how I was able to get papers to come over here. My present wife is a little older than me, not much, but very nice, a very good person. It could never be the same as Laura, of course, but . . . what is the expression? Life had to go on and I couldn't work and look after my daughter.'

'Are they with you here in Los Angeles?'

'Yes. They're waiting for me downstairs.'

'Can I meet them?'

'If you wish. There's just one thing . . . I didn't tell my wife the real reason I came here. I just told her I was seeing you on business. There's no point, is there, in telling other people?'

'No.' I said. 'No point. We can't bring her back just by telling other people.' I picked up one of my letters to her. By chance it was the first I had ever written, and I thought again of that room in the Auberge de Colombier where we first made love and brightness fell from the air. Then I covered the letters with a pile of scripts and together we went out of the room and walked down the single flight of stairs to the visitors' parking lot. The heat hit us like a wall. He led me towards a Volkswagen Scirocco and as we approached a pleasant, buxom girl, totally unlike Laura, got out and stood waiting.

'This is my wife,' Castaldi said. 'Joyce, this is Mr Burgess.'

'Hi. Very pleased to meet you.'

Her hand was moist in mine.

'Have Laura come out and say hello, chérie. Come on, baby.'

His wife released the catch on her passenger seat and reached into the rear of the car to lift out the child.

'Say hello to the gentleman,' Castaldi said.

The child pushed herself behind his wife, but not before I had glimpsed traces of the imperishable gift of my Laura's beauty.

Castaldi lifted her into his arms and she clung to him, burying her face in his neck.

'I'm sorry,' his wife said. 'She's always shy in front of strangers.'

Castaldi stared straight at me.

'Aren't we all?' I said.

BRYAN FORBES

FAMILIAR STRANGERS

The twilight world of Burgess, Maclean and Philby con-
tinues to fascinate both layman and expert. FAMILIAR
STRANGERS, written with fortuitous if uncanny fore-
sight before the Anthony Blunt disclosures, gives an
all-too-accurate glimpse of what lies behind the evidence.

Fiction and truth merge in Bryan Forbes' fascinating,
subtle and brilliantly written spy thriller – the most
challenging book he has yet written in his long and
varied career.

'Brutally frank and compulsively readable . . . a major
novel not to be missed'

The Bookseller

Post·A·Book

A Royal Mail service in association with the Book Marketing Council & The Booksellers Association.

Post-A-Book is a Post Office trademark

MELVYN BRAGG

Coming soon
LOVE AND GLORY

'The glory is Bragg's. It is a novel of depth and richness. The lives of everyday up-market media folk are faithfully recorded in these pages; but love as sexual obsession is archetypal and it is Melvyn Bragg's realization of this theme that gives the book its power.'

Sunday Times

Demotion, a fragile marriage and a dying mother: Willie Armstrong's life seems insupportable. Then salvation: a girl's beautiful smile. Obsessed by Caroline, Willie progresses from jealousy to moral outrage at his lifelong friend, now his rival in love. Ian Grant has lived a charmed, reckless life, but as Willie gains in resolution and stature, so it seems that Ian's credit is finally running out.

'A well constructed, elegantly written traditional novel by one of our most talented and intelligent writers.'

Fay Weldon, Image

CORONET BOOKS

ALSO AVAILABLE FROM CORONET